The American Freshman

Spike Hilton

ONE

"Want t' buy some books?"

"Er..."

"History, yeah?" He pointed to the embarrassingly large pin badge on Dave's shirt, which showed his name and the course he was about to start.

"You'll need some books. They're on the reading list. You didn't read them, did you?"

"No...er...I"

"No one ever does, except maybe someone like him." The cool and confidant 'know-it-all' laughed and pointed towards a thin, spotty, bespectacled youth sipping orange juice on his own in the corner of the Common Room. The youth smiled back at Dave and his book-selling acquaintance, pleased that after nearly an hour of smiling inanely at groups of people, someone had finally acknowledged him.

"Absolutely essential these. What happens is they tell you to read some book, so all thirty of you bugger off to the library and find that the library's only got two copies and those are out. So you all bugger off to the bookshop, where the *Snotty Cow* there tells you it'll take a week to get it and she wants twenty quid off you. So you don't read it and *The Management* think you're a lazy bastard who can't be arsed - then you're fucked! Know what I mean?"

"Er...."

"But if you've got the books, then they think you're one of the really keen wankers who sprinted off to the library to get one of the only two copies available, 'cause you're so fucking interested in what Louis XIV had for breakfast, know what I mean? From then on you're Mr. Golden Balls, know what I mean? One hundred quid, that's what they're worth. Christ, to buy them new from the *Snotty Cow* would cost you...er...godda' be one-fifty! Cock all use to me though, I've had my use out of them. Fifty quid, that's all I'll take off you."

"I'm sorry, but I didn't understand what you just said".

"You're doing History, right?"

"Right."

"Well, to do History you need books, right?"

"Right."

"Well I've got the books you need and I'm letting you have them for the bargain price of only fifty quid."

"'Quids' means Pounds, right?"

"Right."

"But I've only got thirty Pounds... and they're in my room."

"That'll do. You're a Yank aren't you?"

"Yes."

"Whereabouts?"

"Excuse me?"

"Whereabouts in America are you from?"

"Beavers Bluffs, near Omaha, Nebraska."

"You shitting me? There's no fucking place called Beavers Bluffs and Omaha, that's a beach isn't it?"

"Excuse me?"

"Omaha Beach."

"No Omaha, Nebraska."

"Alaska! Fuck me, you don't look much like an Eskimo."

"No, Nebraska."

"Where's that?"

4

"The Midwest."

"Mid West of what?"

"The US."

"Is that near New York?"

"No."

"L.A.?"

"No."

"Middle of fucking nowhere then? So, what ya' doin' here?"

"I won a scholarship and I..."

"Yeah, yeah whatever. Come on then, let's get your cash."

The Bookseller picked up a plastic shopping bag full of books as they left the Common Room and the two of them headed off across the Quad to Dave's room. Sheaf Hall Quad was a grassed area, about the size of a football field, dissected by paths and enclosed by a two-story, gray-brick building. The dormitory, or 'Hall of Residence', looked like a poor copy of the Oxford and Cambridge colleges that Dave had seen in photos.

"Which block are you in?" asked *The Bookseller*.

"Er ... I Block."

The Bookseller roared with laughter.

"You're fucking kidding? You're in with *Brain-Dead*. He's mad! Fucking architect he is. Seven year course those bastards have to do, they all go fucking mad," he laughed again, "and *Brain-Dead's* never left Hall. They'd make him Warden, except he's on another planet."

By now they had reached I Block. Dave pushed on the door and went in. It was gloomily dark inside as all the floors and walls were covered with dark stained wood and the whole place reeked of polish and bleach. Five dark doors faced them. Dave, key at the ready, opened number three and they went in.

The tiny room, on what Dave would call the first floor but the English apparently call the 'ground' floor, overlooked the Quad, was about the size of a prison cell and here again the dark wood and smell of polish was all-pervasive. There was a desk by the window complete with a lamp, dark wood cupboards, a dark wood door that opened onto a sink and a bed with a hideous orange, candlewick bedspread. It was obvious that Dave hadn't settled in as on the bed were an unopened suitcase, a locker bag and the well-thumbed British / American dictionary Dave's mom had gotten him as soon as he heard he was coming to England. Dave had mistakenly thought that the Brits spoke the same language but, after wading through page after page of words he had never heard before and the crazy meanings the Brits gave familiar words, he now knew Brit English was a very strange dialect indeed. Dave had only arrived an hour before and was disorientated and exhausted by jet lag. He hadn't slept on the plane, he hadn't slept on the train and from the moment he had bumped down through the clouds into the gray English drizzle he had been seriously regretting his decision to spend the next three years of his life on this strange, miserable little island far from home, surrounded by people with crazy teeth who spoke crazy English. Ever since his parents and his brother had waved him off yesterday morning at Eppley Airfield in Omaha, he had had a lump in his throat and all his bravado and excitement had been replaced by fear and doubt. This had been amplified by the phone call home he'd just made to let his tearful mom know he'd arrived safely.

"Ever been to Sheffield before?" asked *The Bookseller* as Dave fumbled in his locker bag for his wallet.

"No, never. I've not been to England or even Europe before," replied Dave.

"You'll have a fucking party, *Yank*!" grinned *The Bookseller*.

Back in the Common Room and now the proud, new owner of a bag full of books, Dave continued the nervous first meetings. The formula was always the same; 'What's your name?' 'Ooh, you're American, whereabouts do you come from?' 'Where's that? Why are you here?"

"Dave, come over here."

Dave, who was explaining where Beavers Bluffs was for the twentieth time - this time to the Orange Juice Youth, turned to see *The Bookseller* beckoning him.

Dave excused himself before moving over to join the group *The Bookseller* was in.

"Yank meet Sue, Cathy, *Lard-Arse*, Mike, Angie and Bev."

"Hi," mumbled Dave, having forgotten their names already.

A chorus of greetings and huge, beaming smiles bounced back in response.

"We're off the Broomhill, coming?" asked *The Bookseller*.

"To where?"

"Broomhill, it's an area with loads of pubs. 'Bout ten minutes walk."

"Yeah, OK."

The party made for the door and walked out into the evening light beyond, giving Dave the chance to inspect his fellow students. Mike (was it Mike?) had the sort of looks that made other men jealous; athletic with short, black, tightly curled hair that, although no doubt entirely natural, looked like a craftsman had spent many hours sculpting it into place. *The Bookseller* looked like he rarely saw the sun, ate next to nothing and only changed his clothes when they either dropped off him or caught fire. There was no missing *Lard-Arse*. His nickname didn't do full justice to his gargantuan size yet, although he was especially ugly with copper-red hair, freckles and deathly-white skin, he had the sort of permanent grin that made you smile and feel at ease. Then there were the girls. Two were moderately attractive and two were very good looking. Yet, as the girls laughed and joked among themselves as they walked along, they all seemed incredibly sexy. Maybe their Europeanness, which made them appear cosmopolitan to Dave, and their confidence added to their attractiveness? If that were the case, Dave would be very ugly because he felt very shy and very ill at ease being with a group of friends who obviously knew each other so very well. He felt very far from home.

"A gallon and a 'Botty-Burner', that's what we need," announced *Lard-Arse* loudly.

"What a gent!" exclaimed one of the girls.

"Now David," one of the very attractive girls said, taking his arm as they walked. "I want to know everything about you, and I mean everything!"

Dave was just about to go through his well-rehearsed routine of where he was from etc. when the still evening air was shattered by a howl, apparently that of a wolf. Dave spun around to see where the noise was coming from.

"Oh Christ!" exclaimed his walking companion, "*Brain-Dead's* back."

Suddenly from a darkened doorway came a tall, gangly youth with a peculiarly large head. He was skipping towards them, bent over and with his head on his left shoulder and his arm flaying around. With his other hand he was pulling his mouth to one side. This was obviously his Quasimodo routine. He hopped over to Dave and his companion, which Dave found almost frightening due to this youth's enormous size and manic demeanor.

"Are ya' willin for a shillin'?" he screamed, crouching before Dave's companion.

"Fuck off *Brain-Dead*," she laughed, trying to kick him but missing.

"Oh go on, please," he begged, failing to his knees in front of her.

"Fuck off!" she laughed again.

"Oh Cathy, have pity. I haven't had a wank all summer, just for you. My balls are so big now I've had to keep them in a wheelbarrow."

The whole group laughed, including Dave.

"Fuck off!" Cathy repeated, again trying to kick him.

"Marry me then."

"In your fucking dreams," this time her foot landed in *Brain-Dead's* crotch.

"Arrrrhhhhhh, the jewels, the family jewels. Think of our kids, woman. Little Tommy'll be in a wheelchair now and all because his mother booted his sperm. How could you? Poor little Tommy. You'd better give me a blowjob now. Better safe than sorry!"

Cathy again tried to kick him, but missed.

"You coming to Broomhill, *Brain-Dead?*" asked *Lard-Arse.*

"No!" screamed all the girls in unison.

"Sit in a pub when there are moist freshers in the vicinity? No fucking way."

Then he was off, skipping towards the Common Room.

"Freshers, oh freshers, *Brain-Dead's* got a present for you."

"Oh God," exclaimed one of the girls, "I was hoping he'd have moved out this year."

The group continued out of the grounds of Sheaf Hall and along the road.

"Now, where were we?" asked Cathy taking Dave's arm again. "I want to know all about you David."

"Well there' s nothing much to tell really," replied Dave, but he still managed to fill the ten minute walk to the pub chatting about himself and where he came from. His companion listened intently and laughed in all the appropriate places.

As they walked, Dave had time to start taking in his surroundings for the first time; he had been too jet-lagged and disorientated to pay that much attention on the bus journey from the railway station to Sheaf Hall. He had sat in the front seat on the top deck of the double-decker bus for the novelty value, but had then spent the entire journey worrying about the bus tipping over and ducking every time a tree branch hit the window. This had left him with the impression that Sheffield had more than its fair share of trees, something that was confirmed as he walked with Cathy; but he now also noticed how green it was and more especially just how different it was to anything he had ever seen before. Although it was all 'new' to Dave, the whole place was definitely very 'old'. His hometown Beavers Bluffs hadn't been founded until 1857, yet just walking along the street Dave was passing buildings much older than that. These weren't grand public buildings that he might have expected to be preserved, these were tiny houses clinging to the hillsides, built with huge blocks of black chiseled stone, with massive lintels above the front doors where, helpfully, someone had carved the date they had been built. In a book on Sheffield Dave had read before his journey, he had been amazed to discover that there was a building from 1500 still standing and that only a few miles up the valley from where he was now, there is a two thousand year-old Roman road. A Roman road - how cool is that?

The other thing you couldn't miss about Sheffield was the hills - the place was full of them and steep ones at that! It seemed that any flat area was man-made. 'Built on seven hills and with seven rivers - just like Rome', Dave's book had said. Dave liked the hills and he liked how green and lush and old everything was. Looking down towards town he could see rows and rows of tiny terraced houses, yet looking back up the valley were the bigger houses of the suburbs nestled amongst a forest of trees. Something else he found fascinating was looking above modern shop fronts and seeing old buildings made from brick and stone, often dated and sometimes still carrying the name of some long gone business. But the overriding feeling was that it was all so different and it all served to remind Dave just how far from home he really was. Still there were compensations.

Here he was walking along the street with a pretty English girl who was hanging on his every word, on his way to his first English pub. After a few minutes they passed a sign saying 'Broomhill' and Dave recalled reading some 'blurb' on the place. Broomhill, apparently, was a hill above another area called Broomhall and grew up along the road to Manchester. It was quite a pleasant area, probably the first true suburb you reached as you came out of the city, and it had a nice, sedate atmosphere with its shops, pubs and restaurants.

When they arrived at the pub and settled down with their drinks, Cathy sat next to Dave, still hanging onto his arm. The pub was filling up with what looked like other students and very few locals. As Dave looked around his first English pub he began to feel more confident now he was in such a friendly group and was starting to enjoy himself. The pub wasn't quite how he'd imagined, not as 'olde worlde', but it still had a nice atmosphere - much better than the bars back home. It seemed obvious that the pub had mainly attracted sophomores or seniors (which Cathy had told him were called 'second' and 'third' years in England). They were relaxed and happy to be back at school with their friends again, all laughing and talking loudly about what they'd been doing during the vacation. The few freshmen present, however, were easy to spot. They too had been brought along by people who 'knew the ropes' and sat nervously and quietly, smiling a lot and forcing out the occasional laugh when those around them cracked a joke. Seeing their obvious discomfort, Dave didn't feel quite so vulnerable any more, especially as Cathy was still ignoring everyone except him and he was loving it.

"God, this is great", he thought to himself, "I never got attention like this from the girls at home."

"What ya' doing then Dave?" asked Mike.

"History, European History."

"Lazy cunt," Mike laughed.

"Mike' s a scientist," explained *The Bookseller*. "They get pissed off because where we've got eight hours of lectures a week, they've got forty. It's great! If you ever wake up early enough, you'll see them at a quarter to nine, tramping off to the Science Block in all weathers and all in their blue anoraks, and you won't see them again till nighttime. Pisses you off, doesn't it Mike?"

"Fuck off!"

"Oh, I know what I was going to tell you", continued *The Bookseller* to Dave, "Film Studies."

"What?"

"Film Studies. You've got to have a sub-sid, yeah?"

"A what?"

"A subsidiary subject."

"I guess so."

"Well my boy, Film Studies is the one; a piece of piss. You pick any other and you're fucked. Come the third year, you'll be sweating your nuts off reading all the shit you should have read two years before. But, on top of that, if your subsid's French or something similarly horrific, you've got to read all of that shit too, 'cause it's worth a third of your marks. But if you've got Film Studies, you're laughing. All you do for three years is watch fucking films, then the exam's 'Open Book'. That means you take all your essays, and anyone else's essays you can get your hands on, into the exam and copy them out and they always ask the same questions. Ya' can't fail. And it all counts towards your degree, you know. But you've got to get there early, really fucking early. The English students have cottoned on to it, so you've got to beat those cocky sons-of-bitches to the queue. Go to the American Studies building first thing tomorrow and sign up. If you leave it till later, you've got no chance."

"That's fucking rich, isn't it?" laughed Mike, "A Yank comes all the way over here to sign up for American Studies!"

"Why do I have to beat the English to the American Studies department? You're all English, right?"

"You dumb fucker", laughed The Bookseller, "I meant students reading English, not English people. Bunch of fucking tossers they are, every last one of them."

"Anyway, why did you come all the way over here to Study history?" asked Mike
.

"I won a scholarship."

"Oooh, you must be really clever," cooed Cathy.

"No, not really. I was the only person who applied for it."

Everyone laughed.

"No it's true," Dave continued. "Some guy called Arnold Shuttlebottom came to Omaha from Sheffield, England before the First World War and made a stack of money selling tractors. But he had this wild hare up his ass about the kids in Nebraska not knowing anything about or caring about Europe, so he set up a foundation to send one kid a year from the Omaha area to his home town college to Study European history. Well, Beavers Bluffs is only forty miles from Omaha and there ain't that many folks that are interested in European history or wanting to go to the Univerisity of Yorkshire in England; most people would only have heard of Oxford and Cambridge. So when I applied, I was the only one, so I got it. I thought, 'What the hell?' I get the fees paid, all my travel expenses and my living expenses. I wanted to see Europe anyway and back home I'd have had to work my way through school."

"Yeah, whatever," grinned *The Bookseller*. "Just make sure you get to your Yank ass to Film Studies in the morning, before those English student wankers beat you to it."

"Er... right ... OK I will," Dave stammered. He had heard what The Bookseller had said, but suddenly his thoughts were elsewhere. There was a hand on his leg that was moving to his inner thigh. He glanced nervously at Cathy sitting next to him and she smiled back. Her hand then continued its journey under cover of the table until it reached his, by now, very large erection.

"Jesus," thought Dave, "I can't believe this is happening."

Cathy squeezed him.

"Wow," Dave mumbled.

"What was that, Dave? " asked Mike.

"Er...nothing."

"Come on then young David, your round," announced Mike.

"I'm what?" asked Dave.

"No you dumb-fuck. It's your turn to buy the drinks!" snarled *The Bookseller*.

Cathy giggled and squeezed him again. "Oh Christ," thought Dave, "How am I going to make it to the bar with this?"

He shuffled out from behind the table, bending over to hide his 'embarrassment' and put his hand in his jeans pocket.

He had only gone a few feet towards the bar when he suddenly realized that he had no money. He'd given it all to *The Bookseller*. This was embarrassing. He turned back to the table and suddenly his erection was no longer a problem. He tapped *The Bookseller* on the shoulder and immediately froze. He didn't know *The Bookseller's* name!

"Er...this is really embarrassing but I haven't got any money."

There was a groan from around the table and Cathy laughed.

"I gave it all to you for those books. Could I borrow some till tomorrow?"

"No problem mate," said *The Bookseller*, "but you will give me it back tomorrow, won't you?"

Dave nodded and took the bill *The Bookseller* offered.

An hour later, Dave had calmed down. He'd bought his round, which was an experience in itself, what with the crazily named English drinks the girls wanted, and had a couple of glasses ('pints') of beer. He'd tried an English beer, but it was cloudy, warm and so bitter it made him shudder (how can they drink that shit?), so he reverted to the reassuringly friendly *Budweiser*. Now he was back next to Cathy, her hand was back between his legs and he was starting to enjoy himself immensely. He'd had time to examine Cathy and decided that she was really very attractive. He was getting on very well with everyone and had even started to crack some jokes, which seemed to go down pretty well.

"Curry time!" announced *Lard-Arse*.

Mike and *The Bookseller* nodded in agreement and reached for their coats. The girls seemed less impressed.

"We'll leave you boys to it," said one of the girls.

"Coming Dave?" asked *The Bookseller*.

Cathy gave his erection yet another squeeze.

"Er...no...er..."

Cathy giggled.

"I'd better not. I'm not that hungry and I've got to get up early to sign up for Film Studies, right?"

"Fucking Film Studies! You lazy bastards." Mike was obviously still upset about a scientist's lot in life.

"Come on boys, my Boona's calling me!" moaned *Lard-Arse*.

And so the group split up, the males to get a curry and the females plus Dave to return to Sheaf Hall. Cathy was still clinging onto Dave' s arm as they walked along, with the three other girls twenty yards ahead.

"Fancy a coffee?" asked Cathy as they arrived back into the Quad.

"Yeah sure; that would be great," stammered Dave, his heart racing.

They called 'Goodnights' to the other three girls and entered one of the blocks. As Dave followed Cathy up the stairs, he examined her body as it swayed from side to side in front of him and wondered how far he would get with her. Surely he wouldn't get past first base, not on a first date? But then again, she had been playing with his dick all night. That sort of thing just didn't happen in Beavers Bluffs!

Cathy opened the door to her room and turned on the light. The layout and decor were exactly the same as Dave's, and the smell of polish was still there, but it was so much nicer. Cathy had posters all over the walls, her own bedding and lamps and photos and mementoes covered every flat surface. It looked like she had lived there for years, whereas the reality was that she must have arrived that day, just like everyone else.

Cathy turned on two of the lamps and turned off the main light with its blindingly bright bulb as Dave began studying the pile of CDs. Finding one he liked, he turned around.

"Jesus!" he gasped.

"Got a problem?" Cathy whispered, with her blouse half way off, exposing her bra.

"No, not at all."

"Good. We had a few spliffs before we went to the pub and I'm as horny as hell. You didn't really want a coffee, did you?"

Dave shook his head as Cathy pushed him back on to the bed, where she straddled him. Instead of moving up to his face as Dave had expected, however, she stopped at his crotch and began unzipping his fly. Within moments she was holding his erection in her hand and guiding it into her mouth.

"Oh my God", Dave thought, "this is incredible!"

He had never had a blowjob before, so he lay back on the bed with a huge grin on his face and wondered why they had never mentioned this in the college brochure he'd been sent!

Sunlight burned into Dave's eyelids and woke him up. He sat up with a start, not knowing where he was. Then he saw Cathy asleep next to him in the tiny bed and he remembered all right.

"Wow, what a night," he grinned to himself.

Although he hadn't 'performed' as well as he would have liked, Cathy had seemed grateful enough and he had certainly enjoyed himself. However, now that the lust of the night before had evaporated, Dave's mood had changed. As she lay asleep next to him bathed in sunlight, he thought how beautiful she looked. Not only that, she was such fun. After they had had sex, they had just lain together chatting for hours; chatting about all sorts of things – their families, tastes, homes, ambitions, as they stared at the ceiling in the pink glow of Cathy's lamps. Dave even began to wonder if he was falling in love. This was marvelous; after one night in England (even before the college semester had officially started) he already had a girlfriend and gotten laid.

"I could get used to this!" he thought.

Dave leaned over and kissed Cathy's forehead. She really was so pretty. He imagined what it would be like when he took her home and showed her off to all his friends. Jesus, they would be jealous, and so would all those frigid girls from his high school who had lead him and the guys on for all those years. He settled back under the quilt (something he didn't have at home but was beginning to enjoy) and smiled to himself, taking it all in.

"Oh shit!" Dave cried out loud leaping up. He'd forgotten all about Film Studies. What was the time? Had he blown it?

"Oh God, oh God."

He searched for his watch before catching sight of Cathy's digital alarm clock. Its glowing
 red digits showed 7.32. Was this too late? *The Bookseller* hadn't told him how early 'early' was. He imagined a line of English majors curling around the American Studies building.

Dave leapt out of bed and started fumbling for his clothes as Cathy stirred.

"Off already?" she whispered, opening her eyes but not moving.

"No ... I'm not sneaking out. It's Film Studies, I forgot about Film Studies. I've got to sign up."

"Either you're fucking keen or that's the best excuse I've heard yet," Cathy giggled.

"No, no. I'm not sneaking out. I've got to sign up for Film Studies. See you later?" Dave asked, frantically searching for his shorts in the pile of clothes on the floor.

"Yeah, sure,"

He stumbled down the stairs and out into the cool morning air, pulling his clothes on as he went, before racing down the hill, following signs to the main college buildings.

"Jesus, where is the American Studies department?"

He carried on running without knowing where he was going.

"I've gotta' ask someone."

But who? There was no one about. It was still much too early for students. All the dormitories were still quiet, their occupants still slumbering behind drawn drapes. And what drapes! Who on earth chose the colors of those? Orange seemed to be a favorite, closely followed by brown!

At the bottom of the hill, Dave met a university security guard busily picking his nose.

"Ah hah," thought Dave, "a guy who'll know where American Studies is."

The security guard was in a world of his own, 'Nose-picker Land', and he had obviously just hit a rich seam as Dave approached. He examined his treasure, rolled it in his fingers with a self-satisfied smile and...pushed it into his mouth.

"Oh Jesus," Dave' s stomach did a somersault, but he persevered.

"Excuse me. Could you tell me where the American Studies department is?"

"Tha' wot?"

"Er... the American Studies department," Dave asked again.

The *Nasal-miner* chewed thoughtfully for a moment.

"Come on, you bastard," thought Dave, "this isn't a trick question."

The guard rolled his 'breakfast' over his front teeth with his tongue and gazed thoughtfully skywards. Finally he spoke.

"Tha' gos darn theer," he pointed, "Den tha turns rate, an' it's rate theer."

"I beg your pardon?"

The guard repeated his instructions with an "al rate, yuuth" at the end for heightened clarity.

"Er...thanks," smiled Dave, none the wiser, but making a mental note to sign up for lessons in speaking 'Sheffield'.

Dave charged off down the hill where he ran straight into the American Studies department in all its glory. Well not that much glory really as it consisted of a collection of temporary huts, but Dave didn't care. He had reached his goal and he barged through the door, anxiously looking for the line of English majors signing onto the easiest course in college. But there was no line. There was no one in fact, except an enormous black lady slopping yet more of that omnipresent polish onto the corridor floor from a bucket.

"No one here yet, darlin'," she smiled.

"Oh...er...I'll wait then."

And wait he did, for over an hour, until a professor, who looked like a caricature in his brown cord pants and hideous sweater, appeared and started to fumble in his battered brown briefcase for his office keys. He noticed Dave.

"Er...can I...ah...help you?" he asked, through his serious, though amusing, speech impediment.

"Yes...I've come to sign up for Film Studies."

The professor beamed through his beard.

"An American! Oh...er...jolly good. You're...ah...keen. Interested in er...films are you?"

"Oh yes."

"Excellent...er...excellent. That's my...ah...course. What's er...your favorite film?"

Dave' s mind went completely blank.

"Oh shit," he thought, "What do I say? I can't think of an intellectual movie."

"Er...there' s a whole bunch really."

He cringed. What a stupid thing to say.

"Yes, yes. Of...er...course. My favorite's *Five Easy Pieces*," the professor went on, "It's...ah...one of the films we Study on the...er...course. The first one actually. Magnificent, magnificent."

"Never heard of it," thought Dave panicking.

"Oh yes, great! May I ask where...er...you're from?"

"Beavers Bluffs, near Omaha, Nebraska."

"Not from Hollywood then?"

"No, sorry."

"Oh well, never mind, er...come in young man. I'll...ah...take your details."

Five minutes later it was all sorted. Dave was on the course and had already scored loads of points with the bearded movie-buff by being American. And to heighten his joy, as he was leaving the office, the English majors arrived, hordes of them. It was as though a bus had just pulled up outside and emptied its passengers into the corridor of the American Studies department. As Dave strutted past the line, he shuddered as he was caught in a blast of pseudo-intellectual hot air emanating from a group where everyone was talking but nobody was listening. As they vied with each other for the 'most widely read' crown, each was straining desperately to employ their newly learned 'obscure word of the week', while praying that no one else would recognize it and that they had used it in the correct context. Dave decided at that moment that he agreed with *The Bookseller's* opinion of English majors; they were 'a bunch of tossers'. "And who had tipped them off about Film Studies?" Dave wondered. "Did they receive a secret note with their acceptance letter?"

"Yes!" Dave cheered and punched the air as he left the hut. "What a fantastic start," he thought. Less than twenty-four hours in the country and he'd already got a girlfriend, got laid and had a blowjob and signed up for three years of lounging around watching movies.

There was definitely a spring in Dave's step as he strolled back to Sheaf Hall. It was a beautiful fall day, the sun was shining, the sky was blue, the air was clean and fresh and everything, yes everything, was wonderful. Dave bounded up the stairs to Cathy's room and knocked on the door. There was no reply.

"Oh well," he thought, "she's obviously gone off to her lectures. I'll catch up with her later." And he smiled to himself as he thought about exactly what he'd like to do when he did catch up with her!

He returned to his own room, opened the door and was quite shocked by how cold and uninviting it was compared to Cathy's. His bags were still unopened on the bed; there were no posters, no trendy lamps, no keepsakes. He would have to remedy this, and quickly, so that Cathy would be impressed when she came visit. But, for the moment he had other things to do, the first of which was to shower. He smelled of sex and he needed a change of clothes. He rummaged in his suitcase for his wash bag, his towel and his bathrobe, stripped off and ambled off down the dark corridor to the shower room.

As he pushed open the door, the first thing that hit him was an assault on his nostrils.

"Wooh," he said out loud, "what a fucking stench."

Someone obviously had a serious problem with their bowels and that person had evidently just vacated this cramped room, leaving their 'problem' for him to suffer. The only solution to the problem was to make the aroma his own as quickly as possible and, after scrupulously wiping the toilet seat with copious amounts of toilet paper; he proceeded to do just that.

On his way from the stall to the adjacent shower, something caught his eye. On the huge iron radiator heater, the sort found in old public buildings, were hundreds of small mushrooms. These were unlike any variety Dave had seen back home, these were tiny ones with long, thin stems.

"Bizarre!" thought Dave.

Half an hour later, freshly showered, shaved, powdered, deodoranted and dressed, Dave made his way across the Quad in search of the Refectory. He was starving and he could smell a cooked breakfast wafting around him.

"Whyyooooooo."

It was that wolf howl he had heard the evening before. He spun around and was greeted by *Brain-Dead* bolting out of the door he had just exited and charging towards him.

"Oi fresher, wait for me," yelled *Brain-Dead*.

"Hi," said Dave.

"You're a Yank! And where were you last night? Shagging?" laughed *Brain-Dead*.

"Er"

"You dirty bastard! On your first night."

Dave couldn't help but beam with pride.

"I...er…"

"You were shagging weren't 'ya? We came to your room to take you for the 'Yard of ale' and you weren't there. And you didn't come back, did ya? You were shagging weren't ya?"

"I...er... "

"You dirty bastard!"

By now they had reached the line leading into the Refectory and joined the end of it. *Brain-Dead* tapped a group of girls in front of them on their shoulders.

"His first night here and where was he?" he asked the group, "Shagging!"

Dave blushed. The girls blushed
.

"Who was it?" *Brain-Dead* continued, "Come on, who was she?"

The five minutes it took for the line to reach the serving area seemed like an eternity. *Brain-Dead* had told everyone within earshot in the line and everyone leaving the Refectory his theory.

"Eggs please, darlin', the sloppier the better," *Brain-Dead* demanded of the late middle-aged woman in a pink housecoat who was dishing out the breakfasts, "And give plenty to the boy here. He's been shagging all night."

Head bowed and embarrassed, but secretly proud, Dave collected his very sloppy and barely edible scrambled eggs and soggy toast and sat down on a long wooden bench next to *Brain-Dead*.

"So what' s your name then *Yank*?" *Brain-Dead* asked, spitting bits of egg onto Dave' s plate as he spoke.

"Dave."

"Dave! That's not very American. Why aren't you called Bud or Dwight or Homer or something interesting?"

"My father's called David."

"So are you David Yank the third or something stupid?"

"No, just David. So what' s your name?"

"Everyone just calls me *Brain-Dead*."

"And you think 'David's' stupid?"

"Good point *Yank*, good point. Didn't waste much time coming over here and shagging all our women, did ya?"

"I haven't screwed all of them yet!"

Brain Dead laughed. "Another good point *Yank*. I like you!"

And with that *Brain-Dead*, who'd wolfed down his breakfast, stood up, said 'Goodbye' and left; howling at a pretty young girl who had just entered the Refectory as he left, nearly causing her to drop her tray.

After breakfast, Dave returned to his room, picked up a bag containing a notebook and pen and marched off towards the History Department for the Introduction Meeting. He was now really nervous. Up until now he hadn't given the course a lot of thought or indeed given any of this great adventure much thought if the truth be told. He had applied for the scholarship as a bit of a joke, not expecting to win it, and since then had been swept up in the hype of showing off to his friends, filling in forms and making travel arrangements. Now was the moment of truth and his confidence drained away as a horrible thought occurred to him. At high school he had always cruised through History. Out of a class of fifteen, he had comfortably outshone all the other students. He found the subject easy, relatively interesting and had a teacher who regarded him as the star student. He had been good at English as well, but had chosen to apply for History, because that was the only one on offer for the scholarship. The cause of his sudden crisis of confidence was the thought that he was about to be surrounded not by people who weren't particularly interested or talented in the subject, but by people who, like him, had been the best in their schools. And these were Brits at Brit schools. What were they like? Were they really fucking clever? Did they have two brains? Did they already know all there was to know about European history when he knew next to nothing? Were the lectures going to be difficult? Would he understand the professors' accents? Shit, maybe it wouldn't be so easy after all!

Dave followed the crowds of students down the hill, past the *Students Union* building and under a huge flyover to the enormous Arts Tower where, according to his brochure, the History Department was to be found. It was a strange building, very 1960's, surrounded by concrete, a pond and fountain that, presumably, never saw any water judging by the garbage billowing around it.

Dave joined the stream of students and occasional professor mounting the steps to the building. Once inside, there were two lines. One was waiting by two elevators, both of which seemed to be stuck on the tenth floor. The other line led to the *Paternoster*, which Dave had also read about in his brochure, and this was where all the fun was.

The theory behind a *Paternoster* was fine; have a constantly moving series of cubicle-like elevators, one set going up and the other down, so that people can easily jump on and off on whatever floor they want. No waiting for elevators, no waiting for doors to open; that was the theory. However, the theory didn't allow for freshmen, especially, giggly eighteen-year-old coeds, who were the cause of the queue. Instead of jumping on in groups of three or four whenever a cubicle appeared, the girl at the front would stick her leg out or step forward, then leap back shrieking with fear. Dave watched this for a couple of minutes as the line behind him grew and grew. A student behind Dave was not enjoying the spectacle at all. He was huffing and puffing and finally, with a "Bollocks to this", he left the line for the 'Up' *Paternoster* and jumped into a down cubicle where, of course, there was no line as there was only the basement below.

It was a minute later that Dave saw the light. The student he had watched going down was now in a cubicle going up, with a huge, beaming 'Fuck you' smile on his face. It took only a couple of seconds for Dave to pick his jaw off the floor, think "Why didn't I think of that" and jump onto the down *Paternoster*. Once he reached the floor below, he simply jumped out and jumped into the next upward moving cubicle. As he passed the first floor with the line and the silly girl with her foot out again, he also smiled in that newly learned 'Fuck you' sort of a way.

At the seventh floor (which was really the eighth floor!), he jumped out and walked down the dark corridor to the History Department communal area. It was probably a good idea having all the corridors in the innards of the building so that all the offices on the outside had huge windows, but it did mean that the corridors were grim and dark. Dave did a quick tour of the entire seventh floor before eventually finding the departmental secretary's office and being directed towards the meeting room he was supposed to be in. He pushed open the heavy door and entered a room bathed in sunlight. The room was dominated by a huge table, around which were perhaps thirty nervously smiling, well-scrubbed freshmen. Dave mumbled a 'Hi' and a few responded with their own mumbled greetings as he struggled towards one of the few empty chairs. He sat down and stared out of the massive window with its panoramic view over Sheffield basking in the sunshine. From this high vantage point, the scenery was magnificent, with blocks of gray apartment buildings, the green of a park, rows of tiny houses, cars buzzing down the two lane highway on the wrong side of the road and people the size of insects streaming across the car park past the redundant fountain towards the Arts Tower.

"Hullo," said a cheerful guy next to Dave.

"Oh, hi."

"Name's Paul."

"Dave."

"You're the American from Sheaf Hall, aren't you? I saw you at breakfast this morning. Did you really get your end away last night?"

"Er…"

"You lucky bastard. That was quick work, wasn't it?"

A girl with a beautiful face and a radiant smile on the other side of Dave leaned over.

"That was you, was it? Bloody hell, better watch out for you! I'm Pam." She offered out her hand, "You can shake my hand, but nothing else, you Stud."

Pam and Paul both laughed, Dave blushed.

Thankfully, to Dave's immense relief, the door burst open and a professor leapt into the room, tripping over and falling onto a timid youth sitting just inside the door.

"Fuck!"

The assembled freshmen laughed.
"Sorry, sorry!"

The crash victim pushed his glasses back onto his face.

"Morning everyone, my name's Dr. Devine. Welcome to Sheffield. I hope you all got through the reading list we sent you."

"Yeah right!" Paul whispered to Dave.

"Because we're going to give you a test to see how much you've remembered."

"Oh fuck," Pam blurted out very loudly.

Dr. Devine laughed, "Just joking! Ha ha".

The entire room breathed a communal sigh of relief.

"No, today we're just going to give you your timetables. But, if you want to suck up and create the right impression, you can all attend the History Department' s 'Hello Freshers' cheese and wine evening tonight. It's only £10, it's the highlight of the social calendar and, with delicious sweet white wine and processed cheese, it's the most fun you can possibly have with your clothes on!"

"That's you out then, eh?" whispered Pam to Dave.

"Oh...and if we don't get sufficient numbers signing up, the Head of Department gets really pissed off and insists we really do have that summer reading test. So, who' s up for it?"

Everyone in the room raised their hands.

So, at seven-thirty that evening, Dave, Paul and Pam stepped out of Sheaf Hall heading towards *The Horse and Hounds* pub in Broomhill, the venue for the History Department's 'Hello Freshers' cheese and wine evening. Dave had again knocked on Cathy's door, but yet again she was nowhere to be found. However, Paul and Pam were laughing and joking as they strolled along and he was enjoying their company. Pam was great fun. She was from Newcastle Upon Tyne in the North East of England and had a very strange sense of humor as well as an accent that made her very difficult to understand. Paul said he was from London and his accent was straight from one of those black and white Brit wartime movies that came on TV in the early hours of the morning. Still, he seemed so friendly that didn't matter.

The Horse and Hounds pub duly found, they went in and were guided upstairs by a bartender who issued the instructions without once averting his gaze from the TV on the opposite wall. Upstairs their hearts sank. Dr. Devine's description had been totally accurate. There were indeed several dozen 'gas station freebie' wine glasses filled with urine-colored sweet white wine and two plates of rubber cheese chunks on sticks. The decor was something to behold; tobacco-yellow walls and a hideously garish carpet whose worn-out sections were being held together by black tape. The centerpiece was a very old black, iron, open fireplace where lumps of coal had not been lit properly, leaving plumes of acrid white smoke to billow out from the semi-blocked chimney into the room. Everyone in the room, students and professors alike, looked as miserable as sin.

"Jesus," exclaimed Pam, "Can you imagine what this lot are like when they're not partying?"

"Ah, hello," One of the professors had spotted them and was steaming over. "Welcome, welcome. Come on in. Come on in. Drink? Bite to eat? What are your names them? Settled in yet? Chosen your courses, eh? What d'ya think of the place, eh? Made lots of friends? Name's Rogers, who are you three then? Been to Sheffield much before? Oh well, have fun, enjoy the evening. We'll chat again."

And with that, he turned his back on them and marched off across the room to barge in on someone else's conversation.

"What the fuck was that?" whispered Paul.

"That's the twat I've got for nearly everything this year," moaned Pam, "I signed up for all his courses. Oh God, what have I done? I won't survive a whole year listening to that plonker every day. Do you think I can change?"

All three stood in silence as the cold reality dawned on them. They had all chosen Professor Rogers' courses and it was too late to change them.

"We're well and truly, one hundred percent, totally and utterly fucked!" said Paul after a few moments.

"Oh well," said Pam. "Might as well deaden the pain."

She picked up a glass of wine and took a huge swig. Moments later her whole body shuddered.

"Oh my God, that is awful!"

"I can't speeath. My mouth's been glued together by the cheethe," mumbled Dave.

"Do you know?" declared Paul, "This is so awful, it's actually funny."

"You've got a sick mind," responded Pam

"No, no," Paul protested, "It takes real skill to find a wine like this. Just think how many gnats it took to produce such a vintage. And the cheese, someone actually chose this cheese. And, what' s even more frightening, that person was probably one of our tutors, in whose hands our education and future careers now rest!"

"Jesus," said Pam picking up another glass of wine, "better just get pissed then."

And that is exactly what they proceeded to do, with the result that they soon became the 'life and soul' of the party. The more they drank the more their laughter became louder which, in turn, drew the other students towards their group. Soon they were holding court and Dave, in his semi-drunken stupor, was loving it. In his own mind, he was obviously impressing everyone (especially the prettier women!) with his wonderfully witty anecdotes, amazing range of funny voices and his highly attractive American accent.

"Oh yeah!" he thought as a stunningly attractive blonde joined the group and smiled at him, "I'm on a roll now."

"Well I must say, this is going rather well. Everyone seems to be enjoying themselves, eh?" chirped Professor Rogers, joining the group.

"Fuck off," thought Dave, "I'm the center of attention now and the *Blonde's* getting nicely warmed up."

"So, why did you all choose the University of Yorkshire?" continued Professor Rogers.

"I really liked the structure of the course," replied the *Blonde*.

"Oh me too," squeaked a mousy-haired girl, "that's why I turned down Cambridge."

"Mad tart," laughed Paul, spiking the last piece of cheese with a cocktail stick.

"Well, that and it meant I could stay at home," the *Mouse* muttered.

"Time for some more razor-sharp wit, I believe," thought Dave.

"I won a scholarship," he blurted,

"Oh yes, you're our American aren't you?" smiled Professor Rogers. "Was it an open scholarship or one that specified the University of Yorkshire?"

Dave explained that the scholarship he had won was only open to students from the Omaha area to Study in Sheffield.

"If I was from Lincoln, the state capital of Nebraska, I could have applied for Lincolnshire University because there was a scholarship to go there as well. But nobody applied for it 'cause the entrance exam was too tough."

"Entrance exam? Do Lincolnshire University have an entrance exam now? I'd not heard that," asked Professor Rogers, looking puzzled.

"Yeah," laughed Dave, "you've got to be able to spell your own name and open a cookie jar, but nobody in Lincoln could pass the test. Ha, ha, ha!"

The whole group laughed, including the *Blonde*, spurring Dave on.

"Yeah, I could have majored in brain surgery with Basket weaving minor. But I'd have been wasting my time 'cause I heard that in their bathrooms, above the toilet tissue there are signs saying 'Lincolnshire degrees, wipe to develop'. Ha, ha, ha!"

At this Pam spat a mouthful of wine straight over Professor Rogers' crotch, making him look like he'd wet himself, but he didn't seem to notice. He just stared at Dave, who was bent over laughing and holding his stomach pretending he couldn't breathe.

"I went to Lincolnshire," Professor Rogers hissed, turning his back and walking off.

"Oh, fuck!" exclaimed Dave.

"Congratulations Dr. Kissinger," laughed Paul, "I'm sure a glorious future awaits you in the State Department."

"Oh no, what have I done? What should I do?" blubbed Dave.

"I'd kiss my ass goodbye if I were you," laughed Pam

"Why not apologize?" suggested the *Blonde.*

"Good idea, I'll apologize. That's a really good idea."

So off Dave went, across the room towards Professor Rogers, who was now standing by the fire, talking earnestly to another tutor. However, it was only now Dave tried to walk that he realized just how drunk he was. He could feel himself swerving as he guided himself through the crowd, making exaggerated maneuvers to avoid groups of people. As he approached Professor Rogers, the professor glared at him and continued his conversation.

"Right," thought Dave, "must be diplomatic, mustn't barge in. I'll just hover. Yes hovering's good. Then, when he's finished his conversation, I'll dart in and smooth everything out. That's the best plan."

Unfortunately hovering was not as easy as Dave had hoped. He decided to stand discreetly with his back to Professor Rogers but, what he hadn't planned to do was to rock back and forth as the alcohol swept through his veins and his stomach contents made an occasional escape bid through his mouth, being held back just in time with a burning gulp in his throat.

"Excuse me, excuse me, more refreshments on the way."

Dave turned to see an extremely plump woman, with a face as round as a beach ball, thick glasses and a beak of a nose, wobbling across the room with a tray of rubber cheese held high in the air resting on the palm of her hand. She was obviously impressed with her waitressing skills and was playing to the crowd.

"More cheese anyone? Anyone still hungry?"

"Christ she's ugly," thought Dave. "She's got the face and body only an academic, with no interest in anything but dusty books, could bear to be with. Can you imagine fucking that? Wow!" Dave shuddered and chuckled to himself as he imagined Professor Rogers whipping off his faded white shorts and leaping astride that monster for a spot of 'hide the sausage'.

"'Scuse me, excuse me. More cheese?"

As she approached, the crowd of students parted like the Red Sea for Moses, revealing the true enormity of her bulk. Beneath her blouse, two enormous breasts bounced on her stomach and her dress looked like drapes on a string hanging down from her totally rounded middle. She was a few feet away from Dave when she barged into a group of students who hadn't taken the hint that they should move. In doing so she clattered into the back of the small mousy girl. Everything about this girl said 'Mouse'. She was so petite she looked like a twelve-year-old, she squeaked when she spoke and had huge black glasses perched on her small, pointed 'rodent-like' nose. To try to disguise her diminutive stature she was delicately balanced on perilously high stiletto-heeled black shoes. These were to prove to be her downfall when the full force of the waitress-blimp crashed into her back and sent her reeling. As she fought to regain her balance, she staggered sideways towards Dave and stamped a screwdriver-like stiletto heel right in the middle of Dave's foot.

"Ahhhhhhh fuck!" Dave screamed, as he jumped backwards, writhing in agony. He hopped on one leg, trying to grasp his injured foot, until he in turn collided with someone behind him.

"Oh my god!"

Dave turned around to see Professor Rogers leaping out of the coal fire. He was jumping up and down, wildly shaking his leg and trying to slap away glowing embers from his pants and his shoe. Burning coals were rolling away from the fire across the threadbare carpet as an emergency team of academics and the *Blimp* charged to his rescue, slapping his leg and kicking the coals back towards the fireplace. The *Blimp* dropped the tray of cheese with a clatter onto the floor, grabbed a bystander's glass of white wine and threw it over the professor's smoking leg.

Dave stood with his mouth wide open and his eyes bulging, as his alcohol-dulled brain tried to make sense of what his eyes were telling it. As the commotion died down, Professor Rogers turned round, his face now purple and his piercing eyes focused on Dave.

"You ...you," he shouted with veins bulging out of his neck, "you maniac. You tried to kill me! Are you mad? Are you insane boy?"

"I...er...It was an accident...my foot...I..." stuttered Dave.

"Get out," roared Professor Rogers like an angry lion. It seemed like his mouth was on hinges.

"But...but."

"Get out now!"

The first roar was so loud that most gamblers would have wagered their shirts on a louder roar being physically impossible. Even the most astute bookmaker would have offered very generous odds, but they would all have been out of pocket, because the second roar was more an explosion than a roar. It seemed as if the drapes swayed with its power, leaving a silent vacuum. The room was still as everyone held their breath.

After what seemed like an eternity, the silence was broken.

"Come on *Luv*, let's take you home," Pam whispered softly into Dave's ear, resting a gentle hand on his shoulder and guiding him towards the door. As they moved away, Paul joined them on their journey through a sea of silent partygoers, like a priest and executioner escorting the condemned man on the final steps up the scaffold. Still in absolute silence, they reached the stairs and made their escape. About half way down the stairs, the room behind them suddenly erupted with noise as the partygoers nervously and excitably discussed the scene that had just taken place before their very eyes.

The trio fell out of the pub into the cold, dark night and quickly marched away.

"That's you off his Christmas card list then", laughed Paul, "Fancy a kebab?"

TWO

"Oh my head," Dave groaned as he punched the 'off' button on his alarm clock.

As he struggled to lift his head off his pillow, a shiver ran down his spine.

"Oh fuck. What have I done?"

Holding his throbbing head, he caught sight of his still fully dressed form on the bed. He still had his shoes on, the drapes were open and the one thousand watt light bulb was competing with the sunlight to burn a hole in his brain.

"I need a shower."

He peeled off his wine-soaked, kebab-stained clothes, pulled on his bathrobe, looked at himself in the mirror, groaned and then opened his door and staggered down the hall to the shower room.

As he pushed open the shower room door, the stench that greeted him made him gag.

"Oh my God."

Momentarily he stepped back out into hall to take a lung full of air before persevering back into the shower room. He had to piss like a racehorse, so pushed at the toilet door, but it was locked.

"Top of the morning to ya'!" came a voice from inside the toilet stall.

"Is that you *Brain-Dead*?"

"Ah *Lover boy*, been a' shagging again have ya'?"

"You going to be long? I'm desperate."

"Now ya' wouldn't rush a man's morning dump, would ya'? I've only had half an hour in here and all I've got to show for it is a turtle's head. Tell ya' what though, I could do with another cup of tea, this one's gone cold. Oh, and you could check the Common Room to see if the papers are in yet. *Daily Mirror* would be good".

"Fuck off and just hurry up will you? I need a piss."

"If it's just a piss you need you should be making better use of the facilities."

"What? What are you talking about?"

"My dear *Shag-Monster*, you have a sink in fully working order do you not? Or is there some young filly in your room waiting for her morning porking?"

Seeing that he was getting nowhere, Dave stepped into the shower, locked the door, took off his bathrobe, turned the water on and stepped under the hot water. As he relieved himself down the plughole, he groaned with pleasure before the horrors of the previous evening came flooding back.

Half an hour later he was shaved, dressed and hungry. As he crossed the Quad heading for the Refectory and the distant smell of bacon, *Brain-Dead* caught up with him.

"I was looking for you last night. Out shagging I suppose?"

"No I wasn't actually."

"Well anyway, how d'ya fancy being a professional wanker?"

"What?"

"The pay's good, great working conditions."

"*Brain-Dead*, what ARE you talking about?"

"It was on the radio yesterday, the hospital want wankers. Ten Pounds a shot."

"What are you on?"

"Loads of things, but that's not the point. It's true. The hospital want good manly sperm to squirt up women whose husbands are *Jaffas*."

"What are *Jaffas*?" asked Dave.

"They're oranges without any seeds, geddit? Anyway, the hospital don't want any old sperm, oh no, they only want the best vintage student sperm. So we're starting a club, Sheaf Hall Wankers. That way we can take it turns to take the pots of sponk to the hospital and have a communal porno mag library. What d'ya reckon, can you spare any?"

It was at this point that Dave's gaze was diverted to the door at the bottom of Cathy's block. The door swung open and out stepped Cathy, arm in arm with some huge guy. Dave was glued to the spot. *Brain-Dead*, meanwhile, let out an ear-splitting wolf howl.

"Aaaaaaaaaaaaaaaaaooooo"

And with that he bounded over to Cathy and her hunky companion.

"Catherine, Catherine, great news, great news. We're going to be professional wankers."

"Why does this not surprise me, *Brain-Dead*?"

The *Hunk* smirked in a proud-hunk sort of way. If it was possible, it actually seemed that his anvil-like jaw grew even bigger.

"No, no, you don't understand," *Brain-Dead* continued, ignoring or oblivious to the witty put down. "Ten Pounds a shot. Tell ya' what, we can go into a fifty-fifty partnership, my knob, your mouth. But you MUST promise to spit it into the pot. Whaddya say? In fact, you could be manager for the whole team and do the same for them. You'll make a fortune!"

"Fuck off *Brain-Dead*."

"No, no, you don't understand. Just think about it for a second. If there's ten of us, twice a week, that's £100 a week for you, for no more work than you're doing at the moment."

"Brain-Dead, fuck off!"

"But Cath, it's your hobby. In fact, you could make more. I'll give you a supply of pots, then every time you honk someone like him," continued *Brain-Dead*, flicking his thumb in the direction of the *Hunk*, "you can spit it out into a pot. Then Bingo, ten sobs. Can't say fairer than that now can we? So whaddya' say?"

It was at this moment that the *Hunk* seemed to stir and start to move. It was just as if *Gorro*, the horror movie doctor's evil assistant, had just clicked the switch sending a million volts flowing through the corpse's body, prompting him to sit up on the slab and tighten the bolt in his neck.

"Don't talk to my girlfriend like that," he grunted in a voice so deep that the ground seemed to shake.

Cathy spun round on him.

"Your what? Your girlfriend? Who the fuck do you think you are? We screw once - and not very successfully I might add - and you think I'm your girlfriend. Piss off. Go on, get out of my sight."

"But Cath..." the *Hunk* was obviously wounded.

"You heard the lady," interrupted *Brain-Dead*, "Shagging not up to scratch, so on ya' bike."

Dave actually felt sorry for the *Hunk*. His hatred of only moments before evaporated and was replaced by sympathy for someone who had obviously been taken for the same ride as him.

"Hello David," Cathy smiled.

"Hi," muttered Dave, before striding away towards the Refectory, leaving *Brain-Dead* to sell artificial insemination to Cathy.

After a brief wait in line, Dave surveyed the culinary delights of another Sheaf Hall English breakfast. Hangover hunger meant he had to eat, but the fare on offer looked disgusting and much worse than yesterday's.

"What ya' havin, *Luv*? Come on, son. It'll soon be lunchtime," croaked what looked like a Russian shot-putter with huge throbbing red warts on her face. Her greasy, matted hair was pulled back behind her head and held in place with a brown elastic band. She held an enormous ladle over two huge stainless steel containers. The containers were in turn suspended over boiling water, with steam gushing up between the gaps.

"Er..." Dave stared down into the containers. One was full of huge slices of brown bacon with bits of bone in them, the rind still on and more fat than meat, complete with a strange brown scum. The other was full of a bright red liquid in which peeled tomatoes floated.

"For God's sake son, it's not a hard choice," croaked the *Shot-putter*.

"Bacon and tomatoes please," whispered Dave.

"Good choice son," laughed the *Shot-putter*, "Isn't that amazing, that's just what I would have picked."

Two other witches in filthy white coats behind the counter laughed at Dave as the *Shot-putter* dangled a slice of bacon over Dave' s plate, letting the fat run off before splatting it down. She then scooped up the tomatoes and what seemed like a gallon of red liquid, before splashing them down with such a force that a wave flew over Dave' s hand, up his arm and peppered his white T-shirt.

"Thanks," muttered Dave, thinking 'Bitch'.

With his scalded hand holding the plate and another rummaging for cutlery, Dave then managed to spill some of the tomato juice over his crotch.

"Jesus!" he moaned, feeling particularly sorry for himself.

"Dave, Dave over here." Dave turned round to see Pam calling him across the Refectory. Sitting with her was Paul and the *Blonde* he'd had the hots for the previous evening.

"How 'ya feeling, Darling?" asked Pam gently.

"I've had better days," replied Dave, putting his plate down and sitting on the bench next to Paul.

"That was some apology you gave Professor Rogers last night," the *Blonde* smiled.

"Dave, this is Samantha," Paul interjected

"Pleased to meet you," said Dave, standing briefly to shake her hand.

"Call me Sam. I did feel so sorry for you last night," she whispered sweetly.

"What have you done to your shirt?" laughed Pam, noticing the tomato stain.

"Don't ask," replied Dave as he struggled to prise the inch of fat and rind from his slice of bacon.

When he looked up, having finally succeeded in freeing a piece he could actually eat, he saw Samantha smiling at him. He smiled back.

"God, she's absolutely gorgeous," he thought

"Whyyooooooooo."

The diners in the Refectory all turned in unison to discover the source of the wolf-like howl. Dave didn't need to look up, he knew it was *Brain-Dead*. He prayed with all his heart that *Brain-Dead* wouldn't sit at their table, but he knew that his prayers would be in vain.

"Hey, hey Shag-monster, thought I'd lost you for a moment. Squeeze up will ya'?" bellowed *Brain-Dead*, barging Dave in the back with his backside.

Brain-Dead squeezed onto the bench next to Dave and plunked an enormous plateful of bacon, bread and tomatoes onto the table, spilling tomato juice over the table. Then, to Dave's horror, Cathy settled herself opposite him, next to Samantha.

"Eat up son," *Brain-Dead* prompted Dave through a mouthful of breakfast, spitting bits of bacon and tomato over the table, "Got to keep your strength up now you're a professional wanker."

"A what?" Pam hooted with laughter.

"Didn't ya' know? The *Yank*'s going to masturbate for a living. That's if Cathy can keep his cock out of her mouth long enough."

This was too much for Pam. She keeled over and nearly fell off the bench.

"Just fuck off buddy," Dave snarled at *Brain-Dead*. He looked up at Samantha, who just stared back at him, open mouthed.

"What's he talking about?" asked Paul.

"I really don't know. He was mouthing off about sperm donations, but I've not said I'm doing it. He's probably just jerking my chain," said Dave, replying to Paul, but addressing Samantha.

"It's true, it's true," said *Brain-Dead*, spitting out more food, "There's good money in it. Why not get paid for it. It's like being paid for having a dump or something."

By now Pam was crying with laughter.

"I think it's a good idea," said Samantha, "My sister's having treatment. My brother-in-law and her want kids but can't have them. I think it's great that they can be helped."

"Fuck me," gasped *Brain-Dead*, "If she looks like you, I'd personally deliver her some fresh, free of charge!"

By this point, Dave had had enough.

"Listen guys, I've gotta' go. I've got Movie Studies."

He got up from the table, leaving *Brain-Dead* and Paul discussing the financial benefits of sperm donation and Pam wiping tears from her eyes.

"See you later?" Cathy whispered to Dave.

"Er...I'm not sure," replied Dave, still feeling wounded.

"Dave, wait a minute," called Samantha, "I'm doing Film Studies as well. Can I walk with you?"

"Sure," smiled Dave. His day had just got better.

Ten minutes later Dave, now in a clean shirt, met Samantha in the Quad and they set off together down the hill towards the American Studies department. As they walked, they chatted like they'd known each other for years. Samantha was from Manchester, she wanted to be a teacher, she had two sisters, she had a black Labrador dog called Digby, she loved dancing and skiing and Dave thought she was beautiful.

They arrived at the American Studies Department and found the room their schedules told them they ought to be in. Inside, all the windows were covered with blackout blinds and there were half a dozen rows of plastic chairs all facing a television on a stand with a DVD player beneath it. Already most of the chairs were taken, largely occupied by students Dave did not recognize. He presumed that they must be mainly American Studies majors, but there were also a fair number of English majors he had seen the

day before. Even at home, he'd been warned that English and American Literature and Language majors in college had a reputation for being conceited, partly
because English demanded the highest grades and partly because they believed themselves to be 'beautiful' arty people who could read subliminal messages in books that mere mortals would never see. The medical students had a similar reputation and were known to look down on trainee dentists and vets. God knows why? When the doctors finally made it through the course and found themselves working their internships, doing twenty hour shifts in some scruffy hospital being threatened by drunks, the dentists would be buying their first Porches and spending their evenings screwing their receptionists and counting their cash.

Be that as it may, the English majors had claimed the back rows of the makeshift cinema, like a group of school kids claiming the backseat of a school bus and, to Dave's ears, were sneering at any non-English major who entered the room.

Dave and Samantha took two empty seats in the front row. Dave, by now trying to impress, delved into his bag and pulled out a notebook and pen, just as the professor, bumbled into the room.

"Hi everyone. Ah…welcome, welcome. I'm er...Dr. Marsden, but just call me er...Brian."

"Hi Brian," responded the English majors in unison from the back.

"Er...hi, hi, hi. Anyway, er...welcome to Film Studies. We're...ah...starting with a real...er...treat today, *Five Easy Pieces*. You've er...all probably seen it several times already but I'm...ah...sure you won't mind seeing it again!"

Silence from the room. Dave wrote *Five Easy Pieces* on his pad.

"Ah well, er…as you probably know it stars Jack Nicholson and is er... about the battle between the two halves of his...ah…soul."

"Did he say 'Two halves of his asshole?'" Dave whispered to Samantha.

Samantha giggled but Dr. Marsden scowled. Dave's whisper had been more of a stage whisper, which Dr. Marsden and a few of the other students had also heard.

"Er...anyway. Here we er…go. Fantastic film," continued Dr. Marsden pressing the play button on the DVD.

On the screen, a BBC Christmas title sequence started, featuring a globe topped with skating Santas and reindeer. Dave giggled, imagining Dr. Marsden on Christmas Day, full of Turkey, with a paper hat on his head and, no doubt, slightly drunk crawling over the rug trying to work the DVD Recorder.

As soon as the opening titles started, Dr. Marsden turned the lights off before leaning over to Dave and in a very loud stage whisper said, "Er...good at taking notes in the dark are er...you?"

The English majors thought this was hilarious and even Samantha giggled, much to Dave' s embarrassment. Dave put his notebook and pen down, thankful that the darkness hid his bright red face.

After ninety minutes or so of *Five Easy Pieces* and a good deal of bottom shuffling on the unbelievably uncomfortable plastic chairs, the end credits appeared and Dr. Marsden flicked on the lights, leaving the assembled students blinking and rubbing their eyes.

"Er...wonderful eh?" pronounced Dr. Marsden. "So any ah...comments?"

"I must say I felt very moved by the emotional torment of Jack Nicholson's character as he tried to choose between the staid, middle class piano-playing world of his childhood and the dreadful, violent, working class world of the oil workers," spouted one of the English majors who, for some reason, was dressed like a character from Robin Hood.

"Yes, er...yes, yes, absolutely," enthused Dr. Marsden. "And did you er...notice the director's clever touch at the end of the film?"

Silence.

"You know, er...the end sequence where Nicholson goes into the petrol station and makes up his mind to leave his ah...girlfriend and er...go off to Alaska?"

Silence.

"Did you er...notice what sort of petrol station it was eh?"

Silence.

"*Gulf!*"

Silence.

"Don't you get it? The director didn't just er...choose a *Gulf* petrol station by chance now did he? No, his choice of a *Gulf* station is expressing the 'GULF' between the masculine and feminine worlds. Clever eh? What 'ya think of that eh?"

The English majors nodded and chuckled.

"Bullshit!" whispered Dave to Samantha.

"Er...whaddya say young man?" asked Dr. Marsden turning to Dave.

"I...I...er...just meant that I'm...er...not convinced by that, Sir" stumbled Dave.

"So why did he choose a *Gulf* petrol station then?" demanded Dr. Marsden.

"Er...because it was nearby."

At this the English majors fell about, relishing what they saw as Dave's stupidity.

"Nearby...er...nearby. My dear boy, directors don't just choose things because they're ...er...nearby or handy. They're giving us messages. Well, when I say er...'us' I mean those of us equipped with enough intelligence to interpret the messages."

Dave' s only response was to gulp loudly and turn even redder.

"Maybe you er...need to consider whether you have the intellect to...ah...appreciate this course, my boy. Perhaps you might be happier with something less er...challenging."

Dave gulped again and Dr. Marsden turned to the rest of the class.

"Well that's er...it for today everyone. Same ah...time next week, when we'll be Studying *Gold Diggers of 1933*."

As the class filed out of the room, Dave made sure he was first in line to escape. He waited down the corridor for Samantha to catch up.

"Another stunning example of how to impress your tutor," smiled Samantha as she strolled up. "What have you got against academics?"

"Nothing," muttered Dave, going red with embarrassment again. "I just thought what he said was horseshit. He was a bit up his own ass, don't you think?"

"It's not what I think," replied Samantha. "As he'll be the person marking your exam paper, maybe you should join him up there."

"Guess you're right. You free for a coffee?" asked Dave, changing the subject.

"I can't I'm afraid. I've got to meet someone," replied Samantha.

Dave's heart sank. He'd already decided that he really liked Samantha. For someone so amazingly good-looking, she seemed to have a surprisingly pleasant personality, but he'd hardly impressed her so far, what with the previous evening's debacle and now this.

"Oh, okay then," Dave said sadly.

"Are you doing anything this evening?" asked Samantha.

Dave' s face brightened.

"No, no, nothing," he blurted.

"Would you like to come to a party in my room?"

"Is the bear a Catholic, does the Pope shit in the woods?" Dave replied.

"Do I take that as a 'yes'?" laughed Samantha.

"Yes," smiled Dave.

"Well, I've got one of the double rooms in hall," continued Samantha.

Dave looked puzzled.

"There are two bedrooms and a small lounge between them. Jo, the girl in the other room, and I thought it would be fun to have a few people round, to break the ice and all. We're meeting in the Hall Bar at about eight for a couple of drinks first. That suit you? Pam and Paul are coming; I asked them at breakfast," Samantha smiled with a gorgeous smile that made Dave melt.

"That suits me just fine," he replied.

"Oh, and I'll make sure no academics are invited, so you'll be quite safe!" Samantha laughed. "See you at eight then. Rooms B4 and 5."

"Yeah, see you later," called Dave, as Samantha walked off.

"Yes!" exclaimed Dave to himself, once he thought Samantha was out of earshot.

Samantha turned around, "What did you say?"

"Er...nothing. See you later," Dave stumbled.

Dave stood and watched her walk away until she turned a corner and was out of sight.

"Jeez, she's beautiful," Dave said under his breath.

"Er...yes she er…is, isn't she," said a voice behind him.

Dave nearly jumped out of his skin, before spinning round to see Dr. Marsden standing behind him.

"Listen, I'm sorry about what I said back there," said Dave, regaining his composure.

"That's alright, son. We're all er...entitled to our opinions. I take it *Five Easy Pieces* wasn't exactly your favorite film?"

"Well, it was okay, it's just that I couldn't see the hidden meanings you can see."

"Who knows," said Dr. Marsden, "Maybe it is all er...'bullshit' as you so eloquently put it. Unless we ask the director why he er...picked a *Gulf* petrol station, I suppose we'll never know. So tell me, what is your er...favorite film?"

44

"Honestly?" asked Dave.

"Son, from the little I've er...seen of you, I have no doubt that you'll give me a totally frank and er...honest answer," laughed Dr. Marsden.

Dave blushed.

"*The Blues Brothers.*"

"Ah ha," beamed Dr. Marsden, "a classic film. What a car chase at the end! I love it. It's not a film we Study on the course though, I'm er...afraid."

"Maybe it should be," said Dave, warming to this conversation. "Then we could discuss all the product placement in the movie."

"What er...product placement?" asked Dr. Marsden, looking curious.

"Well, you know the scene where they drive through the mall?"

"Er...yes," said Dr. Marsden, looking quizzical.

"Well they name every store in the mall, before they smash into them. I've always thought that was a way of paying corporations for smashing their stores to bits. Maybe the producer of *Five Easy Pieces* got a bunch of money from *Gulf* to use their gas station?"

Dr. Marsden went silent as he thought about Dave's theory.

"Oh er...bollocks, perhaps you're er...right?" he said after a pause. I'll have to give that some thought."

Dave smiled.

"Well it's *Gold Diggers of 1933* next week. I'd er...be interested to hear your theories on that," said Dr. Marsden.

"You gotta' deal," smiled Dave, "See you next week then,"

It was a much happier Dave that made his way back to Sheaf Hall. On the way back though, he suddenly changed course and diverted to the library to search for a book giving a critic's view of *Gold Diggers of 1933*.

THREE

Dave was certainly in happy mode that evening. Music blared from his mini CD player and he danced and mimed in front of his mirror as he got ready for the party. He lay out his 'coolest' clothes on the bed, hid the rubber he'd bought from a machine in the library bathroom in his wallet (just in case he got lucky with Samantha!) and put on a bathrobe in preparation for a second shower of the day.

As he opened his door to go to the shower room, someone he hadn't met before was struggling up the corridor with a coffee table, which Dave thought he recognized as one from the Common Room. The *Table-carrier* was a thick set youth with greasy blonde hair, wearing torn jeans and a grubby white T-shirt with the words 'Fuck Art, Let's Dance' printed on it.

"Want a hand with that?" Dave enquired as the youth crashed up the corridor, knocking dents into the wooden walls.

"Yeah," the youth grunted

Dave went to help and took one end of the table.

"My name' s Dave," Dave smiled over the table as he staggered backwards. The youth said nothing.

As they arrived outside Dave's room the youth motioned with his foot at the door next to Dave's.

"In there. Open the door, would ya'?" the youth grunted.

Dave, still holding his end of the table, pressed down on the door handle with his elbow and kicked the door open. The two of them lifted the table up onto its side and they maneuvered it into the room, with Dave edging backwards.

"Hello," said a voice behind Dave.

Dave turned around and his jaw fell open.

Standing in the middle of the room was a rather plump girl. She was stark naked with the exception of a pair of very high-heeled black shoes and, even more bizarrely, she had her arms up above her head. Around her wrists was a necktie, which in turn was attached to the flex of the ceiling light, causing the light shade to point up at an angle towards the wall.

Dave put his end of the table down and just stared at this girl open-mouthed. Nobody said anything. The youth began to position the table and the girl just smiled at Dave, her plump nakedness and her black pubic hair facing him.

Finally, having adjusted the table to his liking, the youth stood up straight.

"Thanks," he mumbled to Dave.

"Er...no problem," replied Dave.

"Yeah, thanks," smiled the girl

Then the three of them just stood in surreal silence. Eventually, the youth broke the silence.

"She's kinky and wants me to fuck her on the table," as if this offered to lend some normality to this strange scene. "You can fuck her as well, if you want," the youth laughed.

"Martin!" laughed the girl, as if she found this proposition embarrassing.

At that moment, *Brain-Dead* appeared at the open door.

"Martin," said *Brain-Dead*, "I think these mushrooms are ready, what d'ya think?"

Brain-Dead held out his hands towards the youth, in which he held the small mushrooms Dave had seen drying on the shower room radiator. As the youth examined the mushrooms, *Brain-Dead* glanced up at the naked plump girl dangling from the light fitting.

"Hello Karen," said *Brain-Dead*, with no trace of surprise in his voice.

"Hello *Brain-Dead*," the plump girl replied, with a hint of 'I'm getting bored here boys, could you discuss mushrooms some other time' in her voice.

Martin, ignoring her, continued Studying the mushrooms in *Brain-Dead's*

48

hands. As he did so, *Brain-Dead* turned to Dave.

"Do you fancy going to the football tomorrow, *Yank*?"

Dave, still stunned, took a few moments to reply.

"Er...football, what football?" he asked.

"Sheffield United. They're at home tomorrow, playing Grimsby," replied *Brain-Dead*.

"Er...OK," Dave spluttered, still in shock.

"Good. We'll have an early lunch and then go down for a few beers before the match."

"Martin!" exclaimed the naked Karen, "Come on, I'm getting bored."

Martin, still examining the mushrooms, continued ignoring her. Then, after rubbing some mushrooms between his fingers, finally lifted his head.

"Yup," he said to *Brain-Dead*, "I reckon they're ready. I'll take my half now."

As Martin and *Brain-Dead* began sharing out the mushrooms, Karen turned to Dave.

"Are you the American from next door?" she asked.

"Er…yes."

"*Brain-Dead* says you're a bit of a ladies man," she continued.

"Oh, I wouldn't say that," said Dave, blushing slightly.

"Don't listen to him Karen," laughed *Brain-Dead*, "He's a shag-monster."

"Listen," said Dave, "I've got to get a shower and get ready. I'm off to a party."

"Nice to meet you," smiled Karen, as Dave made towards the door.

"Yeah, nice to meet you too," mumbled Dave as he left the room, shutting the door and the bizarre scene behind him.

"What party?" he heard *Brain-Dead* call after him. But he chose to ignore him

Still in a daze, Dave went into the shower room, turned the shower on until the water ran hot before removing his bathrobe and stepping under the water. After he'd pushed away several discarded shampoo bottles in the shower tray with his foot and pulled a tangle of hair from the plughole to allow the water to drain away, he masturbated furiously.

Once he was dressed and sweet smelling from the copious amounts of deodorant he'd covered himself in, Dave hurried across the Quad to the Hall Bar, eager to meet Pam and Paul and relate the scene he'd just witnessed.

The decor in the Hall Bar was simply horrible, with yellow walls and brown furniture. The seats were made of foam rubber covered with plastic pretend-leather, many of which were ripped. This left the yellow foam rubber exposed, leaving it vulnerable to vandalism where, over the years, the bar patrons had picked huge chunks out. The walls of the bar were covered in badly designed posters promoting terrible university bands, whose only fans no doubt were friends of the band members, and various university societies, all of which seemed to have unfunny mottos such as 'Yorkshire University Miners like going down' and 'Get your rocks off with Yorkshire University Geologists'.

At the bar, where the bartender was a fat, bearded Senior pulling glasses of unheard of beer, was a group of sophomores or seniors dressed in massive hooped shirts, including Cathy's man from that morning, who had persuaded a skinny, lonely freshman to attempt a yard of ale – a long, flower vase sort of glass with a huge bulb at the end containing several pints of beer. They howled with laughter as their pitiful victim tried gulping the beer as it washed over his glasses and face and down his shirt.

Sitting in a corner were Pam and Paul. Paul was rolling a cigarette while Pam was crying with laughter.

"Over here, my son," Paul called to Dave.

As Dave sat down, Pam was gasping for breath through her laughter.

"Tell Dave, Paul. Go on tell him," Pam spluttered eventually.

"Tell me what?" asked Dave.

"I was just telling Pam what my duties as a 'fag' involved at my public school," smiled Paul.

Pam fell about laughing about again.

"You were a fag? Jesus, not exactly a PC way of putting it, but that's fine. Hey, whatever! But you 'ain't no more, right? Not that's it's a problem," Dave blushed. "And public school means private school here, right?"

"That's right, I was sent away to my first school aged seven," replied Paul. "Well, in my senior school we still had 'fagging'; which is where the younger kids were basically slaves to the prefects. Well, my job was to race back to my prefect's room as soon as lessons were finished and warm his toilet seat."

"Say what?" laughed Dave.

"As soon as the teacher let us out of the classroom at the end of the day, I had to run like a crazy bastard back to my prefect's room, put two slices of bread in his toaster and then sit on his toilet, so the seat would be nice and warm for him when he returned for his evening shit."

"Why?" asked Dave.

"Those were the rules. I was his fag," continued Paul, lighting his cigarette. "And if he made it back to his room before me, he'd cane me."

Pam lost it again and nearly fell off her chair.

"Tell him the rest Paul, tell him the rest," she roared.

"Well, after he'd had his shit and eaten the toast I'd buttered for him, I had to wank him off," smiled Paul, puffing his cigarette.

"Jesus," laughed Dave, "crazy English schools! Or was yours like a special gay school?"

"It wasn't a gay school and we weren't gay; that was just normal. Anyway, it could have been worse," Paul continued in a matter-of-fact way.

"Worse?" cried Pam, "How could it have been worse? That's fucking sick."

"Oh, well I didn't have it as bad as one kid. His prefect used to give it him up the arse!"

"Sounds sorta' gay to me," grinned Dave.

"And you know what was really sad?" added Paul.

"No, tell us", said Pam, with tears running down her face, the mascara around her eyes making her look like a panda.

"Well this kid's home was so close to school that he could see his own bedroom window from his dormitory, but his parents still sent him as a boarder."

At this, Pam fell off her chair, knocking her drink off the table and sending it crashing to the floor.

"So your parents sent you away to live in a school like that? Didn't they know what was going on?" asked Dave, horrified.

"I presume they did," replied Paul, gazing thoughtfully at the ceiling, "My dad and my
granddad both went to the school. I never discussed it with them, but they would have been 'fags' in their day."

Away at the bar, a loud cheer went up. Dave, Pam and Paul turned to see the skinny freshman throwing up the beer he'd managed to shallow from his yard of ale all over a girl in a black dress, who'd been queuing for a drink. Both of them stood for a moment staring at each other before they both started crying.

"My dress!" cried the girl, looking at the barf running down her and dripping onto her shoes.

The skinny freshman just stood motionless, sobbing with his bottom lip quivering and a foot-long strand of barf and spit dangling from his mouth.

"You bastards," said a friend of the girl, making her way from the back of the room and putting her arm around the shoulder of the barf-covered girl.

"Woooooh! Keep your hair on darlin'," laughed one of the crowd of men, standing at the bar. The yellow and black-hooped shirt he was wearing made him look like a beer- bellied bumble bee.

"I am not your 'darlin'," continued the girl's friend. "You're just a bunch on bullies, making this poor lad drink 'till he's sick. You should be ashamed of yourselves, you rugby-playing pillocks."

With that she started to guide the barf-covered girl across the bar towards the door.

"Fucking lesbian," the *Bumble Bee* mumbled as he turned to his group of friends, "Who's next for a yard?"

Suddenly, the girl's friend turned around and started back towards the *Bumble Bee*. The *Bumble Bee's* friends began pointing and nodding their heads to suggest that he should look behind him. Once he had finally grasped that they were suggesting he look round, he turned just in time to receive a stinging slap across his face which stunned him to his shoes. The impact immediately left a rosy-red welt on his cheek.

"You fucking bitch," he screamed. "If you weren't a bird, I'd rip your head off and shit down your fucking neck!"

The word 'neck' was still hanging in the air when a blur of the girl's red boot attached to a black-panted leg flew towards him and buried itself in his groin. The *Bumble Bee* crumpled like a bull elephant that had just taken a direct hit in the forehead with a high-velocity bullet. His friends, who formed a semicircle around what now looked like a walrus writhing in agony on the floor clutching his testicles, seemed to have all sucked lemons as they winced at the sight before them.

"Whadda girl!" yelled Pam, so loud that Paul literally jumped up in his seat, dropping what was left of his cigarette in the process.

"Jesus Pam," he moaned, "I think you burst my eardrum."

"But did you see that?" Pam continued. "That's my kind of girl. That rugger-bugger bastard won't find his dick for a month of Sundays."

Once the commotion had died down, Dave made his way to the bar to order some drinks. Against his better judgment, he ordered a pint of the unknown lager beer.

"I've never heard of this beer," Dave said to the bearded barman as his pint was pulled and pointing to the bizarre plastic font containing a smiling Bavarian holding a stein against a mountain backdrop.

"Local brew," answered the barman. "Bloody cheap though."

On sitting down and taking a gulp, Dave suddenly realized why it was 'bloody cheap' and why Pam and Paul had opted for bottled beer. It was disgusting. It was like drinking out of the 'slop tray' with a little soap added for good measure.

"Oh shit, this is awful," Dave spluttered.

"Gnat's piss," nodded Paul, rolling yet another roly.

"We can't take that shit to the party," said Pam. "We'll get some carry-outs of decent stuff."

Dave was back at the bar buying a substitute bottle of beer when a hand tapped him on the shoulder.

He turned to see Samantha, looking exquisite in a red, figure-hugging party dress. Dave's face lit up.

"Hi Dave, recovered from Film Studies yet?" Samantha smiled.

"Yeah, I'm even buddies with Dr. Marsden now," laughed Dave.

"Steady on!" grinned Samantha, "Don't want you getting pally with the academics, do we?"

"It's funny really," Dave continued. "We actually found something we both liked."

Dave failed to mention that the 'something' was Samantha.

It was then that Dave noticed a guy standing just behind Samantha. Then, to his horror, this stranger put his hand on Samantha's shoulder.

"What you drinking, my love?" the stranger whispered in 'melted chocolate' tones.

"Oh sorry, I'm being very rude," Samantha smiled. "Dave, this is Greg.

Greg, Dave."

Dave smiled weakly at Greg, when what he really wanted to do was spit. Not only did Greg call Samantha 'My love', he was another bloody hunk. His chin was square, his figure had that 'I work out regularly' toning, his slicked back, immaculate hair looked like one of those photos in a barbershop window and his teeth simply shone when he smiled at Dave.

Bastard!

"Greg and I were at school together, weren't we sweetheart? But he just couldn't live without his little 'Sammy', could you?" giggled Samantha, playfully pinching his cheek - a feat in itself, finding enough loose flesh to pinch. "So he followed me here."

Dave could not speak. What a total bastard! What a lucky bastard! Miserably, Dave followed Samantha back to the table where Pam and Paul were sitting and plunked himself down next to Pam.

"You alright *Luv*?" asked Pam, noticing Dave's miserable face.

Dave muttered that he was. His answer was ignored, however, when Pam spotted Greg approaching the table
.

"Hello, and WHO are you?" Pam drooled.

"This is my friend Greg," Samantha replied on his behalf.

"And what do you do Gregory?" giggled Pam.

"Medicine," replied Greg, in a voice so deep that Dave was sure the table moved.

"Oooh a doctor!" crooned Pam. "I bet the young nurses wet their knickers when you walk on the ward, don't they Gregory?"

Greg smiled.

Paul and Greg introduced themselves to each other and then the group started chatting, mainly about Dave disgracing himself at the History Cheese and Wine and in Film Studies. Greg laughed but could not keep his eyes off Samantha. Dave did not laugh and could not keep his eyes off Greg. Bastard! No wonder Greg had followed Samantha to college. If

Samantha had been Dave's girlfriend, he would have followed her anywhere to keep other men's 'paws' off her.

The chit chat continued for a while until there came a familiar wolf howl from the doorway. Sure enough it was *Brain-Dead*.

"Christ! Look at that," exclaimed Pam. "What IS he wearing?"

Everyone turned around and gasped. *Brain-Dead* was wearing yellow pants with a gaudy Hawaiian shirt covered in a sunset scene. On his feet he had blue yachting sneakers.
Brain-Dead bounced over to the bar, barging a couple of freshmen out of the way.

"A pint of your delicious Kraut nectar please, my furry friend," he bellowed at the bearded bartender.

"Evening *Brain-Dead*," replied the bartender. "Not been kicked out yet?"

"Not at all my good man. The world of architecture is eagerly awaiting my original designs, like a moist fresher eagerly awaiting my 'length of vein'."

"Cool threads," said Paul to Pam, puffing on his latest roly.

As he was waiting for his pint to be poured, *Brain-Dead* amused himself by extending his enormous tongue in the direction of two girls sitting next to the bar.

"Urrrrgh," giggled one of the girls, "Put it away."

"This is my woman-pleaser," chuckled *Brain-Dead*, "It reaches the parts other tongues cannot reach!"

"Here's your beer, *Brain-Dead*," interrupted the bartender.

"Many thanks, my tubby friend. Remind me to let you have a mushroom, as a token of my esteem. An excellently poured pint, if I may say so. You didn't spit in it, did you?"

"Piss off!" came the reply.

Brain-Dead picked up his pint and began surveying the room. Dave lowered his gaze to avoid being spotted. Unfortunately this proved ineffective.

"*Stud*!" cried *Brain-Dead*, bounding over to the table.

"*Stud*?" laughed Pam Dave blushed and caught Samantha grinning at him.

"You broken in any of these young fillies yet, me ol' beaver bandit?" asked *Brain-Dead* looking at Pam and Samantha.

"Please go away," muttered Dave.

"Go away? Not when I smell a party in the air. Look, I've put on my best shirt to make you feel at home, I've bought a 'jonny' AND I've baked some cakes. I'm your basic party hero. Let me come to the party, please let me come. I'll be good," *Brain-Dead* pleaded.

"Cakes?" laughed Pam, "You haven't baked cakes. Where could you bake them?"

"In the tiny stove in the kitchen, my sweet. I am a fine baker, despite the lack of facilities, as you shall find out if I am allowed to your party tonight," said *Brain-Dead* before turning to Dave and whispering loudly. "Listen, you let me know which piece of meat is on your menu tonight and I promise I'll not whisk her away. She might howl with anguish, she might plead and beg but I'll say 'No babe, you're the *Stud*'s property tonight. No can do.' How about it? Whaddya' say?"

"It's not my party, so I can't invite you," growled Dave, with aggression in his voice.

"You can bring your friend to the party, if you want Dave," grinned Samantha.

"He's NOT my friend!" snapped Dave.

"Oh thank you, kind damsel, you've made an old architect very happy. Your kindness will be rewarded. You will go to heaven. You will pass Go and win £200," shrieked *Brain-Dead*. "So, who are you eyeing up Casanova?"

"I'm NOT 'eyeing up' anyone."

"Ah ha! The field is open then," smiled *Brain-Dead* before turning to Pam and extending his enormous tongue again.

"Hey hey baby, what's your name? I didn't catch it earlier," *Brain-Dead* asked Pam.

"My name's 'Syphilis'," smiled Pam, "Need me to spell it?"

Brain-Dead turned to Dave, "Hey Stud. Can you get syphilis from a bird's gob?"

"Dunno" muttered Dave.

"Oh well," replied *Brain-Dead*, "Worth the risk for such a seeeexxxxy babe! Oh, and before I forget, after we've partied tonight and cheered on the *Mighty Blades* tomorrow, our *Wank-Bank* appointment is on Monday at three o'clock."

"I thought you said he wasn't your friend Dave," smiled Samantha. "You seem to be planning the whole weekend together."

"I've been thinking about this *Wank-Bank*," said Paul, thoughtfully rolling another cigarette. "Ten Pounds a shot, you said didn't you?"

"Ten Pounds of Her Majesty's finest my good man," replied *Brain-Dead*. "COME along with me and the *Stud* on Monday and we'll get you signed up - so long as you're not a *Jaffa*!"

"How does it work?" asked Pam, interested.

"Well," replied *Brain-Dead*, "You take your willy in your hand, like this. Then you rub it until you say 'Oh god baby, yes, yes."

Brain-Dead then proceeded to give a graphic demonstration of masturbating an invisible three-foot penis.

"I know that bit, my dear," interrupted Pam, "I am a woman of the world, you know."

"Doesn't a nurse do it for you?" asked Paul quizzically.

"God, you lazy bastard Paul," groaned Pam. "You'd have a fucking iron lung if you could!"

"I reckon it's a reasonable question to ask," pleaded Paul, looking hurt.

"I don't think that's in the contract," interjected Greg, "But I'm sure a couple of the male nurses would be happy to help you out."

"Presumably they're 'fags', so you'd feel right at home Paul," roared Pam, before collapsing into laughter again.

"We could go in my car," said Paul, ignoring Pam. "Where is the *Bank* by the way?"

"The Fulwood Hospital, Wanking Department," replied *Brain-Dead*.

"Tell me, can the offspring trace you...you know, if you donate?" asked Paul puffing on his cigarette.

"Oh God, I've just had a horrible thought. Some poor wretch is going to give birth to a *Brain-Dead* sprog!" laughed Pam.

"What time should we meet up Dave?" asked Paul.

"Look I haven't said I'm going yet," whined Dave, "I haven't decided."

Dave then winced as he saw Cathy enter the bar with the group from the first evening, including *The Book-Seller*, *Lard-Arse*, Mike and the three girls. The group made their way to the bar with the exception of Cathy who made a beeline for Dave.

"Hello David," Cathy whispered.

"Hello," Dave mumbled.

"I went to your room to look for you, but you weren't in," Cathy continued.

"Er...no," replied Dave, glancing at Samantha.

Samantha, however, was deep in conversation with Greg.

Bastard!

"We're going into town later. Do you want to come?" asked Cathy.

Pam raised her eyebrows at Dave.

"Er...no thanks."

"Oh well, might see you later? You know where my room is," smiled Cathy as she turned back towards the bar.

"Oi *Yank*! You owe me my money," shouted *The Book-Seller* from the bar.

"Oh yeah, I've got it here," replied Dave.

"Needed money for 'jonnies' did ya'?" asked *Brain-Dead*.

Dave ignored him and rose from his chair to go and repay *The Book-Seller*. As he got up, Samantha and Greg also rose out of their seats.

"We're off to my room to get everything ready for the party. See you over there as soon as you're ready?" she said to everyone at the table.

"Yeah, see you soon," replied Pam.

"If you're going for a shower, can I watch?" asked *Brain-Dead*.

"Now *Brain-Dead*, you promised to be good if I let you come to my party," smiled   Samantha, patting *Brain-Dead* on the head.

While Dave was at the bar, repaying his debt to *The Book-Seller* and chatting with Mike, Pam and Paul arrived to buy bottles of beer to take to the party. Dave, after buying some of his own, left with them, leaving *Brain-Dead* to show his tongue technique to the girls.

"Must stop off at the Hall Shop," said Paul, "I've got to get some skins."

They walked out of the main building, nodding 'Good Evening' at the security guard on the front desk, and out into the cold of the night.

"I think this wanking sounds like quite a nifty gig," said Paul, as they strolled across the Quad.

"Boys, boys, change the bloody subject," groaned Pam, as they approached the bright lights of the Hall Shop.

The Hall Shop was rather strange. It was basically a closet that had been converted into a small store. The only window was tiny, high up and had bars so, to compensate for the lack of light, the ceiling was covered in enormously powerful fluorescent lights that made Dave's eyes hurt. Inside was a range of student essentials; notably breakfast cereals, cans of beans, potato chips, a huge selection of chocolate, sanitary towels and tobacco. The shopkeeper was a short, dark-haired girl with terminal acne and her assistant was a Chinese girl with glasses so huge, they made her eyes look about four inches in diameter. The spotty girl had obviously found her vocation in life. She greeted every customer as they took their turn at the counter and then proceeded to give them a running commentary as she picked their purchases off the shelves.

"Ummm tomato *CupaSoup*, this is really VERY nice. I had some earlier and I can highly
recommend it. *Pot Noodle*, delicious! Shampoo? Greasy or normal? This one is excellent and it comes with conditioner in it already, so you're saving money straight away," she bleated on and on.

"An expensive college education over three long years and all this girl wants to do is work in a store," thought Dave.

Quite why the Chinese girl was there was more of a mystery because she just stood and smiled and STARED. Her huge, dark, saucer-like eyes didn't seem to move. Presumably they didn't need to as she had such a massive field of vision. The only contribution she did make was to repeat the occasional word in, what seemed like, a comedy Chinese accent.

"Soup...shampoo...bled," she said at intervals, smiling all the time.

Dave puzzled how someone who patently did not speak much English could be studying at an English college. What course was she on? Moreover, he mused, why was it that so many waiters in Chinese restaurants could barely understand you when you were ordering from their menu? How did these people survive? How did they even get to work?

Paul finally reached the front of the line.

"A packet of skins please," Paul said.

"A packet of what?" asked *Spotty*.

"Papers...cigarette papers, please," replied Paul.

"Oh, cigarette papers. I've never heard them called skins before. What a funny name. I wonder where that name comes from?" *Spotty* asked rhetorically.

"From 'skinning up'," Paul continued helpfully.

"Oh, right," said Spotty, without a clue what he was talking about, "Well, we've got small ones and these enormous ones. The choice is yours, but quite why anyone would want these big ones is totally beyond me. I've never seen a cigarette that big before. Can you imagine how big packets of cigarettes would be if they were all this big. We'd have no room for anything else in the shop," she laughed.

"They're for spliffs," said Paul helpfully.

"Spliffs?" repeated Spotty.

"Spriffs," repeated the Chinese girl.

"I'm not sure what a spliff is and I'm not sure if I want to know," giggled *Spotty* nervously.

"Spriffs," repeated the Chinese girl smiling, seemingly very happy with her new word.

Once outside the shop, Dave turned to Paul.

"Are those really for spliffs?" asked Dave.

"Ah, poor little cowboy," laughed Pam, "The only grass they have in Nebraska is what the cows eat. Isn't that right precious?"

"No...no, I know what a spliff is. Of course I've smoked spliffs," Dave lied.

"I think it's time we got the boy caned, Pam. What do you reckon?" smiled Paul as he rolled a cigarette.

"After hearing about your *Tom Brown's Schooldays* earlier, I reckon getting caned by you is probably the last thing David fancies," laughed Pam.

A few steps later they were at the bottom of the stairs that led up to Samantha's room. On the next landing, they looked around until they found the right number and then knocked.

Greg answered the door.

Bastard!

"Come in, come in. Long time no see," he schmoozed.

"Oh Gregory, you talk so beautifully," cooed Pam, "You make my knees turn to jelly."

Greg smiled at Pam but said nothing. Instead he just opened the door and stood to one side to let them through. As Dave walked past him, Greg gave him a friendly gentle pat on his back.

"Leave my fucking back alone," thought Dave.

Entering the room, Dave gasped. The room was great. Although it was just a lounge with bedrooms at either end and you could spot the standard-issue furniture, it was the other furnishings that took Dave's breath away. There was a rug on the floor, pretty lamps, classy posters on the walls (not the usual student trash) and even an illuminated fish tank complete with goldfish. How did they get all this stuff here? Did they have a truck?

Dave then saw Samantha. She was chatting to a couple in the corner of the room. He could not move. His heart surged. She looked so stunningly beautiful. She had put her hair up since she had been in the bar, which extenuated the delicate shape of her face. He had never seen anyone so beautiful in his life before. Sure, there were a couple of girls at high school whom he had had the hots for. He had been out with one of them for a while, Tammy Tomlinson, and she was certainly very pretty. But the nearest he'd ever been to her panties had been when she was a cheerleader for the school basketball team (christened *The Beavers* in a more innocent age!) and he was sitting courtside when she wiggled her butt in his face. The other one was a cold, hard bitch who knew all the guys had the hots for her, but they didn't dig her nearly as much as she loved herself. But they just were not in the same league as Samantha.

As she was listening to the couple, Samantha caught sight of Dave staring at her and winked at him. He smiled back, but still could just not stop staring. When he eventually came round, he realized that Pam was giggling at him.

"You not stopping *Darling*?" Pam laughed.

Dave was suddenly aware that he was standing in the middle of the room with his jacket on and a plastic bag of bottles dangling from his hand.

"See something you fancy, *Loverboy*?" Pam teased.

"Er..." Dave stuttered.

"Come on, take your coat off and park your arse," Pam smiled.

Dave put the bag on a table, took his jacket off and walked off into one of the bedrooms where he could see a small pile of coats on the bed. He immediately knew that this was Samantha's bedroom from a cluster of photographs on the desk next to her computer. Nosiness got the better of Dave and, instead of dumping his jacket and leaving, he could not help but take a closer look.

One photo was of Samantha with two very similar-looking girls, whom Dave took to be her sisters. All of them were posing for the camera in evening dresses with a Christmas tree in the background. Both of her sisters were stunners as well, they just looked a little older. Dave tried to imagine what her father felt like, having three such beautiful daughters. Christ, he must have sleepless nights! If Dave were in the same position, he'd build a machine gun nest at the end of the drive to deter the certain succession of hormone-crazed teenage boys and hairy-assed bikers whose one ambition would be to get into his daughters' panties. Another photo, which Dave picked up, was of Samantha with an older couple, whom he presumed were her parents, sitting in a garden in the summertime. Samantha had her arms around a large, friendly looking dog. She and her parents were laughing. He took a closer look, examining Samantha's mom and trying to imagine what Samantha would look like in middle age. He was more than reassured by what he saw (for Dave' s mind had already wandered as far as marriage and kids!). Her mother was an elegant, classically beautiful woman with the same sexy smile as Samantha.

"God, I could fuck her as well," thought Dave.

Dave then examined Samantha' s father. He looked like a friendly enough sort of guy, going bald but someone who obviously took care of himself.

"This family could star in a cornflakes ad, they were so attractive and healthy-looking," thought Dave. He imagined himself in the photograph with them as Samantha's boyfriend, enjoying long summer days in a pretty English garden. Then he thought of Greg.

Bastard!

There were no pictures of Greg. Dave shuddered as he realized that Greg could be the photographer and hated him for it.

"That's my Mum and Dad," said a voice behind Dave.

Dave nearly jumped out of his skin, almost dropping the photo in the process. He juggled the photo, yet managed to grab the corner before it hit the ground.

"And that's my dog, Digby," Samantha continued.

"I'm sorry," stuttered Dave, "I didn't mean to be nosy. Er...well I suppose I was being nosy, wasn't I?"

"It doesn't matter," smiled Samantha sweetly, "This one is me and my sisters Fiona and Lucy in party mode. Do you have any siblings?"

"Yeah," replied Dave, "A kid brother, whose greatest achievement to date is the ability to name every model in his massive porno stash by body parts alone and whose main ambition in life is to give himself a blowjob!"

"His hormones must be flowing well, then," Samantha laughed. "Do they run in the family?"

Dave went red. He could hardly admit that his hormones were working overtime at that very moment because of her and were in danger of flooding out of his ears!

"You look so sweet when you blush. Just like a little boy," smiled Samantha.

"Hardly a little boy with this huge erection in my shorts," thought Dave.

Samantha stood on her tiptoes and kissed him on his forehead.

"Come on," she said, "let's get back to the party. You can be my DJ for the evening; just as soon as I've introduced you to my roommate, Jo."

Then, taking Dave's hand in hers, Samantha led Dave back into the lounge. As they entered the room, Dave's eyes met Pam's, who gave him a 'theatrical' wink. His eyes then met Greg's, but all Greg did was smile.

Bastard! He was obviously so secure in his relationship with Samantha that he didn't mind other guys holding her hand. After all, it would be him, not Dave, who would be climbing into bed with Samantha tonight. The very thought made Dave shudder again.

Samantha led Dave across the room to a pretty brunette who was busy pouring potato chips into a bowl at the drinks table.

"Jo," said Samantha, "this is Dave, who I was telling you about."

"Ah ha," Jo laughed, "So this is the famous American Dave. Hello Dave, I've heard a lot about you; you've made quite an impression from what I've heard!"

Dave blushed again.

"Er...hi," he mumbled.

"Dave' s going to be our DJ tonight," said Samantha.

"Oh good," replied Jo, still laughing. "You're not going to get out of your brains on cheese and wine and destroy our room, are you Dave?"

"I'll try not to."

Samantha then led him to the CD player and a stack of CDs, where Paul was already thumbing through the collection.

"Oh hi, my son," smiled Paul. "You know you can tell a lot about someone by their music collection."

"So what does it say to you then?" asked Dave.

Paul took a pensive puff on his cigarette.

"They're birds," Paul announced finally.

"Fuck me, Dr. Freud, that's inspired. It's always a joy to watch a genius at work." laughed Dave.

"Thank you," said Paul seriously.

"So, come on then, what am I going to play?" asked Dave.

"Here you are," replied Paul, "two compilations. That's three hours taken care of. And now I think it's time to build the evening's first 'bifta'!" Dave looked puzzled.

"Drugs," growled Paul in a deep voice.

And with that Paul pulled a black, plastic canister from his pocket and shook it. It rattled.

"Let's get stoned shall we?"

"I don't really smoke that much," replied Dave.

"David, my son, tonight you shall smoke. Tonight you shall enter the whacky world of weed," Paul laughed.

Paul then proceeded to pick tobacco from his pouch and lay it onto one of the enormous cigarette papers. He then opened the canister and pulled out a lump of brown cannabis resin, held it above the flame from his lighter and then sprinkled it along the top of the tobacco. He then ripped a length of card from the cigarette papers packet and rolled it into a tube.

"The roach!" Paul smiled, looking up at Dave.

Finally, he carefully rolled the long joint, put it into his mouth and lit it.

"Woh!" he exclaimed, "Bloody nice! Here you are my son, have a drag on that."

Dave gingerly took the joint from Paul and put it to his lips. Closing his eyes he took a drag. His cheeks puffed up like a hamster's, before he blew the smoke out again.

"No, no, no," huffed Paul, "that's useless. You can't get stoned by osmosis. You're supposed to breathe it in. Try again."

Dave took another drag and sucked the smoke down into his lungs. He held his breath and smiled. Paul, staring at him, put his head on one side, like a quizzical dog.

"Well?" he asked. Dave held his breath until his face turned beetroot red before launching the smoke from his mouth with a hacking cough that was so loud the other people in the room turned to see who was choking.

"Good shit, huh?" smiled Paul.

Dave couldn't reply. His lungs were on fire. He was still gasping for breath like a fish freshly plucked from the water.

"Ahh, there there, you poor little thing," said Pam, who had walked over and was now
slapping Dave on the back. "Maybe you can have another try later, but in the meantime pass that spliff to your Auntie Pam. It's time to stand aside and let the big dogs eat."

Pam took the joint from Dave's fingers, put it to her lips and inhaled massively, dragging the lit part of the joint back towards her fingers at a frightening rate.

"Fuckin' hell Pamela, leave some for the rest of us," said Paul looking horrified, "I've never seen anyone smoke an entire joint in one breath before."

Eventually Pam exhaled.

"Ooooh, that's nice," she croaked slightly before inhaling again and passing the joint back to Paul.

Dave, having now recovered, took a swig on Paul's bottle of beer before looking up to see Samantha approaching with the coats of some new guests over her arm. Samantha smiled at him and he smiled back.

"You OK?" she asked, putting her hand on his shoulder.

"Yeah, fine thanks," Dave replied.

Suddenly the joint was thrust in front of Dave's face by Paul. But before he could react, Samantha's beautiful, elegant hand had lifted off his shoulder and had plucked the joint from Paul. Dave turned and looked up at her as she took a long drag and passed it back to Paul.

Dave stared at her as she held her breath.

"God, she even smokes sexily," thought Dave, before another thought suddenly occurred to him, "I'm not sure if I want my future wife smoking drugs!"

"I didn't know you smoked," said Dave.

"I don't," Samantha replied after exhaling, "apart from the occasional drag on the occasional joint. Anyway, make room on that settee. I'll just put these coats down and then I'm coming to chat to you."

As Samantha walked off towards her bedroom, Dave stared at her gorgeous buttocks moving under the flimsy material of her tight, red dress.

"Make some room, please buddy," Dave said to Paul.

Paul shuffled along the couch, passing the joint to Pam as he went, who was now sitting cross-legged on the floor.

Samantha, reappearing from the bedroom, grabbed a bottle of white wine, two glasses and a corkscrew from the drinks table, before walking over and reversing her sexy ass into the space on the couch between Dave and Paul. It took all the self-restraint Dave had not to grab that ass with both hands.

Now squeezed in next to him, Samantha handed Dave the bottle and corkscrew.

"Will you be mother?" she giggled.

"Oh, yeah sure," Dave replied taking the bottle from her.

As Samantha held out the two glasses, Dave proceeded to botch removing the cork. After much huffing and puffing struggling with the cork, he eventually managed to get it to pop out, but only half of it was on the corkscrew. The other, broken half, was still in the neck of the bottle. So he tried again. When he finally removed the broken half, there were bits of cork in the neck and floating on top of the wine.

"Don't worry. Just pour it," Samantha whispered, seeing the embarrassment on his face.

Dave poured two glasses of wine and cork bits while Samantha held the glasses. She then ran her long finger inside both to mop up the cork bits, flicking them off her painted fingernails, before handing Dave a glass and holding her glass up.

"Cheers," she smiled, "I'm really glad I've met you. I think you're lovely and so funny."

"Is that 'funny ha ha' or 'funny strange'?" Dave laughed, feeling a wonderful warmth inside due to the attention from this beautiful woman.

And so they sat, just chatting and drinking the wine for over an hour. Despite the party going on around them, they took barely any notice of anyone else. Dave did occasionally glance up to check where Greg was and whether he would come and spoil everything for him, but each time he was relieved to see Pam taking all of Greg's attention. She was all over him like a rash, gazing into his eyes, smiling and laughing every time he spoke and not taking the hint as Greg stifled several yawns.

"What's Pam doing with Greg?" Dave thought to himself. "Is she keeping him occupied for my sake or is she really making a play for him? If it's the latter, she's got no chance of attracting him away from Samantha, someone he'd followed to college. Anyway, what about Paul? Surely they were getting something started together? It can't be coincidence that they always appear together."

Dave scanned the room for Paul and spotted him, seemingly quite happily, chatting to a hippy-looking girl Dave had never seen before. Every time Dave glanced over they were either building a spliff or smoking one or both! Relieved, Dave turned all his attention to Samantha. He still had a pang every time he remembered that eventually Greg would come and take her away from him but, until that happened, he was just enjoying talking and laughing with her. She was talking about some of the crazy things she and her sisters got up to when they were young. As she laughed Dave thought to himself, "I wonder how you would react if you knew that all I want to do right now is to kiss you". He knew how Greg would react. He'd punch his lights out!

Eventually, Samantha' s roommate, Jo, came over and kneeled before the couch on which they were sitting.

"Isn't it time you two broke it up?" she smiled.

"No, we're having fun!" Samantha replied.

"Well," Jo continued, "do you realize that you haven't spoken to anyone else but David for over an hour? I don't mind you chatting him up, that's fine by me and extremely good for Anglo-American relations, but I don't know half the people here because you invited them and you haven't even said 'Hello' to them."

"Oh!" exclaimed Samantha, "I'm sorry, that is pretty rude of me. Thanks for covering, I'll come along now."

"It's alright, but there's a weird looking bloke outside, dressed like *Starsky and Hutch* meets *Hawaii 5 'O*, claiming you invited him, that he's baked some cakes and asking me, and I'm quoting him here, if I'll 'suck his knob for a bob'."

Samantha laughed and Dave groaned.

"It's your friend," Samantha giggled, "Go and let him in."

"He's no friend of mine," mumbled Dave, incandescent with rage that instead of Greg breaking him and Samantha up, it was *Brain-Dead*.

"He's a curse, that dude," Dave complained, "Listen, don't let him in for my sake. I can't stand him."

"Now don't be uncharitable," Samantha chided. "He obviously likes you; he's even baked you some cakes. Anyway, Jo's right, I have got to chat to my other guests. But don't go away I'll be back soon."

And with that, Samantha rose from the couch, stroked one of Dave's cheeks and gave him a long kiss on the other.

Dave didn't know what to do, but he instinctively looked up to see where Greg was. Greg was still with Pam. He had obviously spotted Samantha's kiss because he raised his eyebrows in an 'I saw that' sort of way, but then he just smiled and turned back to Pam, who hadn't broken the constant flow of chatter or noticed that Greg's attention was momentarily elsewhere.

"Why isn't he angry?" Dave asked himself, "Why doesn't he want to beat me up?"

And then Dave's heart sank again.

"Because he's no need to be jealous, that's why," he brooded.

Bastard!

And talking of bastards, stupid bastards in this case, *Brain-Dead* came bounding over to the couch.

"Quick, quick *Stud*," he whispered, "Come with me, I need your help."

"For what?" moaned Dave.

"No time to explain; it's urgent!" *Brain-Dead* responded, pulling Dave up off the couch and leading him into Samantha's bedroom. He closed the bedroom door behind them and placed a cookie tin on the bed.

"What do you want?" Dave demanded, "and what' s in the tin?"

"Oh, the cakes are in there, but that's not what I need you for," replied *Brain-Dead*, pulling a small camera out of his coat pocket. "Here take this, it's Martin's."

"So?"

"And this," *Brain-Dead* continued, "is Martin's toothbrush!"

Brain-Dead held a red toothbrush up to Dave' s face.

"So?"

"So...so you've got to take a picture of it," panted *Brain-Dead*, as if time was of the essence.

"*Brain-Dead*, I don't understand what the fuck you're going on about!" said Dave, getting quite angry.

"Jesus, you dumb fucking *Yank*, it's the oldest gag in the book" said *Brain-Dead*, holding Dave's shoulders and staring into his eyes for added clarity, "Martin and Karen are shagging in the shower so, while his door was unlocked, I nipped in and nicked his camera and his toothbrush. And now you've got to take a photo of me with it. But we've got to be quick 'cause they won't be shagging for long and I've got to get it back without him noticing."

"But I don't understand why!" pleaded Dave.

"Jesus, *Stud*!" wailed *Brain-Dead*, now getting quite agitated. "This is Martin's camera, this is his toothbrush, right?"

"Right."

"Well, you take a photo of me with his toothbrush up my arse with his camera, then we put both back in his room without him noticing. When he eventually views his photos, he'll see the photo and realize that he's been brushing his teeth with a toothbrush that's been up my arse! Inspired or what? Anyway, we haven't got all day, so grab this, quick!"

Brain-Dead thrust the camera into Dave's hand and started unbuckling his belt. He then dropped his pants and shorts and bent over, pushing his ass out with his smiling face turned to camera. He then placed the toothbrush on the edge of his asshole.

"Come on," he shouted, "Get snapping. Do a few action shots and get my face in as well as my arse; I want him to know it was my arsehole."

Now finding the whole thing rather funny, Dave started snapping off photos. He started laughing at the crazy scene and giving *Brain-Dead* photographer-like instructions.

"Come on baby, show me that toothbrush. That's it, that's it, stick your ass out and don't forget to smile...yes, that's it, big smile," yelled Dave, getting into the part.

Just then the door opened and in walked Samantha with a couple of coats over her arm.

"What the...?" Samantha screamed.

The whole scene just froze; *Brain-Dead* sticking his ass out towards Dave with a toothbrush in his hand, Dave, now kneeling on the floor, pointing the camera at his ass and Samantha standing, motionless and open-mouthed at the open door.

The scene unfroze with a peel of laughter from the lounge. Dave turned his head to see a sea of open-mouthed faces staring at him with Pam, in the midst of them all, doubled over with laughter. He then saw Paul drop his spliff on the carpet and diving down to retrieve it.

"Oh I am sorry I interrupted you two," laughed Samantha, "Should I close the door again?"

By now there were howls of laughter from the assembled guests.

"I...I can explain," stuttered Dave.

"You don't need to explain anything to me, David," smiled Samantha, "I'm not your mother."

Dave glanced over and saw Greg giggling at him.

Bastard!

"It...er...*Brain-Dead* wanted his photo taken."

"His best side, presumably?" laughed Samantha. "Well, I'll just close the door and let you boys finish what you're doing. Give me a shout if you need anything."

The door closed. Dave dropped the camera, put his head in his hands and groaned.

"Oh God, No!" he moaned, hearing laughter coming from the lounge.

"It's OK," said *Brain-Dead* optimistically, "Don't worry. We got the shot!"

Before Dave could scream at *Brain-Dead* that he didn't give a flying fuck about the shot, *Brain-Dead* was re-buckling his belt and bounding out of the bedroom. As he appeared, the party guests cheered and clapped him. Taking a moment to bow, *Brain-Dead* shouted, "Back in a minute folks. More entertainment and cakes on the way, so stay tuned!" He then ran out of the room, leaving the door swinging on its hinges.

Dave meanwhile, just sat on the bed with his head in his hands, groaning. The laughter died away and was replaced by excited murmuring. After what seemed like an eternity, Dave felt an arm around his shoulder.

"There, there, *Pet*. Are you alright?" whispered Pam.

"I've been better."

"I don't want to pry, but what on earth were you doing?"

Dave explained it to Pam. As he did, Pam's expression turned from concern to mirth, unseen by Dave, who still had his face in his hands.

"I've blown it with Samantha haven't I?" Dave moaned.

Pam, who had been working up to an explosion of laughter could hold it in no longer. So, despite the bad timing (you can't imagine *The Samaritans* bursting into laughter when someone' s world is falling in around them!), she shrieked "That's BRILLIANT!"

Then, grabbing Dave' s arm, she pulled him into the lounge.

"Everyone...everyone...if I can have your attention please," she shouted above the
conversation and music. "Dave feels that he might need to explain what you all just witnessed."

"This should be good!" smirked Paul, dragging on yet another cigarette.

"Thank you Paul. Now please do something useful and turn the music off for a moment," Pam said.

Paul did as he was told. Dave lifted his head up to see a crowd of faces staring at him, some smiling, some with shocked expressions and Samantha, who was standing next to Greg.

"Come on Dave, tell them," whispered Pam, elbowing Dave in the ribs.

"God, this is embarrassing," thought Dave, "I can't stand talking in public, never mind having to explain why I was talking photos of someone with a toothbrush up his ass!"

However, Dave summoned up his courage and, in a faltering voice, he explained to the guests (most of whom he didn't know) what *Brain-Dead's* plan was.

"So that's it," Dave finished.

There was total silence in the room.

"So, that's why it looked as bad as it looked," he finished again.

The silence was finally broken by Paul.

"Hey, that's fantastic man!" Paul shouted and began to clap.

Others joined in the applause.

"He did have a lovely tush, though. Can you get me a copy of the photo?" shouted Greg, to which everyone laughed.

Even Dave laughed and he silently thanked Greg for not sticking the boot in and making light of the situation.

"Here you are, you look like you could do with a drink," said Samantha quietly to Dave, passing him a bottle of beer.

"How embarrassing! I keep making a total dick of myself," moaned Dave.

"You're kidding aren't you? You've made the party. People will be talking about this for years. Can't you see? Most of these people didn't know one another until an hour ago but now they've shared your toothbrush-up-the-bum experience, they're discussing it like old friends. They've bonded as if they've come through a natural disaster or an ordeal together. You' re priceless. You already showed me that you're the life and soul of a party - ask Professor Rogers - that's why I invited you!"

"Oh great," thought Dave, "that's just perfect. The only reason Samantha invited me was because I would make a fool of myself."

Dave smiled a weak smile and just wished the earth would swallow him up. But if that failed, he didn't want to be around Samantha. He was too bruised.

"You'd better put those coats down," he said, pointing at the coats still hanging over Samantha' s arm.

"Oh, yes," Samantha replied, noticing them again, "I won't be a minute".

As Samantha turned to take the coats into her bedroom, Dave scampered in the opposite direction and went to join Paul and the hippy girl. He immediately jumped in on their conversation while, out of the corner of his eye, he saw Samantha returning to the spot he had just vacated. Her mouth was open as if, expecting him still to be there, she was about to say something to him. Finding him gone, Dave could spy her looking around for him. Seeing him with Paul, her expression seemed to drop before she went over to join Greg and Pam.

Try as he might, Dave just couldn't get into the conversation with Paul and the hippy girl. They were earnestly discussing Ry Cooder's early years, interspersed with deranged laughter about things that just weren't funny; they were obviously stoned out of their brains. Dave tried puffing on the spliffs that Paul passed to him at regular intervals, but it always resulted in yet another coughing fit. So he eventually gave up and went to check out the CD collection again, grabbing another bottle of beer off the drinks table. As he sat thumbing through the CDs again Jo, Samantha's roommate, joined him.

"You certainly live up to your reputation, don't you?" Jo smiled.

"A walking disaster, that's what I am," Dave moaned. "I'm not usually like this you know."

"I think you're very funny and Sam hasn't stopped talking about you," Jo replied.

"How long has she been with Greg?" Dave asked.

"Oh, for years I think. They're inseparable."

"Oh," Dave muttered.

Then, before he could say any more, the door flew open again and *Brain-Dead* stormed in.

"Fear not, partygoers. *Brain-Dead* is back. Let the festivities recommence. It's cake time!" *Brain-Dead* shouted.

He then bounded into Samantha's bedroom and collected the cookie tin before touring the room, offering a cake to each of the guests and not taking 'No' for an answer.

"Cake?" said *Brain-Dead*, pushing the tin towards Dave and Jo.

"Ooh, thank you," said Jo, picking a strange-looking thing out of the tin.

"Umm, interesting," Jo said, nibbling on a piece.

"What's in them?" asked Dave suspiciously.

"Ah ha, my secret ingredients, passed down from generation to generation in my family. *Mr. Kipling* can go fuck himself, these are the finest cakes in all of Christendom. Eat one of these and all life's troubles will disappear."

Dave picked a cake out of the tin and nibbled it suspiciously. To his surprise, what he had expected to be sweet was in fact savory. The taste was neither unpleasant nor indeed particularly nice. Before he could pass comment, Paul and the hippy girl had crossed the room to ask *Brain-Dead* for another cake.

"Ah, people with good taste!" laughed *Brain-Dead*.

"Umm, they're just like the ones I had in Amsterdam last year," nodded Paul.

"Oh Amsterdam, my ancestral home. The city of dreams, canals and young fillies desperate for a porking," grinned *Brain-Dead*.

"Are you from Holland?" asked Jo.

"My dear, my very soul belongs to *The Dam*. I pine for her when I'm away and long to be returned to her loving embrace," said *Brain-Dead*, poetically, with a misty look in his eyes.

"We should go!" said Paul, enthusiastically, "I'm up for it."

"A fine suggestion, my good man. A finer suggestion no man has made all day. We shall go, we shall do that thing," shrieked *Brain Dead*.

"And what about you, young *Stud*? Think you could cope with the Dutch hussies?"

"Amsterdam, Holland? I don't know," replied Dave, "I've only just arrived here in England. It's a bit early to be thinking about shooting off again and we've got college work to do."

"Nonsense! Amsterdam is the very place to 'shoot off'. Anyway, you're freshers. Nobody expects freshers to do any work, that's what your first year is for. Indeed, you two are historians, nobody expects you to do any work at all. Take a couple of musty old books on the coach with you, that'll do the trick. So, when shall we go? We can't go tomorrow 'cause the *Mighty Blades* are at home and the *Stud* wouldn't miss that 'for a big clock'."

"What about next weekend?" suggested Paul.

"Another fine suggestion, my posh friend. Have another cake!" replied *Brain-Dead*.

"Can I come?" asked the hippy girl.

"Ha, ha, ha!" laughed *Brain-Dead*, of course not, you silly young filly. You don't take a bird to *The Dam*. It would be like taking coals to Newcastle. No young wench, you shall not go to *The Dam*. The boys alone shall go, to smoke drugs, drink beer and empty their sacks! Talking of drugs, O' posh one, isn't that a spliffette I see before me?"

"Yeah, here you are," Paul replied, passing the joint to *Brain-Dead*.

The hippy girl, meanwhile, huffed and walked away.

"Are you up for a trip to Amsterdam?" Paul asked Dave.

"Gee I don't know," Dave replied, "I'd love to see it, but it still seems a bit soon. How much will it cost?"

"Peanuts my boy," replied *Brain-Dead*. "We shall travel by the cheapest means and stay in a surprisingly cheap yet elegant hotel I know. All arranged for us by a rather dishy thing with enormous tits at the Student Travel Service. We shall book one of their cultural smoking weekends. Anyway, your wanking profits will pay for this and much more."

"It doesn't sound like you'll be taking in much culture, if you ask me," laughed Jo.

"Nonsense, young lady," grinned *Brain-Dead*. "I think you'll find that culture is defined as the customs of a society. You will then have to admit that if it is the custom in *The Dam* to inhale copious amounts of drugs in the pleasant surroundings of a warm canal-side cafe prior to investing in an a ten minute orgy of dirty sex with a young Filipino, then we are indeed bathing in the local culture. Have another cake."

This small group then spent the next hour chatting, drinking, smoking and changing the CD at regular intervals. The mood of the party mellowed, with quiet conversation, occasional laughter and generally smiling faces all round.

Some of the guests even found sitting upright to be too much of an exertion and descended to the floor. After his earlier exhibition, Dave too began to relax.

"This is really nice," he thought. "I'm actually starting to feel at home here."

He chatted with Jo about her home life, with Paul about the merits of masturbating and the Amsterdam trip and he even managed a reasonably sensible conversation with *Brain-Dead*. He occasionally glanced over at Samantha, who was sitting in a group that included Greg and Pam. She still looked so lovely, but she seemed so happy with Greg that Dave decided to give up his hopes of a lifetime of togetherness with her.

"Oh well," he thought, "Plenty more fish in the sea."

He even considered taking Cathy up on her earlier offer. After all, he had had a fantastic lay!

"You've gone very quiet. You OK?" asked Jo.

"Yeah, I'm fine thanks," Dave replied. "I'm really getting into this music though. Who is it?"

"Santana," replied Paul, "*Abraxas*."

"It's really nice and there are so many layers to it; it's so deep. Don't you think?"

"I think you're stoned, man," laughed Paul.

"I'm feeling a bit tipsy myself actually," giggled Jo.

Just then Pam bumbled across the room, looking very drunk.

"Come on then Paul, crash the ash," she laughed.

Paul pulled yet another joint from his lips and passed it to her.

"You calmed down yet?" she asked Dave, dragging on the joint.

"Yeah I have, thank you," replied Dave. "You have a nice chat with Sam and Greg?"

"Oh yeah, they're nice people. Like talking with a married couple though," Pam replied.

"Aren't they just!" laughed Jo. "She even consults him on what she's going to wear."

"You're kidding," exclaimed Pam. "Well I don't think Pamela will be getting into Greg's underpants tonight! I'll just have to make do with you then Paul," as she pinched Paul's cheek.

"What?" Paul spluttered.

Dave settled back once again to listen to the music. It was fantastic. He could feel every note.

"Great hi-fi this," Dave said to Paul.

"Yeah man, whatever you say," laughed Paul.

Dave closed his eyes, but immediately felt the room spinning.

"I must be more drunk than I thought I was. Or was it the drags on Paul's joints?" he thought to himself.

He opened his eyes. This stopped the room spinning but he still felt a bit wobbly, so he picked up the CD cover to read, hoping this would take his mind off it. But as he stared at the cover, the images seemed to move.

"Jesus," he thought, "I am stoned."

He was going to tell Paul, but turning round he found Paul and Pam swapping tongues. Pam had settled herself on Paul's lap and was pulling at his hair in the heat of passion.

"I knew those two were getting it on," Dave smiled to himself.

So he tuned to Jo instead. She was just staring in a trance-like state at the wall opposite. But before he could tell her about the images on the CD cover, she said "That wall's got snails on it."

Dave looked at the wall, but couldn't see anything.

What he did notice however was that his mouth had grown bigger. He knew that didn't make any sense, but it had. Already it was double its normal size and he was beginning to worry that someone would notice, but when he looked around the room nobody was staring at him. In fact, nobody seemed to be doing anything at all. Very few people were talking anymore, most were just staring into middle-distance or had their eyes closed. However, just in case, Dave covered his mouth with his hand. Things were getting out of hand now, his mouth was enormous and it was VERY embarrassing!

Jo turned to him.

"Oh God!" Dave thought, "She's noticed my huge mouth."

Jo smiled at him and started pulling his hand away from his mouth.

"Shit," he thought, "She wants to humiliate me. She wants to show everyone my big mouth."

 For a few moments Dave and Jo struggled until she finally pulled down his hand, but instead of laughing at him, she moved over him and put her lips to his. The two of them then began kissing passionately. This went on for what seemed like an eternity. Dave was enjoying it and it seemed that having a huge mouth - it was about a foot wide by now - was actually a great advantage!

When Dave and Jo finally did come up for air, Jo turned back to watch the wall again and Dave looked around the room. The first person whose eyes he met was Samantha' s. She did not look very happy, in fact she looked VERY upset. Dave immediately covered his mouth with his arm, as this was obviously what had upset her.

Just then there was a howl from another corner of the room. One of the female guests, whom Dave did not know, was wailing and a friend was trying to comfort her.

"I don't understand. I don't understand," she sobbed.

"Come on, I'll take you back to your room," her friend was saying. "What' s wrong? What don't you understand?"

"I'm a lobster and I don't know why!" the girl screamed.

The friend helped the girl up and began guiding her towards the door.

"My coat, where's my coat?" she cried.

Samantha jumped up to help.

"What does your coat look like?" she asked the girl.

"I don't know. Why am I a lobster?" the girl asked.

"It's a blue bomber jacket," the friend said to Samantha.

Samantha then ran into her bedroom and reappeared with the coat, which she draped around the sobbing girl as her friend led her out of the door. Samantha then stormed back across the room to where Dave was sitting. Dave kept his mouth covered, but instead of addressing him, she stood over *Brain-Dead*, who was lying flat out on the floor on his back.

"What did you put in those bloody cakes?" Samantha yelled at the top of her voice.

Brain-Dead did not move or even open his eyes. He just lay there and laughed.

"Don't you laugh at me, you stupid bastard. What did you put in those cakes?" Samantha screamed.

This time *Brain-Dead* did open his eyes and looked up at Samantha.

"Chill out Babe," he laughed, "just a few mushrooms."

"Feels like acid to me," interjected the hippy girl.

"Get out!" Samantha screamed at him, "Get out. The party's over. Get out of my sight."

Samantha then grabbed hold of *Brain-Dead's* hair and pulled him up. She then started hitting him on the back as he retreated to the door.

"You stupid bastard, you stupid bastard. Get out, go on get out!" she screamed, with tears now running down her cheeks.

After she had pushed him out of the door, she turned around.

"Please go everyone. I'm sorry but please just go," Samantha cried.

She then marched back over to Dave.

"And thank you very much for ruining my party. I thought I liked you, but you're just cruel", she cried at Dave before turning to Jo.

"And you," she sobbed, "thanks a lot, FRIEND!"

Samantha then dissolved into floods of tears before Greg walked over and put his arm around her.

"Come on Darling," Greg said gently, guiding her into her bedroom. As she went inside, Greg turned back towards the room and said "I think you'd all better leave now."

Nobody moved for a moment. Then, one by one, people rose from the seats and from the floor, all in total silence. Greg then reappeared at Samantha's doorway carrying a huge bundle of coats.

Dave got up from the couch and went to take his coat off Greg.

"I'm really sorry," Dave said to Greg, still shielding his mouth with his arm, "But I honestly didn't know what *Brain-Dead* was going to do. Will you tell Sam that? I really didn't mean for her to be upset."

"I'll tell her. Don't worry, I'm sure she'll be fine," Greg replied gently. "Are you OK?"

"I'm fine apart from this massive mouth," Dave answered.

"Well take care," said Greg.

Dave turned around and began to put his coat on. Jo had already got up from the couch and was walking into her own room. Once inside, she slammed the door behind her. Dave turned back to Paul and Pam, who were kissing again so passionately that they were practically having sex on the couch.

"Come on you two, it's time to go," said Dave.

They lingered with their mouths clamped together for another moment before prizing themselves apart. As their heads retreated, a string of saliva hung between their mouths.

"Urrrrgh," said Dave.

Pam laughed.

"Has the party finished?" asked Paul, reaching for his tobacco pouch.

"Yeah," replied Dave still covering his mouth with his arm, "Where were you?"

"Sticking his monster up my bum, that's where," laughed Pam, pulling Paul up from the couch.

"What happened?" asked Paul.

"Well, *Brain-Dead* spiked those cookies, one girl thought she was a lobster, I've got a big mouth and Samantha's really upset."

"You're tripping!" laughed Paul. "Those mushroom cakes have made you trip. You OK?"

"I'm OK apart from this enormous mouth," Dave replied.

"You haven't got an enormous mouth, *Pet*," laughed Pam, "you just think you have. Come on, you've got 'The Horrors' from the drugs. We'll take you back to your room."

As the three of them stepped out into the cold night air in the Quad, Dave no longer felt he had to cover his mouth, not that it wasn't still massive, it was, but he now understood why it was. Despite this understanding, he still nearly jumped out of his skin when his mouth shot out from his face and devoured K-Block. Dave screamed.

"What is it? What's wrong?" asked Paul worriedly.

"My mouth just ate K- Block," Dave stuttered.

Pam laughed.

"Chill out man," said Paul reassuringly, "K-Block's still there."

Dave tried to calm himself down, reassuring himself that he wasn't going to die thousands of miles from home. His new friends were with him, they understood what was going on and they would look after him. But he still found the whole experience very frightening and it was one he never wanted to repeat. He took careful, deliberate steps as he walked across the Quad, talking to himself in an effort to keep control. Then suddenly from around the corner, four large men came running past. One of them was the *Bumble Bee* from the bar earlier that evening. They all had striped shirts on, but they were naked from the waist down and (this is the bit that scared Dave out of his mind) they had burning newspapers clenched between their buttocks!

Dave collapsed on the damp grass of the Quad and put his head in his hands.

"Oh God," he cried, "This is awful. I'm tripping again."

"No you're not," laughed Pam, "that really was the rugby team running past with flames coming out of their arses!"

Paul and Pam eventually delivered Dave to his door and found his key for him in his coat pocket. Paul turned on the light while Pam led Dave to his bed.

"You lie down there, *Pet* and get some sleep. Want us to stay for a while? You still got 'The Horrors?'" she asked.

"No, I think I'll be alright. I just feel really tired now," Dave replied, lying on his bed fully clothed.

"Well, we'll leave the lamp on for you and you know where our rooms are if you need us," Pam said gently, stroking his hair.

"Night, Man," said Paul, closing the door.

"Night," Dave replied, his eyes already closed.

The door clicked shut.

"Right," Dave could hear Pam saying outside, "I've got plans for you and that monster of yours. You're coming with me."

"OK," Paul replied.

Dave then heard their footsteps and laughter dying away into the distance. A minute later he was asleep.

FOUR

"*Stud*, Oh *Stud*. Are you awake yet?" a voice sang.

Dave was still mid-dream; a strange, disturbing dream.

"*Stud*. It's time to wake up or you'll miss the *Mighty Blades*," the voice sang again.

Dave opened his eyes, but his head was still glued to his pillow. He stared at the door.

"Wakey, wakey rise and shine," the voice sang, this time with a knocking accompaniment.

"Fuck you *Brain-Dead*," Dave shouted as loud as he could, which wasn't very loud.

"Ahh, don't be like that," *Brain-Dead* chirped, "It's time to go to the football."

"I'm not going and I'm not speaking to you."

"Oh don't be cross with old *Brain-Dead*. If you come out, me and *Lard-Arse* will buy you a *Bumper*," said *Brain-Dead*, as if talking to a baby.

"Leave me alone," groaned Dave.

"Come on Dave," said another voice, presumably *Lard-Arse's*.

"Look, I feel like shit. *Brain-Dead* fucked me over last night and I just want to lie here and die," Dave moaned.

"A *Bumper* will make you feel much better, I guarantee it," said *Lard-Arse*.

Dave pulled himself up off his bed and staggered over to the door, which he opened before stepping backwards and falling back onto the bed. He laid his head back on his pillow, groaned and watched *Brain-Dead* and *Lard-Arse* enter the room. *Brain-Dead* had a huge grin on his face. His mouth seemed too big for his head and (this had nothing to do with mushroom cakes!) he seemed to have double the number of teeth of a normal human being.

Brain-Dead laughed and, although Dave was still furious with him, Dave could not help but laugh as well; his laughter was so infectious.

"You look like boiled shite!" laughed *Brain-Dead*. "Quite a night last night, eh?"

"You are a total bastard," said Dave, trying not to laugh. "You're crazy. Why did you do it? You totally fucked me over last night and I doubt Samantha will ever speak to me again. In fact I'm amazed I'm still alive, I was convinced I was going to do a Jimmy Hendrix and choke on my barf or something. So I've decided that drugs aren't for me, I'll stick to beer. I do not want to go through that shit again, it was awful!"

"Fine words, dear *Stud*, and most understandable. You are, however, overlooking one flaw in your new cunning plan; namely that you are now booked to go to *The Dam* next weekend!" replied *Brain-Dead*.

"Yeah!" exclaimed *Lard-Arse*, "All booked."

"What do you mean 'It's all booked'?" Dave complained. "I never said I was definitely going. I just said I'd think about it."

"Oh, no no no no no!" laughed *Brain-Dead*, "Cub Scout's honor; you said last night that you couldn't wait to go, that you'd learn to roll a good spliff before we go and that your balls were already aching to service a young, Filipino hussy!"

Lard-Arse laughed, but Dave wasn't laughing.

"I don't remember saying a word of that," said Dave, getting quite agitated.

"Cub's honor," replied *Brain-Dead*, making a three-fingered Cub Scout salute.

"Well even if I did, I only said it 'cause I was out of my brains on your fucking mushroom cookies. So it doesn't count, I'm not going!"

"But we've booked for you already. We've been to see *Miss Big Tits* at the Travel Center. It's all sorted. We go next Friday. Wooohooo!" hooted *Brain-Dead*.

"Well you can unbook it," Dave snapped.

"Oh, come on Dave," *Lard-Arse* interjected, "It'll be fantastic, you'll have a brilliant time."

"Anyway, it's all paid for now," *Brain-Dead* added.

Dave thought for a moment, then said "Well, it's tough shit on you *Brain-Dead* 'cause I'm not going and I'm not paying you for something I didn't want."

"I didn't pay for it, *Lard-Arse* did, on his credit card. So you owe him not me and you wouldn't let *Lard-Arse* down, now would you?" *Brain-Dead* pleaded.

Dave went silent.

"He said you wanted to go Dave; you and Paul. So I paid for it," said *Lard-Arse* after a while.

Dave sat on his bed, leaning back against the wall, in silence; thinking.

"I suppose if Paul's going and *Lard-Arse* has already paid, then I'll have to go. How much is it?"

"Woohoo!" yelled *Brain-Dead*, ignoring the question, "We're off to *The Dam*. But before that we're off to *The Lane*, and before that we're off for a *Bumper*."

"What the fuck is a *Bumper*?" asked Dave.

"A *Bumper*, my dear boy, is the finest breakfast known to man," said *Lard-Arse*. "It is a mouth-watering feast that is a tradition on match days. People travel from miles around to sample its delights. In fact, after the war, when the soldiers came home to Sheffield from Japanese prisoner-of war camps, before they saw their loved ones, they stopped off for a *Bumper*. It was the thought of a *Bumper* that had kept them alive. Even today, wise men choose Sheffield over all other cities just to experience the orgasm in your mouth that it creates"

"So get yourself out of bed and get into that shower; you stink," interrupted *Brain-Dead*. "We'll be back in an hour to pick you up. Come on *Lardy*, give the boy some peace."

Brain-Dead then pushed *Lard-Arse* out of the door, before giving Dave a big, silly wave and a big, stupid grin. As they left the room, closing the door behind them, the smile stayed on Dave's face. Even though *Brain-Dead* annoyed him so much, he also amused him, making it impossible to hate him. But then suddenly Dave's mind turned to Samantha and the night before. He groaned out loud and his whole body shuddered. Although it had not been his fault, he could picture the tears rolling down her beautiful face and it still made him feel so guilty. He had to see how she was and apologize to her. Dave jumped up off the bed and removed his clothes from the night before, before looking at himself in the mirror.

"Christ, you look like shit," he said out loud to himself.

He then threw on a bathrobe, picked up his towel and shower gel and opened the door on his way to the Shower Room. As he passed Martin's room, he laughed to himself, thinking about Martin brushing his teeth that morning with the toothbrush that had been up *Brain-Dead's* ass.

Thirty minutes later, Dave was feeling a little bit more alive. He'd shaved, shit, showered and dressed and was now heading across the Quad towards Samantha and Jo's room. He took the stairs three at a time as he bounded up to their floor, but then hesitated before knocking.

"What exactly am I going to say?" he asked himself. "Sorry, I suppose," and he knocked on the door.

There was no reply and he couldn't hear any movement within, so he tried again. But there was still no reply.

"Shit, what do I do now?" he thought. "I know. I'll write her a note."

On his way back to his room, Dave diverted to the Junior Common Room to check if Samantha was in there. He also glanced across at Paul's room, but the drapes were still closed. Dave smiled, thinking about the two 'lovebirds' inside.

Samantha was not in the Junior Common Room and they had stopped serving breakfast in the Refectory ages ago, so Dave went back to his room and sat down at his desk to write the note. He chewed on a pen and stared out of the window onto the Quad, trying to think about what to say.

What could he say? He couldn't say what he really felt; namely that he fancied her to distraction, so why didn't she just dump Greg so they could live happily ever after together. He thought about Samantha and Greg and how close they seemed. He even thought how nice Greg had been to him last night. Of course, Greg's reaction would, no doubt, have been rather different had he known what Dave' s intentions actually were. But the other thing Dave couldn't work out was Samantha having a go at Jo. What was that all about? He considered this puzzle for a few minutes before finally starting to write.

Dear Sam,

This is just a short note to apologize for last night. I honestly didn't know that Brain-Dead was going to bring cookies that had been drugged, but I'm still sorry that it all upset you so much. I know you only invited him because you think he's my buddy, but he's not - I haven't been able to shake him off since I landed in this country.

Anyway, I hope you're feeling better this morning and sorry once again for last night - upsetting you was the last thing I wanted to do.

Love,

Dave.

Dave thought long and hard about the end of the last line and about putting 'Love, Dave', but in the end he decided to go for it. After all, Greg couldn't take offence at that, could he? But he still compromised by not putting a kiss at the end.

"There. That'll do," he said with a flourish, before folding the note and sealing it in the envelope.

At that moment there was a manic hammering on his door, which nearly made him jump out of his skin.

"*Bumper* time, you know, you know it's *Bumper* time!" sang *Brain-Dead* from the hallway to the theme *Hollywood*.

"I'm coming," shouted Dave, grabbing his jacket and opening the door to a grinning *Brain-Dead*.

"We'll have to hurry," said *Brain-Dead*, "*Lard-Arse* hasn't eaten for nearly an hour and I think he's going to faint, or worse, fart!"

As they strode across the Quad, Dave ran off to post the note under Samantha's door. He tried knocking again, just in case she had returned, but there was still no reply. He then rejoined *Brain-Dead* and *Lard-Arse* to walk into Broomhill to the cafe where they produced the legendary *Bumper*. As they were walking along, *Lard-Arse* could talk of nothing else. Dave was getting rather bored with this and felt there was a danger of it being overhyped and, therefore, disappointing. Still, he was hungry and it was nearly twelve-thirty, so a famous English breakfast would be very welcome.

As they approached the cafe, their walking pace quickened. In fact, once they were about a hundred yards away, *Lard-Arse* actually started to run; which was an experience in itself. Watching him reminded Dave of a TV program he had seen where obscenely obese women at a health farm were made to jog on running machines. There were flab, spare tires, tits and asses flying everywhere, all mixed in with copious amounts of huffing, puffing and sweating.

As Dave entered the cafe, *Lard-Arse* was already trying to squeeze his enormous ass between the edge of a table and a wooden bench. This he finally achieved by pushing the table away from him, leaving hardly any room at the other side where, presumably, Dave and *Brain-Dead* were to sit. *Brain-Dead* meanwhile had trotted up to the counter and was now chatting to the chef; you could tell he was the chef, as he was wearing the menu on his apron!

"Tea or coffee, boys?" *Brain-Dead* shouted over.

"Tea," replied *Lard-Arse*.

"Er...I'll try a tea as well please," called Dave.

Brain-Dead nodded and then pulled his wallet out. "What a guy," thought Dave, "he's actually going to pay for it."

Dave looked around the cafe. Half of the tables were occupied. There was a couple of workmen at one table dressed in jackets compete with green fluorescent strips on the back. Why they had not bothered to take their coats off Dave did not know, as the cafe was very warm, but they were just finishing their meal by wiping chunks of bread around their plates to mop up any grease or ketchup they'd missed. One of them even had a cigarette hanging out of his mouth as he performed this procedure. At another table was an old man, who was tucking into an enormous slice of what looked like steak pie, with a mountain of fries, cabbage and gravy failing off the side of his plate. He also had a lit cigarette in the ashtray on the table in front of him that, while still chewing, he picked up and dragged on. Then, ignoring the ashtray completely, he flicked the ash onto a scruffy black dog lying at his feet. As if to protest, the dog released a massive fart that was even audible over the noise of the radio.

"Mucky bugger!" grumbled the old man, giving the dog a kick.

"Na den Jack," shouted the chef from behind his counter, "don't tha' go blaming dog!"

A young couple, who looked as if they had won a lifetime's supply of body piercing, sitting on the table next to the old man both laughed as they drank their tea and smoked their cigarettes. That was until they simultaneously smelled the dog's fart, at which they began to splutter and swear.

"Great place, isn't it?" said *Brain-Dead* plunking copies of newspapers called the *Sun*, the *Daily Mirror* and the *Daily Star* on the table before sitting down.

Dave continued looking around him. On the opposite wall there was an enormous menu giving the prices of everything. All the breakfast variations were there but pride of place was given to the *Bumper*. A separate chalkboard was even dedicated to this culinary delight, proclaiming 'You've not lived till you've had a *Bumper*'. As well as breakfasts, the menu also listed sandwiches and main meals you could have; most of which were fried, and it seemed that 'chips' were mandatory. The menu had obviously been there for some time as each dish had its own mound of stickers roughly an inch high where, over the years, the prices had changed and new stickers put on top of old. Then, right next to the menu, Dave noticed the fan. This was a regular extractor fan except that it was thick with black grease. Not only that, but the grease was actually flowing out of the fan like melted wax down a candle and (and this was what made Dave worry!) nobody had bothered to wipe it away. He dreaded to think what the outside wall must look like if this was just the grease that had failed to escape. As his mind suddenly turned to all aspects of kitchen hygiene, he saw the chef open up a tall, filthy fridge and pull out a massive packet of fat or 'lard'. He didn't bother, however, moving his lit cigarette to his lips or to his other hand, oh no, the cigarette went into the fridge in search of the fat as well.

"Jeez," Dave gasped as the entire block of lard was unwrapped and dropped into a large black frying pan, "do they cook everything in fat?"

"Oh yes indeed," smiled *Lard-Arse*, "that's what gives the Bumper its great taste!"

Dave pulled a face.

"Not only has this boy got a lard arse, but he is also a lard expert. Is this not so, *Fatty*?" grinned *Brain-Dead*.

Lard-Arse nodded.

"I'll have you know that not only does this boy appreciate the use of lard in the cooking process, but he also enjoys a lard sandwich. And we're not talking 'dripping', much beloved by my granny and indeed numerous grannies across the nation. The *Tubster* here lives for a fat sarnie, do you not o' rotund one?" asked *Brain-Dead* again.

Lard-Arse nodded again.

"You're joking, right?" asked Dave in disbelief. "Nobody eats fat sandwiches, do they?

"Oh yes indeed and my Granny's lard eating credentials are but those of an amateur compared to my large friend here," laughed *Brain-Dead*. "My chubby chum does not need the taste of beef interfering with his appreciation of pure, unadulterated lard. He merely opens the packet and tosses a lump on his bread, as a normal person would do with a fine, soft cheese. Is that not right, *Tubby*?"

"Oh yeah," replied *Lard-Arse*, in a matter-of-fact way. "I like a bit of lard."

"Errrrr...gross!" howled Dave.

Just then, three enormous mugs of tea were slammed down on the stained table by an equally enormous woman.

"D' are lads," she said with a brown-toothed smile. "Oh, an tha' needs a clean ashtray."

She picked up the overflowing ashtray and waddled over to counter, threw the contents towards a bin and waddled back.

"D' are," she smiled again, with a certain pride, as though she was thinking 'I have to have everything just perfect for customers in my establishment.'

Dave stared at his unfeasibly large mug of tea, complete with a its chipped rim. It had brown stains inside and out but, as these did not seem to bother *Brain-Dead* or *Lard-Arse* whose were similarly adorned so, like them, Dave took a sip. The tea was delicious.

"Do you lads want t' fat poured on?" shouted the chef.

"Oh, yes please," *Lard-Arse* called back.

"No thank you," called Dave and *Brain-Dead*.

The enormous woman then brought over a plate full of bread and margarine. The bread wasn't cut into slices, they were wedges about an inch and a half thick with a further half an inch of margarine caked on top.

"Ummm, lovely," mumbled *Lard-Arse*, grabbing a piece off the plate and chomping into it even before the plate had landed on the table; leaving his mouth-shaped, teeth marks in the margarine in the process.

"That's what I like to see; a healthy appetite!" the fat woman smiled, with beads of moisture glistening in the black hair of the mustache on her upper lip.

"*Lard-Arse's* appetite is the only thing that is healthy in this place," thought Dave.

She next waddled over with a plate the size of a serving dish and plunked it down in front of Dave. Dave, realizing that this enormous plateful was for him alone, gasped at the amount of food. He also realized why the woman had developed such huge, hairy arms after years of throwing these gargantuan plates around. He stared open-mouthed as he took in what was on his plate. There were two strips of bacon; not a supermarket cut, but the sort a butcher would start with. In other words, the back and the streaky bits still together, complete with half an inch of fat on the top plus the rind. With this came two large fried eggs, two thick slabs of the dreaded blood pudding he'd read about in his guidebook, two fat sausages, a forest of mushrooms, a mountain of baked beans, four halves of tomato, a piece of bread that had also been fried and what looked like two small pancakes.

"What are those?" asked Dave.

"Oat cakes," replied *Lard-Arse*, as a stream of saliva flew out of his mouth and onto the table, as if someone had squirted water from a pipette.

"You slobbering dog," howled *Brain-Dead*. "Easy boy, yours is coming so hang on lad, you can make it!"

Then *Lard-Arse* received his plate. It was exactly like Dave's and *Brain-Dead's* except that the food was swimming in hot, liquid fat to the depth of about half an inch. Dave watched in horror as *Lard-Arse* picked up another chunk of bread and margarine and dunked it in the fat. With fat dripping off the sodden bread, he then transferred it to his opened mouth.

Brain-Dead laughed as he noticed Dave's eyes following this.

"Impressive sight isn't it?" he smirked. "There's no need to cruise the waters of Alaska to catch a glimpse of a feeding whale. Not when there's one right here."

"Fuck off!" mumbled *Lard-Arse*, spitting bits of bread over Dave. "I like my food, that's why I eat too much."

"Your trouble isn't that you eat too much. Your trouble is that you've only got one fucking arse!" laughed *Brain-Dead*.

Before *Lard-Arse* could respond, a bowl of fries, a foot and a half in diameter, landed on the table.

"Excellent," grinned *Lard-Arse*, "I was waiting for these."

All three of them started laughing at this, before silence descended as they got on with the serious work of doing some damage to the pile of food on the plates in front of them.

Twenty minutes later, Dave and *Brain-Dead* had given up. Both had cleared a massive amount of food. Dave had eaten so much, he felt sick, but he had hardly touched the fries.

Lard-Arse, meanwhile, was still going strong.

"How can you leave all that?" he asked Dave, "It's delicious."

"I'm stuffed," replied Dave.

"You leaving that black pudding?" *Lard-Arse* asked *Brain-Dead.*

"The pudding is yours, my fat friend. Have it with my compliments."

"I wish you'd stop calling me fat," *Lard-Arse* protested. "It's only because I've got big bones."

"And a big fucking gut!" laughed *Brain-Dead.*

Eventually, even *Lard-Arse* was finished. He did, however, leave a couple of lonely fries sitting at the bottom of the bowl.

"Not finishing off your chips, *Tubs*?" asked *Brain-Dead*, "You on a diet or something?"

"Fuck off," snorted *Lard-Arse*, wiping his mouth. "So young David, what did you think of your first full English breakfast?"

"Er...well it was very nice, but I don't think I'll be having one every day," replied Dave.

"Not unless you want to end up looking like *Lardy* here," laughed *Brain-Dead*, patting *Lard-Arse's* stomach. "You'd have a bit more trouble finding a bird then, wouldn' t you? You even have trouble finding your cock, don't you *Tubs*?"

"Fuck off, *Brain-Dead*. Just leave me alone, alright?" moaned *Lard-Arse.*

"I apologize, my...I apologize," stuttered *Brain-Dead*. "Anyway gentlemen, it's beer o'clock, so let's vacate this establishment and go get the bus."

The three of them shuffled along the benches, put on their coats and made for the exit.

"See ya' lads," shouted the chef.

"Bye," they all responded.

"Tha's not down t'lane, is tha'?" asked the chef.

"But of course," replied *Brain-Dead*, "Those *Red and White Wizards* await us."

"They're shite. Grimsby'll shit on em'," laughed the chef.

"You Sir may be a culinary genius but, at the end of the day, you are still only a *Pig Fan*. I bid you Good Day," replied *Brain-Dead*, closing the door with a flourish.

"*Pig Fan*?" Dave asked. "Sheffield Wednesday supporter," replied *Lard-Arse* helpfully.

"Wednesday are the other football team in Sheffield and they're known, quite accurately, as *The Pigs* and so their fans are *Pig Fans*."

"Oh, right. And what do Wednesday fans call Sheffield United fans?" asked Dave.

"Oh, they call us *The Pigs* as well," replied *Lard-Arse*.

"Bit confusing, this soccer rivalry," thought Dave.

"Now boys, shall we have some sport in the *Justa Pound*?" asked *Brain-Dead*.

"Oh, yeah!" laughed *Lard-Arse*.

"What sort of fun?" asked Dave.

"You'll see," replied *Brain-Dead*, leading them up the road.

In the middle of a row of shops was the *Justa Pound*. Its windows were covered in massive posters announcing that everything in the shop costs one Pound. Dave peered in the window at the garbage on offer. It looked like a market stall contained within a building. There were awful toys and kitchenware, plastic cutlery, candy and chocolate all spilling out of old cardboard boxes. Dave followed *Brain-Dead* and *Lard-Arse* into the shop, whose bell above the door tinkled as they entered. There was a thin, miserable old man behind the counter wearing a stupid baseball cap with a fan attached to the peak. He didn't say anything as they entered, but just stared as they walked up and down the aisles.

"It's full of crap," *Lard-Arse* whispered to Dave, "and half of the stuff in here costs less than a Pound in other shops anyway! But we're not in here to buy anything."

Dave watched as *Brain-Dead* picked up a toilet brush and started to examine it.

"Excuse me," *Brain-Dead* said to the shopkeeper, "How much is this?"

"It's a Pound," replied the old man.

"And this?" asked *Brain-Dead*, this time holding up a tin ashtray.

"That's a Pound as well. Everything' s a Pound in here," replied the old man.

"How much is this?" shouted *Lard-Arse*, holding a sieve in the air.

"It's a Pound," the old man shouted back.

"And this?" *Lard-Arse* shouted again, this time with a toy car in his hand.

"That's a Pound as well. Look you lot, everything in this shop costs one Pound, that's why it's called *Justa Pound*!" said the old man, exasperated.

"Yeah, but what about this?" called *Brain-Dead*, picking up a child's plastic plate.

"It's a fucking Pound. I've already told you," yelled the old man.

"Ooooh! No need to get stroppy," laughed *Brain-Dead*, "I'll give you 5Op for it!"

"Look you stupid fuckers, every fucking thing in this fucking shop is a fucking Pound alright?" screamed the old man, now with a bright red face and veins standing out of his neck.

Just then, the door opened with a tinkle and two old women waddled in, one pulling a shopping basket. After a couple of moments clucking over a coffee mug, one of them held it up and asked, "How much is this please?"

"What is fucking wrong with you fucking idiots today?" screamed the old man. "Can't you fucking read? In a fucking *Justa Pound* everything is a fucking Pound. Just get that one fucking simple thing into your thick fucking skulls and fuck off out of my fucking shop!"

The two old women just stared at the old man with their mouths open, then one started to cry.

"How rude!" announced *Brain-Dead*. "Gentlemen, we shall leave this establishment and take our valuable custom elsewhere. Good afternoon ladies."

And with this flourish, *Brain-Dead* left the shop followed by Dave and *Lard-Arse*. Once outside, they fell about laughing.

"Quick, run," shouted *Brain-Dead* suddenly, "there's a 51."

Brain-Dead started running up the hill, with Dave and *Lard-Arse* following on behind. Away in the distance a cream-colored bus was waiting at traffic lights and ahead of them was a line of people at a bus stop. The three of them arrived at the bus stop panting, but in plenty of time and they took their place at the back of the line. Several of the would - be passengers in front of them had red and white scarves; some around their neck and some, bizarrely, tied around their wrists.

"Have you got any change?" *Brain-Dead* asked Dave.

"Er...yes, some, " replied Dave, rustling some coins around in his pocket.

"Well chuck a few pence in the *Videmat* when we get on," said *Brain-Dead*.

"The what?" asked Dave, bemused.

"The *Videmat*," repeated *Brain-Dead*, "Just follow me."

Once the bus had pulled up at the bus stop, the line split in two. One went to the driver, who took money and issued tickets. The other, which was the line the bulk of the soccer supporters took, avoided the driver and went to a machine instead. The machine was roughly three feet high and two feet wide, with an opening at the top, into which people threw coins. This done, on pressing a large, round, green button, the machine made a throaty, gurgling sound and spat out a strange ticket. Dave watched as *Brain-Dead* selected a few coins and threw them into the opening, before pressing the button to receive his ticket. Dave then took out some coins, which *Brain-Dead* furtively rummaged through, removing any of even minor value.

"That's it. Chuck em' in there," said *Brain-Dead*.

Dave did what he was told and pressed the green button. The *Videmat* then gurgled, before spitting out a ticket. Dave stared at it. It was a photocopy of the coins he had thrown in.

"Cor ...that's neat," he smiled.

"Yeah, you're supposed to put the correct money in," whispered *Brain-Dead*, "but you can chuck in any old shit, washers, anything you like. No fucking ticket inspector's going to check tickets on a bus full of football hooligans!"

"Move along, Dave," said *Lard-Arse* behind him, barging him in the back to get to the machine.

Dave was still staring at the ticket as he followed *Brain-Dead* towards the stairs on the double-decker bus. As he climbed the metal, spiral staircase, he could hear singing from the top deck.

With a piss, with a piss, with a pistol in our hands,
We'll fight for   the cunt, we'll fight for the cunt,
We'll fight for   the cunter ...ry.

As he emerged onto the top deck, Dave could see it was mainly filled with soccer fans decked in red and white. Some had Sheffield United shirts on, some had scarves and some had no colors, but were still obviously part of the group. They seemed quite segregated, with the younger boys at the front, old men and middle-aged men in the middle (some with their sons) and the youths at the back. The atmosphere seemed raucous and good-natured, rather than threatening and Dave took a seat next to *Brain-Dead* as the next song was started by one youth, with the others soon joining in.

We've travelled far and wide,
We've been to Merseyside,
But there is only one place we want to be
And that's the Shoreham Street
Where it is magnifique
And all the Wednesday fans lay dead at our feet
Nha, nha, nha, nha, nha,nha,
Nha, nha, nha ,nha, nha,nha.

Dave smiled as he watched *Brain-Dead* and *Lard-Arse* join in with the singing and clapping at the end. He then laughed at the thought that 'going to

Merseyside', eighty miles away could be classed as 'travelling far and wide'. Shit, he'd driven that far for a decent burger!

"What's the 'Shoreham Street'?" Dave whispered to *Brain-Dead*.

"It's the Sheffield United kop, the place where all the nutcases hang out, where we're going today. It's the name of the street it's on," *Brain-Dead* whispered back, before joining in the next chant;

Noel, noel, noel, noel
Wednesday's the shit of Sheffield

Which was quickly followed by;

We hate Wednesday and we hate Wednesday
We hate Wednesday and we hate Wednesday
We hate Wednesday and we hate Wednesday
We are the Wednesday .....haters.

Dave was finding all this hilarious. There was a momentary distraction, however, when an attractive young woman got on at the next stop and appeared at the top of the stairs. The singing immediately gave way to wolf whistles and suggestive shouting, before a spotty youth of about thirteen started another chant;

Get your tits out for the lads
Get your tiiiiits out for ... the... lads.

Dave wondered how she would react; whether she would be frighten or intimidated, but she smiled as though she took it as a compliment and giggled with her ugly, fat friend; who in turn seemed pissed off that no one had asked her to get her tits out. Dave smiled and, with chanting in his ears, stared out of the window as the bus meandered past the university and through downtown. In fact, the chanting only stopped on two other occasions. The first was when someone spotted a very attractive girl in a skirt so short that it looked like a wide belt. This caused mayhem on the upper deck, with catcalls, whistles and hammering on the windows. The pretty girl on the bus, whose tits they had all wanted to see only a few minutes earlier, lifted herself out of her seat to see who was causing the commotion, before plunking herself back down again with a scowl on her face, and presumably making a mental note to buy herself a 'belt-skirt'. The second occasion was the spying of a youngster wearing a blue and white Sheffield Wednesday shirt, shopping with his mother. This resulted in aggressive hammering on the windows to get his attention, followed by threats to 'Rip his head off', numerous bared asses pressed against the windows and attempts to spit at him through the narrow ventilation windows. Dave felt ashamed as the boy dived for cover behind his mother, but he laughed when the boy reappeared, once the bus had moved off, to give them the finger. Even some of his tormentors appreciated this and cheered him. His mother, however, was not so impressed and smacked him in the head.

"Come on, this is where we get off," *Brain-Dead* announced after a few minutes, rising from his seat.

"Oh, we here?" asked Dave.

"We're not at the ground yet, but we're at the pub," *Lard-Arse* answered.

Brain-Dead pressed a button to ring the bell and the bus came to a stop. Dave then followed *Brain-Dead* and *Lard-Arse* off the bus and across a main road into a pub.

"I'll get these, what would you like?" asked Dave.

"*Magnet*," replied *Lard-Arse*.

"Excuse me?"

"*Magnet* bitter. You've got to drink *Magnet* on a match day, it's tradition," added *Brain-Dead*.

While Dave ordered, *Brain-Dead* and *Lard-Arse* went to find somewhere to stand, as there were no seats to be had. As Dave stood at the bar, he noticed a couple of dishes containing white and pink objects in some sort of liquid. Occasionally a man sitting next to Dave reached over, fished a piece out of the dish and tossed it into his mouth.

"Excuse me Sir," Dave asked the man, "what's that?"

"Chitterling," replied the man, who was smiling while chewing vigorously.

"Oh, thanks," replied Dave, none the wiser.

A few minutes later, Dave shuffled through the crowd clutching three pints of *Magnet* bitter to join *Brain-Dead* and *Lard-Arse* standing by a fireplace. The two of them were staring at a painting. Once he had handed their pints over, Dave also studied the painting. It was of Bramall Lane, Sheffield United's stadium, on match day and, a small plaque informed them, was by a local artist called Bill Kirby.

"Good innit'?" said *Brain-Dead*. "He's a bit like Lowry, only better."

"Yeah, it is good," replied Dave before noticing that the pub was full of prints in a similar style which, on closer inspection, were all by the same artist.

"If you notice," said *Brain-Dead*, "he often puts himself in the picture, drawing the scene and there's always a red balloon!"

"Why a red balloon?" asked Dave.

"Dunno," replied *Lard-Arse*, "probably artistic"

"Oh yeah, what's chitterling?" Dave asked.

"Local delicacy," replied *Lard-Arse*. "It's lovely!"

"Yeah, but what is it? Dave repeated.

"Raw cow's udder!" answered *Brain-Dead*, sticking out his ridiculously long tongue.

"Jesus!" Dave shuddered, "that's disgusting."

They worked their way down their pints of beer, which Dave still thought tasted terrible, watching the soccer previews on the television where, surprisingly, no mention was made of the clash between Sheffield United and Grimsby Town. Dave was enjoying himself and he liked this pub. Although it was full of soccer fans, it still had a friendly atmosphere. He was also thoroughly enjoying *Brain-Dead* and *Lard-Arse's* company; so much so that the horrors of the night before were melting away. After two more pints of beer (of *Bud* this time for Dave) it was finally time to take to the road and head for Bramall Lane. Dave felt a little wobbly as he walked out into the cold air and immediately needed to relieve himself of at least some of the three pints of beer sloshing around inside him.

"Christ, my back teeth of floating," moaned *Brain-Dead*.

"Mine too," agreed *Lard-Arse*. "Let's nip up this alleyway."

Dave was happy to follow the two of them up between two terraced houses. Then, as all three relieved themselves against a wall, groaning with pleasure, the end of a broom suddenly hit *Lard-Arse* on the back of his head.

"You dirty bastards!" shrieked a voice behind them.

They all span round, without paying enough attention to the direction of their urine. The result was *Brain-Dead* pissing over Dave's jeans, Dave pissing over *Lard-Arse's* pants and *Lard-Arse* pissing straight onto the apron of the growling old woman standing before them holding a broom. The jet of urine subsided and the arc retreated from the old woman's apron back towards *Lard-Arse*. Time stood still. Dave's jaw dropped, *Lard-Arse* said 'Ooops' and *Brain-Dead* said 'Fuck!' Then the old woman's horrified gaze dropped from *Lard-Arse's* face to her drenched apron. She seemed to take a moment to register that her apron was soaked and that the cause of this was in the hand of the fat youth in front of her. Dave, meanwhile, noticed that a torrent of nine pints of recycled beer was now flooding down the cobbled stones of the alleyway and all over the old woman' s slippers.

"You disgusting bastard!" the old woman shrieked, smashing the broom down on *Lard-Arse's* head again.

"Arrrrrhhh," cried *Lard-Arse*, as a blur that was *Brain-Dead* shot past him down the alleyway.

Dave did not hang around either and shot off after *Brain-Dead*.

Lard-Arse, meanwhile, stood around for one last blow to the head before he too decided to beat a hasty retreat. The three of them shot out of the end of the alleyway into the street, all with their manhood hanging out of their flies and with the old woman in hot pursuit. A group of soccer fans across the street cheered at the sight before them as *Lard-Arse* let out a howl as he ran away.

"Oh God, oh God," he yelped, "I've got my foreskin caught in my fly!"

When they were sure they had run far enough and that the old woman had given up the chase, *Lard-Arse* bent over in agony. Tears ran over his chubby cheeks, giving him the look of a cartoon baby.

"My cock, I've caught my cock. What'll I do?" he wailed.

Brain-Dead winced at Dave and then said "Rip the zip down again."

"I can't do that!" blubbed *Lard-Arse*.

"It's either that or we'll all be coming to your bar mitzvah, Heimi!" replied *Brain-Dead*, helpfully.

"Oh God, oh God," cried *Lard-Arse* again, before finally yanking at the zip with a blood-curdling scream.

"It's bleeding," *Lard-Arse* wailed, standing in the street holding his penis in his hand.

"Quick, in there," said *Brain-Dead*, pointing to a branch of *McDonald's* up the street.

Dave supported *Lard-Arse* as he hobbled up the street and *Brain-Dead* opened the door. *Brain-Dead* then ran up to the counter and started yanking paper napkins from a dispenser.

"Can I help you?" asked a youth in a silly hat behind the counter.

"It's alright," replied *Brain-Dead* without looking up, "My mate's got his knob caught and it's spewing blood."

"Oh, OK," replied the youth.

Dave led *Lard-Arse* into the Men's room, where *Lard-Arse* dropped his pants and shorts and held his penis under the cold faucet (what the Brits call a 'tap') in the junior sink.

"Oooooh, that's better!" *Lard-Arse* groaned, as the cold water washed blood down the plughole.

Just then, a little boy walked into the restroom wearing a *Ronald McDonald* hat, followed by his burly father. The boy stopped in his tracks and stared at *Lard-Arse*.

"What the fuck are you doing?" the father snarled.

"Er...my friend had an accident. He caught his foreskin in his fly," Dave replied, not bothering to mention the 'pissing over an old lady' bit.

The father winced.

"Come on son. We'll come back later," he said, guiding the boy out of the restroom.

"But I want a wee-wee," cried the boy.

"Well you'll have to go in the Ladies," answered the father, now somewhat flustered.
"Come in with me," cried the boy, before receiving a shove from his father sending him flying into the Ladies bathroom.

Brain-Dead then appeared with hands full of paper napkins and handed them to *Lard-Arse*.

After drying his penis under the junior hand dryer, *Lard-Arse* wrapped the napkins around his penis and stuffed the bundle into his shorts. He then gently zipped up his fly, wincing as he did it.

"It looks like a fucking codpiece," laughed *Brain-Dead*.

"Thanks a bunch," moaned *Lard-Arse* in reply.

Back out on the street, the three of them made their way slowly towards the stadium. *Lard-Arse* was walking with his legs as far apart as possible, making him look bow-legged. The street was now busy with soccer fans all heading in the same direction, which impressed Dave, who hadn't been in such a large crowd before. He was amazed that so many people would pay good money to watch Sheffield United play Grimsby Town; two teams he had never heard of. When they finally arrived outside the 'ground', the street was full of fans, police (who really did wear those crazy pointed hats), police horses (who didn't), hot dog stands and guys selling Sheffield United scarves and flags. Singing could be heard from inside the stadium, along with pop songs being played over the tinny public address system. Dave followed *Brain-Dead* to an entrance marked 'Shoreham Street Kop - Home Fans Only' and joined a small line. The line edged forward until they reached a turnstile where *Brain-Dead* pushed his money into a hole in a thick, wire mesh screen to a man who looked like he'd smoked a million cigarettes during his troubled life. On receiving his ticket, he then pushed at the turnstile, which made a heavy grinding sound as it turned to deposit him inside the stadium. Dave followed suit and, once inside, bought a glossy program highlighting the afternoon's entertainment, as they waited for *Lard-Arse* to squeeze himself through the turnstile.

Ahead of them were some steep steps with red, metal handrails, leading up a bank towards the stadium. They climbed the steps slowly with *Lard-Arse* still shuffling along with his legs wide apart. Once at the top, Dave could see through an entrance the vivid, green playing field and he felt quite excited. They made their way down steep steps to the row indicated on their tickets and squeezed along it to their seats.

"Oh, this is your seat," Dave said to *Brain-Dead*, who was following behind him.

"Doesn't matter, just sit down," replied *Brain-Dead*.

So Dave sat down on a small, hard plastic seat and said 'Hi' to an old man in a flat cap sitting next to him.

"All rate," replied the old man with a smile.

Dave looked around him at what seemed like a very large stadium. What he found odd about it was that it was made up of four distinct stands that had obviously been built at different times and didn't seem to join onto one another. They were at one end of the playing field in a stand that was quite full. The two sides were half-full, with the occupied seats spreading out from the middle. At the other end of the stadium, however, the stand was largely empty apart from a small circle of people in an area behind the goal.

"Grimsby fans," nodded *Brain-Dead*.

Then Dave nearly jumped out of his skin when someone right behind him shouted at the top of his voice 'Uni...ted. Uni...ted'. He turned around to see a hugely fat man (who made *Lard-Arse* look skinny) in a T-shirt bellowing so loud that the veins on his chubby neck were standing out.

"How can he just be wearing a T-shirt on a cold day like this?" thought Dave.

A few people elsewhere in the stand joined in until it seemed that nearly everyone was singing. Then in a far corner, someone else started singing a song to the tune of John Denver's 'Annie's Song' and, once again, nearly everyone, including *Brain-Dead* and *Lard-Arse*, joined in;

You fill up my senses, like a gallon of Magnet,
Like a packet of Woodbines, like a good pinch of snuff
Like a night out in Sheffield,
Like a greasy chip butty, like Sheffield United, come fill me again
Nha, nha, nha, nha, nha, nha, oooooh
Nha, nha, nha, nha, nha, nha, oooooh, ooooh

"Could you translate that song for me please?" Dave asked *Lard-Arse*.

"Sure," smiled *Lard-Arse*. "A gallon of *Magnet* means eight pints of local beer, a packet of *Woodbines* means a packet of very high tar cigarettes, snuff is...well snuff that you stick up your nose to make you sneeze, a night out in Sheffield is something you've yet to experience and a greasy chip butty is a delicious French fries sandwich oozing with butter and covered in lots of salt and vinegar!"

Dave snickered at this ridiculous song and what John Denver would have thought, before spotting in the distance that the Grimsby fans were holding their black and white scarves over their heads. He thought he could make out the faint sounds of singing, but he wasn't sure. The fans around him were sure though as they yelled abuse and stuck fingers up in the Grimsby fans' direction.

"Nha...you wankers!" screamed *Brain-Dead*, making imaginary masturbating movements.

The fat man behind them also started singing once again joined by the rest of the stand;

Sing when you 're fishing,
You only sing when you're fishing,
Sing when you're fish...ing,
You only sing when you're fish...ing

"Sing when you're fishing?" laughed Dave.

"Yeah," replied *Brain-Dead*, "Their nickname is *The Mariners* 'cause they're from a fishing port!"

Just then there was movement away to the left and Dave turned to see half a dozen young boys charging out onto the playing field. This was a cue for the stadium to erupt. Everyone around Dave stood up and cheered as the team in red and white stripes followed the boys onto the field. Even the old man next to Dave stood up and pulled hands full of ripped up newspaper out of a plastic bag and threw them up into the air.

"Come on you red and white wizards," the old man screamed.

United (clap, clap, clap)
United (clap, clap, clap)

sang the crowd, before changing to boos as the Grimsby Town team ran out.

At the other end of the stadium Dave could just make out their fans jumping up and down. The United goalie ran towards the 'Kop' and waved as the fans cheered and sang his name. Then, after a few minutes of warming up, the referee brought the captains together to toss a coin. The tension and the noise then rose as the teams took their positions and the game kicked off.

It was all very frenetic to start with, with both teams running around like mad things and passes going astray. Each time United won the ball, it brought cheers from the crowd then, when they lost possession again moments later, the crowd booed. The standard of soccer seemed terrible, even to Dave who wasn't really a soccer fan. In fact, he had only ever watched edited highlights of matches on the TV as there wasn't an adult soccer team in Beavers Bluffs and he didn't even know of one in Omaha.

The old man next to Dave, however, was certainly a keen fan and Dave worried about him having a heart attack. He moaned and groaned every time a United player messed up, and cheered and screamed at even a hint of some skill. But, as the minutes ticked by, even the old man calmed down. The singing became intermittent and, after having been so noisy, Dave was amazed how quiet the stadium had become.

Then suddenly, Grimsby were on the attack. A United defender swiped at the ball and missed it, leaving a Grimsby player to run on and slip the ball past the United goalie into the net. The Grimsby fans at the opposite end went crazy. They were writhing about like a black and white snake and, for the first time, Dave could clearly hear them singing. At Dave's end of the stadium, there was stunned silence until someone started a chant of 'United,

United'. The old man next to Dave was despondent.

"I've been coming here for nearly sixty years and they're still shite!" he moaned to Dave. "I've fucking had enough. I'm not coming anymore; wasting me money on these pillocks!"

If the stadium had been quiet before, it was deadly now. Except that is for the singing Grimsby fans. The only other source of noise was a small group at the far end of the right hand stand. Here were about fifty United fans who were taunting the Grimsby fans and, it appeared, throwing objects across the fence at them.

"That's the B.B.C., the *Blades Business Crew*, also known as the suicide squad," *Brain-Dead* informed Dave.

"The what?" laughed Dave.

"Just watch," smiled *Brain-Dead*.

Then all around Dave people began waving their arms above their heads, apparently to the Grimsby fans. To his surprise, several of the Grimsby fans seemed to be waving back. Suddenly, the group of Grimsby fans broke apart, with the majority dispersing to the far corners of their stand. Around Dave, the chants suddenly changed to;

You're going to get your fucking heads kicked in

and

You're going home in a Sheffield ambulance

and

Shoreham agro, Shoreham agro.

Dave could just about make out the scuffles and stand-offs until the police moved in from all over the stadium and began pulling people out and leading them away.

"That happens every time," laughed *Brain-Dead*.

The next twenty minutes were deadly dull with lousy soccer and only the occasional chant. Dave started reading the program, which was also boring, and began to regret coming. Then the noise grew around him and he looked up. The play was at the far end of the field and, from what he could make out, there seemed to be a scramble in front of the Grimsby goal.

'Ooooooh!' sighed the crowd, before bursting into a chant of 'United, United'.

Dave could see one of the United players running over to the flag in the corner with the ball and then the ball flying over towards the goal before the whole stadium suddenly exploded with a roar. Everyone around him began jumping up and down and screaming like maniacs. They jumped on the seats, they danced in the aisles. *Brain-Dead* grabbed hold of him and hugged him, before the old man next to him did exactly the same. It was mayhem. Then, as if after a preset amount of celebration, everyone put their arms in the air and started chanting;

United (clap, clap, clap), United (clap, clap, clap)

Dave did the same. He was caught up in the experience now and couldn't not chant. Everyone around him had broad grins on their faces, everyone was singing. Even the fat man in the T-shirt behind him slapped him on the back and said,

"I told you they'd do it. I told you."

"No you fucking didn't!" thought Dave, though he didn't say it.

"Come on you red and white wizards!" screamed the old man next to him at the top of his voice. "I've been coming here for nearly sixty years, tha' nos!"

Eventually, the madness subsided and people started sitting down again, although they now had smiles on their faces and cheered every time United got the ball.

"Great fucking goal," said *Lard-Arse* leaning across. "What a fucking header!"

Dave nodded, but how anyone could tell what was going on that far away was a mystery to him. After a few more minutes, the whistle blew for half time and a big cheer went up.

"They're only back to where they started," thought Dave, but he still cheered.

"Christ that was great," said *Brain-Dead*, sounding exhausted. "Enjoying it?"

"Oh yeah!" replied Dave.

"This ya' first time?" asked the old man sitting next to Dave.

"Yes it is," replied Dave. "I've just arrived here."

"I've bin' coming for nearly sixty years, tha nos!" said the old man again, proudly.

"Oh yeah?" grinned Dave.

"Aye. Tha' sounds like a Yank, where' s tha' from?" asked the old man.

"Near Omaha, Nebraska," replied Dave.

"Never 'erd of it. Is it in America, like?"

"Yes, the Midwest".

"Well, tha's very welcome lad. Long fucking way to come for a football match though!" the old man laughed.

"Coming for a slash?" interrupted *Brain-Dead*.

Dave replied that he did indeed need the Men's room and all three of them squeezed themselves past people who were sitting reading their programs or had radios pressed to their ears. They joined the line of people making their way up the steps, surrounded by happy voices and laughter. At the top of the stairs a large crowd was gathered around the refreshment hatch.

"Do ya' fancy a pie?" asked *Lard-Arse*.

"You fucking blimp!" laughed Brain-Dead, "You've only just had your *Bumper*."

"I know but they are fucking nice pies here and it's a long time till tea," replied *Lard-Arse*.

"Go on then, I'll have a pie, but I've got to go for a leak first," smiled *Brain-Dead*.

"Pie?" *Lard-Arse* asked Dave.

Dave thought for a moment.

"Oh well, what the hell," he thought; all that beer had made him hungry again.

"Yes please," said Dave, "But I need the bathroom as well."

"You won't find many baths where you're going," laughed *Lard-Arse*, "I'll see you back at the seats." He then disappeared into the throng of people, waving as he went.

Dave and *Brain-Dead*, meanwhile, headed back down the steps towards the turnstiles to find the 'Gents'. What they found was a conveyor belt line of men and boys slowly shuffling into an open-roofed, brick walled Men's room. When they made it inside, they were faced with a line of men and boys all urinating against a brick wall, below which ran a trough overflowing with fast running urine. The place stank! Dave held his breath as he moved into a gap in the line and unzipped himself. When he finally had to breathe, he did so through his mouth. That is until the man next to him shook his penis and, in so doing, flicked drops of urine onto Dave's hand and cheek.

"Oh my God!" Dave howled, still urinating but trying to dry his cheek with his sleeve at the same time. This was not a clever move, as all he managed to do was to urinate over his right shoe and the bottom of his pants. When he was done, he looked around for somewhere to wash himself. Dream on! There was no sink in sight. So on the way back to their seats, he joined the line for the Refreshments, bought himself a bottle of water and took several paper napkins to wash his hands and face. As he arrived back at his seat and *Lard-Arse* passed him a very greasy pie in a paper bag, a cheer went up.

"Wobts that fur?" asked Dave, with a mouthful of pie.

"*The Pigs* are losing," replied *Brain-Dead*, pointing to the electronic scoreboard.

The supporters around him then burst into a quick rendition of 'Wednesday

's the shit of
Sheffield' before starting another chant that was new to Dave. To the tune
of the Christmas carol 'Hark! The Herald Angels Sing', they sang;

Hark now here United sing,
The Wednesday ran away,
And we will fight forevermore,
Because of Boxing Day.

"Boxing Day?" asked Dave, chomping on something worryingly chewy.

"Oh, *The Pigs* shit on us four-nil at Christmas years ago. We haven't got
over it yet and they keep reminding us about it - cunts!" replied *Brain-Dead*.

As he was finishing his pie, the teams came out again to a roar for United
and boos for Grimsby Town. Then, as the Grimsby Town goalie jogged
towards to goal in front them, much to Dave's amazement, everyone
started clapping.

"That's very sporting, very British," thought Dave, wondering if the goalie
was an ex-Sheffield United player or something.

The goalkeeper too seemed pleasantly surprised by this reception and
waved to the crowd to acknowledge their applause. However, the moment
he did this, the clapping turned to jeers and expletives, accompanied by
every offensive gesture known to man.

"They fall for it every time," laughed the old man next to Dave.

And so the game restarted. The quality of the soccer was just the same, but
the atmosphere was much more exciting. The floodlights had been turned
on and, as United were attacking the goal in front of them, every time they
came up the field everyone roared and stood up to get a better view.

Eventually, United broke away and after a couple of passes, a United
forward went around his marker and hammered the ball into the back of
the net. Everyone, including Dave, went mad, jumped up and down and
started screaming and shouting. Dave and the old man hugged.

"They're fucking brilliant, aren't they? I told ya', didn't I? I told ya'," yelled
the old man to Dave, once they had untangled themselves.

Dave was now totally caught up in the passion and atmosphere, singing out the name of the player who had scored at the top of his voice; although he still wouldn't recognize him if he fell over him! They all gave the Grimsby fans a quick rendition of 'You're going down again' and 'What's it like to be outclassed?', before settling down to cheer every pass United made and boo every time Grimsby got the ball. There was now a party atmosphere, something very tribal that Dave had never felt before.

"I'm a Blade now," Dave thought.

After ten minutes of reminding by the United fans, the referee eventually blew the final whistle and the game was over. There was a final cheer and applause before everyone turned away and joined the lines to leave the stadium.

"That was great!" shouted Dave to *Brain-Dead*.

"Come on you Blades," screamed *Brain-Dead* in reply.

"And *The Pigs* lost too," laughed *Lard-Arse*, "What a perfect day! Well, apart from my knob, that is."

"You going to come again, son?" asked the old man, who was right behind Dave as they walked down the steps towards the exit.

"Sure am," replied Dave.

"I think we've got a convert," laughed *Brain-Dead*.

As they were going down the steps, the crowd was pushing them from behind yet there was no room in front. It was in the midst of this melee that the old man slipped and fell into Dave on his way to the ground. Dave stopped to help him up, pushing people back in the process to give him room.

"Oh, thanks son," smiled the old man, now back on his feet. "They won't let me bring my walking stick in here anymore, in case I clobber someone!"

"This way," called *Brain-Dead*, who was slightly ahead of Dave as they left the stadium.

But before Dave could respond, he was suddenly barged in the back.

Turning around, he was confronted by a scrum of youths punching and kicking each other. Being so close to such violence was extremely frightening, as it was so unpredictable and fast moving. Fathers shielded their sons, a young girl was screaming and yet these youths were grabbing each other's hair, punching and wrestling each other. One fell to the ground and was being kicked in the head and body until his friends waded into the attackers. And it seemed to be growing, with more and more people arriving and joining in. Dave looked for a way to get out of the area, but he and the old man were trapped, with a house at their backs and the fight in front of them. Suddenly the fight veered towards them with several youths thrashing around in the gutter right before them. Dave found the whole scene mesmerizing.

He was scared, but also fascinated. The whole unpredictability of this totally alien scene seemed to excite him.

Then Dave got punched full on the nose. The shock of it stunned him before a piercing pain seemed to lift his head off. He held his nose which, even through the tears in his eyes, he could see was bleeding into his hands. Dave felt dizzy as he rubbed his nose to see if it was broken. Just then he received a blow on the head and, before he could react, he felt two pairs of hands gripping each of his arms. He felt himself being lifted off the ground and carried away. As his eyes were still streaming, he couldn't see who his saviors were or where they were taking him. But he was just so relieved to be away from that mayhem. The pain in the back of his head was now competing with the pain in his nose. He could see blood dripping from his nose onto the ground as he was being moved along, but he couldn't wipe his eyes or hold his nose, as his arms were being held so tightly. All around him was white noise of shouting and sirens and all he could see was blurred lights and the shapes of bodies as he was whisked along.
"Thank you," he mumbled to his saviors, but received no reply.

He could now make out a white, square vehicle shape in front of him and its doors being opened.

"Thank God, an ambulance," thought Dave and he imagined himself lying down and being able to wipe his eyes and nose.

The doors were open wide now and Dave was nearly there. However, instead of lifting him gently into the back, his 'saviors' pushed him, face first, against the side.

"Awww!" screamed Dave, as his nose smashed into the side of the vehicle.

His arms were then wrenched behind his back and he could feel some sort of cord being tied around his wrists and pulled tight, digging into his skin.

"What are you doing?" Dave sobbed.

His question was ignored as he was manhandled into the back of the van. His face hit the cold metal floor and the footplate dug into his shin.

"Get in there, you thug!" snarled one his 'saviors', lifting him up by the wrists behind his back and propelling him inside the van.

"Sit up there, you bastard," roared another voice.

Dave lifted himself up and slumped onto a wooden bench running lengthways along one side of the van. He wiped his eyes on his shoulder and timidly pressed his nose gently onto his jacket. Now he could see he looked around him. There were two enormous policemen sitting at either side of the van, next to the doors. Then further up the van were two youths, both had their hands tied behind their backs and one of them, a frightening-looking guy with a shaved head, was wearing a white T-Shirt, jeans and huge, red boots.

"Why have you brought me here? I've not done anything," Dave moaned at the cops.

"Yeah right," snorted of them.

There were no windows in the van, just a revolving vent in the roof, illuminated by a dull yellow light. Outside, Dave could hear sirens and shouting and there he sat, for what seemed like an eternity, with his mind racing with how he had got into this position and what the consequences would be. At intervals, the doors opened up and more youths were pushed into the van. As the occupants got used to their surroundings, they became more vocal, threatening each other and the two policemen sitting with them. After being told to 'Shut the fuck up' by one of the policemen once too often, the skinhead received a blow across his legs with a nightstick for his troubles.

Eventually, the van started up and jumped forward.

"I demand you let me go, I'm a citizen of the United States of America," Dave cried, before adding nervously, "Where are we going?"

"Disney fuckingland!" laughed the other police officer.

"The nick, you thick fucker!" growled the skinhead.

"But ...I've not done anything," wailed Dave, "I got hit. I didn't hit anyone. Why are you taking me?"

The policemen ignored him and the van continued on its way. It drove for about ten horrifying minutes, occasionally turning on its siren, presumably to move pedestrians and cars out of its way. Once away from the crowds, the police van sped up. Dave tried to keep his balance on the wooden bench as the van swayed on its journey. Finally, it swerved around a corner before halting briefly and then reversed before coming to a stop.

"Alright, everybody out. Disneyland's this way," laughed one of the policemen, opening the doors.

Dave kept his head bent so as not to hit it on the roof and jumped down out of the van. In front of him stood a 'welcoming committee' of four massive policemen standing at the bottom of a concrete staircase.

"Inside you lot," bellowed one of the policemen.

Dave moved forward and started climbing the steps.

"I want to see who's in charge. I didn't do anything," he moaned to the policeman walking next to him.

"Yeah, yeah! Move it, asshole," replied the policeman.

Once inside, Dave and his fellow 'prisoners' were led down a narrow corridor. All the walls and doors were painted white, there were burning white fluorescent lights on the ceiling and the place smelled of disinfectant. Eventually, they arrived at an open area and ahead of them was a desk, behind which two policemen in white shirts were sitting.
One of them seemed to be quite senior, judging by the stripes and flashes on the shoulders of his shirt. Dave moved forward to the desk.

"Excuse me but there's been a terrible mistake. I haven't done anything. I was the one who got punched. I...," squealed Dave.

"Shut the fuck up," replied the younger policeman, without looking up from the papers on his desk.

Dave shut up and the policemen carried on writing. Finally, the senior policeman put his pen down and looked up at Dave.

"Right, what were you saying?" he asked.
"Well...I was saying that I'd just come out of the stadium and was going home when someone punched me. That's when you brought me here. You can ask anyone. Ask my
friends, they'll tell you," babbled Dave at a thousand mile an hour.

The policemen smiled.

"Me too, ask my friends," laughed the skinhead behind Dave.

"No, I'm Brian," the other youth joined in, re-enacting *Monty Python's Life of Brian.*

The senior policeman behind the desk turned over a piece of paper and addressed the policeman standing next to Dave.

"Charge?" he asked. "Breach of the peace, Sir," replied the policeman, "I saw him fighting outside the ground and arrested him, *Sarge.*"

"I accept that," replied the sergeant

"That's a lie," yelled Dave, "I wasn't fighting with anyone. I was the one who got punched, you can ask anyone."

"What' s your name?" asked the sergeant.

Dave told him and then told him his university address. As he did so, someone behind him cut the plastic cord around his wrists. Dave, seeing this as a positive sign, sighed with relief as he rubbed the red lines around his wrists before checking his nose again. He was then asked to empty his pockets, which was less encouraging, but he complied. The policeman noted everything down on his piece of paper.

"Now take off you belt and remove your shoe laces," the policeman said gently.

"What?" replied Dave, stunned.

The policeman repeated the request, this time with more aggression in his voice.

"But you don't understand, I haven't done anything. It's not fair," Dave wailed, but he still did what he was told.

"Sign here," said the policeman, turning the paper towards Dave.

"But I haven't done anything," Dave moaned again, signing a list of his possessions.

"Number three, Charlie," said the policeman to the younger officer next to him.

Dave was then held by the arm and walked down a corridor, past two cells until they reached number three. Its thick metal door, complete with spyhole, hung open and Dave stopped as he looked in at the metal bed inside with a blanket on the top. He wasn't stationary for long, as he received a hefty shove in the back to send him flying into the cell. As he turned around him, the door clanged shut.
"Let me out," screamed Dave, "I'm innocent. I want to make my 'phone call. I demand you call the US ambassador. I know my rights."

"Yeah right," laughed the policeman, as he strolled off down the corridor.

It took several moments for Dave to comprehend the situation he was in and he just stood by the door of the cell without moving. He looked at the metal bed, he looked at the bars on a window at least eight feet from the ground, he looked at his bloodstained clothes and his shoes without laces. The smell of the cell was overwhelming. It was a mixture of old socks, urine, barf and disinfectant. Dave was absolutely petrified and he began to sob. He felt so sorry for himself and the injustice his was suffering. If he had one wish at that moment it would have been to be back home with his family and his friends where he felt safe, not rotting in some lousy foreign jail.

The irony was that for the previous few years Dave had been desperate to leave Beavers Bluffs. He and his friend Brad had spent hours and hours moaning about the place. It was so parochial, it was so boring, they knew everybody and everybody knew them. There was no privacy as, no matter where you went, someone who knew you was always watching. His friend Brad had once said, "If I fart in this goddam town, a thousand people will shout 'Jesus, Brad!'"

They had dreamed of moving away to a real city, one bigger than Omaha, one that was alive, like New York or a city with a decent climate like LA and of screwing girls whom they had not known all their lives and whose parents didn't play tennis with their parents. But now Dave longed for the security that Beavers Bluffs brought. Dave would never have been arrested at home for something he hadn't done, as his father was in the same lodge and the same bowling team as the police chief.

He sat on the metal bed and cried. He thought about asking again to make a 'phone call, but who would he call? How could he 'phone home and tell his parents that a week after arriving in England, he was in jail?

"I hate this country," thought Dave as he listened to the sound of traffic outside and the shouts and clanging of doors down the corridor. "Nothing' s gone right for me since I arrived."

And there he sat, head down, with a million thoughts spinning around in his head. What was going to happen to him? Would they make him stand trial? Surely they couldn't convict him for something he hadn't done, could they? When would they let him out? Would they keep him in overnight? Would he get thrown out of school? Would he care if he did? Would getting thrown out ruin his career prospects? What would it be like to have a criminal record in a foreign country? How would he tell a potential wife that he was a convicted criminal?

After half an hour, the spyhole in the door opened. Dave looked up and shouted, "I didn't do anything."

"Tell it to the magistrates tomorrow," came the reply as the spyhole cover closed again.
"Tomorrow? What do you mean tomorrow? You've gotta let me out," yelled Dave at the footsteps retreating up the corridor.

"I've got to do nothing, fuck-wit," came the reply.

Dave lay back on the bed with his eyes closed, listening to the shouting from the other cells and thought about Clint Eastwood in *Escape from Alcatraz*. However, he was soon sitting upright again as the smell of barf and urine on the mattress made him feel sick. After another ten minutes or so (he couldn't be certain as his watch had been taken away), Dave heard footsteps approaching once again. This time, instead of the spyhole opening, he heard a key turning in the lock. The door opened and the sergeant stood in the doorway.

"Come on son, we're taking you home," said the sergeant, in a gentle voice this time.

"What?" spluttered Dave.

"I said we're taking you home," repeated the sergeant.

"Why?" asked Dave, standing up.

"Do you have to fucking argue about everything, *Yank*? This way," the sergeant smiled.

Dave followed the sergeant down the corridor to the open area and the desk. By the desk stood *Brain-Dead*, *Lard-Arse* and the old man from the game.

"Yup, that's him," said the old man, pointing at Dave.

Brain-Dead laughed when he saw Dave.

"Check your possessions and sign here," said the sergeant, pointing at a sheet of paper.

"Did you tell them?" Dave asked *Brain-Dead*, as he signed.

"George did," interrupted the sergeant, pointing his pen at the old man, "He was my sergeant when I started on the force. He's vouched for you."

"Thank you," muttered Dave, almost in tears with relief.

"That's alright, son. See ya' at the Gillingham game?" asked the old man.

"I'll have to think about that," replied Dave.

"We'll take you and your friends home now," the sergeant continued.

"I told you, but you didn't listen did you?" sobbed Dave, now with tears in his eyes. "I'm going to sue you for this!"

"Don't push it son," growled the sergeant, "Just pick up your stuff and this constable will take you home before I change my mind."

Dave retied his shoelaces, put his belt and watch back on and pocketed his wallet and small change, before following the policeman out of the building, back down the concrete steps to a police cruiser in the courtyard. *Brain-Dead* put his arm around Dave's shoulders as they climbed into the back. The car started up as the courtyard gates opened and then sped out into the street before heading off through the city towards Broomhill.

"Bit of luck that old geezer being a retired pig!" laughed *Brain-Dead*.

"Watch it or I'll turn back," snorted the policeman driving the car.

"Yeah, shut up *Brain-Dead*," said *Lard-Arse* from the front seat.

"What happened?" Dave asked *Lard-Arse*.

"Well we saw you getting nicked," replied *Brain-Dead*, "But we didn't see where they took you. Then the old boy said he could help, being an ex-pig...er I mean policeman, but it took us fucking ages to get to the nick; we had to get a bus."

Dave settled back in his seat and watched the city go past as they headed for Sheaf Hall. He was quite amused to see car drivers around them suddenly turn on their best behavior when they saw the police cruiser.

"I wonder if I could make a citizen' s arrest," thought Dave, noticing that the policeman took no notice whatsoever of the speed limit, but he decided to say nothing.

Eventually, they pulled into Sheaf Hall car park and stopped. Dave pulled at the door handle, but the door wouldn't open until the policeman opened it from the outside.

"Thanks, that was great," said *Lard-Arse*, excited at his ride in a cruiser.

Dave said nothing as he got out and just started walking away towards the Quad, with *Brain-Dead* beside him.

"Dave! Is that you Dave?" a voice shouted ahead of him.

Dave looked up to see Samantha. She was walking arm in arm with Greg, but released Greg's arm and ran forwards when she recognized Dave.

"Oh, fucking perfect!" Dave muttered, keeping his head down and marching on.

"Dave, Dave what's wrong? Are you OK? You haven't been hurt have you? Dave, what's happened?" asked Samantha with worry in her voice.

Dave couldn't look at her. He felt ashamed, he felt humiliated and he felt exceedingly sorry for himself and the last thing he wanted to see at that moment was Samantha arm in arm with Greg, witnessing his humiliation.

By now Samantha was striding alongside Dave.
"Dave, speak to me. What's wrong, what's happened?" Samantha pleaded.

But Dave didn't acknowledge her, he just kept on walking.

"What is it?" pleaded Samantha, turning to *Brain-Dead*.

"Oh, he got arrested for scrapping at the footie," laughed *Brain-Dead*, "'Till me and *Lard-Arse* sprang in out of his cell!"

"What?" asked Samantha again, pulling on Dave's shoulder to try to stop him. But Dave shrugged her off and kept on walking towards his block.

"Dave," called Samantha after him, but stopping and grabbing hold of *Brain-Dead* instead.

"Tell me what happened?" Samantha demanded of *Brain-Dead*, "Is he OK?"

Dave heard their voices die away as he pounded across the Quad and into his block towards his door. He then fumbled with his keys, with tears in his eyes, before finally finding his door key and opening his door. Once inside, he locked his door, closed his drapes and stood in front of his sink, staring at his bloodied face in the mirror. He then filled the sink with warm water and gingerly wiped the blood off his face with a washcloth. He gently prodded and wiggled his nose to check it wasn't busted before drying his face and collapsing on his bed with his eyes closed.

After a few minutes there was a gentle knocking on his door.

"Dave," whispered Samantha's voice, "Dave, it's me, Sam. Are you OK? Open the door. I just want to make sure you're OK."

Dave didn't move. He just couldn't face her.

"Please Dave, open up. I'm sorry about last night, I was out of order. I got your lovely note and I just want to say I'm sorry for blaming you. I was upset but now I'm upset that I blamed you. Please open the door," Samantha pleaded.

Dave stayed silent and, after a few minutes, he heard Samantha's footsteps disappearing down the corridor. He just lay on his bed in the dark. He didn't want to see anyone or go anywhere. He just wanted to be alone, get some rest and get his head together.

"I'm going to be dead within weeks if this roller coaster ride continues," he said to himself.

He then heard footsteps coming down the corridor again, heavier footsteps than Samantha's. Dave prayed that they weren't heading for his door, but they were. The footsteps stopped and there was a knock on the door.

"If that's you *Brain-Dead*, just fuck off!" Dave shouted at the door.

"Dave, it's Paul, open up man," came the reply.

"Oh, please leave me alone Paul. I've had the hardest day."

"Oh come on man!" Paul continued, "I've got to talk to you. It's serious!"

Dave sighed, got up off the bed, switched on the light and opened the door. In walked Paul, with a cigarette in his mouth and a four-pack of beer and some CDs in his hands.

"You alright, man?" asked Paul, ripping a can of beer from the plastic ribbon and handing it to Dave.

"No, I've had an awful day, I got..," Dave began to reply until Paul interrupted.

"I'm in the fucking shit, man," continued Paul, ripping a beer for himself and pulling back the ring pull. "Here put this one on, you'll like it, Al Jarreau."

Paul handed Dave a CD, which Dave took, open-mouthed with the unfinished sentence gurgling in the back of his throat. He walked over to the CD player and put the disc on.

"I don't know what the fuck to do," Paul went on. "What do you think I should do?"

"About what? I don't know what you're talking about!" replied Dave, exasperated.

"About Pam, man. I mean I like her. I don't want to hurt her. I think she's great. Know what I mean?" burbled Paul, dragging on his cigarette.

"No I don't know what you mean, you haven't fucking told me what you're going on about.
What's wrong with Pam?"

"It's her pussy; it farted man!" said Paul, deadly seriously.

"Her what did what?" laughed Dave.

"It farted man. Not just a little fart. This was a fucking rasper and it's put me right off."

"Paul, stop! Look at me and tell me what the fuck you're going on about."

Paul lifted his eyes from the floor and looked at Dave, sitting himself on the bed at the same time.

"You got an ashtray?" asked Paul, holding out his cigarette.

"No, but I've got a sink."

"That'll do," said Paul, standing and walking over to the sink to flick his ash in.

"Well I was knobbing Pam last night, right," Paul continued.

"Well, I guessed as much. For the first time?"

"Yeah, first time. Anyway, I was taking her from behind and I noticed her arse."
"You noticed her ass? Aren't you eagle-eyed?" laughed Dave.

"Well," Paul continued ignoring him, "it's pretty fucking big, man. But that wasn't the worst part. When I pulled out, her pussy gave out this monumental fart. Now I'm a man of the world. It's not the first time that a pussy has farted on me and I'm trying to be broadminded and all that, but Jesus this one was so loud I nearly shat myself and I don't know if I can cope with the big arse and the farting pussy; know what I mean. I mean I really like Pam and all that; she gave me a great blowjob and she's great to be with, but shit, man, I can't be expected to cope with that, can I? I mean I like skinny birds usually, but I thought 'Oh, what the hell, give a bigger bird a go for a change'. And she has got such a pretty face; it's just her arse. You're gonna' have to tell her."

Dave spluttered on his beer.

"Me tell her?" Dave gasped, "What am I supposed to say? 'Oh, hi Pam. Listen, Paul really likes you but he doesn't want to fuck you anymore because you've got an enormous ass and your pussy farts like a tugboat. Oh, by the way, you do give great head and you have got a pretty face'. Fuck off!"

"No man, that was great. Just say it like that, she'll understand," said Paul, enthusiastically.

"I'm not going to say anything to Pam, it's up to you. She'll go crazy if she knew you were telling me this shit anyway. You've got to let her down gently. And you can't mention anything about big asses or farting pussies," laughed Dave. "And, just for the record, I don't think her ass is that big."

"Oh come on, man. I'm useless at breaking up with birds. It once took me six months to split up with a girl cause' I didn't want to hurt her," pleaded Paul. "I know what, we'll have a spliff and write a script of what you're going to say. Got a pad and a pen? Nice music this, isn't it? I thought you'd like it."

Dave sighed and went over to the desk in search of writing materials, as Paul flicked his cigarette into the sink before pulling out his tobacco pouch.

"I don't want one of those dammed spliffs, not after last night," said Dave, returning with a pad and pen.

"It wasn't the spliff that did your head in last night, it was *Brain-Dead's* mushrooms. You'll be alright with this. Anyway, we've got to get you in training for *The Dam*. So what are we going to say?" asked Paul.

For the following half an hour Dave and Paul sat on the bed drinking, smoking joints and laughing as they pondered how to let Pam down gently. Finally, Paul got up to change the CD.

"OK, what have we got then?" Paul asked.

"Er...," read Dave, "we've got 'Hi Pam, I need to talk to you about Paul. He's a bit worried because he really likes you as a friend, but his heart is still broken after a failed relationship and he loves and respects you too much to let your friendship fade into bitterness. He can't bring himself to say anything to you, in case it comes out the wrong way..."

"And your pussy farted on him," laughed Paul, dragging on yet another spliff.

"No I don't think we'd better mention that," laughed Dave, "No...in case it comes out the wrong way and you misunderstand how much your friendship means to him'."

"Good one, man. That's sweet. Ah, I'm glad that's out of the way," said Paul, relieved. "Anyway man, you said you'd had a shit day. What happened and what the fuck have you done to your face man?"

"Oh, it doesn't matter now, but I'm exhausted now and could do with some sleep, if you don't mind."

"Yeah, no problem man. I'll shoot. I think I'll wander down to the Uni Bar, to keep out of Pam's way. When will you tell her?" asked Paul.

"Er...I'll track her down tomorrow. I'm too tired now, but you have cheered me up, thanks."

"No problem man," said Paul standing up. "Hang onto the CDs for a while, you'll like them."

Dave saw Paul to the door and said 'Goodbye'. He then closed and locked the door before turning off the light (after cursing the crazy fucking English for having their light switches upside down) and collapsing again onto the bed. He lay in the darkness listening to the music that was still playing on the CD and chuckled to himself.

"Jesus, this roller coaster still goes on," he thought to himself. He'd been so down only an hour ago and now here he was, slightly stoned, slightly drunk and laughing at Paul's situation. Although he'd only known Paul for a few days, it felt like he'd known him for years. He was such an easygoing person and such fun. He could see Paul being a great friend for years and years to come. He even managed a chuckle about *Brain-Dead* and the events of the afternoon.

Then came another knock on the door.

"I don't believe this!" muttered Dave. "Who is it?" he shouted.

"David, it's Pam. Can I come in?" came the reply from the other side of the door.

"Oh fuck," thought Dave, "I haven't had time to get my head together about breaking the bad news to her yet."

Dave got up off his bed yet again and opened the door.
"You OK, Babe" asked Pam, "sitting in the dark like this? Ooh, look at your face! I heard about your fun and games at the football. That's pretty good going. Some hooligans spend years fighting at football matches trying in vain to get themselves arrested!"

"Very funny. I was just chilling out."

"Beering and fagging-it on your own, eh?" smiled Pam, spotting the beer cans and the smoke hanging in the air. "Anyway, I wanted to ask your advice."

"Sure, what is it?"

"It's about Paul. This is a bit embarrassing but I've got a bit of a problem," Pam continued. "You see we ended up honking last night."

"Oh really?" replied Dave, feigning surprise.

"Yeah, well you know how it is, got a bit stoned and horny. Anyway...I don't know how to say this...it's just that...well I really like Paul...I like him a lot. I think he's funny and good company and all that but...but...I don't even know why I'm telling you this...but I don't really fancy him!"

131

"Go on" said Dave, trying to look sympathetic.

"Well, it's just that I like big men with chunky thighs and...you know....big willies!" laughed Pam. "Well, Paul's too scrawny for me. I'm not trying to be rude 'cause I really, really like him, but he's got legs like a...er...chicken. And his willy sort of matches that, you know what I mean?"

"Well, I don't exactly know what you mean, but I'm getting the picture," smiled Dave.

"Well, I don't know what to say to him. I want us to be friends but I just don't fancy him. I don't want to break his little heart. He's so sweet and he was trying his best, but he just doesn't tickle my fancy! What do you think I should do?"

Dave pondered silently for a minute.

"I'll talk to him for you."

"Will you?" asked Pam enthusiastically. "What will you say?"

"Well, I won't say 'Pam's dumping you 'cause you've got chicken legs and your penis is like a pencil!" laughed Dave. "No, I'll say something like your heart is still broken from a previous relationship and it's too soon for you to begin another one right now, and that you like and respect him too much to let your friendship fade into bitterness. How's that?"

"Oh, that's perfect. You are wonderful. Will you really do that?" shrieked Pam, kissing Dave on the cheek.

"Yeah, I'll track him down tomorrow. But in the meantime, I suggest you avoid him. I'm pretty sure he's down at the Uni Bar this evening, so better not go there," said Dave in a serious voice.

"And you'll come and tell me how it went tomorrow, after you've told him?"

"Yes, of course I will. And don't worry, it'll all be fine. You'll both stay the best of friends, I guarantee it," said Dave, in his best reassuring voice.

"Oh, you're so lovely David," cooed Pam, kissing Dave on the cheek again, "Thank you. Thank you so much."

"Now if you don't mind, I could really do with some rest."

"Oh, of course *Darling*. I'll be off then. And thanks once again. You're a star!" smiled Pam as she opened the door and went out.

Dave closed the door once again before changing the CD, turning off the light and settling down on his bed again. But, no sooner had he closed his eyes than there was another knock on the door.

"Jesus," he cursed, "I don't fucking believe this!"

Dave jumped up and threw open the door.

"Hello David," said Cathy, standing in the doorway.

"Oh, hi," muttered Dave.

"I heard that you'd not had a very good day and I thought I'd pop over and try to make it better for you," whispered Cathy seductively. "I'm so sorry that I was horrid to you, so I've put on stockings and suspenders and I thought you might like to tie me up and maybe spank me for being so naughty."

"You'd better come in."

FIVE

Dave was woken the next morning by Cathy shuffling around the room, picking up her clothes and putting them on.

"Good morning!" Cathy smiled.

"Morning," replied Dave, with a grin breaking out across his face as he remembered the antics of the night before.

"David, we have to talk," said Cathy in a serious tone, sitting on the edge of the bed.

"Oh Christ, what now?" thought Dave, propping himself up in bed.

"It's just that I wanted you to know about me," Cathy continued. "I'm a bit of a bad girl really. I adore sex and I like having it with lots of different people. I just wanted to tell you so you don't get hurt or upset. I'm not ready to settle into a relationship with one man yet, I'm too young and I'm having too much fun. You don't mind do you? You won't get all slushy on me will you, or think you can keep me to yourself? I really like you but that's the way it is. You OK with that?"

Dave nodded.

"Oh, goody!" shrieked Cathy. "And can we still screw from time to time?"

"Yeah, sure."

"That's my kind of man," smiled Cathy, leaning forward and kissing Dave on his forehead. "See you around then, Tiger."

Dave nodded again and watched Cathy let herself out of the room. He then snuggled back down in his warm bed and masturbated, before dropping off to sleep again with a broad smile on his face.

It was nearly midday when he woke, yet it still took him another half an hour to come round completely as he slipped in and out of delicious half sleep. But he finally sat up, rubbed his eyes and stood up.

After a shave, shit and a wonderful hot shower, Dave got dressed and strolled out into the Quad in search of the Sunday lunch he could smell

134

wafting from the Refectory. As he approached the double doors he focused on a new poster that had been stuck onto both doors. It took a minute to sink in, but there was his photo (the one from his Student Union card) and his name under bold, black print announcing;

WANTED BY SOUTH YORKSHIRE CONSTABULARY
Have you seen this known football hooligan?
Do NOT approach - armed and dangerous cowboy
SUBSTANTIAL REWARD OFFERED FOR INFORMATION

Dave instinctively turned around to see if there was anyone looking at him. Only then did he see, to his horror, that every window around the Quad was sporting one of these posters, except his own. Above his window was a poster with a big, black arrow pointing downwards.

Dave just stood and laughed.

"*Brain-Dead*, you fucker!" he said out loud, in awe at the ingenuity of getting hold of his photo from the *Students Union* and the industry involved in printing and putting up all these posters. It must have taken him all night and cost him a fortune.

Dave continued into the Refectory and joined the line to be served. A couple of girls in front of him giggled when they noticed who was standing behind them. When it was Dave's turn, one of the servers turned to her colleague and said, "Here Brenda, do ya' think we should serve this dangerous criminal? I hear he's a gun slinger from the Wild West."

"Better had Shirl, there' s no telling what he might do if we don't. In fact, give him extra cause' he'll be on porridge soon!" replied her friend.

Dave took his tray of roast beef Sunday lunch and walked out into the dining area. As he appeared a cheer went up from the diners, which he acknowledged with a grin. His grin soon disappeared though, when he saw Paul and Pam sitting together.

"Oh shit!" thought Dave, "This could be difficult."

However, both of them smiled when they saw him and beckoned him over.

"Hullo," said Dave nervously as he approached the table and sat down.

Both Paul and Pam greeted him with smiling faces and they laughed about

Brain-Dead's posters, before Paul went off to refill the water jug. Pam then leaned over to Dave and said, "Thanks for having that chat with Paul. He seems fine about it. We've agreed to be just good friends."

"Er...no problem," muttered Dave, before Paul returned.

Dave was half way through his meal when Pam stood up.

"Well boys, I'm off. Catch you later maybe?" she announced happily.

Dave and Paul said 'Goodbye' and watched her leave. Paul then turned to Dave.

"Good work, man. Whatever you said has worked a treat," whispered Paul.

"Er...no sweat."

"What ya' up to this afternoon man?" asked Paul.

"I know it'll be a shock to the system, but I think I'm going to have to do some work. I thought I'd get ahead of the game with Professor Rogers. I've got the fucker next week and I've not touched the reading list yet. So I thought I'd cruise over to the library and check out why Loius XIV was such a dick," replied Dave. "I've got some serious butt-kissing to do with Rogers after the other night. What about you?"

"Nothing so mundane for me, I've penciled Tuesday night to sort that crap out. A looming deadline always sharpens my senses anyway. No, I'm auditioning for a band this afternoon."

"Oh yeah?" said Dave, "I didn't know you played. What sort of music?"

"Er...well, crazy sort of jazz I suppose. But they need a bass player cause they've got some gigs and a tour of Bulgaria coming up," replied Paul. "In fact, I'd better shoot. I'll catch you later and thanks again for sorting Pam out. You should be a diplomat! Oh, could you get the Louis XIV books out on your library card, so I can read up on the fucker tomorrow night. And make sure you get Professor Rogers' book, I've heard he always marks you up a grade if you quote him a lot, agree with everything he says and conclude that his big rival, Professor Blakely, is a total cunt!"

Dave smiled as he watched Paul leave before finishing his lunch and strolling back to his room past his wanted posters. After picking up his coat and bag he headed off down the road towards the library. It was a very pleasant stroll on a sunny October day as Dave walked past the shops in Broomhill, the soccer fields, the road that led to the university swimming pool, the museum and the park. Once in the library, with its delicious musty smell and sunlight streaming in through enormous windows, Dave successfully found the History section, the Louis XIV subsection and one of the many copies of Professor Rogers' book on the shelf. Armed with this and three other books, he then found himself a quiet corner, pulled out his notebook and pen and began skimming through the books, making notes as he went. Someone had helpfully underlined key passages in pencil in Professor Rogers' book and scribbled a note inside the jacket assuring future readers that Professor Rogers would 'come in his pants if you include these sections' in any essays.

"Excellent," thought Dave, "that'll save me some work when the time comes."

As he worked, Dave occasionally lifted his head whenever a female student walked past to grade her out of ten. He daydreamed about the position in which he would screw the prettier ones and how drunk he would have to be to screw the 'dogs'. All very entertaining!

Nearly two hours had passed when Dave felt a presence next to him. He looked up from his book to see Samantha.

"Hello," Samantha whispered shyly.

"Oh hi."

"Buy you a coffee?" "Sure, I'd like that," smiled Dave.
Dave put down his book and followed Samantha out of the library and across the walkway into the Arts Tower, where the cafe was situated in the basement. As they walked they said nothing but Dave stared at Samantha's gorgeous backside shuffling inside her tight, faded jeans.

"Christ, that Greg is one lucky son of a bitch!" he thought to himself.

When they reached the *Paternoster*, Samantha pretended to be frightened about jumping into the moving compartments and took hold of Dave's hand. They giggled as they dramatically threw themselves in, crashing against the back wall. Samantha fell into Dave, putting her arms around his neck in the process. They then both stopped laughing and stood motionless, with Samantha looking up into Dave's eyes. In a moment, they had missed the basement and were watching its floor become level with their eyes as they headed downwards.

"Oh God, what happens now?" cried Samantha, pulling herself tighter to Dave.

"The poster said it's totally safe to go right around. You just come up on the other side," replied Dave. But he wasn't entirely convinced as the last sliver of daylight disappeared and they were left in the gloom of a dim yellow bulb, surrounded by the sounds of churning machinery.

"Ooooh, I don't like this," whispered Samantha, gripping Dave even more tightly, "but if I'm going to be minced to death, I'm glad it's with you!"

Of course they weren't minced to death. The *Paternoster* manufacturers had obviously realized that killing passengers who missed their floor might discourage some of the more enlightened potential customers. Instead the carriage moved sideways, before beginning its climb upwards. As they reappeared on the other side, Samantha was still clinging to Dave. He hoped she wouldn't let go but, as the floor level of the basement appeared, Samantha released him, although she did kiss him on the cheek.

"My hero," Samantha laughed as they leapt off together and wandered over to join the line leading to a serving hatch.

"Have you got over yesterday yet?" asked Samantha as they queued.

"I think so, just about. I can't say I'm too keen on repeating the exercise though."

Samantha then asked Dave to explain exactly what happened, which he did.

"Oh, you poor thing! I felt so sorry for you and so guilty for being so horrible to you at the party."

"What do you want, *Luv*?" asked the woman behind the counter.

"Oh, er...what do you want David?" asked Samantha.

"Coffee, please," replied Dave.

"Two coffees please," said Samantha to the woman.

"Do you want anything to eat?" Samantha asked Dave.

"Oh, no thanks."

They both watched as the woman made two cups of coffee and placed them on the counter before ringing the price in the register. It was only after being told the price that Samantha started searching in her bag for her change purse and then began fumbling for the correct change.

"I'll get these," said Dave, quickly.

"No, no, I want to get them," replied Samantha, finally counting the coins out onto the counter.

"Look I am REALLY sorry being so horrible to you, you know," Samantha said once they'd taken their seats at a table.

"Don't worry about it."

"I saw that Cathy girl coming out of your room this morning while I was talking to *Brain-Dead* about the posters. Is she your girlfriend?"

Dave blushed.

"No, no she's not. She just likes...I mean I think she likes me, but she kinda' likes a lot of people," stuttered Dave.

"Oh! I see, or I think I see."

The awkward silence that followed was finally broken by Dave.

"Where's Greg?"

"Oh, he's made a new friend on his course and they're meeting up this afternoon. I'm really pleased for him, and relieved, because he's so shy that I was worried that he wouldn't meet anyone."

"He didn't seem shy to me."

"Well he's certainly not shy when he's with me, but he does feel awkward making...you know...friends," stuttered Samantha.

"Oh OK, I see," said Dave, but he didn't. Greg sounded a bit weird.

"This weirdness could be a chink in Greg's armor, his Achilles heel," Dave thought to himself. "It could allow me to shoot in there and steal Samantha out from under his nose."

"Do you fancy going out tonight?" Samantha asked.
"Er...yeah, where?"

"Just for a drink or something, not in hall or at the Uni. Maybe just wander into town."

"Yeah, sure. Who else is coming?"

"Well I thought just you and me. Is there anyone else you want to come along?"

"No, no. I just thought Greg might be there."

"No, I think Greg'll be with his new friend. He was talking about going to the cinema."

"Sure. You and me, I'd like that. What time?" asked Dave.

"'Bout eight. Do you want to come round then?"

"Yeah, about eight. Then we can take the bus downtown and I'll show you how to use a *Videmat*."

"Sounds interesting!" chirped Samantha. "I've done enough work for one day. Have you got more work to do or do you fancy a stroll home?"

Dave replied that a stroll home would be very pleasant and so they returned to the library to collect the books he needed to check out, before heading home laughing and chatting all the way.

It was five to eight when Dave hopped up the stairs of Samantha' s block and rapped on the door.

"That was an enthusiastic knock," smiled Jo as she opened the door, "Come in."

Dave entered and looked around for Samantha.

"Is that you David?" Samantha called from her bedroom.

"Yes," Dave shouted in return.

"I won't be a minute, I'm just getting ready. Talk to Jo, but no tongues!" Samantha yelled.

Dave went red.

"Oh, that's boring!" Jo grinned. "Sit down Dave, take the weight off. So, have you recovered from all your adventures? You have been a busy boy, haven't you?"

"Just about, I think," replied Dave. "Have you recovered from *Brain-Dead's* party cookies yet?"

"Yeah, I think the hole in my brain has just about healed now. It was quite a trip wasn't it? How's your mouth, back to its normal size?" laughed Jo. "Yes thanks. What a crazy trip though. I won't be doing that again in a hurry," Dave smiled.

The sound of a hairdryer being turned on came from Samantha's room and Dave imagined Samantha sitting in front of the mirror, wrapped only in a fluffy towel.

"So David, what is it with you and all these women? I hear you were 'entertaining' again last night. Are all Americans like you?" Jo grinned.

Dave blushed again. "Oh...er...that was Cathy. She came visit. She likes...er...she likes to visit," Dave stuttered.

"Well you must have something *Loverboy*!" laughed Jo. "Anyway, tell me about your friend Paul. He seemed nice but I couldn't work out if he and Pam are an item. She seemed to be trying to chat up Greg, but then she finished the evening with her hands down Paul's trousers."

"I don't know that much about him. I know that he and Pam are just friends. What else can I tell you...er...he's a musician, he went to one of your expensive private schools. That's it really, he's just a really nice guy."

Before Jo had time to comment, Samantha's door opened and she stood in the doorway.

"I'm ready!" Samantha announced. "How do I look? Will I do?"

Dave's eyes widened. She looked wonderful in a tight-fitting black skirt and half-cut white top, which left her midriff exposed.

"Jeez, you look great!" gasped Dave.

"Are you sure you want to go out with *The Stud* dressed like that, girl?" laughed Jo. "You might end up in his harem!"

"Josephine, behave," giggled Samantha. "Well David, are you taking me out or what?"

"You bet!" replied Dave.

"Have fun children!" called Jo as Dave and Samantha left the room. "Don't do anything I wouldn't do."

Once they had left the block and started heading towards the bus stop, Samantha took hold of Dave's hand.

"This is so weird," thought Dave. "Here I am taking another guy's girl out for the evening. Oh well, what the hell. She seems keen enough."

As they walked along, Dave noticed the reaction of other men they passed. Nearly all turned their heads and followed Samantha with their eyes. Samantha didn't seem to notice the effect she was having and she kept chatting away; but the partner of one of the men certainly did.

"Why don't you just go up and ask her for a photograph, you bastard?" yelled the girl at her open-mouthed boyfriend.

"I wasn't staring," replied the boyfriend.

"You bloody were. You're always doing it and I'm getting fucking sick of it," screamed the girl.

Still Samantha was oblivious to it all. She giggled and talked as they walked, her heels clicking on the sidewalk. Dave could hardly get a word in as she jumped from one subject to another, but he loved it. In fact, he found himself just staring at her beauty and it made his heart ache. He tried to put Greg to the back of his mind, but the black cloud that Greg created kept eating away at him. Even so, he found himself feeling proud that he was with such a beautiful woman and that people, mistakenly, took her to be his girlfriend. When the bus arrived, even the bus driver drooled over Samantha as they boarded and as she giggled over the *Videmat* machine. After they had sat down and Dave began describing the bus journey with the United fans the day before, to the accompaniment of Samantha's giggles, an old lady sitting opposite them leaned over.

"Oooh, you two make such a lovely couple, you know. You remind me of me and my Arthur when we were courting," cooed the old lady. "We were in love just like you two and we stayed in love 'till the day he died, four children later."

"Ahhh, isn't that sweet?" said Samantha.

"Yeah," replied Dave, wishing that they were indeed a couple.

Once the bus reached town, they got off and went into a pub called *The Toad and Parrot*, which was amazingly full and incredibly loud for a Sunday evening - something you just wouldn't find in Beavers Bluffs. Dave left Samantha in a corner as he went off to join the throng around the bar, manically holding out a twenty Pound note in an attempt to grab the attention of the frantically busy bartenders. The bartenders, however, were totally overwhelmed as there were only two of them trying to serve at least twenty people. Dave did get the attention of another member of staff and thought that he was going to get served, but the girl turned out to be a glass washer who was overworked herself, handing glasses directly over to be filled as soon as she had washed them. Eventually Dave did get a reaction from one of the bartenders and shouted out his order; much to the chagrin of a small girl at the bar who had obviously been waiting longer than Dave.

"Well, really!" puffed the girl, giving Dave the evil eye.

Dave shrugged in return, but he did feel guilty and wondered how he would behave on a sinking ship or in a plane crash. Would he clamber over women and children in his hurry to escape? He shuddered as he thought that he probably would! The girl's mood was not helped either, when Dave reached over her head to take his beer and spilled some down her neck. "Sorry," mumbled Dave.

"Wanker! Fucking Yank!" the girl retorted.

Dave then had to squeeze himself through the crowd back towards Samantha, with beer spilling out of the glass held in front of him as he went. As he approached the corner where Samantha was standing, he saw her surrounded by three youths. All three had their freshly ironed shirts hanging over their pants and their short-cropped hair gelled into meringue-like peaks. They were laughing and joking, talking over each other and generally all doing their level best to impress Samantha.

"Fuck off you lot!" thought Dave. "She's mine."

Dave muscled in between them and held Samantha's drink out for her to take.

"Oh, thank you *Darling*," Samantha smiled. "This is Kevin, Wayne and...."

"Shane," mumbled one of the youths, staring menacingly at Dave.

"Yes, Shane," continued Samantha, seemingly oblivious to the copious amounts of testosterone flying around.

"Oh," grumbled Dave.

"These lads were telling me about the parrot. Apparently there really was a parrot here when the pub opened, called Barney," Samantha continued.

"Well, at least that's more original than Polly," laughed Dave, as the three youths started to talk amongst themselves, now with distinctly sullen faces.

"Anyway," Samantha continued, "Barney was a lovely white parrot who used to talk to everyone from his cage that hung from the ceiling but, and this is the really sad bit, Barney's feathers started to go gray and then they fell out until he was totally bald. Then he started to get really grumpy and began swearing at everyone and kicking litter from the bottom of his cage onto people's heads. Then, one day, they found Barney lying dead in the bottom of his cage. He'd died of cancer. Because his cage hung from the ceiling, it was permanently in a cloud of cigarette smoke. He was probably on a hundred
fags a day! Isn't that sad?"

"A hundred fags a day; he was gay was he?" Dave laughed.

144

Samantha looked puzzled.

"He's a fucking Yank," one of the youths muttered to his friend.

"I mean that's very sad," gulped Dave. "But what about the toad, what happened to him?"

"Oh, I don't know about the toad. Was there ever a toad?" Samantha asked the youths.

"Dunno," grumbled one of them.
"So, what do you guys do?" asked Dave, now enjoying their awkwardness.

"I'm at Stannington College," one replied after a pause.

"Oh, what are you studying?" Samantha asked.

"Financial services...A.C.I.I.," he replied, smoothing down his hair and looking proud of himself.

"A.C.I.I., what' s that stand for?" Samantha enquired.

"Another Cunt In Insurance!" laughed one of his friends.

Samantha laughed and then asked what another did.

"I work at Billy Smart's Circus," replied the youth.

"Oooh, that's exciting. Do you really work in a circus? What do you do there?" cooed Samantha.

"E' don't really work in a circus," laughed one of his friends, "Billy Smart's Circus is the nickname o' British Steel Corporation. He digs 'oles an' fills 'em in again. An' I work at HSBC bank in town."

"Aye' doing fuck all," the steel worker interrupted. "They had a 'time and motion' bloke round his place last week an' e' had t' spend all day in t' bog, in case they found out that he did jack shit!"

At that moment, above the noise of the music and chatter came a sound that made Dave's blood run cold.

"Whyyyyyyyyyyyyyyyyyyoo!"

"Oh Jesus, I don't believe it," groaned Dave. "Fucking *Brain-Dead*."

Sure enough, standing in the doorway was *Brain-Dead* with *Lard-Arse*, Cathy, *The Book-Seller*, Mike and the other three girls whose names Dave had forgotten.

"Why can't he just leave me alone?" moaned Dave, praying desperately that *Brain-Dead* didn't spot him. His prayers were in vain, however.

"*Yank!*" shouted *Brain-Dead*, so loud that people in the vicinity turned to see what the commotion was. *Brain-Dead* then bounded over, followed by the others.

"Good evening, *Stud*," said *Brain-Dead* approaching. "Are you joining us on our Sunday curry expedition or do you have porking on your mind? I must say Samantha that you're looking particularly ripe this evening."

"Thank you, *Brain-Dead*. I think," replied Samantha.

"Ah ha, yokels if I'm not mistaken," said *Brain-Dead* turning to the youths. "So, which of you is called Kevin?"

"I am," replied one of the youths. "What' s your fucking problem?"

"I have no problem, young Kev. I am merely curious as to why half of the male population of Sheffield is called Kevin. It's a puzzling sociological phenomenon linked, presumably, to the fact that you're all related to one another. In fact, my theory suggests that if I were to kick one of you, the rest of you would limp. Tell me, my perm-headed friend, is your mother also your sister?"

"Does tha' want a fate? Cause if tha' does, I'll kick ya' fucking 'ead in, ya' fuckin student," growled Kevin, shaping up to *Brain-Dead*.

Mike, however, stepped in between them.

"I'm sorry about my stupid friend," said Mike. "He's got shit for brains."

"Well tha'd better keep him away from me, else I'll fuckin' kill 'im," replied Kevin.

"Come on Kev. It ain't wurth it," said Wayne, pulling Kevin away and leading him across the room.

"Good work *Brain-Dead*," said Mike, "I don't know how you've managed to live so long. Why do you do it?"

"Do what?" replied *Brain-Dead*. "I was simply making conversation with the local populace. So Samantha, I see you've fallen for the charms of young *Studly* here. I do have a request to make though."

"Go on," smiled Samantha.

"It's a simple request really. As the boy' s got his first *Wank-Bank* appointment tomorrow, I would ask that you don't drain him of sponk tonight. Like a finely tuned athlete, the boy must be on the top of his game tomorrow. I know I'm asking you to make a great sacrifice, but your selfish pleasure could deprive the poor boy of a highly lucrative career. I've had to have words with Cathy, who has assured me that she will fight temptation for the greater good."

Dave didn't know what to say or do. *Brain-Dead* was destroying his chances with Samantha.

"Oh *Brain-Dead*," replied Samantha, laughing. "You're asking too much of a girl. I've finally got David out on a date, I've spent hours getting myself ready and now, if I am lucky enough to get him into my bed, you're asking me to keep my claws out of him!"

"*Brain-Dead*, why don't you just go fuck yourself?" said Dave, by now getting very angry and very upset. "Why do you keep following me around wrecking my life? I'm sick of it. You've gotta be the rudist person I've ever had the misfortune to meet. You keep dropping me in the shit, you insult everyone I meet and you create havoc wherever you go. Why? Why pick on me? PLEASE, just leave me alone. Come on Sam, let's get out of here before I lose my temper."

With that Dave held out his hand towards Samantha, who put her drink down and put her hand into his.

"Pretty fair description of you there," said Mike to *Brain-Dead*. "You can be a total pain in the arse. Now it's time to leave Dave alone."

"Goodnight, Tiger," Cathy whispered to Dave as he walked past with Samantha.

Dave pretended not to hear.

Once outside in the fresh air, Dave stopped and turned to Samantha.

"Listen," said Dave. "I'm sorry about that. Yet again I'm apologizing for *Brain-Dead*. You don't mind if we go somewhere else do you?"

"David, stop worrying," smiled Samantha. "I'm a big girl, I won't break. I'm not offended by *Brain-Dead* and whatever he says I don't blame you for it. You're so sweet, do you know that?"

Samantha took Dave's face in her hands and pulled him towards her. She then opened her mouth and began kissing him. Dave opened his mouth to allow Samantha's tongue into his and ran his hand through her hair. She tasted wonderful, she smelled exquisite, her hair was soft and her skin was like a peach. Dave was in raptures. As he kissed, Dave pondered why smell was so important to him. He wasn't kinky about it but, for some reason, if someone's smell wasn't right, then it wasn't right. There was a girl at home, a very attractive girl, whom Dave had once made out with at a school disco. She didn't have BO or anything, but her smell just wasn't right. Maybe it was just that their scents didn't mix well, like if you put two perfumes together. Dave had even been told that women shouldn't use different perfumes without a gap between them for this very reason. Samantha, however, smelled perfect, gorgeous and Dave just wanted to eat her up!

"Weehee, tongues!" shouted a voice from the doorway.

Both Dave and Samantha knew it was *Brain-Dead* and they smiled to each other as they kissed, but neither broke away to respond or even to look at *Brain-Dead* as they heard Mike swearing at him and dragging him back into the pub. They just stood for ages in the middle of the sidewalk kissing and running their hands through each other's hair. They made no effort to move aside when people approached them, forcing the passers-by off the sidewalk into the road.

"Oooh, that was nice," cooed Samantha when the finally unclasped each other.

"It sure was," replied Dave, wiping his lips.

"Shall we go on somewhere?" asked Samantha, taking Dave's hand in hers.

"Er...yeah, why not," replied Dave smiling.

So off they strolled hand in hand down the road with Dave beaming from ear to ear. The world was perfect for Dave at that moment. The evening was warm and here he was walking hand in hand with the most beautiful woman he'd ever seen. As they arrived downtown, they approached Sheffield City Hall where there was obviously some sort of concert taking place that evening, judging by the crowds milling outside. As they got closer it became apparent that the concert was a heavy-metal gig, with masses of youths sporting long hair and jackets with intricately embroidered designs on the back.

"Cor, those jackets are impressive and I'd kill to have hair like some of those lads," said Samantha.

"Yeah, I wonder if they sew their jackets themselves or if their moms do it?" asked Dave. "Hardly fits the macho, head-banging image does it, sitting for hours sewing patterns onto a jacket?"

Dave and Samantha stood and watched the crowd. People were chatting, reading their programs, buying tickets from or selling tickets to the numerous touts, chewing on overpriced hot dogs of dubious origin, buying T-shirts whose motifs would no doubt disappear after the first wash and admiring each others' hair length and needlework. Suddenly from the midst of this serenity a cry went up and a group of about forty people broke away and ran around the side of the building.

"I wonder what's happening?" asked Samantha. "Do you think the band's arrived?"

"Dunno," replied Dave, "let's go check it out."

So Dave and Samantha, still holding hands, jogged around the side of the building, where the group had congregated in front of two huge wooden doors. These doors were one pair of about twenty or so around the building. Each pair was at least fifteen feet tall and, presumably, all of them were fire doors that only opened at the end of the concert to let the concertgoers exit. At the front of the crowd before this particular set of doors were two youths frantically working a metal coat hanger into the gap between the doors, while the group behind them shouted encouragement.

"They're trying to break in!" laughed Samantha.

Her words were still hanging in the air when the doors flew open. The group cheered and pushed forward to charge into the building. Suddenly though they started pouring out and running away as three enormous, shaven-headed bouncers dressed in tuxedos, appeared in the doorway and slammed the doors shut again.

"That's hilarious! Come on," giggled Samantha, pulling Dave along to follow the crowd to another set of doors further along the building.

Here they found what looked like an amateur troupe of acrobats. An enormous man was leaning with his arms outstretched against the wall, his massive beer belly falling out from under his T-shirt and over his jeans. On his shoulders stood a tall, thin youth also leaning against the wall, then from the ground, the crowd thrust up what looked like a child of about nine or ten, dressed in the obligatory denim jacket. Once on top of the fat man's shoulders, he scrambled up the lanky youth, treading on the fat man's head in the process, onto the lanky youth's shoulders. His goal, it seemed, was a tiny open window. As he reached for it, he swayed and nearly fell. The crowd gasped as he clung to the lanky youth's hair; who yelled in pain. Eventually, however, he regained his composure and, with a boot on the lanky youth's upturned face, he squeezed through the window.
The crowd held their breath for a minute before the doors flew open. The child stood in the doorway acknowledging the cheers of the crowd before everyone surged forward into the building.

"Come on, let's go in," squealed Samantha, dragging Dave towards to doorway.

They joined the back of the crowd pouring through the doorway and sprinting up the stairs.

"This is madness!" shouted Dave as they charged up the stairs. "We don't even know who the band is."

"Who cares?" laughed Samantha.

The stairs seemed to go on forever but, eventually, they burst out onto the seats of the Top Balcony. In front of them, people were diving into empty seats and trying to look inconspicuous. The commotion, however, had caught the attention of the bouncers, who were running towards them from every direction.

"Quick, sit here," gasped Samantha, pushing Dave into a seat and jumping on top of him.

She then grabbed Dave' s head and thrust her mouth over his. Behind her, Dave could see people still pouring in through the exit door. Unfortunately for them though, the bouncers had arrived on the scene and were grabbing them as they came through. Other bouncers then began pulling youths from some of the seats, demanding to see their tickets.

Dave's heart raced as he watched a particularly ugly and scary-looking bouncer, with a huge scar running the length of his face, walk down the steps towards them. The bouncer stared hard at Dave and Samantha kissing, before turning his attention to a youth opposite.

"Where's ya' ticket?" snarled the bouncer.

"It's er...here," whimpered the youth, pulling a ticket from his exquisitely embroidered jacket.

The bouncer examined it, grunted and then plodded off. Once he was out of sight, Dave and Samantha pulled apart (even though Dave didn't want her to stop) and looked around them. Directly below was the stage, sporting massive speakers and an intricate lighting grid. In front of the stage was a moat-like gap, peopled by bouncers and two cameramen. Then behind that was the audience, many of whom had already abandoned their seats and were standing ten to fifteen rows deep in front of the stage. Behind this throng, the rest of the seating area was less densely populated. Some people were sitting, some were standing and others were wandering around or talking in groups. The concert hadn't started as the house lights were on and some wholly inappropriate (but slightly homesickness-inducing) country music was playing as scruffy roadies, with big plastic backstage passes hanging off their belts, tested each microphone in turn with a 'One two, one two'.

"Bloody close that!" said a youth sitting a couple of seats down from Dave and Samantha.

"Sure was," replied Samantha, laughing.

" Do ya' want to get downstairs to the Stalls?" asked the youth.

"Yeah, sure," replied Samantha. "But how?"

"Well," the youth answered. "Once you've got through the front doors, they don't check tickets to go upstairs, only to get into the Stalls on the ground floor. I've got mates who've got tickets to downstairs and, if I can get their attention, I'll get one to meet me in Lobby with a few of their tickets, then we can all get in."

"OK. If you don't mind," smiled Samantha seductively.

"No problem," blushed the youth. "You can't head-bang properly if you're upstairs, can ya'?"

"Oh no," agreed Dave.

Dave and Samantha then watched as the youth tried first to pick out his friends near the stage then, having succeeded in that, trying to get their attention. Eventually, one of his friends, who was scanning the upper levels, spotted him and waved back.

"Three, three tickets," shouted the youth, wasting his breath as there was no way his friend could ever had heard him over the noise. However, his friend seemed to understand his hand signals when he held up three fingers and responded with three
fingers himself.

"Come on then," said the youth, rising from his seat and leading Dave and Samantha down the stairs to the Lobby.

Here they waited by the stall selling official merchandise at astronomic prices until the friend appeared and secretly slipped three tickets to the youth. The youth then checked that no bouncers were watching before passing two of the tickets to Dave. All four of them then proceeded to the doors with a 'Stalls' sign above them, where two bouncers were checking tickets. They all held up their tickets, which the bouncers nodded at, and strolled in.

"Oh, thank you. That was really kind of you," said Samantha to the youth once they were out of sight of the bouncers and planting a kiss on his cheek.

"No problem," blushed the youth, who took the tickets from Dave's outstretched hand and then went off to join his friends in front of the stage.

Dave and Samantha stood and drank in the atmosphere without speaking.

They watched the roadies finish their sound checks and the spotlight-operators clamber up fragile-looking rope ladders into the lighting rig to take seats high above the audience. Finally, the house lights went down and the audience cheered and surged forward before an explosion of light and noise blew over them and the band appeared on stage.

As soon as the rhythm of the first song began and the bizarre-looking lead singer started screaming into his microphone, the entire crowd dropped their heads and started head-banging.

"I've never heard of them before, have you?" Dave yelled into Samantha's ear from two inches away.

"What?" Samantha screamed back over the deafening noise.

"I said, who are they?" screamed Dave again, this time cupping his hands over Samantha's ear.

"Oh, I haven't a clue, but they sure are loud," laughed Samantha.

"You can say that again," replied Dave.

"What?"

"Nothing," yelled Dave, laughing.

The two of them stood and watched the scene and took in the strange atmosphere. Each new song was met with a huge cheer as the crowd, now with sweat pouring from their long hair and sticking to their faces, momentarily looked up from their head-banging and air guitar playing. To Dave each new song sounded exactly like the last one and, if it was possible, they seemed to be getting louder. So loud in fact that his ears hurt and he wished they would put the country music back on.

After five songs, Samantha, who by now had her fingers in her ears, turned to Dave.

"Shall we go?" she shouted.

"What?" shouted Dave in reply.

"I said shall we go?" shouted Samantha again, this time pointing towards the exit.

"Yes please!" shouted Dave, taking her hand and leading her through the crowd of head-bangers towards the doors.

Once outside Dave felt like his eardrums had blown up like balloons and were still vibrating to the beat of the bass.

"How do they stand that noise? I've gone deaf," said Dave.

"Eh?" Samantha replied, cupping her ear.
"I said how do they stand that noise?" Dave shouted.

"Eh?" said Samantha again, before bursting into laughter before hugging him.

"Very funny!" laughed Dave.

"Well, that was an experience wasn't it? Come on, let's find a quiet bar," said Samantha, taking Dave's hand and leading him off.

After looking in a couple of scary-looking pubs, they eventually found some steps leading to a trendy, basement bar with reasonably quiet music. Dave left Samantha at a table in a cozy corner while he went off to the bar. Returning with their drinks, Dave gasped as yet again Samantha was being hit on by a couple more *Kevins*.

"I don't believe it," said Dave once he'd sat down and the *Kevins* had moved on, "You're a guy magnet!"

"No I'm not," smiled Samantha, fluttering her eyelashes. "They were really interesting. They're both hospital porters and one of them works in a morgue!"

"Urghhh!" Dave shuddered.

"Yeah," Samantha continued. "He was telling me how he has to put the bodies in a big fridge, you know, like in films, and sometimes he has to get them out for relatives to look at and brush their hair and stuff."

"Christ, why do they want to look?" spluttered Dave.

"I don't know. To make sure they're dead I suppose. Anyway, apparently some of them sit up in the fridge. They're dead and everything, but something happens in the body that causes them to sit up and fart and even speak!" Samantha giggled.

"Speak! You're fucking joking," shrieked Dave. "That sounds like bullshit to me."

"No, he was serious," Samantha continued. "He was telling me about a new lad who had just started in the morgue and had to go onto a ward to pick up a body in his
tin..."

"His what?" laughed Dave.

"His tin," Samantha emphasized, with a very attractive furrow between her eyebrows. "Apparently when a porter has to get a dead body from a hospital ward he puts it in a thing called a tin. It looks like a normal hospital trolley with a pillow and blanket on top, but underneath it's hollow and that's where they put the body. It's so they don't have to walk around hospitals with dead bodies on show, scaring the visitors. Anyway, when he got the body back to the morgue - this was at night and he was on his own by the way..."

"Yeah, of course," Dave interrupted, sarcastically.

"No, he was. Anyway, when he got the body out of the tin and put it on the slab, it sat up and groaned!" Samantha howled. "The poor boy ran away and they never saw him again."

"So tell me," said Dave, when he had stopped laughing. "If this boy ran off and they never saw him again, how did they find out what happened?"

"Oh," said Samantha with the grin falling from her face. "I didn't think of that. Maybe the double-decker tin story was rubbish as well."

"The what?" laughed Dave.

"The double-decker tin. He said that at night, when there aren't any visitors around, lazy porters wait until two people die before they bother going to collect them. Then they put one in the tin and one on top. That's probably rubbish as well, isn't it?" Samantha smiled.

Dave nodded as he laughed.

"Anyway," said Dave, once he'd regained his composure, "how did *Kevin* manage to impart so much information? I was only at the bar five minutes."

"I'm not sure if his name was Kevin, but I just asked him what he did and that's when he told me."

"Don't you get pissed with all these guys hitting on you all the time?"

"Oh, I don't think they're trying to hit on me. They're just being friendly," replied Samantha, apparently in all innocence.

"Trying to get in your panties more like," said Dave firmly. "I should know!"

"Oh yes, David?" laughed Samantha, "Are you trying to get in my panties?"

Dave blushed bright red.

"Er...no not at all, no that's not what I meant," Dave spluttered. "I...I meant I know what they're thinking 'cause I'm a guy."

"Phew, that's a relief," sighed Samantha.

The color disappeared from Dave's face as quickly as it had arrived. The thought 'She doesn't like me after all and doesn't want me to get into her panties!' stabbed Dave's brain.

"I'm glad you're not trying to get into my knickers 'cause they'd never fit you!" Samantha laughed.

"What?" asked Dave, thoroughly confused by now.

"It's a joke David," replied Samantha pitifully. "But, what do you mean you don't want to get into my knickers? Don't you fancy me?"

"Of course I do!" Dave nearly yelled. "To distraction!"

"Oh good, that's alright then," smiled Samantha, leaning over the table and kissing Dave on the lips.

Dave and Samantha then spent the next two hours chatting, drinking and occasionally kissing before the bartender rang a bell to signal last call and they decided to make their way home. They climbed the stairs into the cool night air and the orange neon glow of the streetlights. As they passed stores on their way to the bus stop, they occasionally stopped to inspect the contents of the window displays. One was a huge toy store on the main shopping street, where they tried to decide which toy would best suit each other's personality. The toy Samantha chose for Dave was a *Homer Simpson* figure, due to the number of disasters he'd been having recently. Dave in turn chose a *Barbie* doll for Samantha, as it had a figure women envied. As they moved on they came to the toy store doorway where the sight that greeted them stopped them both in their tracks.

In a dark corner of the recessed doorway a lanky young guy was leaning against the glass door with his pants and white shorts around his ankles. In front of him was a plump, blonde-haired girl on her knees giving the youth a strenuous blowjob, with her mouth pounding along the length of his erection to the accompaniment of loud gurgling sounds. If this wasn't bizarre enough, in the opposite corner stood another tubby girl, smoking a cigarette and looking at her watch.

"'Urry up Karen, we're gonna miss ar' bus," said *The Timekeeper*.

Her busy friend, with her mouth obviously too full to speak, by holding up five fingers still managed to motion that she thought that only five more minutes would be required to quench this particular *Kevin's* ardor.

Stunned, neither Dave nor Samantha could move or take their eyes off the scene in front of them.

"What's 'tha looking at?" growled *The Timekeeper*, before turning to her friend again. "O' 'urry up Karen, I want a kebab before 'bus guoes!"

At this both Dave and Samantha burst out laughing and moved on, as a string out verbal abuse (including at least two 'Fuck off, ya' nosey gets!') followed them.

"Her Swiss Finishing School must be so proud," Samantha laughed.

Within a hundred yards they met two more *Kevins* dressed in cheap, shiny suits and who were absolutely paralytic.

"I fuckin' luv ya', do ya' know that? I fuckin' dus tha' nos!" said one, while the other was busy barfing all over the plastic seats of a bus shelter.

"I 'aint a poof or nuffink, but I fuckin' luv ya'," he repeated, as the object of his desire wiped dribble onto his sleeve.

"What interesting people!" exclaimed Samantha, as the *Kevins* suddenly started fighting each other.

"Yeah right," mumbled Dave, picking up the pace. He'd already been caught in one fight and wasn't too keen on being on the receiving end of another.

When they finally did arrive at their own bus stop, the only entertainment before the bus arrived was a couple of boys, who couldn't have been more than ten years old, arguing over who had the most 'scraps', with their fish and chips.

"What on earth are scraps?" Dave asked Samantha, once the boys had walked past.

"Don't you have scraps in the New World?" Samantha mocked, "Scraps are the bits of batter that get dredged out of fat fryers when they're cooking fish and chips. Am I also to presume that you've never sampled the delights of the battered, deep-fried *Mars Bar* or the battered deep-fried meat pie, both of which are extremely popular in Scotland?"

"I've obviously never lived," laughed Dave.

Samantha then pulled Dave close to her and stroked his cheek.

"There, there you poor little lamb, all lost in this confusing old world," Samantha cooed before kissing him.

As the kiss continued, Dave could feel a mighty erection growing in his pants and tried to push his backside out so that Samantha wouldn't notice it. But she did!

"Easy Tiger!" laughed Samantha pulling away. "I hope you don't think I'm going to give you a bus stop 'knee trembler' like that girl we saw."

Thankfully for Dave, his embarrassment was diluted by the arrival of their bus. After they had got on and had yet more fun with the *Videmat* machine, they climbed the tight spiral staircase to the top deck. It took all of Dave's powers of self-control to keep him from fondling Samantha's gorgeous backside as it wiggled up the stairs in her figure-hugging skirt. Then, as Samantha emerged onto the top deck, with Dave still climbing the stairs, she was met by a chorus of wolf whistles and "Get your knickers off" yells from a group of very drunk *Kevins* on the backseat. Dave could see Samantha smiling as she headed off towards the front of the bus. When he appeared, the *Kevins* started booing and yelled "What's 'tha doin with 'im luv, when tha' can 'ave me?"

"I told you, guy magnet you are," said Dave once they had sat down on the front seat.

The twenty minute or so journey was interspersed with shouts from the back of the bus before Samantha and Dave arrived at Broomhill and got off. They held hands as they strolled back to Sheaf Hall and climbed the stairs up to Samantha's room. By now Dave was wondering if he'd get invited in for 'coffee', yet he'd been scanning for Greg as they had walked across the Quad. Samantha pushed open the door to her room and went in with Dave following.

"Greg!" Samantha shrieked as she entered the room. Dave' s heart stopped as she ran across the room and threw herself into Greg's lap, before kissing him all over his face.

"Watch out, you'll spill my coffee!" said Greg, holding a mug in the air.

"Never mind your coffee," said Samantha stroking Greg's hair. "Tell me about your day. I've missed you so much. How was Charlie? Was he good fun? Where did you go?"

"Calm down," replied Greg, kissing Samantha. "We had a very pleasant day thank you. We went to the cinema and then on for a Mexican."

"And...and?" grinned Samantha.

"There is no 'and'," Greg smiled in return.

"Oh come on," pressed Samantha, "Do you like him? Are you seeing him again?"

"What's this, the Spanish Inquisition?" laughed Greg. "Yes I do quite like him and, as it happens, I am meeting up with him again tomorrow."

"Ooooh!" cooed Samantha, kissing Greg again.

Dave meanwhile was still standing in the doorway, grimacing as Greg and Samantha cuddled. His good mood had crashed and burned and all he wanted to do was to get out of there to go and lick his wounds.

"She's nothing but a dick tease!" Dave thought to himself. "She must be just so used to guys fawning all over her that she leads everyone on, like all the *Kevins* she's flirted with during the evening."

"Anyway," said Greg turning to Dave, "That's enough about me. How was your evening?"

"Er...oh, it was OK," replied Dave glumly.

"OK? Do I only rate an 'OK'?" said Samantha to Dave. "I thought we had a lovely evening. We went to a pub and a bar and even crashed a heavy-metal gig."

"And did you behave honorably?" Greg asked Dave, with a smirk on his face.

Dave stood open-mouthed.

"What the hell do I say to that?" he thought. "Well actually Greg, I've got serious hots for your girlfriend, I've been kissing and cuddling her all evening and, if you weren't here, I'd be doing my level best to ride the fucking ass off her!"

"That's none of your business cheeky!" giggled Samantha, before Dave could verbalize a reply.

"So is Charlie handsome?"

"That's none of your business!" laughed Greg.

"This is just bizarre!" thought Dave. "I've spent all evening fondling his girlfriend and now she wants to know if his new friend is attractive. What sort of a relationship is this? Maybe she's like this with every guy she meets and he knows it? Anyway, who cares? I'm outta here."

"I'd better be off," said Dave.

"Why?" replied Samantha, looking stunned.

"Don't leave on my account," said Greg.

"No, no, I've got an early start. I'll see you around," replied Dave.

"David, don't go," pleaded Samantha. "Stay and have a coffee."

"No, I'm off. I'll see you tomorrow...or whenever!" replied Dave, before turning and walking out of the room.

"Bitch!" said Dave out loud, as he stamped down the stairs and out of the block. "Bitch!" he repeated as he stamped across the Quad, staring at the ground with his hands in his pockets as he made his way back to his block. As he neared the door, Pam's voice made him look up.

"Hello *Luv*," said Pam.

"Oh hi," replied Dave. "You look neat." Pam was dressed to kill. She had some sort of evening dress on and was caked in make up.

"Thanks," replied Pam. "Waste of bloody time though. This was all for Greg's benefit. I waited all bloody night in the Hall Bar for him to make an appearance and he never showed, the bastard!"

"You' re wasting your time there, I'm afraid," moaned Dave. "He's with Samantha."

"Bitch!" moaned Pam. "Oh well, fancy a consolation cup of tea and fag with your Auntie Pam?"

"Sure, why not," smiled Dave, before turning around and following Pam towards her block.

It turned out that Pam's room was in the same block as Cathy's. For a moment, Dave did consider abandoning Pam and knocking on Cathy's door for some mutual gratification. It might help his shattered ego to be with a woman who actually wanted to be with him and Cathy had proved herself to be anything but a dick tease! But he didn't. He didn't have the hots for Pam, but she was great fun and maybe a good chat would do him more good than a screw at this moment in time.

"Here we are," said Pam, opening the door to her room on the top floor of the block.

As they entered, once again Dave was shocked by how nice and cozy Pam's room was. Once again it looked like Pam had been living there for years rather than days.
Pam had adorned her room in the Afghan, hippy style, with a Persian rug on the floor and another hanging off the wall, strange Indian statues and an art deco lamp on the nightstand with a pink bulb giving the room a warming glow.

"This is where I should have been bonking Greg if it wasn't for that bitch Samantha," moaned Pam. "I wonder what he sees in her?"

Dave groaned because he knew exactly what Greg saw in Samantha. It was the same thing that every man saw in Samantha - her wonderful 'fuck me' body and her flirtatious manner. Then he shuddered as he envisaged Greg getting to grips with that 'fuck me' body right at that very moment.

"Bit of Motown?" asked Pam.

"Eh?" replied Dave.

"Motown? Do you fancy listening to some Motown to remind you of home?" asked Pam.

"Yeah, great," replied Dave, not bothering to mention that Beavers Bluffs was a considerable distance from Detroit; further than from Sheffield to Italy in fact.

Pam then went over to a pile of CDs and pulled one out of its case, before putting it into the CD tray and skipping onto a chosen track. As the music started, Pam pulled an enormous red, metal teapot off a shelf, threw in two teabags and left the room to boil some water. Dave sat on the bed, listening to the music and staring, nosily, around Pam's room. He chuckled to himself when he heard the lyrics of the track Pam had chosen. He didn't recognize the singer, but the track was obviously called 'It should have been me' and described a woman who had lost her man to another woman.
He thought about the crazy situation both he and Pam were in. Pam wanted Greg to ditch Samantha, but there wasn't a chance of that happening. Pam had a cute face, but there was no way she was going to compete for Greg's affections with Samantha around. Then there was him. He wanted Samantha to chuck Greg and, likewise, it seemed there was no chance of that happening either.

Shortly, Pam came back into the room with a now full teapot and a small carton of milk. She then took two huge metal mugs off the shelf and poured out the tea, before handing a cup to Dave and sitting cross-legged on the bed.

"So *Darling*, tell me why you're so sad," said Pam, pulling a packet of cigarettes out of her bra and passing a cigarette to Dave.

He had been a committed non-smoker only a week ago but, even though he hated the taste and how they made his mouth feel, he found himself drawn to the cigarette being offered to him. He was already looking on cigarettes as a strange comfort blanket and could now understand why people became addicted to them so easily. Not that that was going to happen to him. No Sir! He could take them or leave them. It's just that he fancied one at this moment in time.

As he coughed over his cigarette and drank his tea, he told Pam about his evening and how it had ended so badly when he returned to find Greg waiting for Samantha in her room. Pam was a good listener and mumbled sympathetic noises at all the appropriate moments.

"Oh well, forget the bitch," said Pam, when Dave had finished his tale of woe, "and I'll try to forget Greg; although he has got lovely arms. I must thank you again though for having that chat with Paul. It could have been really awkward after...you know...our bonk the other night, but he seems to be fine about it. In fact, he spent all evening in the bar being chatted up by Jo. She was all over him. It got quite embarrassing after a while. She was throwing herself at him! I just left them to it in the end."

Dave smiled as he thought how Pam had been planning to do exactly the same with Greg if she'd had the chance. He did start to relax though. Pam rolled a joint, more music went on, more pots of tea were made and they just talked. Pam told Dave about her life in Newcastle, about her family and about having her heart broken by a boyfriend who had dumped her. Dave told Pam about life in Beavers Bluffs and about his family, but didn't go into a lot of detail about his previous love life, as there was very little to tell. When Dave eventually looked at his watch, it was five till two in the morning.

"Shit!" Dave exclaimed. "Look at the time. I'd better go, but thank you for cheering me up."

"It was my pleasure, *Luv*," replied Pam, "thank you for cheering me up."

Dave put his jacket on, pecked Pam on the cheek and left. As he made his way down the stairs his legs felt a little wobbly, thanks to the joints he'd smoked. He stopped outside Cathy's door and for a moment considered knocking, but he decided it wouldn't be a good idea and carried on. Once outside the block, he stopped and looked over towards Samantha's block. His stomach churned as he thought of Samantha and Greg sleeping in each other's arms.

"Bitch," he muttered before staggering on towards his block across the dark and deserted Quad.

"Hey you. *Cowboy!*" came a voice from the shadows.

Dave nearly jumped out of his skin before turning round to see Jo approaching.

"I thought you were supposed to be with Sam this evening, not knocking off that Cathy slag!" hissed Jo.

"I've not been with Cathy," Dave protested.

"Oh yes?" snapped Jo. "Typical bloody man, you're all the bloody same. Just wait till I tell my friend what you're really like."

"Go screw," Dave muttered under his breath. He was too tired and too stoned to persuade her of the truth now. He just wanted to meet up with his pillow.

SIX

"Hey man, wake up. It's ten o'clock. We've got an eleven o'clock lecture."

Dave carried on dreaming.

"C'mon man. Wakey, wakey!"

Dave finally realized that this wasn't part of his dream and sat bolt upright in bed.

"Dave, are you in there man?" came Paul's voice again from the other side of his door.

"Wait up," mumbled Dave, as he pulled back the quilt and staggered over to open the door.

"Hey, great boxers man!" smiled Paul, staring at Dave' s *Mickey Mouse* shorts. "Time to shake a leg, man. We've got The Crusades at eleven and wanking at three."

Dave examined himself in the mirror, as Paul sat on his bed and rolled a cigarette.

"So how was your hot date with Samantha?" asked Paul.

"Oh, well it was going great 'till we got back to find her boyfriend waiting for us," replied Dave.

"Oh, heavy shit man!" said Paul, lighting his cigarette. "I fared rather better, actually. I was in the bar with Pam, hoping the conversation wouldn't turn to *the bonk* and her big ass, when that Joanne bird came over and started chatting me up. No shit! By the end, she was practically giving me a blowjob. Don't think Pamela was totally chuffed with the situation, but shit happens! Nha!"

"Yeah, Pam told me," said Dave, sleepily rubbing his eyes.

"Pam told you?" spluttered Paul. "Jesus my son, you didn't do Pam after Sam blew you out, did you?"

"No I didn't *do* Pam," replied Dave, "I met her in the Quad while you were with Joanne and we had a cup of tea together."

166

"And no sausage-hiding activities took place?" grinned Paul. "You didn't check out the big arse experience for yourself, did you my son?"

"No I didn't. We just drank tea and talked. Anyway, I think Pam's great and, despite her ass, she has got a cute face," replied Dave.

"Yeah, you're right man. She has," said Paul, dragging hard on his infeasibly small cigarette.

"But enough of this idle banter, our education is about to be enriched with tales of Richard the Lionheart and all that shit. So you'd better shift your arse and go and cleanse your smelly body. We don't want the wank-nurse to get to work on your todger later on, only to find half a pound of Gorgonzola lurking underneath the old foreskin, now do we? I've already scrubbed my old man till he squealed. Those fucking scientists woke me up early this morning, crashing about on the way to their fucking nine o'clock lecturers. I reckon they should stuff all the scientists in their own fucking halls, so they don't wake us artists up every fucking morning. Anyway, I'm off to the Common Room to check out the Quick Crossword in the *Mirror*. Sweep by and pick me up when you're ready."

"Hold up a minute," said Dave, "What happened with you and Jo? You haven't told me."

"Well, I didn't knob her!" smiled Paul. "But I do like her and she has got a very fit bod, including her ass I may add. I did think it was a 'game-on' situation when she agreed to come back for a coffee, but she didn't stay long when I realized I didn't have any coffee. She did say, though, that she thought you and Sam were going to get it on. That's why she didn't want to go back to her room too early, you know, to let you two have some time together."

"How wrong can you be!" moaned Dave. "What did she say about fucking Greg?"

"She didn't say too much about him, 'though she did say that he's always round their pad, cluttering up the place, which pisses her off a bit. Better give Cathy another call mate! Anyway, time to mooch. See ya' in a few minutes."

And with that, Paul stood up, threw his cigarette butt in the sink and left the room. Dave smiled as he left. He did like Paul. But then Dave' s face dropped as he contemplated the Samantha situation.

Twenty minutes later, after a shit, shave and a shower, Dave walked into the Common Room to find Paul examining the breasts of a model in the *Sun* newspaper.

"Check these tits out man," said Paul as Dave approached. "Are they real or what?"

Dave studied the photo but couldn't decide. So Paul put the paper down and the two of them set off across the Quad. They had only gone a hundred yards when Dave spotted Greg walking towards them.

"Oh fuck, here's that bastard Greg!" whispered Dave.

"Hello Greg," said Dave politely, as Greg approached.

"I want a word with you, *Yank*," said Greg, gruffly. Dave gulped as it struck him how huge Greg was. "I don't appreciate your behavior with Sammy last night," said Greg in a rather threatening manner. "You should know that that girl means the world to me and if you mess with her, you'll have me to answer to."

Dave gulped again, but didn't say anything. What could he say? He could hardly admit that he'd been all over Greg's girl like a rash. Though he did think it somewhat unfair that Samantha had seemed quite happy with the situation when they were together, but had obviously 'spilled her guts' to Greg as soon as she'd got back.

Greg stood staring at Dave waiting for some sort of reply but, when none was forthcoming, he marched on.

"Heavy shit man," said Paul once Greg was out of earshot. "That's one unhappy dude. Better keep away from that Sam bird, my son, she seems like trouble."

"Yeah, you're right," replied Dave eventually. "Bitch!"

Dave and Paul walked on in silence as Dave mulled over Greg's warning. The more he thought about it, the angrier he grew with Samantha.

"How could she come on to me like that and then play the devoted girlfriend as soon as she saw Greg?" Dave thought to himself.

"You alright man?" asked Paul after a few minutes.

"Oh ...yeah, sorry," replied Dave. "I was just wondering how Samantha could be so two-faced."

"Cause she's a bird, man," announced Paul, rolling himself a cigarette as he walked. "They're all fucking mad."

"Yeah, you're probably right," Dave laughed. "Oh well, fuck her!"

"Or not, as the case may be!" chortled Paul.

"Anyway, I'm being ignorant. How did your audition go yesterday?" asked Dave.

"Err...OK, I think. I'm in the band, I'm going on their tour and we're recording an album," replied Paul nonchalantly.

"Jesus, that was quick work and rates a little better than 'OK'. What happened? Who are they?" asked Dave.

"Well, they're a band called *Noise*. They play fucking weird jazz, they've got a deal with a minor label and, apparently, loads of fans in Eastern Europe for some reason," smiled Paul. "I went along to this rehearsal room and they said 'Just play along'. Then they all started hammering out some crazy fucking jazz. There was no tune or anything; they could have all been playing different tunes. So I thought 'Oh fuck it' and did the same with my bass. Then after about fifteen minutes of undiluted craziness, they said 'Great, you're in'."

"Great!" laughed Dave. "But what about school? Are you going to give it up?"

"I thought about it and thought 'Nah, nobody will miss me for a couple of weeks here and there'."

"You're fucking joking !" laughed Dave. "You'll never get away with that."

"Chill out man," smiled Paul. "We're talking about History here. After you and Pammy have told a couple of the lecturers that I'm ill, I'll be back. I'll spend a couple of evenings scribbling out an essay or two from your notes, then 'Roberto's your father's brother', it'll all be cool."

"You're mad!" laughed Dave.

As they approached the Arts Tower, Dave had a sudden thought that made him go cold.

"Hey, do you know if Samantha signed up for The Crusades as well?" Dave asked.

"Not a fucking clue man," replied Paul. "I suppose she's not exactly top of your list of people you want to see this morning; especially after that Greg bastard threatened to shove your head up your arse!"

"Yeah, you could say that! I think I'll give the crazy bitch a big swerve," smiled Dave. "If she's there I'll be polite, but that's it."

Once the two of them had negotiated the *Paternoster*, employing the 'down-then-up' technique to avoid the crowds, they did a tour of the History floor trying to find Dr. Fleming's room. Dave nervously pushed the door open and peered around the room. This wasn't easy, as it looked like someone had let a smoke bomb off in the room. But, through the clouds of blue smoke, Dave made out half a dozen student faces he recognized from the Cheese and Wine party but thankfully no Samantha. At the far end of the room was sitting a gray haired man with a walnut-like face dragging deeply on a very long cigarette.

"Come in, come in," *Walnut Face* gurgled.

"What did he say?" asked Dave, turning to Paul.

"How am I supposed to know man, I'm in the fucking corridor. It's you who've got your fucking head in the room!" laughed Paul.

"I think he said 'Come in'," replied Dave.

"Well, let's not be rude. Let's go in a say 'Hello' to the man," Paul laughed again.

Some of the girls near the door had begun to giggle at Dave's head hovering in the doorway. Although *Walnut Face* could not, presumably, see that far with enough clarity through the smoke, he would have been aware that the shape in the doorway hadn't moved.

"Come in chaps, come on in. I don't bite," he laughed.
"Er...is this Dr. Fleming's Crusades lecture?" Dave asked *Walnut Face* but scanning the room for Samantha.

"It is indeed," gurgled *Walnut Face*, "and I am the very fellow. And who are you young men? I believe I detect an American accent. Are you our scholar from across *The Pond*?"

Dave confirmed that he was and they both gave their names. Dr. Fleming then put ticks on a piece of paper on the desk in front of him, dropping cigarette ash all over it in the process as Dave and Paul then both sat down opposite each other in the only seats still available.

"Excellent!" thought Dave. "No Samantha."

Everyone in the room then just sat and stared at each other without saying a word. This went on for a good five minutes, but seemed much longer. Paul finally broke the silence.

"Is it alright to smoke?" Paul asked.

"What? Oh yes, of course!" gurgled Dr. Fleming, who was mid cigarette-lighting himself.

"Would you care for one of these, old boy? They're Russian."

"Oh yeah," smiled Paul, leaning over the desk to pull a cigarette out of the packet Dr. Fleming was offering up to him.

"Oh God!" huffed a girl wearing enormous black glasses which made her look like an owl. She then waved her arm and swirled the smoke around in front of her, coughing as she did it.

Paul took no notice whatsoever and proceeded to lean back in his chair and light the cigarette, with a very satisfied smirk on his face.

"Well," gurgled Dr. Fleming, at last. "I think everyone' s here now, so let's get cracking shall we?"

To which everyone pulled out notebooks and pens and, more or less, tried to write down everything Dr. Fleming said. This amazed Dave. Although he did the same, he had somehow expected lectures at college to be different to classes in high school, but they weren't. Just like in high school, the professor lectured and everyone copied what he said. Dave didn't know how else the knowledge would be imparted, but the lack of sophistication disappointed him as he scribbled away.

The lecture itself was very interesting and very entertaining. Dr. Fleming had a very engaging style of oratory. He made the motivations and emotions of the first crusaders very human and, therefore, very understandable. This, added to his very dry and cynical sense of humor, made events seven hundred years ago, which Dave knew absolutely nothing about, appear real and humorous. Even the *Owl* forgot about the smoke, which didn't let up for two hours, and began to laugh as Dr. Fleming spoke. Paul, meanwhile, was like a 'hog in shit'. The only time he didn't have a cigarette in his mouth was when either he was rolling one or when he was leaning over the desk to accept another one from Dr. Fleming. Dr. Fleming's smoking credentials were even more impressive than Paul's. He didn't waste valuable smoking time stubbing one cigarette out and lighting another; he lit each new cigarette from the previous one. When Paul offered to roll a cigarette for him, Dr. Fleming had a cigarette while he was waiting! By the end of the lecture, the bar-style, six-inch square ashtray on the desk in front of Dr. Fleming looked like a mini mountain range and the floor under Paul's chair was strewn with butts and ash.

"Hey, what a fucking cool dude, man. He was the dog's bollocks!" enthused Paul as they left Dr. Fleming's room. "But I thought it was a bit cruel of him, setting us an essay on our first outing."

"Yeah, he was fun but I should enjoy his company while you can. With the amount he smoked I don't think he'll be around much longer. In fact, at the rate he's going, you might have no one to hand the essay in to," smiled Dave.

"Yeah, he could fuckin' smoke for England!" laughed Paul. "And did you hear his voice? He must have tar an inch thick covering his vocal cords. I bet they look like a tanker spill! He'll have to get a fucking voice-box soon, like that Stephen Hawkins bloke."

"Well I don't think it's funny!" interrupted the *Owl*. "I thought this building was supposed to be non-smoking. I don't appreciate having my air polluted."

"Maybe you should take up smoking," Paul replied. "Then you might die early and put yourself out of your misery!"

"Really!" gasped the *Owl*.

"And us out of ours!" Paul continued. She had obviously strayed onto a subject he felt passionately about.

With this comment hanging in the air, Dave and Paul leapt onto a passing Paternoster cubicle and began their descent.

"Wasn't that a bit rude?" Dave asked Paul as they left the Arts Tower. "I haven't heard you speak like that before."

"Yeah, I suppose so," replied Paul, slightly shamefaced. "But fucking, holier than thou, non-bloody-smokers get on my fucking wick. Anyway, enough of this negativity. I think it's time to get back to hall for some serious nosebag to build us up for an afternoon at the *Wank-Bank*! As the French say, 'Let's vont'. As the shepherd said, 'Let's get the flock outta here."

"As the hockey player said, 'let's puck off'!" retorted Dave.

Paul couldn't think of another one.

When they arrived back at Sheaf Hall, Dave asked Paul to go into the Refectory first check if Samantha was there. Paul returned a couple of minutes later.

"All clear on the Samantha front, my son," Paul reported, "but Pamela says you're a big
fucking girl and you're to get your sorry ass in there, or she'll come and kick it in there herself!"

After collecting their food, Dave and Paul joined Pam who, although she had finished her lunch, was waiting for them.

"How was *The Crusades* then boys?" asked Pam, as they sat down.

"Totally cool!" replied Paul.

"Yeah, it was good. Old Dr. Fleming was a nice guy and he actually matched Paul in a smoking competition," laughed Dave. "In fact, a neutral might say that Dr. Fleming possibly came out on top."

"Think I might slip him a spliff next time," smiled Paul.

"Oh you can't do that!" said Dave, concerned. "You might see the old guy off!"

"No chance," exclaimed Paul. "If Dr. Fleming has never checked out a joint or two in his fine smoking career, I'll bare my arse on the Town Hall steps!"

"Oh, you timed your lunch rather well, David," said Pam. "Samantha was in here not five minutes ago, with Greg!"

"Oh yeah?" replied Dave blushing. "Did she say anything?"

"Yes," replied Pam. "She said to tell you that you're a fucking waste of space, that she was so bored on your evening out that she'd rather stick pins in her eyes than see you again and that all she could think about all evening was getting back to enjoy a bit of nookie with Gregory, 'cause he's a real man and is hung like a donkey!"

Paul nearly choked on his *Spam* fritter. Dave turned a brighter shade of red as a pained smile flickered on and off his lips.

"Oh baby!" laughed Pam. "Pamela' s only joking, don't be sad. No, actually they were a couple of ignorant bastards who sat on their own even though they saw me sitting here and they spent half an hour yakking without looking up or smiling once."

"Yeah," interrupted Paul. "Greg was probably working out when he was going to shove your head up your arse for messin' with his wo-man!"

"Ah, you've upset Gregory, have you?" smiled Pam.

"He most certainly has", Paul answered for Dave. "There's not much of a *Special Relationship* there. Big Greg threatened Dave in the Quad this morning."

"Oh well, better forget that one, *Luv*. There's plenty more pebbles on the beach. What about that one over there, she looks like a nice girl?" asked Pam, motioning to particularly ugly girl who was chewing with her mouth open.

"Thanks very much, but I don't need you two to choose a girlfriend for me," replied Dave. "Unless you want me to find partners for you guys."

"Fair point," said Paul, tiring of his *Spam* fritter and rolling a cigarette instead. "And anyway, old David here doesn't need another bird. Samantha was his bit on the side in between knobbing that Cathy."

Before Dave could answer with a witty retort, the familiar wolf howl of *Brain-Dead* made all the diners jump out of their skin.

"Just what I need!" groaned Dave, as *Brain-Dead* and *Lard-Arse* made their way over.

"Greetings fellow masturbators!" shouted *Brain-Dead* as he approached and plunked himself down on the bench next to Pam. "And greetings to you, my Geordie filly," he continued, extending his tongue out towards Pam.

"I have to warn you, *Brain-Dead*, that I have a very sharp knife here and I'm prepared to use it," smiled Pam. "And once I start cutting things off I may not be able to stop myself. Now that would dent your wankability, wouldn't it?"

"Oooh, I love it when a filly plays hard to get," cooed *Brain-Dead*, putting his arm around Pam's shoulders. "Now don't be a silly girl. Just think of all the pleasure you'd miss out on if you cut off my willy. Come back to my room now and I'll service you. We've got five minutes before we have to get off to the *Wank-Bank*."

Not even Pam could keep a straight face at this and she burst out laughing.

"God, you are disgusting!" she laughed.

"Thank you," replied *Brain-Dead*. "Now, enough of this 'Bint-talk'. It's time for *Nursey* to build up her arm muscles on our cocks. D'ya think she'll blow us off if we ask her nicely?
That'd be pretty nifty; a blowjob on the National Health!"

"Hope so," smiled *Lard-Arse*. "I've not had a wank for two whole days now, just to stock up on the old tadpoles!"

"Two whole days?" teased Pam. "However did you sleep?"

"I just got pissed," replied *Lard-Arse* in all seriousness

"Anyway, enough of this tittle-tattle," said *Brain-Dead*. "We have work to do to pay for our weekend in *The Dam*. If my memory serves me correctly, I seem to remember you offering your motor to transport us to our appointment, my spliff-toking friend."

"Yeah sure," replied Paul. "But will we be able to park?"
"Leave the arrangements to me," replied *Brain-Dead*. "I shall navigate. I didn't get a Cub Scout pathfinder badge for nothing you know. We shall meet in the car park in fifteen minutes. Just time enough to give our todgers a final scrub. Don't want the wank-nurse to get anything stuck in her teeth now do we?"

"Oh my god!" laughed Pam. "I've heard enough. I'm off. Have fun boys and come and tell your Auntie Pamela how you got on when you get back."

Fifteen minutes later, the Four Musketeers did indeed meet in the car park.

"Guide us to thy trusty steed so we might be away!" shrieked *Brain-Dead*.

"It's over here," replied Paul, setting off across the car park.

"Is it that one?" asked *Brain-Dead*, pointing at a *Ford*.

"No," replied Paul.

"That one?" asked *Brain-Dead* two steps later, pointing at a *BMW*.

"No."

"This one then?"

"No."

"Are you toying with us?" asked *Brain-Dead*. "Maybe you just dreamt you had a car during a particularly heavy trip."

"Look," snapped Paul, "if you want to get the fucking bus, that's cool with me. If not, just shut the fuck up, OK?"

"Oooooooooh, temper, temper," sniggered *Brain-Dead*.

"Here we are," said Paul, standing proudly in front of a tiny, black, *Fiat* 500 that looked like a *Volkswagen* Bug's smaller, anorexic brother. Dave had never seen such a small car his entire life.

"Where?" asked *Brain-Dead*, pretending not to have noticed the car right in front of him and staring over the top of it.

"Very bloody funny!" replied Paul, opening the driver's door and pulling back the seat to allow *Lard-Arse* into the back seat.

"I'm not sure I can get in there," groaned *Lard-Arse*.

"Course you can *Tubby*!" laughed *Brain-Dead*. "Just slide one of your buttocks onto the seat and the three of us will shove your other buttock in later."

"Fuck off, you bastard!" replied an emotional *Lard-Arse*, who was now determined to squeeze himself in.

"This car is like a motorbike with a roof on it," laughed *Brain-Dead* as he watched *Lard-Arse* struggle.

"Look, I've told you. Shut up about my fucking car or you can fucking walk," snapped Paul.

"Chill, chill, my weed-enriched friend. I mean no offence," pleaded *Brain-Dead*. "I love your vehicle. In future it shall transport all the *Brain-Dead* sperm to *The Bank*, an honor not bestowed lightly. In fact, it's an honor that brings with it the right to display the *Brain-Dead* coat of arms. Unlike our noble Majesty's, the *Brain-Dead* coat of arms features a cock rampant astride two hairy bollocks. I shall also do you the honor of naming this car. From now until eternity, this car shall be known as *Spermy*. God bless this *Spermy* and all who travel in her."

"Just get in the car, you fucking madman!" shouted Dave, who was by now squeezed onto the backseat with *Lard-Arse*.

After several attempts to turn the cold engine over, *Spermy* finally started up and they set off out of the car park. Then, as Paul turned a corner, what seemed like a gallon of cold water poured over *Lard-Arse's* head.

"Fucking hell!" *Lard-Arse* screamed.

"Jesus!" yelled Dave, as *Lard-Arse* crushed into him in an attempt to escape the downpour.

"Oh, sorry about that," said Paul. "The drains from the sunroof are blocked, so water builds up in them."

"I'm soaked," moaned *Lard-Arse*.

"Ignore the fat boy and drive on," laughed *Brain-Dead* to Paul.

Paul drove on without looking at the road in front of him as he fumbled around for CDs on the floor and then fumbled around with the CD player trying to find the track he wanted. *Brain-Dead*, meanwhile, fiddled with everything he possibly could; he hooted the horn, leaned over Paul and put the lights on, opened his window, closed his window, opened and closed the ashtray, opened and closed the glove box and finally opened the sunroof. Dave and a now soggy *Lard-Arse* in the back could only watch the fumbling and fiddling in the front, as they were so tightly packed together that neither could move their arms. In fact the only place to store their arms was around each other which, naturally, *Brain-Dead* spotted.

"Hey, I think we have a couple of gay boys in the back," he laughed. "If you drop your hat, kick it all the way home!"
Once Paul was happy with his choice of music, he turned his attention to driving.

"Where do we go?" he asked *Brain-Dead*.

"Fear not, my faithful chauffeur, I shall direct thee," announced *Brain-Dead*, who then proceeded to stand up and put his head through the sunroof.

As the car was so small, the roof only came up to his waist, giving *Brain-Dead* the look of a tank commander.

"Forward Number One, steady as she goes," directed *Brain-Dead* from above as the car pulled out onto a busy street.

As they drove through Broomhill, shoppers turned to watch and children pointed.

"Are ya' willin for a shillin?" yelled *Brain-Dead* at a couple of giggling teenage girls, before giving a Hitler salute as though inspecting the troops. "Out of my vay, schweinehunds!" he yelled at the traffic in front of them.

"What we need," said *Brain-Dead* leaning down into the car, "is a flashing light and siren now we're in the hospital business."

"I hardly think they're going to give that to a bunch of masturbators on their way to *The Bank*," laughed Dave.

"And why not?" replied *Brain-Dead*. "We should have a cock with a flashing, red bell end on the roof and a siren that goes 'Urrrrgh, Urrrrgh' like someone coming!"

"Sit down you stupid bastard," shouted Paul. "Bandits at eight o'clock!"

Brain-Dead sat down as soon as he saw the police cruiser approaching them.

"Don't want to mess with 'the Fuzz' when we've got a known felon in the car."

"Very funny," replied Dave from the back, sounding annoyed but giggling to himself at the ridiculous position he was in. Here he was cuddling *Lard-Arse* on the back seat of a car no more than two feet wide, that had green moss growing between the metal and glass of the windows and smelled like an old, damp sack, listening to 'dog-done-died blues' through an ancient system that sounded like a transistor radio in a metal cookie tin, watching *Brain-Dead* and Paul bicker in the front as they all made their way to donate sperm to pay for a trip to Amsterdam. Unreal!

In no time at all, the Fulwood Hospital loomed up in front of them. It looked more like a large hotel than a hospital with at least ten floors.

"I knew we should have walked," said Paul. "We'll never find a parking space."

"Have a little faith," replied *Brain-Dead*. "I shall park this midget motor. Now, let's see. Ah yes, follow that 'Staff Car Park' sign, my good man."

"You're joking, they'll never let us park in there!" moaned Paul.

"'Course they will. We're professional wankers now," replied *Brain-Dead*. "We're not patients, are we? We're not visitors? We're fucking staff."

A skeptical Paul followed the road around the back of the hospital until they arrived at a barrier.

"There! I fucking told you, dick brain. Now what?" moaned Paul.

"A minor hiccup," replied *Brain-Dead*. "Where' s your wartime spirit? We can't go through this barrier, we can't go under it - just. So we shall go around it. Flick *Spermy* onto the pavement, my good man."

"Fuck off!" shrieked Paul.

"Have faith and listen to Uncle *Brain-Dead*. Ease ol' *Spermy* onto the pavement and all shall be well," said *Brain-Dead* calmly.

After a moment' s hesitation, Paul reversed before turning the wheel and edging the car's front wheels against the curb. He then depressed the gas pedal and eased onto the sidewalk. Once the front wheels were on, the car sped forward, the back wheels bashed into the curb and the back of the car bumped on as well.

"Jesus!" yelled *Lard-Arse* as his head hit the roof.

The car was so narrow that it fit onto the sidewalk without a problem.

"Forwarrrrrrrrrrrrrrrd!" shouted *Brain-Dead*, standing up out of the sunroof again.

Paul drove forward along the sidewalk and around the barrier, before dropping down from the sidewalk onto the road again.

"Jesus!" yelled *Lard-Arse* as his head hit the roof again.

"Ah ha, I spy our parking space ahead. Position A," shouted *Brain-Dead* from above, pointing to a space against the hospital wall.

"We can't park there," said Paul, "there's someone's name on it."

There was indeed a plaque on the wall with 'Mr. Whittam-Jones' on it.

"Fuck Whittam-Jones," replied *Brain-Dead*. "It's not like he's a doctor or anything. He's only a fucking mister and he's not here, so bollocks to him."

"If I get clamped, you're paying the bill," said Paul, driving into the parking space and pulling up the handbrake.

"Don't they call consultants 'mister'?" asked *Lard-Arse*. "You know, when they're really important."

"Don't talk shite!" laughed *Brain-Dead*. "Anyway, whoever Whittam-fucking-Jones is, he works for the National Health Service, doesn't he? So really he works for us, right? So he'd better not piss off his bosses, eh?"

"Sounds fair enough to me," said Paul, rolling a cigarette.

"Right then men," announced *Brain-Dead*. "Off we go to meet our destiny; or rather to meet our wank-nurse. I hope she's not a pig."

With that *Brain-Dead* flung the car door open, smashing it into a *Mercedes* parked next door.

"Jesus, *Brain-Dead*," yelled Paul, almost dropping his half-built cigarette. "Watch the fucking car."

"It's alright," replied *Brain-Dead*, by now examining Paul's car door. "No damage done."

"Shame we can't say the same about the *Mercedes*," laughed Dave, spotting a very visible dent in its door.

"Oh well, shit happens!" smiled *Brain-Dead*, pulling back the handle on his seat to let Dave out.

After a brief struggle trying to drag *Lard-Arse* from the back of the car, which Paul watched from the sidelines puffing on his cigarette, all four made towards the entrance opposite.

"Aren't you going to lock your car?" asked Dave.

"Nah!" replied Paul. "It's worth more nicked."

Once inside the hospital they looked around for where to go. They tramped up a long, dimly lit corridor until they reached a crossroads with a board displaying a list of departments.

"Uumm, *Wank-Bank*?" mumbled *Brain-Dead* as he ran his finger down the list of departments. "No sign of it here, let's ask this fellow."

An orderly was approaching them pushing a trolley, which Dave was relieved wasn't a 'tin'.

"Ah, my good man, could you please direct me and my colleagues to the *Wank-Bank*?" asked *Brain-Dead*.

"The what?" asked the orderly, before catching sight of Paul's cigarette. "Put that fucking fag out. You're in a hospital, you idiot!"

"Jesus," moaned Paul. "Chill out man!"

"No I won't chill out. Put the bloody thing out," the orderly replied.

A reluctant Paul took two huge drags on his cigarette before dropping it on the floor and crushing it with his foot.

"Now what did you want?" puffed the orderly. "I presume you mean the Fertility Clinic. Third floor."

"Excellent!" said *Brain-Dead*. "Carry on now, my good man."

The orderly rolled his eyes before pushing his trolley off up the corridor. The four of them then followed him in a search for an elevator or some stairs. As it happens the orderly did come to an elevator, with a large 'Staff Lift' sign by it, and pressed the call button. When the elevator arrived, all four walked into the elevator before the orderly could maneuver his trolley in.

"Which floor?" asked *Brain-Dead*.

"You can't use this lift. This is for staff only," growled the orderly.

"We are staff, we're wankers," *Brain-Dead* chirped in reply. "I'd guessed that," sighed the orderly, pressing the fifth floor button.

At the third floor, they left the orderly in peace and followed an arrow pointing down the corridor to the Fertility Clinic. Once there, *Brain-Dead* rapped on the door and marched in.

"Four masturbators ready for action!" he announced to a petite girl behind a desk stacked with papers.

The girl giggled.

"I'll just go and get Sister," she whispered before scampering off.

Moments later a Charge Nurse the size of a tank pounded down the corridor towards them, followed by the giggling girl. She was so wide, her shoulders seemed to touch both walls as she approached and she had an obvious mustache in the middle of her fat, ruddy face.

"Christ, she's not getting hold of my knob!" whimpered *Lard-Arse*, his face turning ashen.

"Hello boys!" boomed *The Hulk*, in a thick Scottish accent. "I'm Sister Lee, but you can call me Brenda. Here to sign up for sperm donation, are you?"

"We are indeed Brenda, my old girl. Sign us up and get to work," replied *Brain-Dead* jauntily.
Sister Lee laughed a booming laugh.

"My, we are keen, aren't we?" she laughed. "If you'd like to come this way Gentlemen, I'll run through the procedures and the forms you've got to fill in."

"Come that way?" sniggered *Brain-Dead* like a naughty schoolboy. "Don't you have a pot or something for me to shoot in?"

Sister Lee laughed again so hard the building seemed to shake.

"I like you!" she boomed. "Most lads who come in here are shy but you're not, are you sonny? I think we're going to have fun together."

Sister Lee then turned and led them off down the corridor.

"Tell me *Nursey*, do you have any other uniforms?" asked *Brain-Dead* walking behind her. "I mean, I like the old nurse's uniform, especially if you're webbed up with stockings and suspenders under there, but it could get boring five times a week. You got any dominatrix or rubber gear you could slip on occasionally, to keep the old man pert and ready for action?"

Dave winced, not believing his ears, but Sister Lee just howled with laughter.

"What do you think I am, young man; a milk maid?" she laughed. "Sorry to disappoint you but I'm afraid it's you who' s got to do all the work. That's why you get paid."

Although *Brain-Dead* appeared disappointed at this news, *Lard-Arse* was visibly relieved as they entered a small meeting room. Once inside, they sat down to listen as Sister Lee explained the procedure. They had to have blood test today and then every two months.
They had to have a sperm test to check their sperm count and make sure they were all 'swimmers'. If they failed either of these two tests then the gig was up! They had to sign forms signing away their rights to the sperm, but also guaranteeing that they wouldn't get a knock on the door in the future to find some kid shouting 'Daddy!' They couldn't donate more than twice a week. They weren't to donate on any day they'd had sex or masturbated, or even the day after. After today, they could masturbate at home into supplied jars, but the donation had to be at the clinic within half an hour. And their sperm would be stored and wouldn't be used for six months, just in case they were carrying some awful disease that hadn't shown up yet.

Sister Lee then opened a cupboard and pulled out her 'blood sample collection kit', before calling them one by one to raise their sleeves.

"OK, that's that done," said Sister Lee when she'd taken blood samples from each of them. "Now, if you want to take one of these little pots each and pop into the small room opposite, you can give us a sperm sample. You'll find some literature in there to help you along. Unless you all want to do it together, you can fill in your forms while you wait your turn. Any questions?"

"Yeah, when do we get the cash?" asked *Brain-Dead*. "It's just that we're off to *The Dam* at the weekend and could do with a spot of dough."
"Unfortunately, you won't get paid until you're accepted and that won't happen until we get the results of your tests back," replied Sister Lee.

"No chance of a sub then?" *Brain-Dead* persisted.

"'Fraid not," laughed Sister Lee.

"So this first shot's on us then?" asked *Brain-Dead*.

"I hope not. I hope it's in the pot," she chortled, leaving the room. "Give me a shout when you've all finished."

When she left, the boys all stared at each other in silence; each holding a form and small, clear plastic jar.

"So who' s first?" asked *Brain-Dead*.

"I'll go first," replied Paul, putting his form down and heading for the door.

It soon became obvious why Paul had volunteered to go first when, moments later, the smell of cigarette smoke began wafting from under the door.

"Oi you! You can have a fag after your wank," shouted *Brain-Dead*.

The door opened revealing a grinning Paul with a cigarette in his mouth and holding a jar half-filled with white liquid.

"I've wanked already," he announced proudly.

"Fucking hell, that was quick," laughed Dave.

"No problem to a public schoolboy," replied Paul. "In the dorms, last one to come on the piece of bread had to eat it!"

"My turn," announced *Brain-Dead* taking Paul's place in the room before flinging the door open again moments later. "This porn' s shit! It's just tits and bums stuff. I want
farmyard animals, golden showers or, at the very least, a few up-the-ass shots. D'ya reckon they'll sell some real porn in the hospital shop?"

"Oh yeah, very likely," laughed *Lard-Arse*. "You mean the shop that's run by the Women's Institute. Just get back in there and start wanking. This is embarrassing enough without you prolonging it."

Five minutes later, *Brain-Dead* emerged with his filled jar and a self-satisfied look on his face.

"Check this out, *Hippy*," he said to Paul, holding his jar up to the light.

"Loads more sponk than you. Bigger balls you see."

It was Dave's turn next. He entered the room and locked the door behind him. The room was like a doctor's consulting room, with posters about sexual diseases on the off-white walls; a real turn on! A bed was against one wall, which looked particularly uncomfortable with its plastic-covered mattress and paper sheet much higher off the ground than a normal bed. Next to the bed was an armchair, not a big comfy one but typical hospital-issue, with three well-thumbed 'adult' magazines on a small table by the side. Dave decided to go for the chair option and dropped his pants and shorts and tried to make himself comfortable to get to work.

"Christ, this is surreal," he thought.

Then, bizarrely, he shuddered as he thought what his mom would say if she could see him now, in an English hospital, penis in hand, trying to masturbate with *Brain-Dead* knocking on the door asking him if he'd finished.

"Fuck off!" he shouted at *Brain-Dead*.

He tried to concentrate on the women in the magazine but they were too plastic-looking. They'd been photographed through some sort of filter and Dave found this off-putting. So he skipped the models and went for 'Readers' Wives' at the back. These certainly weren't shot through filters. These photos looked like they'd all been shot on *Polaroid*, but that wasn't the problem. The problem was that the wives were fat or ugly or both. A few had donned some fetish gear for their husband's kinky photo shoot, but this didn't help; they were still fat and ugly.

"Why do they do it?" thought Dave. "Do their husbands bully them into it or do they just like the idea of a load of guys jerking themselves off over their photos? What happens if someone they know spots the photos of them in their kinky gear with their big asses sticking up in the air? What would they say? They'd probably say 'It's you who's jerking yourself off over it, so fuck off!'"

This was getting Dave nowhere. *Brain-Dead* would be knocking on the door soon and he was nowhere near finished. He closed his eyes and tried to imagine doing it with Samantha. He pictured himself pulling down that sexy skirt she had on last night and tugging at her sexy panties, but that was no good either, he just saw Greg's ugly face grinning at him. So he reverted to

'Readers' Wives' and imagined doing it with some fat, old, ugly friend of his mother's. He realized this was kinky, but it did the trick and he was soon aiming his ejaculation at the small jar.

"I'm surprised you had any left in you, *Stud*," smiled *Brain-Dead* a few minutes later, staring at Dave's jar. "Come on *Tubby*, it's your turn. Don't be long."

As they watched *Lard-Arse* disappear into the room, *Brain-Dead* turned to Paul who by now was sitting on a desk, blowing cigarette smoke out of the window.

"If you fancy a break from the shit they serve up in the Refectory, we can crash the Staff Canteen here. The grub's excellent and it costs fuck all. I've been here before with a couple of medics."

"Are we allowed in there?" asked Dave, examining his sperm jar by holding it up to the light.

"Sure we are, we're staff now," replied *Brain-Dead*, who then spent the next ten minutes waiting for *Lard-Arse* rifling through the drawers in the room for interesting surgical instruments. When he became bored with this, he hammered on the door opposite.

"Hurry up *Tubby*!" he yelled through the door. "What are you doing in there, playing with yourself?"

"Ah, fucking hell *Brain-Dead*. I was nearly there and you've gone and ruined it. Now I've got to start all over again!" moaned *Lard-Arse* from the other side of the door.

"Here's an incentive for you, my fat friend. If you get a move on, there' s a slap-up feed waiting for you in the Staff Canteen," laughed *Brain-Dead*.

"Be with you in a minute!" came the reply.

Sure enough, five minutes later *Lard-Arse* appeared clutching his jar.

"What the fuck is that?" laughed *Brain-Dead*, staring at the contents.

"What?" asked *Lard-Arse*, puzzled.

"That pathetic attempt. There's nothing there. You can't put that in, they'd have to save up three weeks' worth of your donations to get a single shot," laughed *Brain-Dead*.

Lard-Arse stared at his jar and even Paul jumped down from the windowsill to join in the examination.

"Is that all you could manage, man?" asked Paul.

"What' s wrong with it?" moaned *Lard-Arse*, looking worried.

"There's just not enough, my bloated buddy!" laughed *Brain-Dead*. "Your body obviously devotes too much energy to fat production and not enough to wank-making. There's no other choice, you'll have to spit in it."

"What?" blubbed *Lard-Arse*.

"Spit in the pot. That'll make it look more," urged *Brain-Dead* helpfully. "Otherwise *Nursey* will boot you off the team."

Lard-Arse hesitated as he considered this suggestion.

"Don't listen to him," said Dave calmly. "I'm sure it's the quality not the quantity that counts. There's no point diluting it with spit. They'll test it, see what you've done and think you're mad!"

"Yeah, you're right," smiled *Lard-Arse* after a pause.
"Oh well," said *Brain-Dead*. "Ignore me at your peril. You know this quality-over-quantity bullshit is only put around by blokes with small knobs, don't you? On your head be it. Come on then chaps, let's go find *Nursey*."

Back at the front office they found the petite desk clerk busily typing.

"Kindly inform Nurse Brenda that we have returned armed with three and a half pots of the finest sponk," announced *Brain-Dead*.

The desk clerk blushed and giggled before rising from her chair and disappearing into an office. Laughter boomed from the office before Sister Lee appeared before them.

"Success?" she asked. "Mixed," replied *Brain-Dead*. "My tubby friend here only managed a half portion."

"It's not the quantity but the quality that counts," replied Sister Lee.

"Fucking told ya'," grinned *Lard-Arse*, jabbing his finger into *Brain-Dead's* ribs.

"What you fail to understand *Chubster*," smiled *Brain-Dead*, "is that when they examine the contents of my pot, they'll find grade-A sponk and copious amounts of it! When they get yours under a microscope, all they'll find is two or three whale-like, fat bastard sperms that are too fucking flabby to swim anywhere. And not even the thought of the biggest egg supper they've ever imagined will make those fat bastards get off their fucking arses and swim."

Sister Lee nearly wet her panties laughing a laugh so loud that Paul and Dave covered their ears.

"Oh, you boys are soooo funny!" she shrieked.

"Thank you, you're not bad yourself, even with that stupid doily on your head," replied *Brain-Dead*, pointing at her uniform. "Now if you don't mind, could you please point us in the direction of the Staff Canteen. We intend to replenish our energy levels after all this knob exercise."

"I was about to tell you that the Staff Canteen is for staff only, but I suppose I'd be wasting my breath. So, go up two floors, turn left and you can't miss it. If you write your names on your pots, we'll contact you when the sperm tests have been completed. It could be as early as tomorrow."

And so, after writing their names on the plastic jars of sperm and handing them over to the blushing desk clerk, the four of them bade Sister Lee a cheery goodbye and headed off for the cafeteria. Dave hesitated as he approached the double doors with huge 'Staff Only' lettering on them. *Brain-Dead*, however, marched in, throwing the doors open as if entering a saloon in a Western.

"Great! That'll help us keep a low profile," thought Dave, as every head in the cafeteria turned to see the cause of the banging doors.

Brain-Dead, as expected, was totally oblivious to the diners' reaction and marched straight on to join the line of people waiting to be served. Dave followed him at a distance with his head down, but secretly scanning the diners to see who might question their right to be there.

"We don't look much like doctors," he whispered to Paul.

"Chill out, man. They'll think we're medical students. They're a bunch of scruffy herberts as well!" replied Paul as they picked up their trays and stood in line behind *Brain-Dead*.

Lard-Arse, meanwhile, was staring open-mouthed at the food on display.

"Looks fucking great grub!" he whispered to Paul. "What ya' gonna have?"

"I dunno, I'm not that hungry yet. Think I can smoke in here?" Paul replied.

"In your fucking dreams," hissed Dave.

The line edged forward until *Brain-Dead* was finally asked 'what he fancied' by a lady in a white uniform and a hairnet.

"Ummm," pondered *Brain-Dead*, "what shall I have? I've been chopping up stiffs all day and it's given me a real appetite. What can you recommend, my good woman?"

"Er...the special today is T-bone steak, if you fancy that, Doctor. Or the coq au vin is very nice," she replied.

Dave glanced up at the 'Specials' board to check out the price of the T-bone steak which, to his great relief, was extremely cheap. *Brain-Dead*, meanwhile, was still pondering.

"Hurry up *Brain-Dead*, I'm fucking starving!" moaned *Lard-Arse* from behind.

"Ummmm, yes you've tempted me. I'll go for the T-bone," said *Brain-Dead* eventually.

"It'll take a few minutes *Luv* but, if you take a seat, I'll bring it over to you. How do you want it cooked?"

"Just wipe its arse and drag it through the kitchen," replied *Brain-Dead*.

The server looked shocked.

"I'll have the same," called *Lard-Arse*, even though it wasn't his turn to be served.

"What would you like with that?" asked the lady, ignoring *Lard-Arse*.

"Chips...er...and roast potatoes...er...and peas. Lots of peas," *Lard-Arse* shouted.

"Look you fat fuck," snapped *Brain-Dead*. "The dinner lady's not asking you, she asking me. So wait your fucking turn. I'll have chips and peas, please."

"And for you, *Luv*?" the server asked Dave.

"I think you'd better ask him first," said Dave, pointing at *Lard-Arse*. "He's desperate!"

The server duly wrote down *Lard-Arse's* order.

"Can I have a chip butty and a sausage while I'm waiting, please?" asked *Lard-Arse*. "With lots of butter on the bread."

When all the orders were made and they'd chosen drinks, they went in search of an empty table, with *Lard-Arse* nibbling fries as they walked. Paul followed behind with a sad-looking, cellophane-covered tuna sandwich. He had a cigarette hanging from his mouth as a comforter, even though he knew he couldn't light it. *Brain-Dead* found a table for them, right next to four young nurses.

"Helloooo nurses!" he beamed.

"Hullo," one replied.

"I haven't seen you on my rounds. Which wards are you on?" *Brain-Dead* asked.

They all ignored him.

Dave sat down at the table and rolled his eyes at Paul, to which Paul smiled and nodded in return, as *Brain-Dead's* excruciating attempted pick-up continued. Three of the nurses had decided that either they didn't like the look of *Brain-Dead*, that he was talking absolute garbage or that they wouldn't respond to a pain-in-the-ass doctor when they were on their own time. The youngest student nurse, however, seemed flattered that a doctor was being so friendly to her and listened intently as *Brain-Dead* described all the complex, life-saving operations he'd performed that day.

Lard-Arse meanwhile had finished his fries in a bun and was busily chewing on the sausage speared on a fork in front of his face.

'D'ya think they're going to be long with our steaks?" he asked Dave. "They're taking ages and I'm starving. D'ya think they've forgotten about us?"

"You are incredible!" laughed Dave. "You without food is like Paul without nicotine."

"Bloody right," moaned Paul. "When can we get out of here and have a fag?"

Thankfully for *Lard-Arse*, he had timed finishing his sausage perfectly with the arrival of the steaks.

"Excellent! 'Bout' time too," he exclaimed, still chewing.

Brain-Dead, however, failed to notice the approaching restaurant staff laden with platters, as he was trying to persuade the student nurse that a bit of personal coaching was what she needed to help her sail through her exams. The student nurse's friend, though, was not convinced and seemed to be getting rather agitated. She kept muttering to the other two nurses at the table and shooting vicious glances at *Brain-Dead*. When she heard *Brain-Dead* arranging to come to the Nurses Home that evening she'd had enough.

"Come on Sally," she announced, pushing her chair back with a teeth-torturing scrape. "Let's go."

"But..." Sally protested.

"I said let's go, now," she said firmly, pulling Sally up out of her chair by her arm. "He's not a doctor. None of them are doctors. He's been talking absolute bullshit since he arrived."

"How DARE you Madam!" screamed *Brain-Dead*. "You shall be hearing from my lawyers unless you retract that scurrilous and libelous statement immediately. You'll never work in this town again!"

"Fuck off, asshole!" the nurse screamed back, causing everyone in the cafeteria to turn round, before dragging student nurse Sally towards to door.

The cafeteria staff didn't know what to make of the scene before them, so they just stood back, holding the steak platters. *Lard-Arse* wasn't happy with this and reached up to take his platter. Dave, meanwhile, held his head in shame.

"Just wait 'till I talk to Matron about her," said *Brain-Dead*, addressing the waitresses. "The girl's insane. She shouldn't be allowed near patients. Ah food. Yes, that one's mine. Thank you, my good woman."

Dave's heart was pounding, he was red with embarrassment and he kept taking furtive glances around the cafeteria to check if they were still the center of attention. Thankfully, after a minute of so, their fellow diners turned away and got on with their meals and the waitresses left them to their steaks. *Brain-Dead* was happily tucking into his meal and *Lard-Arse* was over half way through his gargantuan feast when Dave finally picked up his knife and fork.

"This looks good!" he said.

"Ish bruudy gweat!" smiled Lard-Arse, spitting pieces of roasted potato at Dave from, what looked like, a cement mixer full of pigswill.

Dave picked up his knife and fork and sliced a piece of meat off his steak. It was nearly at his mouth, when a voice from behind him made his nearly jump out of his skin.

"What the hell are you lot doing here?" boomed the voice.

Dave didn't need to turn around to know that the voice belonged to Greg.

"I said what are you lot doing here? You're not allowed in here," Greg boomed again, this time so loud that once again they were the center of attention in the cafeteria.

Dave still didn't turn around, but he was now too on edge to bite into the steak sitting on the end of his fork. *Brain-Dead* and *Lard-Arse* continued eating, totally ignoring Greg, while Paul rolled the unlit cigarette around his lips.

"Are you deaf?" boomed Greg, getting even louder. "I'm talking to you I asked..."

"Look *Bone-Head*," interrupted *Brain-Dead*, finally looking up. "We're staff now, so why don't you and your friend just fuck off and leave us alone. We're trying to eat our dinner."

Dave could have kissed *Brain-Dead* and he just had to see Greg's reaction to this retort, so he turned to see a rather taken aback Greg with his mouth open. Greg was dressed in a white coat, as was a very handsome black guy standing with him. Dave lapped up every second of Greg's discomfort. Greg obviously did not know how to react to *Brain-Dead*. Dave was sure that if it had been he who'd insulted Greg, Greg would have had no hesitation in taking him on. But *Brain-Dead* was obviously a different prospect. For a start, *Brain-Dead* was very tall, even taller than Greg, and although he was quite awkward, in that his long arms and legs sometimes seemed uncoordinated, he wasn't skinny and, no doubt, could pack quite a punch.

The other thing that crossed Dave's mind, and was possibly what Greg was currently considering, was *Brain-Dead's* 'madness'. Although not in the 'loony' category, *Brain-Dead* was certainly in the 'strange, borderline loony' camp and these people could be very dangerous. Dave remembered a boy from high school who shared some of *Brain-Dead's* characteristics, except that where *Brain-Dead* had humor, this boy had had aggression. Dave remembered a time when this boy, who was always getting himself into trouble, did exactly that with a gang of six visiting *Hells Angels* in downtown Omaha. 'Round One' of the fight they had ended with this boy getting beaten up so badly that his left arm was broken and his face was left black and blue. But, instead of taking himself to hospital, the boy got a bus home, armed himself with a kitchen knife and got a bus back downtown to find the gang. He stabbed three of them before the police arrived and arrested him. He eventually ended up in the state penitentiary for it, but it was the fact that he was mad enough to go back, that was the point. He didn't know when he was beaten, when the odds stacked against him were too high, when self- preservation should have stepped in.

Also, on a family holiday on to Mexico when Dave was young, there'd been a local lunatic in the town where they were staying. He was probably in his late teens and everyone kept out of his way. Dave and his family had been sitting outside a cafe one day, when the lunatic just strolled up and drank Dave's soda. Dave was devastated, until the bar owner replaced it. The bar owner had told Dave's dad that it was better not to argue with the lunatic as when he got angry, he had the strength of ten grown men.

Dave stared at Greg who, for a good couple of highly enjoyable minutes, was weighing up how to respond to *Brain-Dead*. Finally, he plucked up his courage and said, "What do you mean you're 'staff'?"

Brain-Dead sighed then, through a mouthful of peas, replied, "As I told you the other night, we're wankers at the *Wank-Bank*."

"Why does that not surprise me?" Greg laughed to his friend.

"Look asshole," said *Brain-Dead*, sounding angry now. "We're staff eating in the staff canteen. Now, just because you're upset that the American *Stud* here shagged the arse off your bird last night, there' s no need to piss on everyone's parade. So be a good boy and fuck off, will you?"

Greg went purple with rage.

"Come on Greg, leave it," whispered Greg's friend, pulling him away by the arm.

"I tell you Charlie, he never touched Sammy," yelled Greg as he was being led away. "He never laid a hand on her."

Brain-Dead responded by pushing his cheek out with his tongue and holding his hand, with fingers curled as if around a penis, in front of his mouth doing an impression of a blowjob. *Lard-Arse* then decided to join in the fun, amazingly ignoring his food for a minute, by leaning over the table with his ass in the air, while *Brain-Dead* pretended to screw him from behind.

"Oooooh *Stud*, give it to me hard big boy!" cooed *Lard-Arse* in a high-pitched voice.

"Take that Samantha, you dirty bitch, you know you want some Yankee cock," *Brain-Dead* grunted.

"Oh *Stud*, please don't stick your huge cowboy cock all the way in. I can't take any more. Greg's dick is only half this big!" laughed *Lard-Arse*.

Greg, however, was not laughing. His head seemed close to exploding and he was wrestling with his friend to get back into the cafeteria. His efforts though were more symbolic than real as he waved his fist before being shoved through the door.

195

Brain-Dead and *Lard-Arse* were crying with laughter and even Paul seemed to have forgotten about his cigarette temporarily. Dave was smiling a nervous smile as adrenaline pumped through his veins. It was all very well for Greg to be taunted while Dave was surrounded by three friends, but what would Greg do when he caught him on his own?

Eventually, *Brain-Dead* and *Lard-Arse* stopped laughing and returned to their meals, but Dave just stared at his.

"You not eating that?" asked *Lard-Arse* glancing up from 'the trough'.

"I've lost my appetite," replied Dave.

"Ah, come on *Stud*," smiled *Brain-Dead*. "Don't worry about that Greg wanker, he's all wind and piss. Now eat up; you'll need your strength later when you're fucking his bird."

"Look, let's get one thing straight. I've not slept with Samantha," Dave protested.

"Yeah, right!" grinned *Brain-Dead*. "So why's sonny boy so upset?"

"Can I have your steak if you're not hungry?" interrupted *Lard-Arse*.

"Sure, help yourself," replied Dave, pushing the plate towards a delighted *Lard-Arse*.

"Come on, man. Let's go outside and get some fresh air," whispered Paul. "We'll see you boys by the car."

"Don't you want your sandwich?" asked *Lard-Arse*, still scraping the contents of Dave's plate onto his own.

"Jesus, you fat sod!" laughed *Brain-Dead*. "Don't you ever stop eating? What happens when you're asleep, d'ya have to have a drip or something?"

"Ah, leave me alone. It's just that it would be a shame to waste it, wouldn't it?"

Dave and Paul left *Brain-Dead* and *Lard-Arse* arguing and made their way towards the door. The occupants of every table stared at them as they passed, with a mixture of curiosity and hostility on their faces. Dave found this experience embarrassing but Paul didn't seem to notice; he was presumably preoccupied with the thought of a cigarette outside. The second they reached the exit, Paul lit his cigarette and took a huge lung full of smoke, then immediately began rolling another one. He'd chain-smoked six cigarettes before *Brain-Dead* and *Lard-Arse* appeared through the doors.

"Right boys, time to get back to Hall. We're in perfect time to get ourselves ready for *The Polish,*" announced *Brain-Dead*.

"The what?" asked Dave.

"The Polish Social Center," answered *Lard-Arse*.

"Oh yes! Monday night is *Pull a Pig* night down at The Polish," smiled *Brain-Dead*. "It's serious work, with a lot of money riding on it. It's basically a disco, but a lot of Sheffield's ugliest women congregate there on a Monday night; so we all put a quid in the pot and whoever pulls the ugliest pig wins it. It's excellent sport and is a fine Yorkshire University tradition."

"Sounds a bit cruel," puffed Paul.

"No, no, not at all my liberal, *Guardian*-reading, brown rice-munching, hippy chum. Think of it as a social service," smiled *Brain-Dead*. "Once a week, all us handsome, eligible chaps put on our best bibs and tuckers, slick our hair back and go and chat up some lonely pigs. Just think of it from their point of view. Say you're a female version of *Lard-Arse,* you squeeze your fat butt into a pair of hot pants every Friday and Saturday night, spend hours slapping on your make up before paying a fortune to get into some club, where you stand for five hours holding your gut in, hoping someone will chat you up. Now the best that you can hope for is that some pissed-up cunt asks you for a last dance fumble in your knickers before he throws up all over you and you spend a fortune on a taxi home covered in puke. On a Monday night, however, you spend a fraction of the cost to get into *The Polish* and suddenly loads of handsome blokes are all over you like flies on a turd. All we ask for this act of charity is a bit of harmless sport and the chance of a small wager. Think of it like charity bingo; it's all for a good cause."

"I like *The Polish* night," smiled *Lard-Arse*. "I sometimes win."

"Ah yes, this is a strange phenomenon," laughed *Brain-Dead*. "Some of the poor, fat souls can't believe their luck when they get chatted up by someone attractive and become strangely suspicious. So instead of grasping their good fortune with both hands, they spurn the opportunity of a lifetime and look for one of their own kind instead. Here's where *Tubby* here comes into his own. In him they can see a *blubber buddy*, someone with whom they have an affinity and they start imagining romantic winter evenings sweating together by the fire, stuffing their faces and swapping 'feasts I have had' stories."

"Fuck off!" snapped *Lard-Arse*. "You're just jealous 'cause they fancy me and not you. You frighten them 'cause you're mad!"

"What's that?" interrupted Paul, pointing towards his car.

"What?" asked Dave.

"That, on my windscreen. I've got a bloody ticket. I told you I shouldn't have parked there."

"That's not a ticket, it's a note," announced *Brain-Dead* as they approached, before picking the piece of paper from under a windshield wiper. "Ah ha, it's a letter from our friend Whittam-Jones. He says:

Who the hell are you?
Can't you read? This is my parking space.
What department do you work in?
I demand you contact my secretary.
I've got your number

Whittham-Jones.

Fuck him!"

"Still, we'd better get outa here," said Dave,

"Wait one moment!" announced *Brain-Dead*. "Anyone got a pen and a piece of paper?"

Paul replied that he had both in the glove compartment, which he duly retrieved. Then, after scribbling circles on the paper for ages to try to get the ink running, *Brain-Dead* wrote out a note:

Sorry about the dent in your car. All my fault.
Spare no expense putting it right and send me the bill.

198

Brain-Dead then slipped the note under the wiper of the dented *Mercedes*.

"That'll fix the bastard! Now, into *Spermy* and let us away!" yelled *Brain-Dead* with a flourish. "Oh Christ, we've got to get *Fat Boy* in the car again. This could take forever now he's had four dinners. Eh *Fatty*, how about you jogging home?"

"Fuck off," replied *Lard-Arse*, who was busily trying to squeeze into the back seat again, this time head first.

This technique had its disadvantages however; the most obvious of which was presenting *Brain-Dead* with an irresistible target in the shape of *Lard-Arse's* gargantuan backside. Within a blink of an eye, *Brain-Dead* had his foot on *Lard-Arse's* behind to push him into position. Despite *Lard-Arse's* screams and Paul's protests that the seat would be broken, *Brain-Dead* was on a mission and didn't let up until *Lard-Arse's* nose was pressing into the fake leather of the backseat. Soon, Dave and *Lard-Arse* were cuddling again on the back seat, the barrier had been bypassed and *Spermy* was heading back towards Sheaf Hall.

SEVEN

That evening, against his better judgment, Dave was following *Brain-Dead* and *Lard-Arse* up some steps into the Polish Social Center with Paul close behind him. An ancient doorman, who looked like he'd been sitting in the same position since World War II, was sitting just inside the door with a small cashbox on a table. They followed *Brain-Dead's* lead by paying him the required pittance, received a green ticket in return and then marched on up a corridor towards the bar. On the walls of the corridor were black and white photographs of Polish servicemen in uniform standing by ancient airplanes and tanks. These were interspersed with posters in Polish, many of which were drawn in a Soviet style, advertising who knows what.

In the enormous bar, the tables were occupied by people of the same generation as the doorman, muttering in Polish (presumably) and drinking dark, forbidding beers from bottles whose brands Dave had never seen before. The place smelled musty with a hint of stewed vegetables, but the people seemed quite friendly and a few smiled at Dave as he walked by. It was hard to believe that this was the venue for a 'happening' night out, never mind a *Pull a Pig* contest. At the far end of the bar, their march led them to a flight of narrow, worn, wooden stairs.

"Surely the disco can't be up here?" thought Dave. "What would happen if there was a fire?"

The place was a disaster waiting to happen and Dave imagined TV News reporters asking why people had been so stupid as to squeeze themselves into such a deathtrap. At the top of the stairs, however, they emerged into an unfeasibly large room, with a cloakroom and a bar at one end and a mobile disco and dance floor at the other. It was obviously the same surface area as all the rooms downstairs put together, but it felt like it was the same surface area as the entire block! Thankfully, there were also double fire doors half way down one wall. Near the bar were a number of tables and metal frame chairs with stretched fabric, the sort that seem so popular in church halls. The bar area was already well populated and there were a few circles of girls on the dance floor, dancing around their handbags. The mobile disco was quite a sight. A three-foot square, homemade lightbox at the front proudly proclaimed that this was called *Solid Rock* - not very encouraging! Multicolored bulbs behind a sheet of white, opaque plastic flashed in a circle around the logo, behind all of which stood an enormous man with a blonde 'Afro'. He'd obviously perfected the deep-voiced, local radio, mid-Atlantic chat, which he was using to flirt with the girls on the dance floor, who giggled as he complemented them on their dancing. He did overcook it, however, when he 'crashed' the lyrics of the song he was introducing but, in his own mind at least, he made up for this lapse by turning on a feeble smoke machine which puffed two cheeks-full onto the dance floor.

Brain-Dead went to the bar and ordered pints of beer for them all, plus a packet of dry roasted peanuts for *Lard-Arse*. He then directed them over to a table positioned on its own at the side of the dance floor. Sitting behind the table, all facing the dance floor, were three students looking very officious with notebooks and pens next to their half -drunk beers.

"Evening *Brain-Dead*, back for another year?" one asked as the others smiled.

"Evening Barney. Wild horses wouldn't keep me away. Are we on for a good turnout?" asked *Brain-Dead*.

"Dunno," replied Barney. "The first few competitions of term can be a bit quiet until the freshers hear about it, but we seem to be doing alright. We've got sixteen so far and it's still early. Hello *Lard-Arse*, not exploded yet?"

"Very bloody funny," muttered *Lard-Arse*, as he nibbled on a peanut.

"What' s the field looking like?" asked *Brain-Dead*.

"Not bad," replied one of the other 'judges'. "We've got a couple of 'slappers' in already, but give it time, the pubs haven't chucked out yet. Allow a few minutes for them to get a bag of chips and they'll be here. Are all four of you in?"

They all nodded.

"That'll be a Pound each then please. What are your names?" Barney asked Dave and Paul. They said their names and handed over their money. "Have the rules been explained?"

"Er...a bit," replied Paul.

"Well," continued the final judge, "you have until one forty-five to pull the worst pig. Just having a dance doesn't count, you have to snog it at least. If you do manage to fuck your pig you'll get serious bonus points, but this must be witnessed by at least one of the judges. So, if you think you're getting close to a 'game-on' situation, you must tip us the wink before you go outside for a 'knee- trembler'. We recommend the area by the bins at the bottom of the fire escape, as it's dark enough for your pig to feel comfortable but still affords us enough illumination to make an accurate judgment. *Disco Dave* has agreed to put the 'smoochies' on a little earlier this year to give you time to work your pigs up before the deadline. The presentation will be made when the lights go on at two and, as always, winner takes all and the judges' decision is final. That only leaves me to wish you the very best of luck Gentlemen and happy hunting."

They thanked the 'judges' and made their way to the tables by the bar. When they had sat down, Paul asked, "Why do girls come here for a Pull a Pig contest?"

"It's not advertized as a *Pull a Pig* contest, you dumbfuck!" laughed *Brain-Dead*.

"No, it's basically a good night out; the best you'll find in Sheffield on a Monday night," continued *Lard-Arse*, pouring the leftover brown scraps from his packet of dry roasted peanuts into his palm, before lobbing them into the back of his mouth. "It's all a bit 'Secret Squirrel' really; bit like having a Masonic meeting in the middle of a party. We all know what' s going on, but the civilians don't."

"Ah yeah," mused *Brain-Dead*, "you've got to be canny about it. Ya' can't just steam in and start chatting pigs up straight away; they'd get suspicious. You've got to bide your time, recce the prime candidates, let 'em dance on their own for a bit, then time your approach to perfection. The pig's gotta think you've had a frustrating evening and you're chatting them up 'cause you're getting a bit desperate. It's a bit like fishing, I suppose. You don't just chuck a fucking great big hook into the water and expect some huge, motherfucking trout to gobble it up. No, you've got to be subtle. You disguise your hook with a fly and you flick it over the water for hours on end till your trout thinks 'I'm going to have that stupid big fly if it's the last thing I do'."

Having been suitably enlightened, the four of them sat at their table drinking beer and watching the dance floor. Occasionally, someone would come along to say 'Hello' to *Brain-Dead* or *Lard-Arse*. Some would chat about the 'form' on offer that evening and some were obviously just 'civilians'. All the time, the room was filling up with, it has to be said, some very attractive girls.

A few groups of *Kevins* also appeared and stood by the bar, drinking beer out of bottles. But it was the groups of girls appearing at the top of the staircase that dominated the conversation, especially if one of their number was particularly fat or ugly.

"Oh yes, come to Daddy!" exclaimed *Brain-Dead* when an enormously fat girl puffed into room. "You're mine, you lucky broad. You just don't know it yet."

"I'm not sure I totally approve of all this," Paul said to Dave, tugging on the end of a cigarette.

"It is a bit crazy!" replied Dave. "But what the hell, eh?"

"Yeah, I suppose. What the hell."

"There's no dissension in the ranks on the other side of the table, is there?" asked *Brain-Dead.* "You boys need to be focused. You need to steel yourselves, or get pissed, before you grit your teeth and march over the top. You could always warm yourselves up with a semi-pig if you need to, but that can be a dangerous strategy. You might get too preoccupied by the semi and miss out on a total sow."

They were then distracted by *Disco Dave*, who was having a few problems. He'd obviously taken a shine to some girl on the dance floor and he'd put on an extended dance version of a chart song before creeping out from behind his kit to ask her to dance. His pitiful victim was apparently impressed and accepted his overtures. But then he stared dancing!

"Check out that knob!" laughed *Brain-Dead.*

They watched open-mouthed as *Disco Dave* performed some well-rehearsed dance floor moves. No doubt in his own mind, he imagined he looked like John Travolta in *Saturday Night Fever* but, in the real world, he had all the poise of a dancing elephant. He bit his
bottom lip seductively and kept running his fingers through his afro, as the sweat built up on his forehead and in his armpits. Then they all gasped in unison as he clenched his crotch. By now the girl's friends were wetting their panties laughing from the side of the dance floor, some imitating *Disco Dave's* moves. The girl herself was horrified. Three minutes ago she'd been honored that the DJ had picked her as his dancing partner, now she was praying that the floor would swallow her up. Her prayers were answered, however, when the speakers started to crackle. The crackle became a fizz

before they finally gave up the ghost altogether.

The *Kevins* by the bar all cheered as *Disco Dave* left his poor, tormented dance partner and ran behind his kit. She saw her chance of freedom and dashed off to be amongst her friends.

"This guy's terrible!" laughed Dave. 'Who is he?"

"*Disco Dave?* Oh, he's a total wanker," laughed *Lard-Arse*. "He was a student years ago, but he decided he'd make his fortune being a DJ. He does a show from three till six in the morning on *Sheffield FM*, when nobody' s listening, does the lunchtime show on the university station and he still lives in the same student house he did ten years ago. The trouble is he still thinks he's a cool nineteen-year-old, not a sad, old fucker. The funniest thing was last year when he won the *Pull a Pig*. He went mad 'cause he'd not been in the competition and thought she was a stunner!"

The *Kevins* gave *Disco Dave* another cheer when he reappeared in front of his kit with a soldering iron and dragging an extension cable behind him. He then proceeded to solder wires together from the 'spaghetti' bulging out of his decks. After a good five minutes soldering, to an accompaniment of slow hand clapping by the *Kevins*, *Disco Dave* flicked on a switch and the speakers boomed back into life. A newly arrived *Kevin* nearly shit his pants when the base bin speaker he was leaning against suddenly belched back into life. He dropped his nearly full bottle of *Budweiser* on the floor, which exploded over his white pants. He was not a happy *Kevin*!

"Ya' fucking Muppet!" *Kevin* screamed at *Disco Dave*. "Tha' oowes me a *Bud*."

"Sorry about that small technical hitch Ladies and Gentlemen," boomed *Disco Dave* into his microphone, with his best American accent and totally ignoring *Kevin*. "I'll be having words with my roadies later I can tell you! Still, the sensational sounds go on, as we say in show business. Here's Michael Jackson."

"His 'roadies' my arse", laughed *Brain-Dead*. "He's the only fucking roadie. I should know. When he got pissed last year, he paid me to help him pack up his gear and lob it into his knackered old *Transit* van. Jesus, it was horrible. His speakers and wires were all covered in beer and someone had puked all over his lightbox."

"Oi cunt, I'm talkin' t' thee," the *Kevin* continued. "Tha'd better get me another fucking *Bud* or I'll kick tha' fuckin' ed in."

Disco Dave, finally acknowledging the presence of the threatening *Kevin* standing in front of him, turned and said, "Don't you threaten me. I only have to say one secret code word and Security will come down on you like a ton of bricks and throw you out."

Dave turned around to spot 'Security', but the only staff he could see was a seventy-year-old man by the cloakroom dressed in a jacket and tie and puffing on a pipe. The *Kevin*, however, fell for it and trudged off to buy himself another *Bud*.

By the time the boys had consumed a couple more drinks, the hall had filled up considerably. The dance floor was now full and the bar was three rows deep. *Brain-Dead* announced that the time was now ripe to make a move as he'd spotted a likely candidate.

"This I've gotta watch," said Dave, getting up from the table to see *Brain-Dead* in action.

Paul and Dave followed *Brain-Dead* at a discreet distance as he homed in on his target pig.

"This is so cruel," groaned Paul before grinning.

Brain-Dead's candidate stood out a mile. She was an enormously fat girl who had squeezed herself into a blouse and leather pants at least two sizes too small for her. The buttons on her blouse were straining to contain her massive breasts, which could quite clearly be seen through gaps where the material had been pulled apart between the buttons. She had chosen to wear a black bra, which in itself was quite a feat of engineering, under her white blouse. The V of her crotch was nearly a foot wide and she'd somehow managed to stuff part of her stomach inside her leather pants, leaving a single button straining to hold back a huge wall of flab. If the button were to give way and fly off, it could be quite dangerous given the force behind it. The rest of the flab, of which there was still copious amounts, hung over the waistband of her pants. Her ass was gargantuan; the size of a small state. The saddest thing though was that behind the rolls of fat on her neck, she actually had a very pretty face.

Brain-Dead smoozed over to her as she stood on her own at the side of the dance floor.

"Hello gorgeous, what's your name?" asked *Brain-Dead* seductively.

"Tha' wot?" asked the *Blimp*.

"I was just wondering what your name was sweetness. You see I've been admiring you from afar and have been building up the courage to ask you to dance."

"Is tha' takkin the piss?"

"Oh, no no!" pleaded *Brain-Dead*. "Do you come here often? It's just that I know if I'd seen you before I'd have remembered such a pretty face. Would you do me the honor of dancing with me?"

"It's not that fuckin' *Pull a Pig* competition is it?" growled the *Blimp*. "Cause if it is, I've won it twice before!"

Dave and Paul couldn't help but fall about laughing. *Brain-Dead*, for once, didn't know what to say. He just spluttered.

"Look," continued the *Blimp*. "I'll do ya' a deal. You can snog me at t'end if tha' splits ya' winnings with me."

"Er...er...I'll come back to you on that, *Luv*," coughed *Brain-Dead*.

Dave had tears rolling down his cheeks by this point and turned to Paul. Paul, however, had stopped laughing and was staring towards the cloakroom.

"Jesus man, it's Jo," said Paul.

Dave looked across and saw Jo. His heart missed a beat as he strained to see if Samantha was with her.

"Can you see Sam with her?" he asked Paul.

"No man. Looks like it's all clear on the Sam front. I'm going to say 'Hello', you coming?"

"Er...no, I'll give that a swerve if you don't mind. I don't particularly feel like hearing about Greg screwing Sam," replied Dave.

"Fair enough man. You don't mind if I go and have a quick chat do you? I quite fancy her."

"No, chat away. I'll see if I can find myself a hog."

Dave watched Paul amble across the room towards Jo, rolling himself a cigarette as he went. Jo was with a group of girls Dave had not seen before.

"They must be from her course," thought Dave.

Paul strolled up and tapped Jo on the shoulder. Even from a distance it was clear that Jo was pleased to see Paul. She pecked him on the cheek, took his arm and headed off to the bar; ignoring the girls she'd arrived with.

Dave now turned to find *Brain-Dead* and *Lard-Arse*. He spotted *Lard-Arse* sitting at a table with a plump girl, sharing a bag of chips. *Brain-Dead*, meanwhile, was prowling the edge of the dance floor. Now alone, Dave decided it was time to pluck up the courage to ask someone to dance. He'd never been very good at hitting on girls he'd never met before. It was different in Beavers Bluffs; he knew them all. What were you supposed to say? It was bad enough talking to someone you were attracted to, but what do you say when you've got to hit on someone you find repulsive? The *Brain-Dead* pick-up wasn't his style; he couldn't do that.

"Just ask one of 'em to dance," he muttered to himself as he scanned the room for a likely candidate. He spotted a girl who looked like a man in drag, another with a long, black mustache and one who looked like someone's elderly mother. As he was trying to choose which one to go for, someone pinched his ass. Spinning around he found Pam grinning broadly at him.

"Hello *Gorgeous!*" said Pam, planting a kiss on his cheek. "Thanks a bundle. You all piss off for the evening and leave me searching for you amongst the wallies in the Hall Bar. Bastards!"

"Sorry," Dave spluttered. "it's just...it's just that it's a guys' night out. *Brain-Dead* brought us."

"Well I like boys' nights out as well, you know. How else is a girl gonna find some willy?" laughed Pam. "I see Paul's homed in on Josephine. Left you all alone, has he?"

Before Dave could reply, *Brain-Dead's* circuit of the dance floor had brought him to them. His eyes lit up when he saw Pam.

"Ah ha Pamela," he grinned as he approached. "Are ya' willin for a shillin'?"

"It'd have to be more than a bloody shilling with you!" Pam laughed back.

"Oh come on Pamela, just one little dance. What harm would that do?" begged *Brain-Dead*. "Please!"

Pam thought for a minute.

"Go on then, just the one dance. But not to this, I can't stand this track."

"Er...no, don't dance Pam," interrupted Dave. "I'll buy you a drink."

"Oh no, have a drink in a minute", screamed *Brain-Dead* dropping to his knees and clutching Pam's legs. "I'm begging you, just one little dance. I promise I won't feel your arse or anything."

"My, aren't I popular all of a sudden. It was a different bloody story when you bastards all pissed off and left me in hall. Ooh, I like this one. Come on then, you," she said to *Brain-Dead*, grabbing his hand. "Just this one dance, but you'd better keep your bloody hands to yourself or I'll rip your goolies off!"

Brain-Dead grinned at Dave over his shoulder as he put his left arm around Pam's waist and began waltzing, even though *Disco Dave* had just put another Michael Jackson track on. The dance floor was so packed by this point that Pam and *Brain-Dead* just sort of waltzed on the spot, right next to where Dave was standing and, even though *Brain-Dead* was keeping his hands to himself, he still stuck out his snake-like tongue towards Pam's face.

"Tempting eh girl?" he grinned.

"Fuck off. It's no good having a tongue the size of a willy and a willy the size of a tongue, you know," laughed Pam.

Brain-Dead spun Pam around with a flourish and shot a grin at the 'judges' sitting at the table by the dance floor. He then let go of Pam's waist and pointed at her from above her head. All three of the judges laughed before shaking their heads and giving a 'thumbs down'.

"Why are those boys laughing at us?" asked Pam, spotting the gestures.

"Oh, it's just that we're having a *Pull a Pig* competition and you're my pig!" grinned *Brain-Dead*.

Dave, being only a couple of feet away from them and hearing every word, shuddered.

"What?" asked Pam, the smile crashing from her face.

"I said that we're having a *Pull a Pig* competition and you're my pig," repeated *Brain-Dead*, still smiling.

His smile didn't last very long though, as Pam rocked back on her heels and swung her arm around in a wide arc before her palm landed with an almighty smack on the side of *Brain-Dead's* face. Dave flinched at the power of the slap and then groaned nearly as loud as *Brain-Dead* screamed, when Pam reached down and crushed *Brain-Dead's* testicles in her clenched fist. *Brain-Dead* fell in a crumpled heap on the floor as the horrified 'judges' looked on. Pam, however, simply smiled down at the writhing mass on the floor, before turning to Dave.

"You can buy me that drink now David."

Dave nodded, still staring at *Brain-Dead*.

"Unless that makes me YOUR pig."

Dave shook his head and they turned away and headed for the bar.

"Giving you the thumbs down meant that you weren't a pig, you know," said Dave helpfully as they queued at the bar.

"Oh Jesus, you're not in this *Pull a Pig* competition as well are you?" Pam groaned.

"Er...well, yes I am," replied Dave.

"That's terrible! Don't you think it's just a little childish?"

"Er...'suppose so."

"Whaddya win?"

"Money."

Dave felt more than a little embarrassed and forced himself forward through the crowd towards the bar to avoid Pam's censure. He returned a few minutes later to where he'd left Pam, clutching two bottles of beer.

"I suppose I should be grateful that you didn't invite me out with you tonight. It would have been awful if you' d brought me 'cause you thought I'd win it for you," Pam laughed.

As they drank their beers, they watched *Brain-Dead* being carried from the dance floor by two of the judges and being sat on one of their chairs. Pam then squealed with delight.

"Ooh, he's here!"

"Who is?" asked Dave.

"That hunk over there, just coming in. I met him in the coffee bar this afternoon and nearly talked him into my knickers. Coooeee, over here. Hi!" Pam waved at the object of her desire. "Isn't he a hunk o' love?"

Dave examined the dopey-looking guy who was waving back at Pam. He wasn't hard to spot, as he was about eight feet tall.

"He's a monster," laughed Dave as the *Hunk o' love* clumped over towards them. He was obviously conscious of his height as he kept his head bowed in an attempt to look normal.

"Bet he's got a monster willy though," whispered Pam out of the side of her mouth as he approached. "We meet again. You following me?"

Hunk o' love chuckled in a voice so deep that it must have had whales around the world covering their ear holes with their flippers.

"Nah, I didn't know you were going to be here," *Hunk o' love* chuckled, rattling nearby tables and chairs. "Would you like a drink?"

"Got one," replied Pam.

"Would you like to dance?"

"I would like to dance, but first I need you to tell me everything you know about *Pull a Pig* competitions," said Pam.

"What's one of those?" asked *Hunk o' love*.

"Correct answer, let's dance!" smiled Pam, handing her bottle of beer to Dave and pulling *Hunk o' love* towards the dance floor.

"I haven't taken my coat off," gurgled *Hunk o' love*.

"Well hurry up and hand it in over there. I'm waiting so be quick about it," Pam ordered.

Hunk o' love chuckled to himself as he gamboled off towards the cloakroom.

"Isn't he a love?" Pam said to Dave.

"Jesus Pam, he's a jerk. Look, he even walks like a gorilla. Do ya' reckon he's got curvature of the spineor something? Or is he hiding a hump under his jacket?" laughed Dave.

"Maybe, but just think how huge his willy is?" Pam replied.

"They gave me a ticket for my coat," grinned *Hunk o' love* when he returned moments later.

"Gee, congratulations!" laughed Dave.

"Well done, big boy!" said Pam, glugging down the contents of her bottle. "Let's boogie."

Dave stood and watched the two of them move onto the dance floor and start dancing. To be totally accurate, Pam was dancing, *Hunk o' love* was merely rocking on the spot, occasionally lifting one of his size sixteen clown-like shoes off the floor before slamming it back down again; once onto Pam's foot. Ignoring this, Pam pulled him close to her and began thrusting her groin into his, in time to the music. *Hunk o' love* was smiling but he actually looked scared.

"Poor guy," thought Dave. "He doesn't stand a chance."

Finishing his beer, Dave returned to the main business of the evening; the pigs. He scanned the bar area, where Paul and Jo seemed to be getting on like a house on fire. There were quite a few pretty girls around the place and Dave was tempted to give up on the *Pull a Pig*, but then he spotted the perfect candidate. She was quite monstrous! She must have weighed in at a good two hundred and fifty pounds, she was wearing a white summer dress through which her circus tent-sized, apple catcher knickers could clearly be seen, thanks to *Disco Dave's* ultraviolet light. She had chosen to go braless and her massive breasts were hanging down to her waist, where they had settled on her beer gut. Her face was perfectly round and her cheeks were so fat she looked like a hamster who'd just taken a month's supply of food on board. She seemed to be with a short, ugly friend, but they weren't talking. They were just staring at the dance floor looking bored and sipping occasionally on their fluorescent cocktails; goldfish bowls of pink liquid with umbrellas and slices of pineapple sticking out of them.

Dave ambled over towards them.

"Excuse me, but would you like to dance?"

They both looked shocked.

"Who me?" asked the potential winning pig.

"Yes."

"Wi' you?"

"Yes."

"Ere Babs, 'old me drink."

Babs didn't look too keen.

"You won't be long will ya'?" she asked.

"No, just wait 'ere. An' don't drink any, I know 'ow much I've 'ad."

After the drink had been handed over, Dave took her hand and walked her to the dance floor. Once there, they stood about a foot apart and began dancing.

"What's your name?" asked the candidate, leaning towards Dave and shouting over the music.

"Dave and what's yours?"

"Shelly."

"Hi Shelly, nice to meet you."

"Nice t' meet you too. 'Aven't seen you 'ere before, are you new?"

"Yes, I've just arrived at school here in England."

"School? Ya look a bit old for that, like?"

"I mean university, I'm at the university."

"Ooooh, you're a *student*. Ya' must be dead brainy then!"

"Not really. What do you do?"

"I work in a pork pie factory."

"Oh OK, that's interesting. Do you eat many?" Dave asked and then regretted it. He blushed as his eyes were instinctively drawn to her massive stomach.

"Nah, not many, I'm on a diet. Only half a dozen a shift," replied Shelly, not appreciating the irony.

They carried on dancing for another song and large sweat patches began to appear under Shelly' s armpits. When the song finished, Shelly wiped her forehead with the back of her hand.

"D' wanna sit down now?" she asked.

"Yeah, why not," answered Dave and followed her off the dance floor back to where Babs was standing.

"Yuv' drunk some, 'aven't ya'?" Shelly yelled at Babs.

"Aven't!" shrieked Babs back, obviously upset at this slur.

"You 'ave, I can tell. It were up ta' there on me pineapple when I left."

"You can fuck off, I'm goin'," screamed Babs, thrusting the glass into Shelly' s hand and marching off towards the door.

"She's only jealous 'cause I've pulled," smiled Shelly to a shocked Dave as they watched her go. "Let's sit down 'ower there."

"So tha's a student eh? O' what?" asked Shelly after they had sat down at a table awash with spilled beer and half-empty glasses.

"My major's History."

"Ooooh, 1066!"

"Excuse me?"

"1066. William the Conqueror. That's the only history I know."

"Ha ha," laughed Dave nervously, realising she was serious. "And what do you do at the pork pie factory?"

"I squirt the jelly into the pies."

Dave spluttered as he tried to suppress a laugh.

"Ya' ave t' be careful 'cause the jelly' s fucking 'ot. It comes down from the ceiling in pipes t' ya gun and it can sometimes squirt up ya' arms."

"Really?"

"Aye. With the little 'uns ya' poke an 'ole in one side, then ya' squirt jelly in t'other. But we don't just do little 'uns, oh no. We do big lattice 'uns as well. They're a piece of piss. You just fill 'em up till ya' reach the top o' sides. We make 'em for all the supermarkets tha' nos. They send round inspectors to make sure we're all wearing us 'ats and 'air nets."

"How long have you been doing that then?"

"Five year. I started there a few months after me baby were born. I were dead lucky to get the job. Me dad knew this bloke who were a blue 'at at factory an' e' got me in."

"A blue hat?"

"Aye. If I play me cards rate, they might make me an orange 'at soon!"

"No shit...what's an orange hat?"

Shelly laughed at Dave as though he was stupid.

"An orange 'at is somebody what's in charge of a line. A blue at' runs a shift and the manager 'as a white Trilby. They get loads of money, but ya' ave to be a real bastard to be one of 'em. It's a rate laugh though. Me an' the girls are always 'aving a laugh and takin' t' piss out of lads in t' factory. An' on Wednesday nite, we 'ave fish an' chips."

"You work nights?"

"Oh aye. The money's shite if tha' only works days. But I'm lucky 'cause me mam looks after me little 'un when I'm at work an' she's usually asleep anyway. So where are you from? Ya' don't 'ave a Sheffield accent. Let me guess, are ya' from Australia?"

"No, I'm American. I'm from the United States. A little place called Beavers Bluffs, Nebraska."

"You're shitting me!"

"Excuse me?"

"You're takkin' piss outta me. Theere' s no place called fucking Beavers Muff."

"Beavers Bluffs. And I'm serious. It's near Omaha."

"Omaha? That's in Hawaii, ya' cheeky fucker. D'ya think I'm that fucking daft?"

"No honestly. That's the name of my home town."

"Is it near Orlando?

"No."

"We 'ad an holiday in Orlando once. We stayed in a 'otel. It were beautiful and dead posh. It were one of t' best weeks o' me life. We went t' Disney

215

Wurld, Seawurld, 'Ollywood Studios Toor n' everything. An' they had some lovely grub, them Yanks. Pancakes for breakfast with syrup from a fucking tree!"

"Maple."

"No, it's true. And the best thing were that no matter where I were, there were always some Yank bigger than me, so I didn't worry nor nothing, I just relaxed."

As they chatted Dave began to forget about the *Pull a Pig* competition. He went to the bar and got them some drinks and, by now getting a bit tipsy, he was just enjoying chatting to Shelly. They had absolutely nothing in common; in fact they could have been from different planets, but it didn't matter, she was a lovely, funny girl with a wicked, razor-sharp sense of humor. She lived with her mom and dad and her baby on a 'council estate' or housing project in a part of Sheffield Dave had never heard of. The father of her baby had 'done a runner' the second he found out she was pregnant, but Shelly had decided to keep the baby because she thought it would be fun! She had a brother in the Navy who was based in Plymouth, Devon, but she'd never been there. They must have spent an hour or so drinking and chatting when *Disco Dave* started playing the smooch records and dimmed the lights.

"D' ya fancy another dance?" Shelly asked. "I really like this one and I've never danced wi' an American before."

"Yeah, sure," replied Dave, wobbling with the drink as he stood up.

Shelly led him onto the dance floor and immediately wrapped her arms around him. As they rocked to the music together, Dave could see *Brain-Dead* dancing with a girl with a plum-colored birthmark on her face. Spotting Dave, *Brain-Dead* gave him the 'thumbs up' behind the girl's back. Shelly then grasped one of Dave' s buttocks and pulled him even closer to her, her massive breasts pushing into his chest. Dave could feel an erection growing in his pants and wondered if Shelly had noticed it. Moments later she did.

"Ooooh hello," Shelly cooed, dropping her hand to his crotch where she began rubbing his penis. With her other hand, she grabbed the back of Dave' s head and pulled his mouth towards hers.

Dave felt dizzy as Shelly's tongue danced with his in his mouth. By now her hand was down his pants and inside his shorts grasping his penis and gently pulling his foreskin forwards and backwards. Dave was quite worked up and reached behind Shelly to fondle her ass, as his whole body was now thrusting in time with Shelly's hand. Suddenly he felt his whole body shudder as an ejaculation started from deep within his balls but, not wanting to come, he pulled away and grabbed Shelly wrist to stop her hand moving. As he pulled his mouth away from hers, he looked up and stared straight into Samantha's eyes.

Dave froze and his erection fell away, like the air going out of a balloon.

"What? What is it?" asked Shelly, looking up at him.

Dave couldn't answer. He just stared open-mouthed at Samantha, who was no more than three feet away at the side of the dance floor. Samantha just stared back at Dave, her eyes bulging. Then, after what seemed like an eternity, Samantha dropped her head into Greg's chest, who was standing next to her and now put his arm around her. Greg snarled at Dave with gritted teeth before turning Samantha away and leading her, still head down, away through the crowd.

"What is it? What's wrong?" asked Shelly.

Dave still couldn't answer but was saved by *Disco Dave* turning on the fluorescent house lights.

Everyone in the hall blinked and some covered their eyes as they adjusted to this harsh light. The lights of the disco, which had seemed so bright only seconds ago, were now washed out and pathetic-looking. The people on the dance floor suddenly looked pasty and white with sweaty hair and crumpled clothes. Shelly, still with her hand down Dave's pants and still holding onto what was left of his erection, looked upwards and puckered her mouth for another kiss. She looked awful. Her make up was running down her face, her dress was wringing with sweat, her hair looked like it hadn't been brushed for a month and, if possible, she looked even fatter than she had two hours previously.

When Dave didn't respond to her 'kiss me now lips' she opened her eyes and caught the look of horror on his face. Looking hurt and embarrassed she let go of Dave's penis and pulled her hand out of his pants. Dave winced as the now foreskin-less end of his penis chafed against the material of his shorts.

Shelly opened her mouth to speak when both of them were suddenly aware of being surrounded. The three 'judges', complete with clipboards, had left their table and had made their way across the emptying dance floor to where Dave and Shelly were standing. One of the judges coughed a pretend cough to get their attention.

"Congratulations David," he smiled. "It is my pleasure to inform you that you are the glorious winner of this year's inaugural *Pull a Pig* Contest!"

"Well done lad," nodded the second judge.

"Here's your winnings," said the third judge, holding out some rolled up bills to Dave.

Dave winced and held his breath, expecting a slap like the one Pam had given *Brain-Dead*, but no slap came. As he turned back to Shelly, tears began to roll down her face, following the same course as the rivers of sweat from her forehead.

"Oh please God, swallow me up!" Dave prayed. But God clearly wasn't listening and he was left staring into Shelly's pitiful face as judge number three again pressed him to take him winnings. Dave altered the prayer and this time begged for Shelly to hit him or swear at him, but she didn't. She just kept staring at him with a 'How could you?' look on her chubby face, which was much worse. Eventually, she turned and walked away, her shoulders jerking up and down as she sobbed. Dave wanted to run after her and say something to her like 'I might have picked you for the *Pull a Pig* Competition but I've changed my mind and I actually think you're really nice.' But he knew this would sound like horseshit and he was better saying nothing. What he did do though was to tell the judges that he didn't want the money, before joining the throng heading for the exit.

It took a good ten minutes to reach the narrow stairs and another five to file out through the bar into the cold night air. Dave shivered as he tried to remember which direction he should head in to get back to Sheaf Hall. He looked around to see if he could spot Shelly, but she had disappeared.

"Over here *Stud*! Hey *Stud*, over here."

Dave looked up to see *Brain-Dead* and *Lard-Arse* waving at him from a bus stop at the other side of the road. Although he didn't feel like talking to them, at least they knew how to get back, so he dodged the traffic to join them.

"Bloody impressive work that *Stud*. No one's won the comp on their debut before" grinned *Brain-Dead*, who had his arm around the shoulders of the girl with the birthmark.

"What competition's that then?" asked the girl, smiling up at *Brain-Dead* who towered above her.

"Oh, nothing *Luv*," spluttered *Brain-Dead*.

"No, come on, tell me," she giggled, poking a flirtatious finger into *Brain-Dead's* ribs.

"Dancing," *Lard-Arse* interjected.

"Oh?" the girl said, looking puzzled. "I didn't see any dancing competition. Did they have that before I arrived?"

"Oh yeah, It's always early in the evening," said *Brain-Dead*, looking relieved. "The *Stud* here's a great dancer. Aren't you *Stud*? Won loads of competitions back in Hicksville, didn't you *Stud*?"

Dave didn't respond.

"Why do they call you '*Stud*'?" asked the girl.

Dave still didn't respond.

"It's 'cause he's hung like a donkey and the babes can't get enough of it," laughed *Brain-Dead*.

They waited nearly twenty minutes for the bus to arrive, during which time Dave became colder and colder and seriously regretted not bringing a jacket. *Brain-Dead* and the girl passed the time giggling and flirting like a couple of newlyweds on their honeymoon. Dave was sickened. As they climbed onto the bus, *Brain-Dead* squeezed the girl's backside.

"Hey, watch it you. I'm not that kind of girl!" she giggled.

Brain-Dead turned back towards *Lard-Arse* and Dave and stuck out his monstrous tongue.

"Not many!" *Lard-Arse* whispered to Dave.

Brain-Dead and the girl headed up the narrow spiral staircase with *Brain-Dead* cupping her buttocks as they went.

"What's he doing with her?" Dave asked *Lard-Arse* as he watched them go. "*The Pull a Pig's* over, isn't it?"

"Oh yeah," nodded *Lard-Arse*, dropping some coins into the *Videmat*, "but he hasn't had a shag in ages, so he's planning on giving her one!"

Throughout the bus journey Dave and *Lard-Arse*, from their seat behind, were forced to witness *Brain-Dead* nibbling the girl's neck and fondling her thighs. She giggled incessantly and occasionally, but unconvincingly, told him to stop. This only seemed to encourage *Brain-Dead*, who kept winking at *Lard-Arse* and Dave over the girl's shoulder. The walk back was no better. The two of them walked like they were contestants in a three-legged race, their arms entwined around each other.

"I've got some crisps in my room and there's a loaf of bread in the kitchen. D'ya fancy a crisp sandwich and a cup of tea?" *Lard-Arse* asked Dave as they entered the Quad.

Dave, who by now was starving, replied that he did. So they agreed to meet up in the kitchen in Dave's block. *Lard-Arse* went off to fetch the potato chips, while Dave went to put the kettle on. As he approached his block, Dave made out Pam heading towards him through the darkness.

"Hello *Luv*," said Pam as they met.

"How did your *Pull a Pig* go?"

"A disaster, I won," replied Dave, gloomily. "How did you get on with the *Hunk o' love?*"

"Bloody disaster," said Pam, the smile falling from her face. "I got into his pants and he shot his load all over my hand. Christ, aren't there any real men in this dammed place? Was that *Brain-Dead* I just saw heading towards his room with some poor, unsuspecting girlie under his wing?"

"Yeah, he picked her up in the *Pull a Pig* but he's kept her on 'cause, and I'm quoting *Lard-Arse* here, 'he hasn't had a shag in ages'. We're going to have a crisp sandwich and a cup of tea, you like some?"

"I sure do," replied Pam. "I could eat a scabby donkey. It doesn't do a girl any good to get all worked up and then get nothing, you know. It's not surprising that we find solace in food."

As they passed *Brain-Dead's* room en route to the kitchen, they could clearly hear giggling.

"Oh poor, misguided wretch," moaned Pam. "Do you think I should go and warn her about what she's letting herself in for?"

But they carried on into the kitchen and began making three cups of tea, before *Lard-Arse* walked in with a family-sized bag of chips. As they prepared their 'Midnight Feast', they speculated on the depravities taking place down the corridor.

"I just hope she doesn't find his pajama bottoms," said *Lard-Arse*, looking concerned.

"Oh yeah, why?" asked Dave, as he squashed a pile of chips between two slices of bread.

"'Cause he wanks into them," laughed *Lard-Arse*, shoving a handful of chips into his mouth to keep him going until his sandwich was ready. "He reckons he's been wanking into them at least once a day since he was fifteen and hasn't washed them once."

"Oh my God, that's disgusting!" shrieked Pam. "That poor girl."

Dave, who had been lifting his sandwich to his mouth, had to put it down again because he was laughing too much. It was at that moment that *Brain-Dead* walked into the kitchen wearing nothing but a tiny, silk robe.

"What are you doing here?" asked *Lard-Arse*.

"I've bloody come already, haven't I," grumbled *Brain-Dead*. "Two bloody strokes and that was it. Has the kettle just boiled?"

"But you've only been in there two minutes. What happened to foreplay?" asked Pam.

"Bollocks to that. It's not like I want to see her again, is it?" replied *Brain-Dead* taking a cup from the cupboard and dropping a teabag into it.

"You total bastard!" snapped Pam. "But at least you're making the poor girl a cup of tea, though it's hardly adequate compensation for her having you flying up her like some dog on heat."

"This isn't for her," grunted *Brain-Dead*, as he poured hot water on the teabag. "This is mine. I'm knackered and I want some sleep."

"What?" shrieked Pam.

Dave, who had just taken his first bite of sandwich, spat chips over the kitchen floor. *Brain-Dead* just stepped over them to get a bottle of milk out of the fridge, which he sniffed to make sure the milk wasn't off before pouring some into his cup. He then turned, his 'frank and beans' swaying below the short, silk robe as he moved, and headed back down the corridor.

"He's not serious?" Pam asked, horrified.

"He looks serious to me," laughed Dave, wiping tears from his eyes.

"No, he can't be THAT much of a bastard, surely to God?" Pam asked, but she knew the answer.

"I gotta' watch this," said *Lard-Arse*, setting off after *Brain-Dead*.

Pam and Dave followed and saw *Brain-Dead* opening the door to his room.

"Are you still here then *Luv*?" *Brain-Dead* asked from the doorway.

"I don't believe it, I really don't believe it!" exclaimed Pam.

Moments later, the sobbing girl came running out of the room, carrying her shoes and pulling her dress down as she went. She barged past Dave, Pam and *Lard-Arse*, who were standing open-mouthed in the corridor, and flew out into the Quad. Pam watched her go before kicking *Brain-Dead's* door open and marching in.

Dave and *Lard-Arse* followed in hot pursuit to watch Pam storm up to *Brain-Dead*, who by now was sitting up in bed sipping his tea, and slap him across his face for the second time that evening.

"You bastard!" she screamed at him. "How could you be so cruel to that poor girl?"

"You're not jealous are you Pamela?" grinned *Brain-Dead*, rubbing his cheek.

Pam slapped him again, so hard that the tea flew out of his mug and splattered against the wall.

"I'm going to make it my life's work to get you castrated, you horrible man. In fact, I'm going to start a petition right now and I'll insist that I get to perform the operation with a rusty pair of garden shears or a couple of bricks. That poor girl, how' s she supposed to get home? And you just lying there, you piece of shit!" yelled Pam, before storming out of the room.

Brain-Dead watched her leave before turning to Dave and *Lard-Arse*.

"Women, eh? Any chance of another cup of tea, lads?" he asked.

Both Dave and *Lard-Arse* just laughed before leaving the room and heading back up the corridor towards the kitchen. Pam was there, shaking with anger as she tried to drink her tea.

"What a bastard," she muttered. "You boys wouldn' t do anything like that would you?"

"Oh no!" Dave and *Lard-Arse* replied in unison.

EIGHT

"Oh Jesus, just five more minutes," Dave mumbled to himself as his hand searched for the blaring alarm clock.

It had been three-thirty in the morning when he'd finally got to bed and even then he'd not been able to sleep; he'd had to jerk himself off first. But he knew he had to get up, as today he had to face Professor Rogers and Samantha at the same time! After silencing the alarm, Dave crashed back onto his pillow and groaned as he covered his eyes with his hands. After a few minutes feeling distinctly sorry for himself and shuddering as he recalled how horrible he had been to Shelly, Dave finally forced himself out of bed.

"You look like shit!" Dave said out loud to himself as he stared into the mirror. He pulled a lower eyelid down to reveal a bloodshot street map of veins and groaned again. He then pulled his towel off the radiator, pulled his bathrobe on and grabbed his washbag before heading off to the shower room.

As he pushed open the door the horrific, but now familiar, scent of *Brain-Dead's* morning 'dump' filled his nostrils.

"You're not in there again are you, *Brain-Dead?*"

"Ah, Good Morning Master Pig Puller," came the reply from behind the toilet door. "I trust you're refreshed and ready to face another fun-packed day."

"Will you please hurry up in there," replied Dave.

"You can't hurry a good shite. Be warned my impatient colonial cousin, if you strain a shite out it'll only end in the tears of everlasting painful piles. No, tis far better to let gravity and Mother Nature do the work and simply let the turd fall with a gentle splash into the waters below. So, please avail yourself of the shower or your sink 'cause I may be some time."

"I can hardly shit in the sink and I'm desperate."

"Well, may I suggest you pop upstairs and shit on the girlie's pot."

Dave hesitated but then decided that desperate times required desperate measures and hurried upstairs to the women's shower room. He edged the door open to make sure it was empty before dashing in, slamming the toilet door behind him and settling himself down with a relieved sigh. When he'd finished, he unlocked the door, stepped out and walked straight into Karen, who had just entered the room.

"Oh, hello!" smiled Karen.

"Er...hello," replied Dave, his cheeks reddening on being caught in the Ladies shower
room, due to the smell he'd created there and due the fact that the last time he'd met her she had been tied naked to a light fitting. "I was just er...I had to..."

"Oh don't worry," whispered Karen. "I was just going to take a shower. You can rub my back if you want."

With that, Karen untied the belt on her bathrobe and pulled it open to reveal her nakedness.

"No, no, I've got to go...sorry!" replied Dave, barging past her out of the door and into the corridor where he met *Brain-Dead* bent over with laughter.

"Bastard!" said Dave, hopping down the stairs to the Men's shower room.

Once he had showered and dressed, Dave got his bag together including his Louis XIV notes and stepped out into the sun-drenched Quad. He decided he would go and get Paul and Pam, as they were both in Professor Rogers's class and he needed their support for the coming ordeal. He looked over at Paul's room which still had its drapes closed.

"Lazy bastard," thought Dave as he entered Paul's block and hammered on his door.
Dave could hear stirrings behind the door.

"Come on Paul, you're going to be late!" Dave called through the door.

Eventually, the door opened to reveal an exhausted-looking Paul in his shorts, his hair knotted and plastered to his to head.

"Hi man," smiled Paul.

"Come on, we've got Professor Rogers in and hour and...oh hi Joanne."

"Good morning David," smiled Joanne, whose head had appeared from under the duvet.

"I'm sorry, I didn't know you were...I mean I didn't mean to disturb you...I just ..." spluttered Dave.

"It's OK man. Give me ten minutes and I'll be with you," replied Paul.

"Bye David," called Joanne, giving a little wave.

"Er...bye Joanne," replied Dave, pulling the door closed.

Dave then went off to get Pam. He hopped up the stairs in her block and knocked on her door.

"Who is it?" Pam asked from behind the door.

"It's me," replied Dave. "Good fucking job I know who 'me' is?" laughed Pam as she opened the door. "Bet you're looking forward to this morning's lecture."

"Oh yeah! I'd sooner have a red-hot knitting needle through both nuts," moaned Dave.

"Well just take deep breaths. After all, what can he do apart from making your life hell for the next three years?" Pam laughed.

"Thanks for that. I feel a whole lot better now."

By the time Pam had put her coat on, fumbled around in her handbag, checked her hair, locked her door, opened it up again to get the notebook she'd forgotten, re-locked the door and gone downstairs, Paul was already standing outside his block.

"Howdy Tiger!" laughed Dave.

"Er...morning man, morning Pam," smiled Paul, lighting a cigarette.

"How did it go with Joanne, *Loverboy*," laughed Pam.

"Er...OK," replied Paul, looking at Dave. "How did the *Pull a Pig* go?"

"I'll have you know that David here is the *Pull a Pig* Champion and I was one of the bloody contestants!" said Pam.

Paul struggled to for something to say. He patently didn't know whether to congratulate Dave or to ask Pam if she was the prize-winning pig.

"Er...er..." he spluttered.

"It's OK," said Pam, recognizing his awkwardness, "Dave didn't win with me as his pig."

Paul took a huge breath and the three of them walked off towards the Arts Tower. Once they'd found the lecture room they were to be in, Dave pushed Paul in front of him in as if to shield himself from Samantha' s gaze; presuming that she was indeed already in the room. He walked in with his head down, not looking up at all until he had taken his seat between Paul and Pam. When he did look up, he found he was looking straight into Samantha's eyes, who was sitting directly opposite him

"Great seating position, buddy. Thanks a lot, good work!" Dave hissed at Paul.

"Oh shit!" said Paul, looking up and spotting Samantha.

Dave spent the next five minutes (which seemed like five hours!), arranging and rearranging his notebook, his pen and his Louis IX notes in an attempt to avoid Samantha. Meanwhile, his heart was pounding as he waited for Professor Rogers's entrance like a condemned man on a scaffold awaiting the executioner. To add to the sense of doom, the lecture room was deadly quiet. No one was talking. The only sound was the sniffle of a girl with a cold sitting at the other end of the room slowly working her way through a box of tissues. It was as if the whole room was waiting for the execution as well. Dave told himself he was just being paranoid and then realized that they probably were awaiting Professor Rogers's entrance with as much anticipation as he was, as they'd all been at the Cheese and Wine Party!

"Are you scared yet?" asked Pam, loudly breaking the silence.

The whole room laughed.

"Bastards! They are waiting for me to face the music," thought Dave, grimacing at Pam.

Then the door opened.

The room took a collective intake of breath and Dave's pulse raced. A brown shoe gently pushed the door opened before a frightening-looking Professor Rogers edged into the room carrying a brown folder under one arm and glass of water in the other. His features seemed sharper than Dave remembered and his eyebrows seemed much more aggressive. In fact, his face distinctly resembled a bird of prey. As his eyes met Dave's, Dave gulped but Professor Rogers kept an icy, 'you're mine!' sort of stare.

"Oh fuck, does he look pissed or what?" whispered Paul, shielding his mouth with his hand.

Professor Rogers moved his foot clear of the door to let it close behind him, before making his way down the row of chairs that included Dave's. Dave looked down at the table and held his breath, waiting for Professor Rogers to pass behind his chair. He could sense him approaching and then stopping directly behind him.

"Come on you piece of shit, move on," Dave prayed.

But his prayers were not answered. Instead Dave suddenly jumped out of his skin as the sharp shock of ice-cold water running down the back of his neck hit his senses.

"Jesus!" he yelled, spinning in mid air to see a grinning Professor Rogers standing behind him with an empty glass of water.

"Oh, I'm most terribly sorry old chap. Purely accidental you understand," smiled the professor. "Good morning everyone."

There were a few murmured 'Mornings' from the assembled students, but the majority was far too shocked to say anything. That majority, however, did not include Pam who, after shaking with silent laughter for a few moments, finally let it all go and howled with tears running down her face. This was the cue the rest needed to join in and before Dave knew it, the entire class was laughing at him too.

"Oh I'm sorry, *Darling*", sobbed Pam, not looking particularly sorry.

Even Professor Rogers, who by now had taken his seat at the top of the table, was smiling a satisfied smile.

Dave scanned the room as his blush turned from red to purple before his gaze settled on Samantha. She was the only person who wasn't laughing. Instead she was just doodling in her notebook, before looking up at him. Dave tried to read her expression but couldn't.
She didn't look pleased at his discomfort; she just looked sad. Dave couldn't decide if he should leave the room to go and dry his sodden back, but eventually decided just to try to ignore it rather than giving Professor Rogers the pleasure of seeing him leave. Professor Rogers, after waiting for everyone to get the laughter out of their systems, finally coughed a loud cough to get their attention before opening his brown folder and starting a very boring and very dry two-hour lecture.

"Christ that was boring!" grumbled Paul, rolling a cigarette as they waited in a throng for the elevator.

"You dried off yet, dear?" asked Pam, pushing her hand up underneath Dave's jacket to feel his back.

"You have to hand it to the old bastard, that was pretty fucking cool!" grinned Paul, shuffling into the crowded elevator.

"Oh yeah, totally hilarious," moaned Dave, squeezing in after Pam and Paul.

Just as the elevator doors were closing, Samantha squeezed in to squash up against Dave. As their noses were about an inch apart, there was no way that Dave could avoid her this time.

"Hi," Dave mumbled.

"Hello," replied Samantha, with her nose sticking up in the air. "You seemed to be having a nice time last night."

"Oh...er...yeah, that was just...that was...er...," spluttered Dave.

"I was wondering if you'd do me a favor?" Samantha continued. "I would be very grateful if you wouldn't claim me as one of your conquests. I had thought that you were quite nice, but I now see that there's another side to you, which isn't so pleasant. So, if you wouldn't mind..."

Before Dave could protest his innocence, the elevator doors opened and Samantha was the first to step out. Dave, still spluttering, turned to see that, once again, he was the center of attention.

"Don't worry man. I'll get Jo to put her straight," said Paul reassuringly, once they were out of the elevator.

"Oooh, lardy bloody dar. You'll get Jo to put her right eh?" laughed Pam. "You and Jo an item are ya? My, that was quick work."

"Forget it," replied Dave, ignoring Pam and watching Samantha striding off into the distance. "I never claimed I laid her, so she can think what she likes. Bitch!"

As they tramped up the hill back to Sheaf Hall for lunch, the heavens opened and the three of them got thoroughly soaked. The weather seemed to reflect Dave's mood and the city didn't help by showing its ugly side. The university stood on the edge of the downtown area, with the dormitories or 'halls of residence' in the Broomhill area, the start of suburbia. Beyond Broomhill, towards the *Peak District National Park* with its moors and reservoirs, were the classy areas of Fulwood and Lodge Moor. Yet behind the university, Dave could see rows and rows of black terraced houses stretching off into the distance. There never seemed to be a shortage of a view in Sheffield, even in this weather, due to the hills, but the view today was very grim, dark and 'Old Country'. It reminded Dave of black and white films of Europe in the 1930's depression; so Northern European and industrial, where the swollen skies had been squished down on top of the old stone houses. It struck Dave how different it all was to Nebraska which, even in the rain (and my God could it rain!), was blessed with skies that went on forever, where you couldn't help but be in awe of the vastness of nature all around you. Dave pitied the people who woke up every morning to this view. The air may be clean now, but centuries of industrial smog had smothered these houses in black coats which, on a day like today, made the whole place seem so miserable. His mood wasn't helped by the fact that, not only were his pants and coat wet, but so was his back, thanks to Professor Rogers.

The three of them hardly spoke as they trudged up the hill, walking in single file along the sidewalk to avoid being splashed by passing traffic. Yet as they approached Sheaf Hall, Dave looked up to see *Brain-Dead* standing, dripping wet, in the middle of the Quad.

"Great news, we all passed!" he yelled as they approached. "We're not *Jaffas*."

"What?" asked Dave, with rain dripping off his nose.

"The wanking! We all passed the sperm and blood tests. So here's your pots boys, let's get to work," *Brain-Dead* grinned, handing jars to Dave and Paul.

"I thought we had to wait six months to check we don't have any diseases or anything," said Paul desperately trying to light a soggy cigarette.

"Luckily for you, the blood test obviously didn't include a drug test, my spliff-toking friend, otherwise you'd be out on your ear. However, I've been a busy boy this morning. I phoned *Nursey*, who told me we'd all passed - even *Lard-Arse*, which was a shock. She said we could get wanking as soon as we liked and, more importantly, they'd start paying us, even though they would store our shots for a few months. So, despite the inclement weather, I charged off and collected a month's supply of pots and purchased the start of our porn stash on the way back. *Lard-Arse* has already gone off to his room to make a start, taking *'Fetish Magazine* - the monthly guide to rubber and latex' with him. But I still have '*Spank* - the hot bot digest', *'Pony Girl* – for horseplay lovers' and *'Up the Ass* - for all the chocolate starfish fans amongst us', so take your pick!" grinned *Brain-Dead*, pulling three magazines from inside his coat.

"You depraved animals," shrieked Pam. "Whatever happened to love and romance?"

"My dear girl, love and romance may be employed to entice a bird into getting her kit off, but it has no place in a professional organization like ours. What we need are results. We're on a mission and hardcore porn is merely one of the tools of our trade. However, if you were to strip off and give us a floorshow, I dare say we could be persuaded to cut you in on a percentage of the action!"

"Fuck you, *Brain-Dead*! I'll see you wankers later, I'm off to get dry and get some lunch," said Pam, heading off towards her block.

"Women!" exclaimed *Brain-Dead*, watching her leave. "Pity, I bet she'd do a great show. Anyway, back to the work 'in hand'. Here, take a pot each. Which mag do you want?"

"I'll take Up the Ass if no one else wants it," replied Paul, quite matter-offactly as he blew embers out of his crooked, wet cigarette.

"Good choice, Sir!" smiled *Brain-Dead*. "And you *Studly*, spanking or horses?"

"Jeez, I don't know. Horses, I suppose, only 'cause I don't know what you're talking about."

"Yeah, yeah, I know it's your secret fetish, being a cowboy an' all. Cathy told me. She said you begged her to whinny as you took her from behind!" laughed *Brain-Dead*. "That's what you all do out on the range, isn't it? Get a bit horny round the campfire of an evening, miles away from your ranch, you just lasso a passing steer or pork your horse!"

Paul raised an eyebrow towards Dave and smiled. Dave smiled back and shook his head.

"OK then team, quick wank then reconvene in the *Slopatron* in fifteen minutes."

"The what?" laughed Paul.

"The Refectory," smiled *Brain-Dead*, walking off and leaving Dave and Paul standing in the middle of the Quad with a porn mag in one hand and a plastic jar in the other.

"What the fuck are we doing, man?" grinned Paul.

"Christ knows, but I'm getting soaked. I'll see you at lunch. Happy jerking off!" laughed Dave, before turning and heading off after *Brain-Dead* towards their block.

Once inside his room, Dave threw his bag, the magazine and the jar onto the bed, pulled the drapes, flicked on the light and started stripping off his sodden clothes. The cleaner must have been in while he was out as the smell of polish in the room was overwhelming and there were still wet patches on the floor. This particular method of cleaning apparently consisted of opening the door and throwing a bucket of polish into the room, as there were splash marks on the door, the legs of the bed and even on the sneakers he'd left under the bed. The smell was now clawing at the back of his throat so, being naked, Dave had to slip his hand under the drapes to reach up to open the window, before settling back on the bed with his plastic jar and his magazine.

"Now how the hell am I going to do this?" he thought to himself. He could hardly adopt his usual laid-back position for masturbating as, although he could aim the sperm into the jar, it would just fall out. So he plumped up a pillow and positioned it against the headboard, before propping himself up and opening *Pony Girl*. It was then that he caught sight of himself in the mirror and laughed.

"They should put a photo of this scene in the College brochure!"

Dave flicked through Pony Girl in utter disbelief. Its pages were filled with women dressed in harnesses, some with blinkers on, some pulling naked fat guys in traps having their asses whipped, some eating out of nose bags and even some with pretend hooves on their feet. Unfortunately, however, it was more humorous than erotic so, after a few minutes trying very hard to concentrate, Dave gave up and threw the magazine on the floor. In the absence of any mainstream porn, he was left with just his imagination and decided to fantasize about Samantha. This didn't work either. His mind just kept reverting to all the disasters, which totally put him off his stroke. So he settled instead on what degrading acts he could perform with Pam and before long was firing a quite respectable quantity of his finest home grown into the jar.

After wiping a slight spillage off the side of the jar with his towel and screwing on the lid, Dave washed his hands, threw on some dry clothes, slipped the jar into his pants pocket and set of for the Refectory. Once he'd queued for his *Spam* fritter and fries, he quickly spied his fellow masturbators sitting at a table at the other side of the room. Paul, *Lard-Arse* and *Brain-Dead* were already there tucking into their lunch and laughing with Pam, who was sitting with them. Right next to them, three jars of sperm were prominently positioned on top of a huge radiator.

"Greetings fellow wanker!" yelled *Brain-Dead* at the top of his voice across the packed dining room. "You took your time, didn't you? What happened, did you get too engrossed in *Pony Girl* magazine?"

Dave's face reddened as heads turned and some people started giggling.

"COME, COME, don't be shy!" hollered *Brain-Dead*, warming to his task, seeing the embarrassment he was causing. "COME over here and take your place on the Sheaf Hall Wankers' table."

"Excuse me, I'm not one of you bloody wankers", laughed Pam, punching *Brain-Dead* in the arm.

"COME on, put your sample on the radiator. Got to keep those little babies warm and snug before Hippy gets 'em to *Nursey's* gaff. Can't present her with four pots of dead sponk; not on our first outing," *Brain-Dead* laughed as Dave approached.

After he'd put down his tray, Dave pulled his jar from his pocket and added it to the collection on the radiator.

"Pleasant wank?" asked Pam, grinning.

"Yes thank you," smiled Dave in return, wondering what her reaction would be if she knew she'd been the subject of his fantasy.

"It certainly gives you an appetite," said *Lard-Arse* through a mouthful of food.

"Name one thing that doesn't give you a fucking appetite," laughed *Brain-Dead*.

"Pam, can I ask you a favor?" asked *Lard-Arse*, ignoring *Brain-Dead* but still chewing.

"You can ask?" smiled Pam.

" It's just that I'm going fishing this afternoon..."

"Fishing?" laughed Paul. "Where the fuck are you fishing?"

"Up at Redmires reservoir. The 51 bus goes nearly all the way, past Lodge Moor. Then it's only a fifteen minute walk to the reservoir. It's very relaxing up there, you know. It's so quiet and beautiful. You can come along if you want."

"No thanks, man. I'm off to band practice. It's my first gig tonight in the *Students Union*. I hope you'll all pop along, it should be good!" replied Paul.

"Your first gig? How can you be having your first gig, you've only just joined the sodding band? What about learning the songs?" laughed *Brain-Dead*.

"Oh, that's not a problem. We play experimental jazz, so you don't really have to learn anything, you just sort of do your own thing."

"Fucking hell, that sounds great. Book me a fucking ticket in the front row, NOT!" grinned *Brain-Dead*.

"I'll be there, *Darling*," Pam smiled to Paul. "Anyway *Lard-Arse*, what favor did you want? Do you want me to go fishing with you?"

"Well not quite, it's just that...well it's a fact that, for some reason, women tend to win fishing competitions, whether they know how to fish or not. They just cast off and suddenly all the fish make a beeline for their hooks. It's very frustrating for the blokes. There are some champion fishermen at these competitions and they just don't stand a chance. Well, I've been reading about it in one of my fishing magazines and this scientist reckons it's down to women' s pheromones, you know, their smell."

"Yeeesss?" grinned Pam. "So?"

"So, I was...er...wondering if you wouldn't mind ...you know..."

"Come on *Lard-Arse*, spit it out."

"If you wouldn't mind just...er...running my fishing line through your mott"

Paul looked horrified, Dave spluttered on his *Spam* fritter and *Brain-Dead* literally fell off his chair onto the floor, clutching his stomach laughing, with tears running down his face. Pam, however, was stony-faced.

"I think I must have misheard you *Lard-Arse*. For a minute there I thought you asked me to take one of your fishing lines and run it through my pussy, 'cause you believe the fish up at Redmires reservoir will be attracted to my scent. Is that correct? Is that what you are proposing?"

"Er...yes," replied *Lard-Arse* sheepishly.

Pam took a deep breath, as though she was giving the request serious consideration. *Lard-Arse*, noting this, seemed encouraged and gave her a little smile.

"FUCK OFF!" Pam screamed at the top of her voice, causing everyone in the Refectory to jump out of their skins and look round. You could have heard a pin drop, the silence was deafening.

Eventually, a red-faced *Lard-Arse* plucked up the courage to speak.

"Should I take that as a 'No' then?"

Dave winced as he steeled himself for Pam's reply and Paul covered his eyes. Pam stood up and slapped the table with both hands.

"Take it as a 'No'? Dammed fucking right you can take it as a 'No', you sick bastard," she screamed. "In fact, you can take your fucking fishing line and shove it up your arse and see what the fish think of that!"

With that, Pam grabbed her bag and marched off across the Refectory.

Lard-Arse watched her go before turning back to the boys.

"I only asked," he moaned. "Women!"

"Well, thank you chaps," smiled Paul, picking the sperm jars off the radiator. "Thank you for another highly entertaining luncheon. I'm off. I'll drop these off at the *Bank* and then go on to my band practice. Don't forget, eight o'clock tonight in the bar at the *Students Union*."

Dave watched Paul go before turning to *Brain-Dead*.

"What is it about this place and fucking *Spam* fritters?" he asked, chewing frantically.

"They're cheap, that's what it is, laughed *Brain-Dead*. "The money they have to spend on grub is slightly less than in a Bolivian prison. So it's balls and brains, lips and arseholes all the way. You'll soon learn that their descriptions of foodstuffs don't stand up to scrutiny either. If the menu says 'steak', it'll taste like no fucking steak you've ever tasted. And be very afraid when they go all cosmopolitan, like giving us pretend Chinese food or a curry. That's just a cunning plot to recycle the pigswill bins and give us back what we scraped off our plates the week before. You'll soon learn to love *Spam*, my dear boy, or 'plastic pig' as it's more affectionately known here in *Blighty*. Isn't that right, *Lard-Arse*, my swill-guzzling friend. You love your *Spam* fritters, don't you?"

"Sure do! Why does someone not want theirs?" asked *Lard-Arse* eagerly.

"That's hardly a recommendation," laughed Dave.

"Very true, dear boy. Lunching with *Lard-Arse* is like being in a prison movie. You know, when the new arrival can't stand the crap food 'cause it's got cockroaches crawling in it. There's always an old lag who gratefully gulps down any scraps that are left. If *Lard-Arse* were a *Michelin Guide* reviewer, every restaurant would have "They had food - fucking great!" listed by it. All except Nouvelle Cuisine, that is. You're not very keen on Nouvelle Cuisine, are you *Lardy*?"

Lard-Arse sat bolt upright and the veins in his neck stood out.

"Fucking Nouvelle Cuisine, it's just a big con. My uncle took me to a fucking Nouvelle Cuisine restaurant and we thought they were taking the piss. There was just a speck of food in the middle of my plate and it cost a sodding fortune. Japanese food, that's another waste of time. Have you seen their portions, bloody disgrace!"

"Ah yes, on a trip to London to watch the rugby last year, we made the mistake of going into a Sushi restaurant. You know, one of those trendy ones where the dishes come past your table on a conveyor belt and you take off what you fancy. Well people further down the conveyor belt thought the chef had died 'cause there weren't any dishes reaching them. *Lard-Arse* had taken them all and chucked them into the black hole that is his stomach. It was like one of those comedy sketches where hundreds of people climb into a mini. That was all well and good till we got the bill. They charge by the plate you see and *Lardy's* stack of plates was as high as an elephant' s eye and it ended up costing him a fortune!"

"Yeah, it cost me a month' s curry allowance. Bloody Japs, no wonder they're all so small, they eat fuck all," added *Lard-Arse*, obviously still bruised.

"Well guys, I'm off," announced Dave as he pushed the remains of his *Spam* fritter across his plate. "Enjoy your fishing, *Lard-Arse*. I'm off to the library to get this Crusades essay sorted out. Are you going to Paul's gig tonight?"

"Damn right! I wouldn't miss The *Hippy* making a total prat of himself for all the tea in China," laughed *Brain-Dead*. "In fact, I might bring some hecklers along with me, just to spice it up a little. You finished with *Pony Girl*? I might get some practice in this afternoon and then I might even join you in the library. We've got a new lecturer this term who's too bloody keen for my liking. Apparently, he expects us to do some work, the bastard! So it'll be another quick wank for me, then head down and write some shit about buildings not falling over."

Dave stood up and said 'Goodbye' and promised *Brain-Dead* that he'd push *Pony Girl* under his door. *Brain-Dead* waved and *Lard-Arse* mumbled, stabbing the remaining fritter on Dave's plate with his fork.

The rain had stopped as Dave strolled across the Quad to his room. Once inside, he picked up the copy of *Pony Girl* off the floor and turned around to go to *Brain-Dead's* room. Just outside his room, he bumped into Karen.

"Heelloooo, are you following me?" she cooed, before spotting *Pony Girl* in his hand. "Oooh, that looks interesting. Is that what you're into? I could dress like that for you, you know. Then you could ride me and whip me."

As she was speaking, Martin appeared out of his room and stood listening to his girlfriend. This made Dave somewhat nervous as he wondered how Martin would react to her talking like that to another guy, but he needn't have worried.

"She will ya 'know," grinned Martin, in a crazy, axe murderer sort of way.

"An' I can watch ya'! I've watched her fuck wi' loads of blokes."

"Er...no thanks. You see, it's not mine. It's *Brain-Dead's*. I was just...er...minding it for him," spluttered Dave.

"Yeah right!" chuckled Martin.

"Well the offer's open, if you change your mind," cooed Karen. "Don't be shy."

Dave hurried off up the corridor and pushed the magazine under *Brain-Dead's* door, before charging back to his own room and locking himself in. He decided he would wait for a while until the coast was clear before setting off for the library. So he lay on his bed and put the radio on. As it was still set to KQBW FM, his local radio station in Omaha, all he got was white noise, so he turned the dial to see what there was in Sheffield. The first station he tuned into was *Radio South Yorkshire*, whose presenters and phone-in guests spoke in such thick Sheffield accents that Dave at first thought it was a comedy sketch. The phone-in was called 'Compliment or Criticism', which gave the local populace the chance to express their opinion of the local soccer teams. From what Dave heard, there seemed to be an awful lot of criticism going on and not many compliments. Apparently, Sheffield United, Sheffield Wednesday, Barnsley, Rotherham, Chesterfield and Doncaster were all 'crap' and all the respective head coaches should be fired. All the players were overpaid, lazy good-for-nothings and the fans were no better as they never 'got behind t'lads'. Dave could stand only a few minutes of this as, even when he could make out what was being said, he didn't know who they were talking about. So he moved the dial on until he came to a track that he liked and decided to keep it on this station for a while. When the track finished, there was the most stupid jingle he'd ever heard in his life:

You get the news,
You get the news five minutes early,
On Sheffield FM

"What?" laughed Dave.

Sure enough, the news then came on at five minutes to the hour, so Dave turned the dial again. The next station he came had a voice he recognized. He spent a few moments wracking his brain trying to place it. Then those mid-Atlantic tones gave it away, it was
Disco Dave from the *Polish Club*! This was obviously *Yorkshire University Radio* as *Disco Dave* was giving a rundown of all the events taking place on campus and making dedications to people in the various dormitories. Dave had to admit that both *Disco Dave*, and some girl who read the campus news after him, sounded very professional; better than either *Sheffield FM* or *Radio South Yorkshire* in fact. Then, however, some guy called Ian Lambing came on. He was terrible. No, he was worse then terrible. He was so nervous it sounded like someone was holding gun to his head as he presented his show. He was trying to sound cool, presumably attempting to copy *Disco Dave*, but he sounded like an idiot with a speech impediment. His voice kept warbling as, no doubt, sweat was pouring down his face.

"Maybe this guy is *The Management's* secret weapon to get the students off their asses and off to class," Dave laughed to himself.

However, he was SO bad that Dave found it compulsive listening. Even when he wasn't speaking, DJ Ian still managed to screw everything up. He spoke over the songs, he played two jingles at once, he left his microphone on when a track was playing, so you could hear him rustling around and swearing to himself in the background, until a door opened and someone came in to tell him. And he said he was going to play one track, then proceeded to play a different one. But his 'pieces de resistance' were his jingles. Somehow he'd managed to con a number of famous people to endorse his show which, presumably, they'd never listened to. He'd obviously accosted visiting rock stars and showbiz personalities (sometimes in the street, as you could hear cars roaring by on some of them) and shoved a microphone under their noses.

'When I'm in Sheffield I always listen to Ian Lambing on *Yorkshire University Radio*,' said one.

'Don't touch that dial! Don't you realize you're listening to Ian Lambing on *Yorkshire University Radio*,' said another.

'I'm thinking of moving to Sheffield, just so I can listen to Ian Lambing on *Yorkshire University Radio*,' said another.

"My left nut!" said Dave out loud.

Eventually Dave became too embarrassed for Ian Lambing to listen to any more and got his bag together for the library. As he left the block, a girl from upstairs ran out in front of him in a *Girl Guide's* uniform. At first Dave thought she must have dressed up for some kinky sex game but then, pulling himself together, he began to worry that he was actually thinking like that at all.

"There must be thousands of normal people at this college," he thought to himself as he walked off towards the library. "It's just that I've only met the crazy ones."

He wondered if the *Girl Guide* from upstairs had any idea what depraved acts were taking place within a few feet of her room. Was she oblivious to it? Did she realize that Martin was tying his girlfriend to the light fitting under her bedroom floor, or that *Brain-Dead* was masturbating every night into the same pair of pajama bottoms stoned on magic mushrooms, as she cuddled up to her teddy bears and dreamed sweet innocent dreams. He decided that he was just getting a jaundiced view, caused by hanging around people like *Brain-Dead*. Most people here would be horrified if they knew what a very small minority was getting up to, with their *Pull-a-Pig* competitions and their sperm banks.

Dave was still pulling himself together as he walked across the Quad. As he approached the car park, he came across a line of six students (all guys, some of whom he recognized from meal times) all very smartly dressed in shirts and neck ties. They all started clapping politely as a car pulled into the car park.

"What are you guys doing?" Dave asked one of them as he passed.

"Oh, we're welcoming Dougie's Mum and Dad," answered the youth.

"See!" said Dave to himself, "I told you there were perfectly respectable people here - VERY respectable in fact."

Dave didn't quite understand why they were all dressed up. Maybe they were private school boys and that was the sort of thing they did. He stood and watched as the car pulled into a parking space and came to a halt. The clapping continued as out of the car stepped a middle-aged man and woman and an old lady with a walking stick.

"Dougie' s parents and grandma," Dave thought.

Dougie's mom smiled with pride as she helped his granny out of the car. This completed, they walked towards the applauding youths. Then suddenly, one of the youths shouted "Now!" and they all turned around, pulled down their pants and shorts and pointed their bare asses at the approaching family. On each of their butt cheeks they had drawn letters spelling out

HE LL OM UM &D AD

The party of three stood and rocked on the spot as they beheld the vision before them. Mom went white with shock, dad smiled, but granny, after faltering for a moment, unbent her warped back (probably for the first time in years), raised her walking stick and shot off towards the buttocks as though she were leading the cavalry into battle. As she approached, waving her stick above her head, the 'honor guard' made a tactical retreat, dragging up their pants and laughing as they went.

Walking to the university was a pleasant downhill stroll and Dave enjoyed it, especially as the sun was coming out. He hummed to himself as he went and laughed out loud at the thought of *Lard-Arse* and his fishing line. Once inside the library, he found himself a secluded cubicle, plunked his bag on the chair and trotted off to collect some of the books he was supposed to use as reference. This task completed, Dave sat down and, for the next hour, scanned the textbooks for suitable sections he could steal to insert into his essay. He was storming through this and was totally engrossed when a hand patted him on the shoulder.

"Jeez, *Brain-Dead*!" cried Dave, returning to his seat after jumping several feet into the air. "You shouldn't sneak up on people like that. I nearly shit myself."

"Sorry *Stud*, but you'll never guess who I've just seen."

"Surprise me."

"Your bird! I've just seen her in the *Students Union Bar* with that Joanne filly and she's absolutely shit- faced."

"What?"

"Samantha, she's totally lashed. She's as pissed as a fart and she...talk of the devil, here she is now." Dave looked past *Brain-Dead* to see Samantha staggering towards them and boy was she drunk! She looked like a pinball as she bounced off desks and bookcases, apologizing to both people and inanimate objects as she went. This would have been amusing had Dave not seen a steely stare focused on him as she approached.

"Obviously not a happy drunk," whispered *Brain-Dead*.

"There you are!" yelled Samantha at Dave from ten feet away.

A student in the next cubicle to Dave poked her head out and 'shushed' Samantha.

"Don't you shush me," Samantha hissed at her, before staggering up to Dave' s cubicle. "I want a word with you."

"Hello," smiled *Brain-Dead*.

"Not you *Dead-Brain*, him!" she slurred at *Brain-Dead*.

"Sorry," said *Brain-Dead*, moving aside to give her full access to Dave.

"You wanna' know what I wanna' know? Eh? Eh? I wanna' know why you're so horrible to me?" said Samantha, trying to whisper but not achieving this.

"I..."

"Don't interrupt me when I'm talking to you! I want to know why you've been so horrible to me, that's all. I thought you were really nice, but you've just been...horrible yes horrible to me and it's not fair."

Dave recoiled as Samantha leant down and blew alcoholic breath over his face.

"Jeez Sam, you're drunk!"

"Don't change the subject. I might have had a few drinks but it's my birthday so I'm allowed. You' re not telling me I can't have a drink when I want to, are you?"

"No, no, I…"

"Shut up! I'm talking to you. Will you stop interrupting me when I'm talking to you! Where was I? Oh yes...that's a nice shirt you're wearing."

"Thanks."

"There you go again. You're interrupting me again. Why do you keep interrupting me when I'm talking to you?"

Samantha was now propping herself up on Dave' s desk and swaying from side to side. *Brain-Dead* meanwhile was standing behind her laughing silently and doing drinking imitations for Dave's benefit.

"I really really fancied you, you know. I thought you were really nice, but you're just a shit. Yes, you're ...you're a big shit!"

The *Head* once again appeared from the next cubicle.

"Will you please be quiet! I'm trying to work. This is a library after all."

Samantha spun round and hissed at the girl.

"Look, I've already told you once. It's my birthday and I'm trying to sort things out, so just piss off will you?"

The *Head*, accurately judging Samantha' s mood and deciding that a tactical retreat was the order of the day, withdrew back into the cubicle, leaving Samantha to carry on.

"I thought you wanted to go out with me. We had a lovely evening and then...then you just dumped me for that slag. Or should I say 'slags'. I can't keep up with all the slags I keep seeing you with. That wasn't very nice was it? Eh? Why did you do that? Why were you so horrible to me? Do you just like slags or something?"

"I do not like slags," pleaded Dave.

"My arse!" laughed *Brain-Dead*.

"Shut up!" both Dave and Samantha said in unison.

"But I can't date you," Dave protested, "because you're dating Greg!"

"Ha! You stupid boy...I'm..."

Once again Samantha was cut off in her prime, this time by the noisy approach of a dwarf librarian.

"Hey, hey you. What's all that noise? You can't make all that noise, this is a library," yelled the *Dwarf*.

The *Head* re-emerged from the cubicle with a huge self-satisfied smirk on its face.

"Told you!" grinned the *Head*.

"Fuck off!" Samantha snarled at the *Head*, causing it to disappear once more.

"And you can't use foul language like that in a library either, young lady," the *Dwarf* added.

"This just isn't fair," wailed Samantha, with tears welling up in her eyes. "It's my birthday and...and I'm just trying to sort things out. He's been really horrible to me..." Samantha pointed at Dave, "...and he's an idiot. D'ya wanna know why he's an idiot? I'll tell you why. He thinks I'm going out with Greg when really Greg's..."

Dave, *Brain-Dead* and the *Dwarf* were all staring intently at Samantha when suddenly Samantha wasn't there anymore. Her words were still hanging in the air, but where Samantha's head had been there was now only empty space. All three blinked in unison as their brains tried to catch up with events. Finally, they all followed the movement blur downwards, to find Samantha lying in a crumpled heap on the floor.

"Jesus!" muttered *Brain-Dead*. "She went down like a sack of potatoes. It was just like she'd been hit by a sniper's bullet straight through the forehead."

"Oh my God!" screamed the *Dwarf*.

"Shush!" hissed the *Head*. "I'm trying to work here."

"Don't you shush me, you little shit. Can't you see this girl's ill?" the *Dwarf* screamed that the *Head*. "Oh God, oh God, what are we going to do?"

Dave knelt down and whispered in Samantha's ear, but she didn't respond.

"She's still breathing," *Brain-Dead* noted.

Dave put his hand under Samantha's head to cradle her in his arms.

"What do we do now?" he asked the other two.

"I'll loosen her clothing," grinned *Brain-Dead*.

"Fuck off!" Dave yelled at him.

"Rub her wrists, rub her wrists," suggested the *Dwarf*.

"Rubber wrists?" laughed *Brain-Dead*. "Where do you expect us to get rubber wrists at a time like this?"

"Cut out the jokes *Brain-Dead*, you ignorant fucker!" snarled Dave. "Do you think we should call an ambulance?"

Before either had time to answer, Samantha let out a massive fart, which echoed around the library.

"Whoa!" laughed *Brain-Dead*. "Good work girl. I'd have been proud of that one myself."

"Right, that's it. I'm leaving," exclaimed the *Head* from the next cubicle, throwing her books, notebook and pen into a backpack before storming off.

"Come on Sammy, wake up," Dave whispered into Samantha's ear as he stroked her face.

Samantha's eyes flickered and then opened.

"I don't feel very well David," she whispered, staring up at him. "I think I've drunk too much."

"I think you have too," Dave smiled. "We'd better get you home."

"She's drunk!" squealed the *Dwarf.*

"Oh, brilliant deduction Sherlock!" mocked *Brain-Dead.*

"If she's ill in my library because she's drunk, she'll be in big trouble. I'll report her, you know."

"Leave her alone, will you. It's her birthday," snapped Dave. "Come on *Brain-Dead*, help me lift her up."

Brain-Dead took hold of Samantha's arms and heaved her up as Dave pushed from below. Samantha, meanwhile, had now closed her eyes again and began to snore very loudly. Dave jumped to his feet and took hold of her right arm, while *Brain-Dead* took hold of the left. They then wrapped her arms around their necks, leaving Samantha dangling between them.

"Christ, she weighs a fucking ton!" puffed *Brain-Dead* as they staggered towards the exit.
"How can she weigh so much, there' s not a pick on her?"

"Dead weight," explained Dave.

"Well next time you're knobbing her, make sure she doesn't fall asleep on top of you afterwards. Otherwise, it'll be you that'll be fucked!"

"Come on Sammy wake up," whispered Dave.

But his efforts were in vain. Samantha was snoring loudly and was so unconscious that, as they walked her along, the toes of her shoes were dragging along the ground behind her.

"Jesus. I wonder how much she drank. This is industrial quaffing!" noted

Brain-Dead, obviously impressed.

They managed to carry her out of the library, with the help of a friendly soul who held the door open for them. Then came the next obstacle.

"Oh shit, stairs!" cursed Dave, staring at the flight of steps before them.

As they pondered how to navigate the steps a group of high school students marched in, walking in line behind a tour guide.

"And this is the library and as you can see..." the guide stopped in mid-sentence, staring up the stairs at the three of them.

"Is she OK?" he asked.

"Oh yeah," smiled *Brain-Dead*, "just absolutely lashed. You lot wouldn't give us a hand, would you?"

The high school students swarmed up the stairs in an excited gaggle and each took hold of a piece of Samantha. She was hoisted up and her handbag was laid on her stomach. Then between them they carried her down the stairs, like a group of management trainees on an out-of-bounds group-bonding course carrying a log across a stream.

"If you come to university, you can get lashed like this ya' know," laughed *Brain-Dead*.

"That isn't quite what we would encourage!" spluttered the academician guide.

But the giggling school kids had already decided that Yorkshire University now seemed like the ideal institution.

At the bottom of the stairs, Samantha was propped upright and Dave and *Brain-Dead* once again took up their positions on either side before heading out across the car park. Every few yards they had to stop and lean against a car to catch their breath. Behind them, they could make out two parallel lines where Samantha's toes had been dragging along the asphalt. Then, with a final effort, they eventually made it to the main road and leant Samantha up against a wall.

"We need a taxi," puffed Dave.

"I just hope she appreciates this when she sobers up," gasped *Brain-Dead*. "You deserve a bucket-load of kinky shags off her for this. In fact, I deserve a few as well!"

Naturally, they had to wait for what seemed like an eternity for a taxi to come along. *Brain-Dead* was appointed taxi spotter while Dave tried to coax Samantha to wake up. She occasionally opened her eyes momentarily, before drifting back into her drunken stupor. At last a taxi did appear and pulled up.

"Sheaf Hall in Broomhill, my good man," grinned *Brain-Dead*.

"What' s wrong with her?" asked the taxi driver. "Is she pissed?"

"Absolutely not! Perish the thought," retorted *Brain-Dead*, acting horrified.

"She looks pissed to me. Why's she asleep then?"

"It's the anesthetic. She's just had a wisdom tooth out and the anesthetic hasn't worn off yet," *Brain-Dead* explained. "Why did they let her out then?"

"Shortage of beds."

"What?"

"The hospital, there's a shortage of beds, so they booted her out to give her bed to someone else."

"That's a bloody disgrace! They shouldn't be allowed to get away with it, tha' knows. I was just reading in my paper that some old dear was kept waiting on a trolley for three days in a hospital down South 'cause they had no beds. This country's going to the bloody dogs. Don't know what they spend all our bloody taxes on, the robbing bastards. They squeeze you for all your hard-earned money, then you can't even get a bloody bed in a bloody hospital. You know what I'd do with them? I'd line all of them up against a bloody wall and shoot the whole bloody lot of them, that's what I'd do. Are you sure she's not pissed? She looks pissed to me."

"I assure you, not a drop has passed her lips. In fact, she's teetotal," *Brain-Dead* assured the taxi driver as they bundled Samantha into the back of the cab.

"Why does she stink o' booze then?"

"Antiseptic."

"What?"

"Antiseptic. They washed her mouth out with antiseptic once the tooth was removed."

"Oh rait," nodded the taxi driver. "But if she pukes in my cab, there's a fifty quid charge tha' knows. It's always the birds, tha' knows, they're the ones that puke in ya' cab. The lads can be rude fuckers when they're pissed, think they're funny an' all that, and some of em' try doin' a runner, fuckers. But it's the lasses that puke. Fucking terrible it is, cleaning all that shite out o' ya' cab. In fact, I'll tell tha' wot. Sat'dy and Sun'dy neet most of us cabbies keep us' lights turned off and only pick up the ones that don't look too bad and we always steer clear of groups of pissed up lasses at all bloody costs."

"This is all very interesting my good man, but do you think you could drive while you talk?" asked *Brain-Dead*.

"Oh yeah, rait!"

Dave tried propping Samantha up against the back seat, but it was no good, she was like jelly and her head kept falling forwards, so he held her head gently in his lap and stoked her hair. She smiled occasionally but still didn't open her eyes.

"What the fuck are you doing?" Dave hissed at *Brain-Dead*, who had his hand up Samantha's skirt.

"Sorry *Stud*. I was just having a quick feel. Can't look a gift horse in the mouth and she has got gorgeous legs. I mean, a bird like this would never let me have a grope if she was sober, would she?"

"Just keep your hands to your fucking self."

"Ooooh, *Mr. Possessive*! Can you imagine what you'd be like if you really were going out with her?"

As the taxi made its way up the hill towards Broomhill, Dave stared at Samantha's face cradled in his arm. Even hopelessly drunk, stinking of booze and with mascara running down her face, she was unbelievably beautiful. As his eyes made their way over her perfectly shaped breasts and down to her incredible thighs and legs, he could understand *Brain-Dead's* impulse to touch her. But Dave suddenly felt protective towards her. In this state she just needed looking after and he was the man to do it. He even wondered if this was how you felt when you fell deeply in love with someone. Sure he wanted to sleep with her, but not now. Now she was vulnerable and he would do anything to keep her safe.

The taxi pulled into the car park at Sheaf Hall and Dave paid the driver before he and *Brain-Dead* wrestled Samantha out. They then dragged her across the Quad to her block and, taking rests ever three or four steps, carried her up the stairs. Once they reached her door, Dave kicked it.

"Joanne. Joanne, are you in there?" yelled Dave.

"No," came a muffled reply.

"Come on, open the door. We've got Samantha here and she's drunk."

"I know she's drunk. I'm drunk too."

"Well just let us in. We can't carry her for much longer."

"I can't let you in."

"Why not?"

"'Cause I'm not in. I'm in the toilet and I don't feel very well. In fact, I think I'm going to be sick again!"

They then heard Joanne sobbing before she made some very painful retching sounds, which were followed by the sound of liquid being fired into the toilet bowl at very high velocity.

Brain-Dead fumbled for the door handle which, thankfully opened, allowing them to stagger into lounge before making for Samantha's bedroom. Once inside, they dropped Samantha onto the bed with a little less subtlety than they intended and she bounced as she hit the mattress. They hadn't meant to be so uncaring, it was just that they were absolutely exhausted. After resting on the edge of the bed for a moment, they shuffled Samantha around so that her head was on the pillow and her legs were stretched out.

"What do we do now?" asked Dave.

"I reckon we should loosen her clothing," grinned *Brain-Dead*.

"Oh come on," pleaded Dave. "Please just be serious for a moment."

"Well we should turn her over, so she doesn't choke on her puke. Don't want her doing a Jimmy Hendrix do we?"

Dave agreed and they rolled Samantha onto her side.

"What about the handbag?" asked *Brain-Dead*.

"Yeah, you're right", agreed Dave, lifting her head to untangle the strap from around her neck.

Dave put the handbag at the end of the bed before deciding that she would be more comfortable if he took her shoes off. So he knelt down and began fighting with the fasteners on her shoe straps. He had just managed to unhitch the first shoe, which he tossed over his shoulder when a familiar voice barked at him. Just because the voice was becoming familiar didn't mean that it was any less shocking or any more welcome.

"What the fuck are you doing, you bastards?" yelled the voice.

Dave looked up to see Greg towering over them with his hands on his hips and steam coming out of his ears. He then glanced at *Brain-Dead*, who had hands on each of Samantha's breasts but which he quickly removed. Dave was about to scream at *Brain-Dead* for fondling Samantha's tits when he realized that from Greg's angle, Dave appeared to be staring straight up Samantha's skirt.

"I said what are you doing to her, you perverts?" screamed Greg again.

Dave was speechless but *Brain-Dead* calmly rose to his feet and stood with his face an inch away from Greg's.

"I'll tell you what we're doing, asshole. We're looking after your fucking bird, that's what we're doing. She got totally shit-faced in the *Uni* at lunchtime, before nearly getting herself banned from the library and finally falling unconscious, leaving us to carry her home. Now, as her boyfriend and being a supposed medic, it should be you making her comfortable and ensuring she doesn't choke on her vomit. However, as you're a twat and obviously can't be arsed looking after your bird on her birthday, me and

Dave here, out of the goodness of our hearts, have stepped into the breach to do your job for you. So fuck you!"

Greg's mouth fell open at the end of *Brain-Dead's* speech and, for a minute, he didn't utter a sound. Finally, his gaze fell away from *Brain-Dead* to Samantha and he dropped down beside her.

"Oh Sammy, I'm sorry. I forgot your birthday. I'm so sorry!" he whispered into her ear.

As Greg pleaded with Samantha to open her eyes, Dave and *Brain-Dead* quietly left the room.

"You know, I really don't like that Greg fucker!" said *Brain-Dead* as they walked out into the Quad.

"I know exactly what you mean," replied Dave.

NINE

It was now seven o'clock and Dave and Pam were heading back down the hill towards the university. Dave was bringing Pam up to speed with the goings-on of the afternoon and she was 'Ooohing' and 'Aaaahing' sympathetically in all the right places. It felt good to get it off his chest, but it still didn't make Dave feel any better about the situation.

"What I can't understand is why, if she's going out with Greg, she bothered to come and give you a bollocking?" said Pam.

"'Cause she was drunk", Dave grumbled.

"Yeah I know she was pissed, but 'in vino veritas' my dear."

"What?"

"People often say what they really mean when they're pissed, 'cause all their inhibitions have gone. I think that..."

Pam was cut short by a scream of "Are ya' willin for a shillin?" coming from a passing bus. Looking up, they saw *Brain-Dead* with his head on an angle, yelling out of a tiny window at the back of the bus with a gargantuan bare ass, that could only be
Lard-Arse's, pressed against the glass below him.

"It's so nice to be mixing with such refined and cultured company," said Pam as the bus disappeared down the hill. "You know, when I was at home in Newcastle and I imagined university life, I had visions of earnest political discussions into the early hours with men with beards and women with sandals and unshaven armpits, of walking around with a university scarf wrapped around my neck and a pile of impressively weighty books under my arm and of forging lifelong friendships with future political and industrial leaders. Not being 'mooned' at from the top deck of a bus by a whale who wants to run his fishing line through my pussy, while his imbecilic friend is suggesting to the unsuspecting populace that not only am I a prostitute, but that my rates start at five pence."

"They probably will end up as politicians or captains of industry."

"God help us all!"

When Dave and Pam arrived at the concrete monstrosity that was the *Students Union*, *Brain-Dead* and *Lard-Arse* were waiting for them at the front door with Paul who, if it were at all possible, was smoking even more furiously than usual.

"Excellent. Glad you could make it," puffed Paul.

"No problem *Darling*," replied Pam. "but you needn't have met us outside. You could have just put our names on the guestlist."

"Oh, there is no guestlist," replied Paul. "You don't have to pay to see us, we're just playing in a corner of the bar."

"You don't think anyone in their right minds would pay to watch the *Hippy* and his spaced-out pals abuse some poor innocent instruments, do ya'?" asked *Brain-Dead*.

"I think that's a little harsh!" Paul protested.

"Ignore him, my love. Come on in and I'll buy you a drink," said Pam.

"I'll be in in a minute. I've got to wait for Joanne," replied Paul, glancing around.

"You'll be waiting for a long fucking time," laughed *Brain-Dead*. "She was 'on the lash' all afternoon with *Stud's* Sam bird; probably trying to build up enough Dutch courage to watch you play. Anyway, she got so pissed she ended up chucking her guts up in the bogs."

"Oh!" said Paul, looking somewhat shocked and not a little disappointed.

"Never mind *Babe*, we're here," smiled Pam.

Paul led the way into the *Students Union*, through double doors with two identical posters taped to the glass.

NOISE
Last chance to see them before their sell out European Tour!
Tonight Only Yorkshire University Students Union Bar

"Sell out?" noted *Lard-Arse*.

"Total bollocks!" replied Paul. "But no one's going to fly to Bulgaria to

check, are they?"
As they walked along the corridor towards the bar, there was a *Noise* poster every ten feet.

"Fucking hell, have you put up all these posters *Hippy*?" laughed *Brain-Dead*.

"Yeah."

"What's the fucking point?"

"What?"

"What's the fucking point of putting loads of posters up in the *Students Union*, when you're playing in the *Students Union*? I mean, it's not as if anyone could avoid you even if they wanted to, 'cause you're playing in the fucking bar!"

Paul looked embarrassed, but said nothing and marched on towards the bar. When they'd got their bottles of expensive Czech lager (which Pam bought), they sat down at a long, wooden table with benches in the corner of the bar, near to where the instruments were set up.

"God, this is a stroke of luck! Fancy being able to get so near the front at a *Noise* gig. I wonder where all the fans who've camped out all night are?" laughed *Brain-Dead*.

"Look man, if you don't want to be here, just leave. You're really starting to wind me up!" muttered Paul. He was becoming visibly upset, with his hands shaking so much that he was spilling tobacco onto the floor as he rolled himself a cigarette.

Brain-Dead decided to suspend the goading of Paul for the time being and they all settled down to their drinks. As they chatted (mainly about Sam and Jo's session earlier that day), even *Brain-Dead* could not have helped but notice that the bar was filling up. Dave wondered what was attracting so many people to the *Students Union Bar* on a Tuesday evening. Surely it wasn't Paul's band? But then again, if *Noise* wasn't the attraction, then why were these people standing in a crowd in front of the instruments?

"Are you the only band on this evening?" Dave asked Paul.

"Yeah man," replied Paul, gathering together a pile of cigarettes he had just rolled. "In fact, I'd better make a move, 'cause we're on in a couple of minutes."

He then climbed off the bench and ambled off towards a door behind the instruments. At that very moment, two couples approached the table.

"Do you mind if we share your table?" asked a very attractive girl, possibly in her mid twenties.

"No, not at all, help yourself," Pam replied, smiling.

The girl, her equally attractive friend and two guys put their drinks on the table and squeezed onto the benches.

"Are you here to see the band?" asked *Lard-Arse*.

"Oh yes!" grinned the second girl. "It should be quite an exciting evening. They've got a new bass player."

"I don't fucking believe this!" *Brain-Dead* whispered to *Lard-Arse*, his eyes widening.

"You've seen them before then?" asked Dave.

"At least twenty or thirty times," replied one of the guys.

"And we're got all of their albums," added the first girl.

As she was speaking, the lights at their end of the room dimmed and the audience started clapping and cheering. On the wall behind the instruments the word *Noise* was weakly projected. A minute later, the band walked through the door and made their way to their instruments, waving to the audience as they went. A squat, dark-haired drummer wearing sweatbands on his wrists entered first, holding his drumsticks up to the audience, before sitting down and repositioning one of his cymbals. The tall, skinny keyboards player followed and ambled into position, seemingly unaware that the audience was there at all. The guitarist was next in line. He obviously fancied himself (without just cause, according to Pam later), running his hand through his long hair before plugging his guitar in and dramatically stamping on the pedals on the floor in front of him. Paul followed next, complete with cigarette drooping out of his mouth, to cheers and wolf whistles from the table he had recently vacated. He hitched the strap of his electric bass around his neck before fiddling with the amplifier behind him. Finally, the saxophonist, who was clearly the leader of the band, appeared to cheers from the audience. He stamped out to the front, bizarrely, dressed like Clint Eastwood with an enormous cowboy hat on his head and elaborate boots on his feet. He waved the two saxophones he was carrying, then took his position at the front microphone and clipped one sax onto a strap around his neck.

"Hello. We're *Noise*," he yelled into a microphone.

The crowd cheered and clapped as the band started up, but it was a sound quite unlike any that Dave had ever heard. For a start, it was so loud that it made Dave's entire body vibrate and tingle. Added to this was the total absence of any sort of tune. It was exactly how Paul had described it, as if were all playing different tunes at the same time. In fact, it was worse than that. Some of them didn't seem to be playing any tune at all, but simply making their instrument generate the loudest possible noise. This went on unabated for at least fifteen minutes. Dave looked across at his three companions, all of whom were open-mouthed and staring straight ahead without blinking. The two couples that had joined them at the table, however, were yelling, cheering and clapping as they swayed to some beat that remained hidden from Dave. He stared at his friend in disbelief. Even an unbiased observer would have had to admit that Paul looked extremely 'cool' and appeared totally proficient as he slapped his bass. When the first number came to an end, the girl next to Dave literally jumped off the bench and began screaming and whistling.

"Oh yeah! Woah! Aren't they great?" she yelled at Dave.

"Oh yeah!" replied Dave.

"The new bass player's fucking superb!" added her boyfriend.

"And quite a dish," grinned the other girl.

"It seems 'ol chicken legs' has hidden talents. I'm starting to see him in a different light. But just check out that sax player. Girlies always fancy a sax player and this one's already making me moist!" Pam shouted into Dave's ear.

But it wasn't the sax player that Dave was interested in, it was Paul. If Paul had been performing to a hundred thousand people at a stadium gig, Dave could not have been more amazed or proud. Paul, meanwhile, unstrapped his electric bass, before wrestling an enormous double bass away from the back wall.

"Look," screamed the first girl. "He plays double bass as well!"

Brain-Dead and *Lard-Arse* still said nothing as the saxophonist clipped a second sax to his neck strap and started the second number by playing them both at the same time. The long-haired guitarist strutted around behind him as if he was playing a solo for the Rolling Stones rather than for some crazy, modern jazz band. The drummer, who was as wide as he was tall, was building himself into a sweaty frenzy next to a keyboards player, who still looked like he was practising in his bedroom. But, although the sax player was the showman and the main crowd-pleaser, to Dave it was Paul who was stealing the show. He looked so at ease and happy as his fingers flicked along the strings of the massive instrument, smiling every so often at the drummer.

The gig lasted for nearly an hour and a half, during which time *Brain-Dead* and *Lard-Arse* sat motionless like rabbits in car headlights. Dave was simply mesmerized by Paul's performance. If he had been given a recording of the gig, he would have turned it off after a minute. But, as he was only watching Paul, he found that he actually enjoyed it. Pam, meanwhile, was positively drooling over the saxophonist. As the band took a bow at the end of the gig, she stood up on the bench and wolf whistled with all the gusto of a worker on a construction site spotting some 'hottie' in a low-cut blouse.

After a few minutes in the back room, Paul reappeared and joined them at the table.

"I want that sax player!" hissed Pam as he approached.

"What?"

"The sax player, bring him over here so I can get my claws into him."

"But he's married with two kids."

"So? He's a bloke isn't he? Since when has a bloke turned down a shag?"

Paul looked shocked.

"You were great!" said Dave.

"Thanks man. Did you all enjoy it?" asked Paul, turning to *Brain-Dead* and

Lard-Arse.

"It was shit," replied *Brain-Dead.*

"Oh...thanks a lot," said Paul, looking very hurt.

"But I have to admit, *Hippy*, that you were surprisingly unshit," continued *Brain-Dead.* "What drugs did you have to take to play that well?"

" I thought it was amazing." added an ashen-faced *Lard-Arse.*

"Thank you," said Paul, smiling.

"I thought the music was shit, but it was still amazing." *Lard-Arse* continued. "Anyone hungry?"

"I'm hungry for some pork sausage," declared Pam. "So get that hunky sax man over here, will you? And tell him to keep his hat on."

Dave asked everyone what they wanted to drink and set off for the bar with *Lard-Arse* in tow, whose mission was to ensure adequate supplies of dry roasted peanuts, *Scampi Fries* and *Pork Scratchings* were bought. On returning with the drinks spilling around on a metal tray and with pockets full of snacks, Pam had indeed enticed Clint to the table and was gazing into what she could see of his eyes under the incongruous Stetson. *Clint* was busy congratulating Paul on his performance, while Pam's hand was very obviously working its way up his thigh. Every time he praised Paul, Pam praised him and, although *Clint* seemed to be starting to enjoy Pam's attentions, *Brain-Dead* clearly wasn't.

"Why do birds always fancy bloody sax players?" he whispered loudly to Dave. "It's not like it's difficult or anything. And you know what they say, 'If you can't fight, wear a big hat'."

"Fuck off *Brain-Dead*", Pam replied, without averting her gaze from *Clint.*

"And he's bound to have a small cock," *Brain-Dead* continued, unperturbed. "Blokes in big boots always have small cocks."

"It's big enough to make two kids!" smiled Pam, still without turning around.

The following hour passed in much the same way. More and more drinks were consumed at quite a frantic rate, *Lard-Arse* worked his way through every snack that the *Union Bar* had to offer (including two jars of cockles in vinegar and three pickled eggs), *Brain-Dead* became more loudly offensive towards *Clint* as he became more drunk, but *Clint* ignored him completely and conversed only with Paul, with Pam cooing into his ear. Finally, *Brain-Dead*, who'd been getting more and more agitated, could take it no longer and stood up.

"I've had enough, I'm off!" he declared.

"See you," smiled Pam, waving but still not turning towards him.

"Kebab?" asked *Lard-Arse*.

"You coming, *Stud*?" *Brain-Dead* asked Dave.

"Er...what are you doing?" Dave asked Paul.

"I've got to help get all the gear packed up and into the van."

"Need a hand?"

"No thanks, man. The boys will give me a lift home after we've sorted everything out. I'll see you back there. Thanks for coming."

"Could you squeeze me into your van?" Pam asked *Clint*, fluttering her eyelashes.

"Oh, I think I could give you a squeeze, if you had a mind for it!" smiled *Clint*.

"Right, that's it. I'm off!" snarled *Brain-Dead*.

"You said that already," giggled Pam. "Don't let me keep you."

Brain-Dead tried to make a dramatic exit but, unfortunately, was too drunk to pull this off and tripped up over the bench. Pam laughed very loudly, which didn't improve his mood any and he stormed off towards to exit. Dave and *Lard-Arse* said their goodbyes before joining an angry *Brain-Dead*, who was marching up and down outside the *Union* building.

"Fucking bitch! Did you see that? Fucking bitch! She gonna' shag him ya' know? That fucking...cowboy...bastard – no offence *Yank*. She gonna fucking shag him."

"Yeah, we know," replied *Lard-Arse*. "Can we go for a kebab now?"

"I've been working on her all bloody week and do I get a shag? Do I bollocks. But some twat in fancy bloody dress shows up and she's got her bloody legs behind her ears before you can say 'hard on'. Bitch!"

"Come on, let's go for a kebab."

Brain-Dead kicked the wall before ripping a *Noise* poster off the door.

"I'll wipe my arse with this one later," he snarled.

It wasn't until they started walking that Dave realized how drunk he was. He found himself laughing at the most stupid things and crashed off walls and cars as they made their way up the hill towards Broomhill. *Brain-Dead* and *Lard-Arse* were no better. *Brain-Dead* had to stop and urinate every few hundred yards, while *Lard-Arse* couldn't stop farting.

"Umm, what do you reckon to that one boys?" he asked. "I think that one's *Scampi Fries*, what do reckon *Stud*?"

"Perhaps, but maybe there' s a touch of picked egg in there somewhere."

"And that one?"

Dave sniffed the air.

"Definitely *Pork Scratching*."

"Umm, perhaps you're right, although I thought I could detect the sea in that one. I think we've got a touch of cockle in there somewhere."

As they approached Broomhill, they decided that they could squeeze one last beer in before closing time and voted unanimously to dive into the pub next door to the kebab shop. As it was *Lard-Arse's* round, he pulled out a note and waved it at the enormous girl serving behind the bar.

"Cor she's fit!" exclaimed *Lard-Arse*.

"What?" laughed *Brain-Dead*.

"Check out the arse on that!" *Lard-Arse* continued.

"It's difficult not too, my flabby friend, her arse is all I can see. You know how a horse can see three hundred degrees, or whatever it is, and the only blind spot for a horse is the middle of his back - that's why the put policemen there, so the fucking horse isn't embarrassed - well, if I was a fucking horse I'd be panicking now, 'cause all I'd be able to see would be her arse!"

"Well I think she's cute. What do you think *Stud*?"

"I usually associate cute with small pretty things, you know, cute little dogs and such. Well I don't think even her best friend would describe her as 'cute'."

"Well fuck you boys. I think she's gorgeous."

"I tell you what *Lardy*, you'd have a dead cert if you bring her to next week's *Pull a Pig*," laughed *Brain-Dead*.

"She's no pig. Just look at that pretty face!"

"Not a pig? Jesus man, if you get into her knickers you'll find she's got *Danish* tattooed on her arse!"

"Shut up you bastards, here she comes!"

She waddled over to them to take their order before waddling back with three pints of beer, giving *Lard-Arse* a big smile as she placed them on the bar in front of him.

"Look at that boys, a bird who can carry three pints at once!" smiled *Lard-Arse* before turning back to her. "Er...and a packet of cheese and onion...oh and whatever you're having."

She smiled.

"Oooh, that's kind of you. I'll have a packet of C and O with you."

Brain-Dead fell about laughing.

"Jesus fatty, she's definitely the bird for you. I've never met a barmaid who'd choose a packet of crisps instead of a drink. I wonder if she can fart a menu as well, like you?"

As they drank their beers, *Lard-Arse* and the barmaid kept chatting, in between her serving other people. It was confirmed that *Lard-Arse* had definitely pulled when he agreed to meet her outside with a large doner kebab with extra peppers and chilli sauce, once she'd 'washed the pots'.

"I hope you're not planning to shag her in your single bed back at hall. It just won't take it. If you two start 'buffing uglies' on it, you'll end up with a pile of fucking matchsticks in the morning," laughed *Brain-Dead*. "How do whales do it, *Stud*? I'm sure it must involve a cock half a mile long and a lot of salty water. It certainly doesn't involve a university single bed and a cock the size of a peanut."

"Will you just fuck off," moaned *Lard-Arse*, while motioning to the Turkish man with an unfeasibly long mustache behind the counter to continue slopping radioactive-looking chilli sauce onto the two kebabs he'd ordered. "You're only jealous 'cause Pam's blown you out for 'Billy-the-fucking-kid' and there's a chance that I'll be shagging while you're wanking into those crispy pajama bottoms of yours!"

"Oooh, harsh words there, *Fat Boy*. The night is still young and sweet Pamela might yet be treated to a length of BD vein!"

"Twenty fucking sobs says she won't," laughed *Lard-Arse*, slamming a note on the counter, which the Turkish kebab man duly picked up and rammed into his register.

"I think I'll have to have a piece of that bet as well," mumbled Dave, chewing on an extra long and greasy piece of meat, that subsequently flapped against his shirt leaving a strange red stain and which, even though he was drunk, he knew would never wash out.

"Boys, I accept your bets and want no blubbing when Pamela is riding my greasy pole later on 'ce soir'!"

As they left the kebab shop, Dave saw the owner give a sigh of relief that the drunks had left without causing trouble or subjecting him to the usual racist abuse that normally resulted in him having to flash his two foot kebab carving knife. On the wall outside the pub, they gorged themselves on whatever it is that doner kebabs are made out of, trying not to think about how many bugs had barfed on it or what strain of botulism they would probably contract. Just after all three paper bags had burst, spilling kebab remains and salad onto the ground, the lights in the pub went out and the barmaid appeared.

"Oooh, that's kind of you!" she grinned at *Lard-Arse* through freshly applied lipstick.

"It's probably a bit cold by now," said *Lard-Arse* handing over her package.

This didn't seem to bother her, however, as she had unwrapped the paper and sank her teeth into the pita bread before he'd finished the sentence.

Lard-Arse's chest swelled with pride.

"Well, we'll leave you two lovebirds to it," grinned *Brain-Dead*.
"Don't forget our wager, *Mr. Zero*," yelled *Lard-Arse* as Dave and *Brain-Dead* walked off. "It counts for fuck all if Dave doesn't verify it!"

As Dave and *Brain-Dead* made their way up the hill towards Sheaf Hall they tried to hail a couple of passing taxis; not because it was that far away, but because they were so drunk by now that for every step forward they took two steps sideways.

The cab drivers, however, quickly spotted this and decided that the likelihood of cleaning barf out of their cab wasn't worth the potential gain of a five minute fare. When they realized that this was the case, *Brain-Dead* decided it would liven up the walk home if they lifted 'For Sale' signs out of people's yards and moved them to houses that weren't for sale. This seemed hilarious for the first three attempts, but Dave tired of the practice when *Brain-Dead* clocked him heavily on the back of the head with a sign. When, finally, they staggered into Sheaf Hall car park, *Brain-Dead* cursed at the sight of a battered *Transit* van with *Noise* painted on the side with as much precision as on the wall at the *Students Union*.

"I think you owe me twenty bucks," smiled Dave.

"Faint heart never fucked a pig!" grinned *Brain-Dead*, marching towards Pam's block.

"What are you doing?" Dave asked jogging after him.

"I'm going to show young Pam the error of her ways."

"You're joking?"

"Follow me *Mr. Adjudicator* and you might learn something."

Dave struggled to catch up with *Brain-Dead* as he stormed into the block and strode up the stairs, three at a time. By the time Dave arrived at Pam's floor, *Brain-Dead* was pushing Pam's door open. Dave gasped as his eyes focused on the softly-lit scene beyond the door. Pam was on all fours on the bed with her dress hitched up around her shoulders, displaying an old and rather ragged pink bra and a bare ass. Behind her, *Clint* was kneeling up and was humping away 'doggy fashion', causing Pam's more than ample buttocks to change shape with each thrust. If this wasn't enough to make Dave wince, the fact that *Clint* still had his hat and his boots on (with his jeans and shorts scrunched up around the top of his boots) certainly was. At first, it appeared that neither Pam nor *Clint* had noticed the door open. This appearance dissolved, however, when *Brain-Dead* spoke.

"Pam, when' s it my turn?"

Pam's head span towards *Brain-Dead* with a look of absolute outrage, or as much as Dave could discern through the tangled, sweaty hair covering her face.

"Fuck off Brain-Dead!" Pam yelled.

"Fuck off, you bastard," growled *Clint*, pausing mid thrust.

"Arrrh Pam, you don't want to be fucking him when you could have this!" laughed *Brain-Dead*, pulling his erect penis out of his fly and pulling back the foreskin.

"Oh my God!" laughed Pam.

"Just look at that beauty Pam. Just look at what you're missing," grinned *Brain-Dead*, stroking his erect dick.

Dave was too shocked to say a word.

"Just fuck off will you!" hissed *Clint*, patently not knowing whether to pull out or not.

"Oh yeah, and what you gonna do about it, *Cowboy*? Wife know you're here, does she?" grinned *Brain-Dead*, before extending his tongue towards Pam. "Come on Pam, you know you want it. Tell you what, you give me a blowjob while he's fucking you and we could spit roast ya'. How about that?"

Pam, by this time, was laughing into her pillow.

"This is ridiculous," she howled. "Oh and thanks a bundle 'friend' for stopping this daft twat," she continued, spotting Dave in the hallway. "Is anyone else with you? Have you brought any buddies from the bar to check out some cheap porn?"

"Sorry Pam, I couldn't stop him," muttered Dave. "Come on *Brain-Dead*, enough's enough, let's go."

Dave pulled *Brain-Dead* back towards to door, with *Brain-Dead* still hanging onto his manhood. *Clint*, meanwhile, remained silent; no doubt wishing he'd not chosen this particular night to 'play away from home'. After Dave finally succeeded in dragging *Brain-Dead* away and waiting for him to stuff his penis back into his pants, the two of them made their way across the Quad towards their block.

"Fancy a little number for the road?" asked *Brain-Dead*.

Dave agreed and followed *Brain-Dead* into his room and sat at his desk. *Brain-Dead* then proceed to pull out a bizarre contraption from his wardrobe. The base was a glass amphora with two finger holes around the stubby neck, which Dave recognized as an item used in the production of home-brewed wine (his father had gone through a stage of buying some sort of syrup in tins and making his own wine which, naturally, was absolutely undrinkable). The amphora was filled with brown cloudy water with a fowl-looking sludge at the bottom, which in turn sent wisps of debris into the water as it was moved. Sticking into the neck were two clear plastic pipes with a small metal bowl on top of one of them.

"What the fuck is that?" Dave asked.

"It's my hubbly bubbly pipe, also known as a bong. It'll melt your brain."

"Doesn't look very clean."

"You don't clean a hubbly bubbly pipe, *Dumbfuck*. You'd be wasting all the *dooby* that has amassed in the bottom. Me and *Lardy* dredge it occasionally when times get hard and we can't afford any fresh stash. It also comes into its own when the opposite happens, in other words you've got the cash but there' s no stash to be had. Now just watch and you might learn something."

Brain-Dead heated up some resin with his lighter and sprinkled a few bits into the bowl. He then lit this and dragged on the other pipe. The air above the water inside the amphora filled with gray-blue smoke before disappearing up the pipe and into his lungs.

"Woah!" he squeaked. "Your turn."

Dave leant over and took the pipe from him, before putting his mouth around the now wet end. He took a deep breath and watched the approach of the smoke. As he breathed in the fowl air, he started choking. He dropped the pipe with his lungs on fire, his eyes watering and sweat poring from every pore. At that very moment, he could just about discern, through the water in his eyes, Pam kicking open the door and storming into room. She marched over to *Brain-Dead* and punched him on the nose. The bizarreness of this sight was heightened by the fact that she had tucked her dress into her massive knickers.

"You piece of shit!" she screamed at *Brain-Dead*.

"What?" asked *Brain-Dead* looking bemused.

"What do you mean 'what', you stupid shit-for-brains-son-of-a-bitch. I'll tell you what. I'm having the first decent shag since I arrived in this God-forsaken place, when some fucking halfwit bursts into my room and starts flashing his cock around. Not only that but", looking at Dave, "someone I regarded as a friend finds the whole thing so amusing that he doesn't lift a finger to prevent this. To make matters even worse, I'd just been getting warmed up when my shag decided, unsurprisingly, that he couldn't go on, seeing as the place was full of crazies, and has now fucked off home to his bloody wife and kids! So what are you gonna to do about that then, eh?"

Pam put both hands on her hips and scowled at *Brain-Dead* as Dave, still choking, tried to explain that he had been powerless to intervene.

Brain-Dead merely grinned at Pam.

"Don't you grin at me, you crazy bastard, I asked you what you were going to do about it," Pam smirked.

Dave, who hadn't realized that Pam's anger was turning to something else, continued apologizing.

"Dave," said Pam.

"Er...yeah?"

"Shut the fuck up and leave me to deal with this sorry excuse for a human being."

"What?"

"Dave, just go to bed, will you?"

"Oh yeah, right...OK," replied Dave, puzzled.

"Night Dave," said Pam.

"Er...goodnight," replied Dave, standing up and walking to the door.

Brain-Dead got up as well and walked with him.

"Goodnight *Studly*," he said, smiling at Dave before extending his tongue out in his obscene fashion and winking as he closed the door.

"Goodnight *Brain-Dead*, sleep well," he replied to the closed door.

As he staggered along the corridor towards his room, he heard Pam giggling.

TEN

Dave surfaced just after eleven. He woke with a start and a panic before dropping back down onto his pillow and smiling. He was smiling, even with a slight headache and hangover, because today was Wednesday. Even though it was his first full Wednesday at college, he knew this was going to be his favorite day of the week, because on Wednesday he had a totally free schedule. Somehow he felt Wednesdays were even better than Saturdays because there was something delicious about lazing around when everyone else was working and he congratulated himself once again on picking History as his major. Naturally, the academic establishment hadn't written this break into Dave's schedule to allow him to convalesce after drinking far too much and coughing his guts up after smoking from *Brain-Dead's* bong. No, they had decided that History students needed this time to read around their subject and do some independent research in the lower vaults of the library. Yeah right! Dave lay there wondering if any of his fellow History students were indeed in some dark dungeon, sweating over a hot book. Perhaps one or two of the owly, ugly broads were; the ones who had no prospect of having any sort of social life at college, so they may as well work their tits off for *Summa cum Laude* honors (what the Brits call a 'First class degree').

His mind wandered from the subject of Wednesdays and landed, with a crash, on the subject of *Brain-Dead* and Pam. How remiss of him. How could he have not awakened thinking of this? Then there was *Lard-Arse*. How had he got on with *Miss Piggy*? Both of these questions were going to have to wait, however, as Dave was bursting for the bathroom. He leapt out of bed and, after giving brief consideration to using the sink, opted to go out to the shower room, just in case he was moved to take a dump while he was there. So he grabbed his bathrobe and opened his door, at the very moment that Pam was exiting *Brain-Dead's* room, dressed in one of his huge T-shirts and with a teapot in her hand.

"Morning David," she grinned

"Morning Pamela. Good night?"

"Surprisingly good, actually. I wasn't sure at first whether, because I was in such a state, that a ride on a washing machine or a good cucumber would have done the trick, but I have to say that the boy certainly has stamina and not a little technique. How surprising! And I won't be able to watch him doing his stupid tongue trick in future without getting just a little tingle downstairs."

269

"Now that's more information than I need," laughed Dave.

"Fair enough my sweet. Would you care for a cup of tea? The kettle's going on."

"Sure, that'd be great, I'm just off to take a leak."

"Now that's more information that I need to know. I'll leave it outside your room 'cause I'm going to see if I can milk any more out of Casanova in there."

When Dave had relieved himself (he did decide to go for the 'dump' option after all), he returned to find a cup of tea outside his door. He took the tea inside and got back into bed, just because he could. He propped himself up against the headboard sipping his tea and thought about Pam and *Brain-Dead*. Try as he might, however, the very concept was just too surreal; it was like trying to imagine your parents 'doing it'! By the time he had finished his tea his hangover was starting to subside and his mind turned to how Samantha's head was feeling this morning. Dave shuddered at the very thought of it.

Eventually he decided that he must get up and do some work on the essay he was attempting the day before when Samantha had interrupted him. So, once he had shaved and showered, he threw open the drapes and sat down at his desk at the window. He hadn't even opened the first book when *Lard-Arse's* face appeared in front of him. *Lard-Arse* mouthed something that Dave didn't understand and then disappeared. Moments later he was at the door.

"Morning Dave."

"Hi. How did you get on last night with Miss P...er...with the bartender?"

"Very well. Got a BJ!"

"A blowjob? How romantic."

"Well not really. We finished our kebabs and chatted for a while and then she gave me a
blowjob against a grit bin."

"A what?"

"You know; a big, yellow bin full of salt. You won't know what they are 'cause it's always hot in cowboy country, isn't it? I've seen your gaff in Westerns; all those red rocks and shit. But they're all over Sheffield for when the snow comes and you have to chuck salt on the road to get your car up the fucking hills."

"Never snows in Nebraska, eh? I fucking wish!"

"Anyway, she couldn't be arsed walking all the way back here and we couldn't go to her house 'cause her mum was up watching the boxing, so we popped round the corner and I leant against a grit bin and dropped my trolleys and she blew me off."

"Didn't anyone see you?"

"Only a few people."

"And was it good?"

"It was alright."

"Only alright?"

"Well the trouble was she'd had so much chilli sauce on her kebab that it was still in her mouth and it made my cock sting like hell."

"Jeez, that would be a first for a sex therapist. Are you seeing her again?"

"Dunno. Perhaps. There are plenty more fish in the sea."

Dave considered making a crack about there not being many whales, but decided against it.

"Anyway," *Lard-Arse* continued, "I presume we're twenty quid richer this morning."

"I'm afraid not!"

"What? You're fucking joking me. He shagged Pam?"

"He's probably still screwing her now for all I know. She came out for a tea break about an hour ago and went back in for more."

"Oh no, this is disastrous. *Brain-Dead* getting his nuts off, we'll never hear the end of it. Why did she do it, is she mad? Was she pissed? His mum will kill him."

"What?"

"His mum; she drives down from Bradford every weekend to bring his washing. He's scared shitless of her and she'd kick his ass if she knew he was fucking about."

"You are joking me, right? I thought..."

"Think again. You wait and see. It'll be worth twenty sobs, just to watch that."

"I wonder what Pam will think about her sex bomb with the nine inch tongue when she finds out about this?"

"Watch this space."

They were then interrupted by a knock at the door and Samantha entering to Dave's 'Come in'.

"Oh helloI " said Samantha quietly to *Lard-Arse.*

"Hello," *Lard-Arse* replied, before slipping quietly away.

"Dave, I've just come to say 'thank you' for helping me out yesterday. I don't remember exactly what I said, I was very drunk..."

"You sure were," laughed Dave, before shutting up again when he saw how serious she looked.

"Anyway, I just came to say that I thought it was very kind of you, you didn't have to do it. Oh and thank *Brain-Dead* for the breast massage, I'm sure that helped," she smiled.

"Er...how about going out for a beer sometime?" asked Dave, quickly trying to change the subject. "Oh, maybe not a great suggestion today."

"I'd love to go for a drink with you but I can't today."

"Hangover and all that?"

"Well yes, but that's not the reason. I've got to go home. My Dad's been taken into hospital. That's my sister, Lucy. She's come to give me a lift home."

Samantha pointed out of the window at a very attractive woman pacing around the quad, who Dave just about recognized from the photo in Sam's room. She was obviously older than Samantha, but still hot. Dave wondered if this was the married sister, the one trying to have a child without much success. She was very elegantly dressed in clothes that, although casual, looked stiff enough to be brand new. Dave wondered, with looks like hers, if she'd had to work very hard for her expensive clothes or if she'd just 'sat on the right cock!'

"We don't know how serious he is but Mum's very upset," Samantha continued, interrupting Dave as he was mentally undressing her sister (he'd just reached the designer French underwear).

'Oh Jeez, I'm sorry to hear that."

"Thank you, you're really sweet. Maybe I can take a raincheck on that date till I get back. Anyway, I've got to go, but I just wanted to thank you."

Samantha leaned over and gave Dave a peck on the cheek. Dave responded by giving her a very brief cuddle, to which Sam started crying.

"Don't cry. I'm sure it's all going to be OK. If there' s anything I can do..." said Dave, before thinking what a ludicrous thing that was to say; what could he do?

Samantha then started for the door and for some reason Dave followed her out into the Quad as she went to her sister.

"Luce, this is David," said Samantha as they approached.

"Hello David," said the sister, "You're the American we've heard so much about from Sammy, but I'm still pleased to meet you...I think."

Dave didn't quite know how to take this, (was it Brit humor?), but Lucy smiled a very cute smile and held out her hand for him to shake.

"Bye then David. I'll see you when I get back," said Samantha as they headed towards to car park.

"Bye and good luck!" Dave called after them. Although he felt guilty about the timing, their father being at death's door and all, he couldn't help himself imagining what a 'kinky threesome' with those two sisters would be like. He watched as they climbed into a brand new, top-of-the-range yellow sports coupe and drove out of the car park, before returning to his desk and staring blankly at the papers in front of him. Although he tried to concentrate, he couldn't stop thinking of Sam and what she'd said.

"Date, what did she mean 'date'? What about Greg?" He was totally confused.

He stared at his papers again for a couple more minutes and tried to read one of the textbooks he's bought from *The Bookseller*, but it was no good. So he closed the drapes again and settled back on his bed to masturbate, dreaming of that 'kinky threesome'.

Once he had relieved himself and pottered around his room, played a couple of CDs and tidied up a little, it was lunchtime. So, leaving his papers still unread, he sauntered over the Quad to the Refectory. After collecting a portion of some strange looking stew, he spotted Paul, Joanne and *Lard-Arse* at a table and went over to join them.

"Great gig last night," he said to Paul. "Get back OK?"
"Yeah fine, I got a lift in the van."

"How are you today Joanne?" Dave asked.

"A little delicate, Sam certainly had her drinking head on yesterday and I got so bored listening to her rattling on about you that I had to get pissed," moaned Joanne.

"About me?"

"Damn right. I wish you'd just make your mind up about that girl and put us all out of our misery."

"It's not me that needs to make their mind up..."

"Goooood afternoon everyone!"

Dave was interrupted by the approach of Pam, sporting a grin from ear to ear.

"I'm bloody starving. Nothing like a bit of nookie to give a girl an appetite!" she beamed.

"Where's *Brain-Dead*?" asked *Lard-Arse*.

"Here's *Loverboy* now," laughed Pam, pointing over her shoulder to the pitiful sight hobbling across the refectory.

Everyone stared open-mouthed at the cripple that was *Brain-Dead*, sliding his feet along the floor, grimacing with every step. He was ghostly pale, with dark bags under his eyes and a hangdog look on his face.

"Are ya' willin for a shillin'?" laughed Joanne.

"Don't say a fucking word, you bastards!" he moaned.

"You look shagged, old man," *Lard-Arse* grinned.

"Only because I am. Gave the old Geordie tart a good seeing to, didn't I *Luv*?"

"Whatever you say, dear!" giggled Pam. "You Yorkies just can't stand the pace, can you lad? I'm ready to go again, if you're game big boy!"

"Noooooo!" *Brain-Dead* wailed. "My knob' s red raw."

"Well I never thought I'd live to see the day," laughed Mike (one of the seniors from Dave's first evening in Sheffield, who was sitting with *The Book-Seller* and one of the girls at a nearby table).

"I want to shake you by the hand," the girl said to Pam, standing up and offering her hand. "For two years we've had to put with endless sexual innuendo from this pervert and all any of us girls needed to do was to fuck his brains out."

"I'd snap your fucking hips if I knobbed you, Beverley. She's no normal bird," said *Brain-Dead* pointing at Pam, "She's a bloody machine. Oh God my cock hurts!"

275

"Ahhh, shall I kiss it better for you *Luv?*" asked Pam, puckering her lips.

"Keep your bloody mouth away from my todger, you animal," *Brain-Dead* shrieked.

Pam picked up the banana she had on her tray, peeled it and took a very violent bite out of it.

"You sure?" she grinned, squeezing banana pulp through her teeth.

Brain-Dead winced.

"I hate to remind you, old fruit, but we're supposed to do a *Wank-Bank* trip this afternoon, if we're going to build up the finances for *The Dam*," said *Lard-Arse*.

"The what?" asked Joanne, staring at Paul.

"Er...Amsterdam. We're going to Amsterdam on Friday," smiled Paul weakly.

"Oh yes, and when were you going to tell me about this? I had plans for us this weekend."

"Give the bloke a break woman. You sound like a married couple but you've only been together two days and for one of those you were pissed," snapped *Brain-Dead*, expressing what Paul thought but daren't say.

"Follow my lead girl. Fuck him senseless for the next two days, then he won't be able to get up to any funny business over there," Pam said to Joanne.
Paul grinned but Joanne didn't look convinced.

"Hey hey," yelled *Lard-Arse*, "I've just remembered what day it is. It's curry night! God, I've missed curry night. Right through the vacation, when it got to Wednesday night, I could cry knowing it was curry night."

"You're not really telling me that you went for three fucking months without sticking a curry down that fat throat of yours, *Tubby*," laughed *Brain-Dead*, perking up.

"No, it's just that...well it wasn't the same."

"Arhhhhhh Tubby, did you miss us?"

"No...well...I just missed our curry nights, that's all. Hey Mike, are you up for curry night tonight?"

"Wednesday wouldn't be Wednesday without one," Mike shouted back. "I bet *The Savera* will welcome us back with open arms."

"*The Savera's* great," *Lard-Arse* explained to the uninitiated freshmen. "Whatever you order, they'll bring you more rice and sauce for free till you're full!"

"Stupid fuckers!" laughed *Brain-Dead*. "Oi *Hippy*, cope with a curry, can you?"

"Of course," replied Paul.

"They don't do brown rice ya' know."

"I'll have you know that I'm a regular down Brick Lane, my son."

"Brick fucking Lane, what's that? You've never had a curry till you've had a Bratford curry, you southern puff!"

"A what curry?"

"It's a curious fact that residents of Bradford in Yorkshire can't actually pronounce the name of the town they live in. For some reason, and we can only presume it's the years of inbreeding taking its toll, they pronounce it Bratford," *Lard-Arse* interjected.

"Well, I don't know about Bratford mate," Paul continued, "but the best curries in the country are to be found in Brick Lane. They were making curries in Brick Lane when all you lot knew about was Yorkshire Pudding, you sheep-shagger."

"I hope you're not referring to me!" laughed Pam.

"Fuck off, Nancy Boy. When you go for a curry in Bratford, you don't get any cutlery. They just slam it down on the table with a naan bread and ya' have to fight the cockroaches for it."

"Why does that not surprise me?"

"And it's so fucking hot, it'd blow your softy southern sphincter clean out of your ass! In fact, at one of our better restaurants, if you manage to eat the hottest curry they do, they give it you for free and you get a T-shirt."

"What does the T-shirt say 'For the first time in my life, I've had a meal that didn't start with Yorkshire Puddin'? You don't know what hot is, you northern tyke. I've had curries down Brick Lane that'd have you crying for your mummy."

"Right, tell you what, you Cockney twat, tonight we're going to order the hottest curry that *The Savera* can make and then we'll see who can handle a curry."

"You've got a deal!"

"Boys, boys, this is pathetic!" sighed Joanne. "Who cares?"

"Bloody men, they're so competitive," agreed Pam.

"Oh that reminds me," said *Brain-Dead*, smiling at Dave and *Lard-Arse.* "You boys owe me twenty sobs. Come on you twats, pay up. There's no arguing, I did her."

Lard-Arse and Dave both grumbled as they pulled out their wallets to hand over the twenty Pound bills.

"What's that for? Did what?" asked Pam.

"Not 'did what?' my darling," smiled *Brain-Dead*, taking the notes. "'Did who?' I did you, so the boys have to cough up twenty sobs each."

Dave grimaced, waiting for Pam to explode, but she didn't. She just ripped both twenty Pound bills out of *Brain-Dead's* hand.

"If we're going to have this right, I think you'll have to agree that I did you and, therefore, these belong to me!"

"Oi Bitch!" exclaimed *Brain-Dead.*

"Now, now *Lover*, should I keep these crisp twenty Pound notes or shall I tell the good people here what you said when I wanted to go for it again in the small hours?"

"Er..."

"Thought so."

"I'd pay you twenty sobs to find out what he did say," smiled Mike.

"Aren't you offended, as a woman, that this piece of shit was betting on whether he could bed you or not?" asked Joanne, obviously horrified.

"My dear, he didn't 'bed' me, I 'bedded' him. Not for a posh meal out or a ride in his flash car, but because I wanted to shag him. And now the poor fucker can hardly walk, but I've been satisfied and I'm forty sobs better off. The sooner you realize that blokes' tiny brains live in their underpants, the happier you'll be!"

Joanne didn't argue, she simply turned to Paul and raised an eyebrow. "I want you to know, and let there be no doubt about it whatsoever, that I didn't go to bed with you for a ride in that crappy car of yours," she said to Paul, who was clearly horrified by the conversation.

"I'm sorry to break up this repartee but I've got a lecture to go to," said *Lard-Arse*. "So what' s the plan for this evening?"

"Well," replied *Brain-Dead*, "how about we meet chez moi about eight, do a bit of bong, then mootch down to *The Savera* in the *Hippy's* chariot? You up for that, Cockney?"

"Sounds good to me," smiled Paul.

"Oi Mikey Mike, meet you in *The Savera* about nine-thirty?" shouted *Brain-Dead*.

"Yup!"

"Good. Bring some Kleenex for the *Hippy* to blub into when his arse is on fire!"

"Can I just ask how all of us are going to get into Paul's car?" asked Joanne.

"Oh ye of little faith!" laughed *Brain-Dead*. "Just turn up, Babe, and you might learn something."

After lunch Dave decided that he really must do some work, so he gathered his papers together and caught the bus down to the library. He found himself a quiet cubicle and got his head down. Paul turned up about an hour later, said 'Hello' and took the booth next to him. But, other than that, there were no interruptions until he looked up to find *Brain-Dead* and *Lard-Arse* grinning at him over the partition.

"Wank o' clock," grinned *Brain-Dead*, waving a plastic jar at him.

"Excuse me?"

"*Tubby* was right. We've got to get some wanking in today so we can collect our earnings tomorrow."

"But we're not supposed to do it if we've had sex," said Dave.

"Oh yeah *Stud*, and who have you been servicing in the last twenty-four hours?"

"Er...I wasn't thinking about me, I was talking about you, you were screwing this morning."

"Oh well, they'll never know. I must admit that my bollocks are like a couple of walnuts after the *Geordie Tart* had her evil way with me, but my knob's recovered enough for a tug. It's not like they're going to check every shot. I mean, they checked that we aren't *Jaffas* and we're not. Maybe some bird'll get a shot with a few less swimmers than usual, but that's just tough shit, I need the brass. So chop chop, let's go."

"Go where? I can hardly wank in the middle of the library!" said Paul.

"They've got toilets haven't they? Me and *Lardy* have made full use of the facilities in the Science Library, so off you go boys and don't be long."

So five minutes later, despite their initial protests, Dave and Paul found themselves occupying adjacent booths in the men's bathroom, masturbating into plastic jars. As Dave tried to concentrate on the 'job in hand', which wasn't going to be particularly easy as he'd been masturbating only a few hours before, all he could hear was the blowing of the hand dryers, pissing into the urinals, the door opening and closing and some guy noisily trying to squeeze out a shit in the stall next to his. He shouted over to Paul about how degrading it was, but Paul had finished ages ago and had already left.

"Is that all you could manage?" asked *Brain-Dead* when Dave eventually returned with his jar.

"I'm surprised you could manage any at all, after the night you had," replied Dave, staring at *Brain-Dead* respectable jar full.

"I had to borrow some of *Lardy's*."

"You are joking," exclaimed Paul horrified. "You're not telling us you poured some of *Lard-Arse's* sperm into your pot?"

"Of course, why not? Look, here's a biology lesson for you *Hipster*. Only one fucking sperm makes it all the way to the bull's eye, right? Well, it doesn't fucking matter whether it's all mine in the race or a mixture of mine and the *Tubster's*, does it? Same fucking result! It's not like the bird who's copping for it has chosen my sperm over *Fatty's*. It's not like choosing fucking wine, it's take it or fucking leave it. They say 'Look, sorry love but your old man's a *Jaffa*. All is not lost, however, as we've got some grade-A student sponk in the fridge over there. Now this stuff is none of your rubbish, this is hand-milked from one of the top fucking five percent of society, he's as fit as a fucking flea and has more brains than you can shake a stick at. So, hop up there, open up and brace yourself 'cause it might be a little cold'. They don't say 'And this one, Madam, is *Lard-Arse's*. Cop for a shot of his and your kid'll look like a fucking Zeppelin before his fifth birthday'. She's not looking at our photos in a fucking catalogue. So my point is, there's no fucking choice. One day she could get a shot of mine, the next day a shot yours, then a shot of the *Yank's* then, God help her, a shot of *Whale-Boy's*. So what's wrong with mixing it up a little? Nothing! So, now that's all sorted, off you trot to the *Bank* and don't worry your Save-the-fucking-whale, wolly-hatted, pinko-voting little mind about it, okay?"

"When did you jerk off in the Science Library?" asked Dave.

"When was it, *Fat Boy*?" *Brain-Dead* asked *Lard-Arse*.
"Er...an hour or so ago."

"Yeah, an hour or so ago. We went for a coffee afterwards, to refresh ourselves after all the exertion."

"But we're supposed to get it to the bank within half an hour," said Paul.

"Oh well, shit happens!"

Dave volunteered to go with Paul to the *Bank*, so that Paul wouldn't need to park *Spermy*. Once they'd pulled up outside Dave, very self-consciously, walked through the hordes of people in the hospital lobby and on towards the *Bank*. It wasn't as if anyone could see the four jars in his plastic carrier bag, but he felt embarrassed because he knew they were there. When he arrived, Sister Lee herself was sitting behind the front desk.

"My, we are keen aren't we?" she boomed.

"Yeah," replied Dave shyly, "we're off to Amsterdam, Holland on Friday and we need the money."

"Och, you be careful out there, laddie! I don't want any of my boys catching a dose off one of those hussies," she laughed. "Well, I dare say we can stretch the rules a little and get you paid today. Will you be taking your friends' money with you?"

"Yeah OK," replied Dave.

"Here you gooo then," she smiled, counting out the bills "Have a goood time and remember what I said."

Dave returned to the car to find Paul puffing away on a cigarette with *Miles Davis* blasting from his tinny system.

"Mission accomplished, my son?" Paul asked, opening his eyes.

"Absolutely, we've even been paid."

"Oh well, makes it all worthwhile," smiled Paul, starting the engine.

At just after eight that evening, Dave knocked on *Brain-Dead's* door. Then he had to knock again to be heard over *Frank Zappa* at full volume inside.

"Hey hey, *Stud*!" grinned an obviously stoned *Brain-Dead* as he opened the door.

Through the pall of smoke inside, Dave found Pam, Paul and *Lard-Arse* sitting around the room, all with stupid grins on their faces. Joanne was there as well, but she was only sporting a dirty scowl.

"Bong or spliff?" *Brain-Dead* asked.

"Er..."

"Don't even think of taking a toke out of that disgusting contraption," giggled Pam. "I dread to think what's swimming around in the bottom of there. Here you are *Luv*, have one of Aunty Pam's."

Pam handed Dave a very long joint.

"I'm surprised at you Dave," growled Joanne. "I didn't have you down as a pothead like all these idiots."

"Now, now *Mrs Killjoy*, just because you've got a broom up your arse, doesn't mean you can piss on everyone else's parade," said *Brain-Dead*.

Joanne went back to her sulk while Dave tugged on the joint and had his usual coughing fit. Joanne raised her eyebrows at him in a 'Told you so' sort of way. She was right. As Dave did more coughing than smoking there was no way he was going to end up on the same planet as the others. Before long they'd reached the laughing at anything stage, which left Dave perplexed and Joanne downright annoyed. After an hour of Joanne bleating on about being hungry, it was time to set off for the curry.

"How are we getting there?" asked Dave.

"In *Spermy* of course!" giggled Paul, having a joint 'for the road'.

"You are joking!" snapped Joanne. "You can't drive, you're out of your brains!"

"I drive very well when I'm stoned, I'll have you know," replied Paul, his face covered by a cloud of blue smoke. "Tell you what, if you don't like my driving, you can take over."

She didn't look convinced and she was even less so when they stumbled out into the car park to the waiting *Spermy*.

"There's no way we're all going to get in there!" she said, pointing at *Spermy*.

"'Course we will, woman," said *Brain-Dead*, as Paul unlocked the car and opened the doors. "You birds can slip your sweet little tushes in the back,

Fat Boy has to go in the front so he can rest his gut on the dashboard and me and the *Yank* will go on the top deck."

"What the fuck are you talking about?" moaned Joanne.

"Just get in woman, you might learn something!" grinned *Brain-Dead*, pulling the passenger seat forward to give her access to the back.

Once she was in and Pam had squeezed in to join her, Paul, with a joint still dangling from his mouth, pulled back the canvas sunroof.

"Hop up there, *Studly*," laughed *Brain-Dead*.

"Where?" asked Dave, bemused.

"Fuck me, use your loaf," huffed *Brain-Dead* before standing on the driver's seat and jumping up onto roof. There he sat, on a narrow strip of metal between the sunroof and the back window, and dangled his feet inside the car.

"Watch your sodding feet, *Dipshit*," shouted Pam, narrowly avoiding having a size thirteen planted in her mouth.

"Sorry *Lover*," called *Brain-Dead* from above. "Come on *Laddy*, we haven't got all night!"

Dave didn't bother arguing. He climbed up next to *Brain-Dead*, taking great care not to kick Joanne, as that would not have improved her mood. The front seats were then clicked back into position and Paul and *Lard-Arse* sat in and closed the doors.

"All aboard!" yelled Paul. "Hang on up top."

With that he started *Spermy* up and she jerked forward, nearly sending Dave and *Brain-Dead* flying down the back of the car.

"For fuck sake *Hippy*, gently does it!" screamed *Brain-Dead*.

"Sorry," called Paul, turning the music up.

And off then went, not very quickly it has to be said as *Spermy's* tiny engine struggled to cope with the weight. However, as they drove out of the car park and into the traffic, even Joanne started to see the funny side.

"This is ridiculous!" she howled with laughter.

Dave was still sober enough, however, to be not entirely amused. He was hanging on for dear life and panicking about falling under the wheels of the car behind. He looked round to see puzzled looks from the driver and passenger, while the two kids in the seats behind them pointed and squealed. The father at the wheel just shook his head. *Spermy* got up speed as they went down hill which, with the wind whistling through his hair, Dave started to find rather exhilarating as well as frightening. It felt a bit like being on a white- knuckle ride at an amusement park, but without any assurance that he was going to survive. Just then, Paul slammed on the brakes. *Brain-Dead* and Dave struggled to grip the roof to stop themselves flying over the hood.

"Owww!" screamed Pam from inside the car. "You just kicked me in the face, you great oaf!"

'Wasn't my fault, it was the crazy *Hippy* braking like that!" yelled *Brain-Dead*.

"Sorry," sang Paul happily.

They had reached a traffic jam and stayed motionless for over ten minutes.

"I'm hungry," wailed *Lard-Arse*.

"I'm squashed," moaned Joanne.

"What' s the traffic look like?" Paul shouted up to Dave and *Brain-Dead*.

"Fucking brake lights as far as the eye can see," came back the report. "Alright, everybody out," announced Paul.

"Oh good, are we walking?" asked Joanne, climbing out from the backseat.

"No chance," replied Paul as the car emptied. "Right, grab a corner boys, we're going to put her on the pavement."

'What?" asked Joanne, stunned.

No one answered her, however, as the four guys lifted the surprising light *Spermy* onto the sidewalk with such ease it looked like a well-rehearsed routine.

"OK, as you were," announced Paul with a grin.

Everyone took their previous seats, even Joanne, and Paul set off along the sidewalk.

"Alright!!!" shrieked *Brain-Dead*, as the passed the stationary traffic, much to the annoyance of the trapped drivers and the occasional pedestrian, who had to leap into the street. One old lady nearly shit herself when Paul hooted her from behind, sending her and her shopping trolley into a hedge. Dave looked behind him as she held up a clenched fist and sent a tirade of expletives after them. Apart from that, everything was going swimmingly well. There weren't many obstacles on the sidewalks as it was past nine o'clock and they sailed along. Paul even managed to steer them across a couple of junctions, using pedestrian crossings to avoid any high curbs. Then it all went horribly wrong. They were passing a line of cars with Paul head down trying to light a cigarette, when they glided past a police cruiser. Dave could see the look of total incredulity on the policemen' s faces as *Spermy* shot past them on the sidewalk. He followed the eyes of the cop on the passenger side as he glanced up to him and *Brain-Dead* sitting on the roof.

'Oh shit, that's torn it," mumbled *Lard-Arse*.

"What' s torn what?" asked Paul, looking up and blowing glowing embers out of the end of his now- lit cigarette.

"We've just passed a car full of pigs!"

At that moment, a police siren started up, followed by the flashing lights on the roof and Dave turned to see the police cruiser pull out of the line of cars and come after them.

"I warned you. Don't tell me I didn't warn you," hissed Joanne from the back seat. "You've done it now. Don't come running to me when they lock you up and throw away your licence!"

"Be cool. Just be cool," Paul whispered, bringing *Spermy* to a halt.

The cruiser edged back into the line of traffic and pulled up next to them. Immediately both policemen, one old timer and a younger man, opened their doors and stepped slowly out of the car. They ambled slowly over to *Spermy* with, it has to be said, rather stern expressions on their faces. As they approached, *Brain-Dead* tried to give them a winning smile, but their expressions didn't crack.

"What the hell do you think you are doing?" the first, older policeman said in slow, quiet, measured tones as he leant down at the window.

"Er...good evening Constable," smiled Paul in his finest private school accent.

"I wasn't asking how the evening was. I wanted to know why you were driving this car on the pavement and why you have passengers sitting on the roof!"

"It's all my fault, Officer," smiled Pam sweetly from the back.

"And why' s that, young lady?" asked the officer, less aggressively this time.

"It's *Rag Week* officer and we're raising money for the Children's Hospital. I know it seems a bit daft now, but it was my idea and we've raised over £120 so far," Pam simpered. "Please don't blame Paul. I talked him into it by telling him about all of those poor children we are raising money for."

"*Rag Week?*" asked the younger policeman. "Is it *Rag Week* already? I thought you lunatics had only just got back after the summer holiday."

"Oh yes, Officer. Our hall always starts early. We raise more money that way!" Pam grinned.

Joanne remained stony-faced while Paul, *Brain-Dead*, Dave and *Lard-Arse* all had the sense to remain silent.

"Do you think it's clever to drive on pavements?" asked the first policeman, staring at Paul.

"No Sir."

"Did you even consider that you could have killed someone?"

"No Sir."

"Have you been drinking?"

"Absolutely not Officer."

"Well, we're going to have to check. Would you step out of the vehicle, Sir?"

Paul opened his door and climbed out, while the second policeman went back to the cruiser for the breathalyzer.

"I told you lot it would end in tears, didn't I?" hissed Joanne, as the policeman explained to Paul what would happen if he gave a positive test or failed to blow into the machine properly.

"Just shut the fuck up," whispered *Brain-Dead*, leaning down into the car.

The first policeman returned with the breathalyzer, pressed a couple of buttons on the side and held it up for Paul. Paul blew into it with all the breath he could muster. Unfortunately all he could muster wasn't enough and the policeman warned him that if he didn't give an adequate sample this time, then they would arrest him. Paul, now sweating, tried to put half a lifetime of smoking behind him and blew for all he was worth. The second policeman's face dropped when, not only did he blow the required amount, but the test was negative.

"Well," said the first policeman, "it appears that you haven't been drinking and, because I'm just driving in after a long, hard shift and I can't be arsed extending it for a bunch of stupid fucking students, I'm going to let you off with a warning."

The second policeman seemed to be going to say something before changing his mind, although the bitter disappointment registered on his face. Paul, meanwhile, sighed gratefully.

"Oh thank you Officer, that's very kind of you. It won't happen again!" Pam beamed.

"Have you been smoking any of that 'whacky backy'?" asked the younger policeman to Paul.

"Certainly not!" replied Paul, as if mortally offended.

"Right," said the older policeman, "you two idiots get down from that roof and you (pointing at Paul) NEVER, EVER, PULL A STUNT LIKE THAT AGAIN! Do you understand me, *Lad*?"

"Yes sir," mumbled Paul.

Dave and *Brain-Dead* stood with Paul by the side off the car as the cruiser moved away and turned its flashing lights off. The younger policeman pointed to his eyes and then at them as if to say 'I'll be watching you'.

"Yeah, yeah, fuck you, fuck you," *Brain-Dead* whispered under his breath as he watched them leave.

"Jesus that was close!" Paul exhaled violently. "I need a drink and a spliff."

"You've got to admit, it was good of the old boy to let you off. I thought the young gun was going to chew your balls off," said Dave.

"Well I hope you're proud of yourselves," hissed Joanne, pushing the front seat, recently vacated by *Lard-Arse*, forward and climbing out of the car.

"Well, I spy *The Savera!*" grinned *Lard-Arse*, ignoring her.

Joanne turned to look down the street to see an odd shimmering sign, a collage of tiny pieces of metal in a mosaic forming the word *Savera Tandoori*. No doubt this sign had looked very impressive when it was first attached to the brick wall on which it hung, but the ravages of time and Sheffield winters had taken their toll and its faded colors said nothing but decay.

"Is that it?" asked Joanne.

"Mumm heaven," muttered *Lard-Arse*. "God, I've missed this place."

Dave thought he could see a tear appear in *Lard-Arse's* eye.

"Looks dodgy to me," moaned Joanne.

"Look Bird, you've been a killjoy all bloody evening. If you want to cheer up, I'll treat you to a poppadom. If not, please just piss off!" said *Brain-Dead* before turning to Paul. "Sorry if that cost you a shag Hippy, but it had to be said."

Even Joanne seemed to admit that it needed saying and, after looking to Paul for support and receiving none, she accepted what *Brain-Dead* had said with surprisingly good grace and resolved to cheer up for the rest of the evening.

"Come on girl, let's give it a try," Pam whispered to Joanne, taking her arm and leading her down the road.

After Paul had parked the car in a side street, the guys followed the girls into the *Savera Tandoori*. Dave gasped as he followed *Lard-Arse* through the door. There was no one there! There were a couple of very tatty tables with a very visible layer of dust on them and a decrepit bar in a corner, about three feet in length and totally devoid of drink.

"Is this it?" he asked *Lard-Arse*.

"Oh no," laughed *Lard-Arse*. "This is just the reception area. All the action goes on downstairs. Follow me!"

Dave couldn't remember seeing *Lard-Arse* move as fast as he covered the ten yards from the front door to a narrow staircase at the opposite end of the room.

"Prepare to be slimed by *Mr. Slime*," laughed *Brain-Dead* as they made their way down the staircase.

"What?" asked Dave.

But *Brain-Dead* didn't have time to answer as they had reached the bottom and found themselves in a very busy restaurant with tables in the middle of the room and booths down both sides. From a well-stocked bar at the opposite end of the room, next to a door leading to the kitchen, a small Asian man in a black suit darted towards them with his arms in the air and a huge grin on his face.

"Oh welcome, welcome! Welcome back *Mr. Arse*, welcome back *Mr. Dead*. We have missed you most very much. Oh oh," he wailed before hugging *Lard-Arse*.

If he had been *Lard-Arse's* favorite multi-millionaire granny, *Lard-Arse* couldn't have been more pleased to see him either. The two of them stood in the middle of the restaurant hugging each other, much to the amusement of the diners around them.

"Arrh isn't it touching?" laughed Pam, pretending to wipe tears from her eyes.

When they eventually disentangled from each other, the restauranteur turned his attentions to *Brain-Dead*.

"Oh *Mr. Dead*, I am most pleased to see you sir. I trust you had a most enjoyable summer and that you are most refreshed," he cooed, grabbing *Brain-Dead's* hand and covering it with both of his own.

"Yes, yes, thank you. Thank you *Mr. S.*," laughed *Brain-Dead*, obviously trying to pull his hand away without any success. "*Mr. S.* I'd like you to meet friends of mine. This is *Mr. Stud*. He's come all the way from America to see you."

"Oh *Mr. Stud*, I am most pleased to welcome any friend of *Mr. Arse* and *Mr. Dead* into my most humble restaurant, most pleased. But your coming all this way, is most gratifying."

He grabbed Dave's hand and at that moment Dave realized why he was called *Mr. Slime*. Not only was his display of affection over the top, but he had the sweatiest palms Dave had ever come across. It was just like he'd pulled them out of a dishpan!

Brain-Dead hooted with laughter at Dave's reaction and wiped his own hands down the front of his shirt, behind *Mr. Slime's* back. When, eventually Dave broke free, the sliming moved onto Paul, who seemed stunned by the whole experience, and then to Pam, who, still stoned, couldn't stop laughing, and finally to Joanne, who actually curled her lip up with an "Errgh" before regaining her composure.

Finally, *Mr. Slime* let them join Mike, Bev, one of the girls whose name Dave could never remember, *The Bookseller* and Cathy, who were sitting at a long table and had been laughing throughout the whole episode.

"Why don't you come and sit down next to me David," smiled Cathy.

Dave did what he was told and the others took their places at the table. A young Asian man in black pants and a white shirt then approached the table, sporting a friendly smile.

"Welcome back you lot," he grinned. "You really are cruel, ripping Uncle like that. We've had a quiet summer and he's been counting down the days till term started again. Here are the menus, can I get you any drinks?"

"Greetings Mohammed," said *Brain-Dead*, "good to see you again. Yes, I think drinks are in order. What are we having, lager?" Everyone nodded. "Yup lagers all round, please."

"Pints for the gents and halves for the ladies?" asked Mohammed.

Everyone nodded again except Pam.

"I'll have a pint, if it's all right with you," she bleated.

"Oh, sorry Madam," said the waiter, obviously upset that he might have caused offence.

"Don't worry about her, Mohammed," laughed *Brain-Dead*. "She's no lady, she's my bird!"

Mohammed laughed as Pam punched *Brain-Dead* in the arm.

"Any poppadoms and chutneys?" he asked.

"Yeah," yelled *Lard-Arse*, jumping in from the far end of the table, "six please, three spicy and three plain. Anyone else want any?"

Everyone around the table laughed.

"What?" asked *Lard-Arse*, looking puzzled.

As they studied the menus that Mohammed had handed out (with the exception of *Lard-Arse* who didn't need to look at his), *Brain-Dead* turned to Paul.

"You still up for this, *Hippy*? You can bottle it now if you want to, before your arse gets set on fire."

"I never felt more up for it, *Northerner*! " grinned Paul.

"You stupid little boys aren't really going through with your childish game, are you? It's pathetic!" said Pam.

"Very juvenile" agreed Joanne.

Paul just nodded at *Brain-Dead*, who called Mohammed over.

"Mohammed, my good man, I want you to bring me and this Cockney 'girl'

292

here, on one plate to share, two portions of the hottest curry your chef can make. It can't be in two dishes, as one portion might be cooler than the other."

"You're kidding right?" laughed the waiter.

"Nope, I've got to teach this young upstart here a lesson."

"You're talking *White-Boy* hot, right?"

"No, you heard me, a plate full of the hottest possible, with two spoons!"

"You've got to be joking!" Mohammed laughed before going around the table taking everyone else's order.

Before he reached Dave, it was Lard-Arse's turn.

"Umm," smiled *Lard-Arse*, "I'll have my usual. I've been dreaming about this. I'll have Chicken Tikka Shahee with Pilau rice, Bombay potatoes, a sag bajee, a Keema Nan and two plain Nans please."

"What' s Chicken Tikka Shahee?" asked Dave, his one and only experience of Indian food being three weeks before in the *Indian Oven* restaurant in Omaha. He had been on a shopping trip with his family, when his mom insisted they have Chicken Tikka Massala for lunch, as she'd read that it was the most popular meal in England. It was very tasty, but not terribly spicy.

"It's Chicken Tikka cooked in mincemeat," smiled *Lard-Arse*. It's fucking delicious."

"I'll have one of those as well, please. And can I just get some rice with that?" Dave asked the waiter.

Mohammed went away with the orders and the menus before returning two minutes later following *Mr. Slime*.

"Oh *Mr. Dead*, you cannot really want this curry you ask for sir!" he wailed.

"Just bring it on *Mr. S*."

"But Sir, it will make you very ill. Not even I would eat such a curry. Please Sir, I bring you a very nice Vindaloo."

"No *Mr. S.* I want that curry and I want it to be the hottest your chef can make. I take full responsibility for my actions and I challenge the chef, as a man of honor, to prepare me the hottest dish he can make. If he fails in this, I shall never darken this establishment's door again and will hold you up to the ridicule you would so rightly deserve. Oh, by the way, we don't care what meat it is, we'll never taste it!"

Brain-Dead folded his arms and leaned back into his seat, leaving the poor restauranteur with no option. So *Mr. Slime* headed back towards the kitchen shaking his head and moaning.

After the party had munched their way through the big crisp poppadoms and drunk most of their beer, the table was cleared for the main event. First of all, all the regular meals were brought out, then came *Lard-Arse's* gargantuan feast. Finally came a large bowl carried by Mohammed, which he placed between *Brain-Dead* and Paul. Behind Mohammed came a still-moaning *Mr. Slime* and the chef.

"Right *Cockney*," said *Brain-Dead* picking up a spoon and staring at the oily, red and black mass in the bowl before him, "these are the rules; one spoonful each at a time, no drinks, no rice, no yoghurt. Deal?"

"Deal," replied Paul, picking up his spoon.

"Then let us begin!"

No one, with the exception of *Lard-Arse*, could touch their food, so mesmerized were they by the duel before them. Both *Mr. Slime* and the chef tried one last time to talk them out of it. Mohammed just laughed. Paul and *Brain-Dead* stared at each other one last time, holding their spoons in the air before dipping them into the curry. In perfect harmony they lifted a spoonful out and held it in front of their faces. Then slowly, staring at each other, they put their spoons in their mouths. By now the whole restaurant was deadly quiet except for the sitar music blaring out of speakers on the walls. Dave was sure he heard a gasp from the fellow diners as their mouths closed around the spoons and they began to chew. Everyone studied each of them for any signs of pain before they swallowed, once again in total unison.

Brain-Dead's eyes bulged.

A smile appeared on Paul's face, before a line of sweat appeared on his upper lip and the smile faded. Both gulped.

"Delicious!" *Brain-Dead* squeaked.

"I've had hotter," Paul gasped.

"You can give up now *Cockney-Boy*," said *Brain-Dead*, with a touch of pleading in his voice.

"Never!" replied Paul, wiping his forehead with his napkin.

And so it went on, spoonful by spoonful. Their companions could only pick at their own dishes, so absorbed were they in the contest. By the third spoonful, both Paul and *Brain-Dead* had bright red faces, down which torrents of sweat poured incessantly, and each of them shuddered in pain before they put the next spoonful into their mouths. By the time they had reached half way, their bodies were obviously involuntarily reacting to the poison being poured into them and they gagged continuously. Then *Brain-Dead*, followed by Paul, developed uncontrollable hiccups and shivering, but they persevered until the entire bowlful was gone.

"Ummm," said *Brain-Dead* touching around his mouth with his napkin as though he had just finished a particularly crumbly canape, "not bad for a Southern puff."

"Not so bad yourself, for a Northern tyke," replied Paul, leaning back in his chair and gasping for breath.
The two of them sat motionless for a moment before *Brain-Dead* suddenly threw his chair backwards, leapt in the air and bolted across the restaurant. A woman, who had been waiting for the (only) tiny bathroom to be vacated by a male diner and was just closing the door behind her, was suddenly grabbed by the arm and thrown back into the restaurant with such force that she tumbled into a table. Her husband stood up and shouted 'Oi' at *Brain-Dead*, but he was already inside, tugging down his pants in full view of the diners as he struggled to close the bathroom door at the same time.

"Oh god, oh God" he screamed, trying to disrobe and sit down before the exploding torrent of excrement came shooting out of his trembling sphincter.

Paul watched this with a smirk on his face until *Brain-Dead* had succeeded in closing the door and he was sure he could no longer be seen. He then stood up and grabbed a jug of water off the table and poured the entire contents, ice and a slice of lemon included, down his throat. As the water spilled down his front, he slammed the jug down again on the table and frantically started scratching at his tongue with his fingernails, screaming as he tried to remove the source of the pain, with tears pouring down his face.

The noises from the bathroom, meanwhile, were frightening the civilians in the restaurant. Even before its present incumbent arrived, the bathroom had left much to be desired. It was so small and in such close proximity to the tables that even careful occupants couldn't help but be heard within then restaurant and, when the thin door was opened, toilet smells filtered out to the nearby tables. Now, however, despite *Mr. Slime* turning the sitar music up to full blast, the sound of screams and aquatic explosions were audible to all. A party of four asked to move tables, holding their noses, and a couple, who had wandered down the stairs, turned on their heels and retraced their steps with sheer horror written on their faces. *Mr. Slime* watched the devastation in his restaurant with tears in his eyes. He could see his business disappearing with every flush and with every jug of water that Paul poured over himself as if he were taking a shower. Even *Lard-Arse* looked up occasionally to take in the scene, before getting his head down again and ordering more sauce and rice. The rest of the Sheaf Hall party just laughed uncontrollably, with the exception of an embarrassed Joanne, and Pam, who muttered that 'tonight's shag had just gone down the toilet.'

Dave decided to steer Paul outside into a tatty backyard where, *Mr. Slime* informed him, a 'tap' ('spigot' to Dave) could be found, partly to help Paul and partly to get away from Cathy, who was coming on to him again. Once outside, it took a full fifteen minutes of constantly pouring water over Paul to calm him down.

"Oh god man, I feel awful. What have I done?" moaned Paul sitting down on a step next to the spigot and beside large tins of ghee butter.

"You've just had one motherfucker of a curry," laughed Dave. "I don't envy you when you take a shit!"

"There is no way I am taking a shit for a week," replied Paul, listening to *Brain-Dead's* howls emanating from the restaurant.

"Shall we try to get you home?" asked Dave.

"Yeah, good idea, I need to lie down."

So Dave went inside to rejoin the others who, by now, had finished their meals. The check was then asked for and subsequently divided and paid for. After taking *Brain-Dead's* share out of his jacket pocket, Pam walked over to the bathroom.

"It's time to go now," she whispered at the door.

"I can't move", came a whimper from the other side.

"You can't stay here all night."

"I've got no fucking choice. Every time I try to stand up, my guts turn head over heels and 'wham' I fill the bowl again. Oh god, my arsehole's red raw."

"Ah, a romantic meal out with my new lover. What a lucky girl I am. Come on, you've got to move. *Mr. Slime's* sharpening his knives 'cause you're ruining his business."

"But I can't move!"

"You've got to move, or I'm going home without you," said Pam, getting angry.

"Don't leave me!" *Brain-Dead* was actually crying big, hot tears now.

"Clean yourself up and get out now, otherwise you're on your own, *Buddy Boy.*"

There was a rustling and the toilet was flushed yet again, then came the sound of the lock being opened. Slowly the door opened and *Brain-Dead's* head poked out. He looked so white and ghostly that Pam gasped, before laughing.

"Oh shit!" he yelled again, before disappearing back inside to 'fill the bowl' again.

When he did finally make it out, he was walking like an old cowboy who'd spent a lifetime in the saddle. He was so bowlegged, you could have driven a car through them and he was bent over as if he had curvature of the spine. Everyone in the restaurant laughed and even *Mr. Slime* had to cover a grin with his sleeve.

"Fuck off, you bastards!" he yelled to the restaurant without looking up.

"Do you want any more of that sauce, it's free!" laughed *Lard-Arse.*

"*Fatty*, when I can walk again I'm going to shove that fat head of yours so far up your fat arse..."

"Bit hot for you was it?" asked Paul, who'd regained enough composure to make it back into the restaurant to collect his belongings.

"Is that you *Hippy*?" asked *Brain-Dead* who, being unable to lift his gaze above waist height, couldn't see that Paul looked like he'd taken a shower fully dressed. "It wasn't the heat of the curry that was the problem, the chicken must have been off. I've got food poisoning."

Two more prospective diners disappeared up the stairs on hearing this and *Mr. Slime's* face rippled with anger for the first time in all his years of putting up with drunken racism and people trying to run off without paying.

"*Mr. Dead*, that is a most unfair thing to say about my restaurant. I would ask you to please not say such things again."

"Apologize to the man right now," snapped Pam.

"Sorry," mumbled *Brain-Dead.*

"Louder!" ordered Pam.

"I'm sorry *Mr. S.*," said *Brain-Dead* loudly, but still unable to look up.

"Thank you *Mr. Dead*," smiled *Mr. Slime.* "I will be most honored to serve you in my restaurant again. But next time you have a Korma."

The Sheaf Hall party all laughed and thanked *Mr. Slime* and Mohammed before trooping across the restaurant and up the stairs; only *Brain-Dead* didn't troop, he hobbled. By the time he'd made it up the stairs, it had been decided that Paul would drive *Brain-Dead*, Pam and Joanne home and that the others would walk. As they were saying their goodbyes outside, however, *Brain-Dead* had to shoot behind a bus shelter and discharge another gallon of liquid. Unfortunately for him, as he was crouched with his pants and shorts around his ankles and with a stream of liquid pissing out of his skinny white ass, he was caught in the headlights of a bus pulling up at the bus stop. More than a dozen people getting off the bus then had to walk straight past him, pointing and laughing.

"Farewell love's young dream!" sighed Pam, covering her eyes before going back into the restaurant to ask for some paper napkins for *Brain-Dead* to wipe his ass on.

The rest of the party waved their goodbyes as they set off up the hill and Dave quickened his pace to catch up with *The Bookseller* to thank him for his Film Studies advice but, more importantly, to escape Cathy's attentions. There had been literally hundreds of times in the past that he would have given his right arm for a guaranteed screw with someone as good-looking as Cathy, but tonight his mind was too full of Samantha and her talk of a 'date'. When they reached Sheaf Hall, Mike invited everyone to his room for a coffee and Cathy invited Dave to her room for a 'nightcap', but Dave made his apologies and wandered off to his room to try to figure out the meaning behind Samantha's words.

ELEVEN

As Dave opened the door to the shower room the following morning he could hear a faint sobbing noise coming from behind the locked toilet door.

"Hello," he said to the door.

"Is that you *Stud?*" came the pitiful reply.

"Yes, *Brain-Dead?*"

"Yes."

"You okay?"

"No, I'm not very well."

"Is your ass still sore?"

"Still sore? It's an open wound. I've been in here all fucking night. Every time I try to get up, I shit again. The furthest I've made it is to the sink to fill up my glass with water, just to give my body something to shit."

Brain-Dead then began sobbing uncontrollably. Dave could only laugh.

"You' re not laughing at me are you, you bastard?" wailed *Brain-Dead.*

"No, no, of course not. Is there anything I can get you?"

"A new arsehole! You are laughing at me aren't you, you fucking *Yank.* Just you wait till I get out. You'll be second on my list after I've wrung that fucking *Hippy's* neck."

Dave had to leave to laugh outside in the corridor, which was where he met Pam.

"How's the patient?" Pam asked with a grin.

"Not happy. He says he's been in there all night."

"Yeah, I can vouch for that. I stayed with him till about two-thirty, but the smell became so bad that I had to leave. Does it still stink in there?"

"No, it's perfectly safe."

"Oh well, I'd better go and mop his fevered brow. They don't tell you about this in *Mills & Boon* do they?" Pam laughed before pushing the door open. "Good Morning my love, *Nursey's* here!"

Dave left them to it, to go shit and shower in another block before going in search of Paul.

"Come in," Paul shouted to Dave's knock on his door.

Dave entered to find Paul lying on his bed.

"How are you this morning?" Dave asked.

"I've been better, man. I managed to get some sleep, but my stomach was bubbling all night and I thought my arse was going to explode on more than one occasion. Have you seen any sign of *Brain-Dead*?"

"Yeah, he's been in the can all night, crying his eyes out."

Paul smiled, but it was a worried smile.

"He was in a terrible state on the journey home. I had to stop the car three times for him to leap out for a shit. On one of those occasions he wasn't quick enough and shit in his pants! That's why I daren't go for a crap. I know if I do I'll be in agony, so I've decided just to lie here till it all calms down."

"You're not coming to breakfast then?"

"Oh no way, man. Joanne's gone out to get me some diarrhoea tablets to bung me up and some more *bakky*."

"You're not coming to Dr. Devine's lecture then?"

"No, I think I'll have to take a raincheck on that as well. It's just too risky. Send him my love though, will you?" Paul grinned.

After Dave had breakfasted, he returned to his room to find Pam with her coat on outside his room.

"I was looking for you. I thought we could wander down to Dr. Devine's lecture together," said Pam.

"Yeah sure, but how's the patient?"

"Somewhat sore around the rim, but he's made it back to his room and is even muttering about going to some party tonight!"

"You are joking?" Dave laughed, opening his door to collect his papers.

"No I'm not. Apparently he has a friend called *Muppet*, who's rated even higher on the loony scale than *Loverboy* in there; hard to comprehend I know. Anyway, *Muppet* always has a start-of-term party in his house, which by all accounts, makes the last debauched days of the Roman Empire seem like a puritan prayer meeting. We're all invited, which is no great honor as, from what I can gather, the entire world is invited. Oh yes, I almost forgot, he says you need to pack for Amsterdam tonight 'cause your bus leaves at five in the morning."

"What?" replied Dave, dropping the papers he was shoveling into his bag. "What time did you say?"

"Five in the morning," Pam repeated, "from the coach station in the center of town."

"The coach station? Surely we're not going by tour bus, it'll take forever!"

"That's what I thought he said. In fact he's planning to take his bag to the party and just go straight from there to the coach station. But you'd better check it out for yourself. Pop your head around the door as we're passing."

Dave finished packing his bag, locked the door and strolled along with Pam to knock on *Brain-Dead's* door.

"*Brain-Dead*," Dave whispered at the door, in case he was asleep.

There was no reply, but Dave thought he could hear the sound of running water. He was just about to call again when Pam pushed past him, opened the door and marched straight in.

"What the fuck are you doing, you crazy bastard?" laughed Pam.

Dave followed her in to see *Brain-Dead* sitting with his bare backside in the tiny sink with the cold faucet running, his feet were propped up on the back of his chair and he had the copy of *Pony Girl* open in his hands.

"My bum is so sore, I thought I'd cool it off under the cold tap, if you must know," *Brain-Dead* scowled.

"But we can see your 'block and tackle' hanging out and everything!" giggled Pam.

"My dear woman, if you had not barged into my boudoir you would not now be staring at my 'block and tackle'. However, since you arrived unannounced and since the university authorities decided against fitting bidets in all our rooms, decorum has had to take a back seat, leaving me no choice but to utilize my sink as a bum-basin, so that my poor, raw undercarriage may be refreshed by the cool and soothing waters."

"And THAT magazine?"

"Purely academic interest, my young filly. Unless, of course, you have equine tendencies!"

"Pam says we're going by tour bus to Amsterdam," Dave interrupted. "That's not right is it?"

"If by 'tour bus' you mean 'coach' then it is indeed correct my colonial friend. Unfortunately, our flabby companion shits his pants at the mere thought of travelling *par avian*. However, the coach is also the cheapest mode of transport, leaving us with more cash to splash on drugs and hussies!"

"On WHAT?" growled Pam.

"Naturally, when I spoke of hussies, I was referring to the bachelors in the party, my sweet, and not to myself. Now that I have lost my heart to you, you *Geordie Temptress*, I no longer have a need to empty my sacks into some Filipino whore; even if she is all dressed up in high heels, stockings and a basque and is begging for it. Oh no, I shall be found pining over a lonely beer in some dark corner, counting down the minutes 'till I may gaze upon your beautiful countenance again, my love. So, coming back to our mode of transport *Studly*, worry not about the coach, for you will find that it will prove to be a source of great pleasure. Think of it as a party on wheels. Whilst we imbibe humongous quantities of beer and spliff with like-minded folk, we will be transported magically to *The Dam*. Despite the early start, you will discover that the journey is one of the highlights of the trip. So, pack your belongings tonight, enjoy *Muppet's* hospitality 'till dawn, then we shall leap upon our magic carpet to the *Promised Land*!"

"Still sounds a bit goddam early," grumbled Dave.

"Come on David, time to make a move. Dr. Devine and *The Origins of the Cold War* await us," said Pam. "So farewell my love. I hope your bottom recovers enough to give me a shag tonight before you bugger off to Amsterdam and leave me all alone."

Brain-Dead wiggled his fingers in goodbye as they made towards the door, before opening up *Pony Girl* again.

After breaking the news of *Muppet's* party and Friday's early start to Paul, Dave and Pam set off down the hill to the Arts Tower. They still had plenty of time before the lecture so they just ambled in the fall sunshine. Dave did enjoy Pam's company; she constantly made him laugh, whether she meant to or not. But between the jokes today, Dave saw a melancholy side to Pam that had not been evident before. This morning Pam described to Dave how much she adored her father, despite his obvious weaknesses, and the problems she had relating to her bullying, vindictive mother. It appeared that she had spent most of her childhood trying to protect her father from a constant barrage of verbal and sometimes physical abuse emanating from her mother. Her father had never had any ambition further than a quiet life, growing his vegetables and his comfy chair in front of the television. Unfortunately for him, his wife saw life from a different perspective, wallowing in self-pity thanks to her 'champagne taste and beer money' and despising the husband whom she blamed for her predicament. She hated her home, was jealous of any neighbor who appeared more successful than her and constantly threatened to leave without ever lifting a finger to improve her lot or lift the gloom that surrounded her. Pam's brother had escaped from this living hell as soon as he was old enough, only returning under sufferance for an annual visit. Pam, meanwhile, had only ever once seen her mother happy, when she got drunk one Christmas and danced around the kitchen with the uncooked turkey. The family was made to pay for this episode of light relief, however, when she awoke the next day with a monumental hangover and blamed her husband for her affliction, making everyone's life even more of a misery throughout the 'festive' period and into New Years. Pam's gaining a place at college, instead of being a source of pride, as it was to Pam's father, merely caused her mother to reflect on how she had never had to same opportunities as her daughter. She had then spent the few weeks before Pam left home trying to persuade her daughter to turn her back on university and take a job in a department store in Newcastle, so that she wouldn't be left on her own with Pam's father.

Dave listened to Pam's story in silence, reflecting on how lucky he was to have supportive parents and marveling at how Pam had managed to develop and maintain such a wonderful sense of humor. Even as she related her story, Dave noted that there was no bitterness, just regret that her mother had ruined her own life and cast a dark shadow across those around her, especially Pam's father.

"Maybe that's why I've taken so quickly to that dickhead who, at this very moment, is reading porn with his arse in a sink; he's so full of life," Pam mused as they sat down in the lecture theater.

"Morning campers!" grinned Dr. Devine, striding past them to the lectern at the front. "I trust you all enjoyed the Cheese and Wine last week."

This was met with a few muffled giggles from the assembly.

"And I must thank you, young man," Dr. Devine said turning to Dave. "I've dreamed of pushing Professor Rogers into a fire for years but never had the bottle. So I take my hat off to you; good work! Now though, let us turn our attention to the origins of the Cold War which, for you, will be the start of two years of unbridled pleasure and academic fulfillment."

Later that evening Dave was sitting in a pub in Broomhill with a rejuvenated *Brain-Dead*, Pam, *Lard-Arse*, Paul (who still hadn't had a shit) and a stony-faced Joanne. Dr.
Devine's lecture, which had promised so much, had been as dry as a mouthful of crackers and had bored everyone senseless; something that did not bode well for the next two years. However, at this moment, Dave was in a self-righteous mood. He'd left Pam after the lecture and spent all afternoon in the library working on his now completed Crusades essay. It wasn't the finest work he had ever produced, but he figured it would certainly suffice and it freed him from any feeling of guilt about taking off to Amsterdam for the weekend. He had then packed a bag ready for the early start in the morning and was looking forward to the mayhem that *Muppet's* party promised.

While Paul was busy complaining to *Brain-Dead* and *Lard-Arse* about having to get up at four o'clock (something he'd never had to do in his life before) and exploring pointless alternatives, Dave was in deep conversation with Joanne about Samantha. Much to Dave's delight, Joanne informed him that Samantha was constantly talking about him and that she thought he was cute. However, she had also said that she thought Dave was toying with her; especially after Joanne had told her she'd seen him coming from Cathy's block only hours after their first 'date'. Although the news that she thought he was cute made Dave's heart miss a beat, Joanne could still not explain Samantha's relationship with Greg. When Joanne had pressed Samantha on it, she had become very defensive and told her that 'her friendship with Greg was non-negotiable',

"What the fuck does that mean?" Dave asked, exasperated.

"You tell me," replied Joanne.

"I mean, how I can I be toying with her when she's fucking with him?"

"Dunno, I've never seen them fucking. He's always around, but I've never seen them at it."

"You don't expect them to sell tickets do you?" Dave was nearly shouting by this point.

"It's no good getting cross with me, David. You asked me what I knew and I'm just telling you. There's no point shooting the messenger."

"Sorry. It's just that I find the whole thing bizarre and frustrating. She may be good looking, but I think she's a goddam headcase!"

Before Joanne could respond, however, the tranquility in the pub was suddenly broken by the entrance of a large, black gorilla. The gorilla burst through the double doors and ran up to a very large dude standing at the bar drinking with three equally large friends. The gorilla then danced about on the spot in front of the bemused drinkers before giving a rather muffled rendition of 'Happy Birthday'. The recipient of this attention clearly did not appreciate the gorilla's musical gift, which was evidenced by bulging of the tattoos on his neck. His mood then took a distinct turn for the worse when the gorilla finished singing and began throwing bananas at his face.

"What the fuck does tha' think tha's doin, twat?" growled the drinker.

The only response was in the shape of another banana, which bounced off the drinker's nose. This was patently too much for the drinker to bear as, in a flash, he began beating the crap out of the gorilla. The screams from inside the costume didn't deter him. In fact it only seemed to spur on the drinker's friends to join in the gorilla-bashing and, before long, the gorilla was on the floor taking a flurry of boots to the abdomen.

"Stop! Stop!" came a scream from the other side of the room, as a young woman ran over and started pulling the assailants away by their sleeves.

"Leave him alone, you bastards, that's my gorilla!" she yelled.

Eventually, the beating subsided and the assailants, after one more kick each for luck, returned to their drinks, leaving the gorilla in the fetal position on the floor with his arms around his head.

"You're from *Mike's Gorrillagram* yeah?" asked the girl.

"Yes," came the muffled and sobbing reply.

"For Houlden, Laurence Houlden?"

"Yes."

"We've been waiting for you. You're in the Lounge Bar and he's in the Public Bar. Follow me and I'll point him out to you."

"No fucking way!"

"What? What do you mean? I've paid for you."

"Well I fucking resign!" said the gorilla, gingerly getting to his feet.

"You can't resign, I've paid for you...it's all arranged for Laurie's birthday," pleaded the girl.

"Tough shit!"

"But what'll I say?"

"Tell 'Laurie' from me to go fuck himself, I'm going home," said the gorilla, dusting himself down.

"You bastard!" yelled the girl punching the gorilla full on the nose and, as he slumped to the ground yet again, she began kicking him in the abdomen with more venom than any of the previous assailants.

"Dangerous work being a gorilla," noted Paul, dragging on a roly before continuing his argument with *Brain-Dead* about coach travel.

This argument continued for the best part of an hour before Paul finally had to concede that it was too late to make any changes and that, if he wanted to go to Amsterdam, he had to be at the bus station at five in the morning. Once this had been settled, a new argument began over who had eaten the hottest part of the curry the night before. There was no resolution to this argument, however, and the protagonists eventually had to agree to differ, as it was time to buy some liquor and set off for *Muppet's* house. As they marched along, through a dark, deserted, litter-strewn   shopping center, where Lard-Arse had to stop and piss into a shop doorway despite the fact that he had left the pub only two minutes before, they joined groups of other people also heading to the party. As more and more people appeared from different directions and joined the throng, it reminded Dave of the crowd heading to the soccer match.

"How many people has *Muppet* invited?" Dave asked *Brain-Dead*.

"Shit loads," came the reply.

"Does he live in a big house?"

"Oh yeah, he lives with six other students, but they'll have invited shit loads of people as well and then all those people will bring their friends along too," grinned *Brain-Dead*. "I don't think the neighbors will be getting much sleep tonight!"

At that very moment, they turned a corner and saw a line of people snaking across the road to a large house on the corner. Every room in the house was lit up and, even from such a distance, the music was so deafening that the house seemed to be jumping. There was obviously a blockage in the funnel of people trying to squeeze in through the front door and it took over ten minutes to go the short distance from the gate to the door. The yard, or rather the scrubland that in the house's heyday had been a garden, was filled with partygoers who had either given up trying to reach the house or who had decided that the house was too full and had escaped outside. Here they were sitting on the wall or standing around sucking on cans of beer, being constantly jostled by the prospective entrants.

As Dave tumbled through the doorway, being pushed from behind by a wave of humanity, he lost his footing and fell face-first into someone's breasts.

"Gee I'm so sorry," he cried, looking up at a not unattractive girl.

"No problem," the owner of the face-cushion yelled over the din, "it's a bit crowded in here, isn't it?"

"Sure is," smiled Dave, resisting the temptation to add 'Nice tits!'

Dave was almost upright again when he received another push from behind which, once again, sent him flying into the same girl. This time he instinctively put out his hands to try to keep his balance, but only managed to find her breasts.

"Tit man are you?" the girl grinned.

"David!" laughed Pam.

"Jesus *Stud*, you don't waste any time do you?" grinned *Brain-Dead* from behind him.

"I'm sorry, I'm so sorry. I didn't mean to..." spluttered Dave.

"It's alright," smiled the girl. "You're the American doing Film Studies, aren't you? My name's Nicola. I saw you the other day, so I know how accident-prone you are. Written many more essays in the dark have you?"

Dave's attempted reply, however, was drowned out by *Brain-Dead* screaming *'Muppet'* so loud that even the sound system couldn't compete. The recipient of the scream was impossible to miss. He was at least seven feet tall with a face two feet wide and topped off (quite literally) with a mop of straw-colored hair that looked like a haystack after a particularly stormy night. As *Brain-Dead's* call met *Muppet's* ears, he turned his enormous bulk with all the finesse of a supertanker and bellowed a delighted *'Brain-Dead'* back, revealing an array of tombstone-like yellow teeth. Then, in a manner that reminded Dave of a giant or a nuclear blast smashing everything in its path, he set off through the crowd of partygoers towards *Brain-Dead*. As he ploughed along, scattering guests like an icebreaker through pack ice, he seemed oblivious to the carnage he was leaving in his wake. People were crashing into one another and into walls, drinks were flying and guests, who had finally made it to the doorstep, were launched back into the yard by a wall of escapees desperately trying to avoid being trampled underfoot. The next person to feel the force of this human tornado was Nicola, who was lifted clean off her feet and sent hurtling through the air - destination Dave! She took him out, like a defensive tackle getting a hit on a quarterback, and sent him sprawling backwards onto the floor. Luckily for Dave, his head was saved from a Humpty Dumpty experience by a soft landing on *Lard-Arse's* gut which, only moments before, had positioned itself on the hard, linoleum floor. *Lard-Arse* emitted a winded 'Ooooff!' as the back of Dave's head buried itself into his rolls of flab, before receiving the full force of a flying Nicola landing on Dave with the precision of a jet onto an aircraft carrier. *Muppet*, meanwhile, had reached *Brain-Dead* and had lifted him in the air as if he was a child in the arms of an over-affectionate uncle.

"You made it, *Bud*," bellowed *Muppet*, planting a huge kiss on *Brain-Dead's* cheek. "I love you *Bud*!"

"Sure did, *Mup*. Love ya' too man," croaked *Brain-Dead*, as if the lifeblood was being squeezed out of him and dropping his Amsterdam bag to the floor.

As *Muppet* swooped in to plant another kiss on *Brain-Dead's* rapidly whitening cheeks, *Brain-Dead* managed to escape asphyxiation by motioning towards Pam.

"Is this the bird?" asked *Muppet*, grinning down at Pam.

"Yes," panted *Brain-Dead*.

"Hullo *Bird*," bellowed *Muppet*, dropping *Brain-Dead* to the floor in a crumpled heap and extending a plate-sized hand towards Pam.

"Hello *Muppet*," smiled Pam sweetly as she watched her hand disappear into his massive paw.

"So you're the one who' s finally managed to trap my buddy *Brain-Dead*?" gurgled *Muppet*.

"Less of the 'trapped', if you don't mind," smiled Pam looking up at this enormous beast, who had made her over-large boyfriend look like a dwarf.

"Ho ho, I love you too *Babe*!" boomed *Muppet*, lifting Pam off the ground and kissing her on the cheek.

Dave, meanwhile, still had Nicola lying on top of him staring into his eyes as they, in turn, lay on the human equivalent of a waterbed, i.e. *Lard-Arse*.

"We mustn't keep meeting like this," grinned Nicola.

"When you two have quite finished, would you kindly bugger off and let me get up," puffed *Lard-Arse*.

"What' ya doin' on the floor *Lardy*?" asked *Muppet*, still holding Pam in mid air as one would hold a drink.

"Trying to fucking get up, that's what!" groaned *Lard-Arse*.

As Nicola and Dave disentangled themselves and climbed off *Lard-Arse*, *Muppet* dropped Pam and held out his paw to *Lard-Arse* before yanking him off the floor and into the air.

"Love ya' *Lardy*!" said *Muppet*, planting another sloppy kiss on *Lard-Arse's* cheek.

While *Muppet*, *Brain-Dead* and *Lard-Arse* continued this 'love-in', Dave, Paul and Joanne set off to find some space away from the crowds in the hallway. Clinging onto the drinks they'd brought, they joined the line of people that was shuffling its way towards the kitchen. Worryingly there was an equally slow line pushing its way in the opposite direction. When finally they arrived in the kitchen, they realized why. The kitchen was every bit as crammed as the hallway and they now had to execute a turn and retrace their steps, pushing against the tide in the process. As this took some time, Dave had plenty of opportunity to take in the squalor that surrounded him and give thanks that he was not a resident of this particular student house. The kitchen did an excellent impression of a Mumbai slum. Where, presumably, the trash can should have been, there was a midden; a pile of garbage four feet across and three feet deep, taking up an entire corner of the kitchen. Although the party could account for a few of the beer cans and bottles nestled on top of this pile of stinking detritus, it could not account for the rotting takeout food containers, newspapers and chicken carcasses that made up the bulk of the heap. The sink, meanwhile, was an overflowing sewer of dirty cups and plates in a sea of jet-black water, covered with a thick layer of strangely orange-colored fat and grease. In the opposite corner was the toilette of some wretched feline, who must have to climb to the top of a foot- high pile of now-solid cat litter and turds every time it needed a shit. Just then Joanne shrieked with horror at the sight of the stove.

"Oh my god, look at the state of that cooker!" she wailed, putting her hand over her mouth.

The stove was indeed worthy of a shriek. It was a museum piece, circa 1930, with strangely shaped gas knobs and was blackened through years of abuse, with congealed fat pouring down the sides and the back plate beneath the grill like wax down a candle. In the tray holding the gas rings was a two-inch deep lake of fat, punctuated with islands of long-forgotten foodstuffs and even the handles of submerged items of cutlery.

"Only men could live like this," pronounced Joanne.

"Sorry to blow your theory out of the water, my dearest," smiled Paul, "but *Brain-Dead* told me that there are two female residents in this particular house."

"Well they should make them honorary blokes. Do you think this is a 'squat'? Surely no one would pay to live in a house like this?" asked Joanne puzzled.

Nobody answered her. Instead they pressed on with the tour of the kitchen and made for the front room. The lounge was only slightly less crowded and was also the home of the hi-fi, which was pumping out music so loud that they had to cover their ears as they entered. This room somehow managed to be as disgusting as the kitchen without the obvious advantage of the rotting food. It attained this unlikely feat with a combination of downright seediness and pure filth. Every wall had been painted a different but equally garish color, presumably several years before, but apart from that, the walls were bare. The dangling lamp shade must have been the height of fashion in the 1920's, but now was torn and battered with a lace trim dangling from it and the bodies of a hundred bugs submerged and semi-submerged in a blanket of dust. Above this, an impressively large slug was busily drawing abstract patterns of slime on the ceiling. They jumped off the human conveyor belt and pushed their way to a corner by the window, where they could just about stand without being barged every few seconds. There was still no room to take their coats off, but they did manage to put their cans of beer on the floor between their feet.

"Great carpet!" said Paul,

"What?" shouted Joanne.

"I was just admiring the carpet," Paul yelled back.

Joanne squinted her eyes, trying to focus on the only patch not being trampled upon.

"What are you talking about? It's disgusting."

"Yeah, but it must have been a lovely carpet when it was new," pleaded Paul.

Dave and Joanne exchanged glances of sheer disbelief. To their eyes, it was an ancient Persian rug, so tatty and threadbare that there was more 'bare' than 'thread', exposing acres of black floorboards and sporting an immense oil slick stain.

"I sometimes worry about you," replied Joanne, rolling her eyes.

"Paul, you can't be serious; it's terrible. It looks like someone's stripped a car engine on it," laughed Dave.

"No, no I like it. I like this house, it's got character!" said Paul, in all seriousness. "Maybe we could live here next year when we move out of hall."

Dave looked around him, desperately trying to see what Paul was seeing, but the only thing that came into view was a highly suspicious gas fire with lumps of a black substance clinging to the grid and bars, indicating a lethally blocked chimney.

"I can't stand this," screamed Joanne at the top of her voice. "Get me out of here!"

"Chill out Babe, we've just arrived and the party's only just started. I'll roll you a spliff," said Paul helpfully.

"I don't want one of your bloody spliffs, I just want to go home. I tell you Paul, you're in for a bloody shock if you ever sober up long enough to see what the world really looks like," hissed Joanne.

Paul, looking very hurt, did manage to persuade Joanne to stay while they drank a couple of cans of beer but, although the crowds died down slightly and they could now nearly hear each other speak, he finally had to concede defeat and agree to take her home.

"Are you coming back with us, man?" Paul asked, obviously annoyed that he was being robbed of a good party.

"No thanks. I think I'll stay on for a while," Dave replied.

The two of them then agreed to meet in Sheaf Hall car park at four-thirty in the morning and that Paul would order a taxi to take them down to the bus station to catch the Amsterdam bus. Dave waved them off, before going off to explore. He first tried the kitchen again, but failed to meet anyone he knew and instead met a group who stopped talking and stared at him when he entered. Taking the hint, and bursting for a piss, he climbed the narrow stairs in search of a bathroom, which he found occupied. Unfortunately his brain had informed his bladder that relief was imminent and it came as a crushing blow to find that it wasn't. His bladder was not at all happy with this development and was threatening to explode. Dave was trying to distract it by hopping from foot to foot and massaging his penis, when the lock clicked and the bathroom door opened.

"Hello again!" Nicola smiled sweetly from the doorway.

"Hullo," grimaced Dave, still hopping.

"I was looking for you, where you've been?"

"Downstairs...look I'm sorry but I'm really desperate!"

"Oh sorry," laughed Nicola, standing aside as Dave charged in and flicked the lock behind him.

"Oh God, oh God," cried Dave, struggling with his fly, still hopping and with sweat now pouring down his forehead. He could now feel the urine making its journey from his bladder and knew there was no stopping it - this was a race, pure and simple. Would he manage to get his penis out and point it in the right direction in time, or would he wet himself? He yanked his penis out from the depths of his shorts just as his foreskin inflated like a balloon from the pressure of a tsunami of urine. His sigh of relief was short-lived, however, because the end of his foreskin was in hibernation mode and was curled up and stuck to the side of his penis like a sleeping dog. The net result, as it unfurled itself, was that although he was pointing it directly at the porcelain, a stream of yellow urine shot off at forty-five degrees onto the floor to the right of the toilet. An expert in prostrate exercises and bladder control might have been able to stem the flow, but

Dave was neither; not after several pints of beer. Knowing this, his only course of action was to spin around forty-five degrees to his left to correct the alignment. The stream was now heading in the right direction, but at the wrong trajectory, causing Dave to thoroughly soak the bottom of the raised seat. Still standing at right angles to the toilet bowl, he aimed lower to finally get some in the bowl, but it was still like firing at a moving target. As his foreskin kept unfurling, it was like moving a finger over the end of a hosepipe and Dave had to keep moving to compensate. When the flow subsided, he was left to examine the dripping mess.

"Oh shit!" he moaned.

He would have mopped up using the one and only roll of toilet paper but, as there was no toilet roll holder, it was on the floor to the right of the toilet and he'd pissed all over it.

"What the fuck do I do now?" he asked himself.

There was a towel slung over the side of the bath, but he could hardly use someone's towel to mop up piss and he could hardly ask *Muppet* for a mop and bucket without acknowledging what he'd done. Relief came when he stopped panicking and took a good long look at his surroundings, realising that the bathroom was in such a disgusting state already that no one would actually notice his contribution. The toilet itself was encrusted with oddly colored fur deposits, which hadn't been attacked with disinfectant in a generation. The wall behind the toilet had solid waves and splash marks of dried urine from years of near misses, making it look like paint that had run before drying. And, even though Dave had soaked the carpet to the right of the toilet bowl, when he pressed his foot on the left hand side, it was like treading on soggy, stinking moss. Further afield, the bathtub had obviously received as much love and attention as the toilet. Anyone stupid enough to bathe in it would certainly emerge dirtier than when they went in. The sides were layered with black tidemarks, beneath the faucets were brown teardrop-shaped stains and an overall layer of dust and grime finished it off to a tee. Cheering up, Dave decided that there was nothing he could do but beat a hasty retreat. His one concession was to leave the toilet seat up to allow it to drain. He would have washed his hands, but there was no soap, so he just flushed the toilet, zipped himself up and went for the door.

As he stepped into the hall, a girl took his place and locked the door behind her. Dave winced as he heard her yelling "Oh my God, what a disgusting mess!" moments later.

"It is pretty horrible in there, isn't it?" smiled Nicola, standing a few feet down the corridor.

"Er...yes, yes it is," stuttered Dave.

"I don't know how anyone could live like this. I know I couldn't," Nicola continued.

"Er...no, me neither."

"You coming downstairs?"

"Er...yeah," replied Dave following her.

Nicola led Dave into the kitchen and introduced him to the group who had been so pleased to see him a few minutes before. They were predominately from Rivelin Hall, with a few pompous English majors thrown in for good measure. Dave didn't know if he had done something to upset them, if they disliked all Americans or if they were just rude to everyone; for a moment he even wondered if they somehow knew about his toilet accident. They just carried on talking amongst themselves, totally ignoring Dave, who just stood on the fringes smiling inanely and sipping his now-warm beer. He tried to interject into the conversation on two occasions, but his supposedly witty remarks brought nothing but distain and 'who said you could talk?' looks in return. There's only so much of this a man can take and in Dave's case that was about ten minutes. He didn't bother saying 'Goodbye', he just ambled away to go and look for Pam, *Brain-Dead* and *Lard-Arse*.

He didn't have to look very far, as all three plus *Muppet* and a couple of other people Dave didn't know were in the front room he had vacated earlier. The crowds had certainly dissipated, leaving enough room to stand and there was even a vacant chair. His friends were sitting on and around a sofa that looked as if it had been reclaimed from a garbage dump, passing round an unfeasibly large joint.

"*Stud!*" screamed *Brain-Dead*, seeing Dave approach.

Dave smiled. After the hostile reception in the kitchen, it was a relief to feel wanted again and *Brain-Dead*, for all his faults, was like a faithful dog that had been waiting all day for his beloved master to return home.

"*Muppet*, this is *Stud*, he's only a fresher but he's a Yank and he's a bird magnet. He's nailed several already, the dirty bastard!" grinned *Brain-Dead*.

"He's done what?" asked Pam.

"Nailed a few fillies?"

"What a horrible expression! Does that mean that you've 'nailed' me then?" asked Pam scornfully.

"Baby I nailed you good and proper!" laughed *Brain-Dead*, extending his monstrous tongue.

"Pleased to meet you *Stud*," smiled Muppet, standing up and once again startling Dave with his size as he shook Dave's hand.

"Pleased to meet you as well *Muppet*," replied Dave, watching his hand being swallowed. "Nice house!"

"It's a shithole but we love it," laughed *Muppet*. "The nice thing about living in a shithole like this is you never worry about tidying up and you can have as many parties as you like 'cause it can't be trashed any more than it is already."

"Grab a pew and take a toke on this," smiled *Lard-Arse*, handing Dave the spliff.

As Dave sat down on the edge of the sofa and took the joint off *Lard-Arse*, Nicola walked into the room and approached Dave.

"So this is where you skulked off to as soon as I turn my back," she said to Dave.

"See what I mean *Muppet*? The boy' s insatiable," laughed *Brain-Dead*. "Hey *Bird*, you do realize what you're dealing with don't you?"

"Are you talking to me?" asked Nicola.

"Nicola, this is *Brain-Dead*. *Brain-Dead* this is Nicola," Dave interjected.

"Yeah...Nicola, I'm just warning you that you're playing with fire here. This shy-looking, apparently innocuous chap before you is in fact a sex beast, who will have your knickers off and you ankles behind your ears before you can yell 'Mummy'. Just thought you ought to know."

"*Brain-Dead*!" spluttered Dave.

"Well thank you...'*Brain-Dead*', but I am a big girl and I think I can look after myself; if it's alright with you."

"Ignore him, he's always like this. I should know because he's 'nailing' me apparently. Anyway my name's Pam, pleased to meet you. Come and join us. Come on *Lard-Arse*, squeeze up a bit," said Pam, pushing *Lard-Arse* along the sofa to give Nicola somewhere to sit.

"Thanks," Nicola smiled at Pam, taking a seat.

The group then spent the next hour or so chatting, drinking and smoking, interrupted only by changing the music occasionally (which thankfully was down to a level that didn't make your ears bleed) and by guests saying 'Goodbye' to *Muppet*. Dave, who had been chatting away to Nicola for most of this time, eventually glanced at his watch.

"Jesus, it's half past twelve!"

"Well, you're not going to turn into a pumpkin or something are you?" laughed Nicola.

"No, no...it's just that I've got to be up at four to leave for Amsterdam."

"I told you you should have brought your bag with you," scolded *Brain-Dead*.

Dave acknowledged that *Brain-Dead* was right but, be that as it may, he still had to get back and get his head down.

"You can walk me home," announced Nicola, standing up as well.

"Hey hey!" howled *Brain-Dead*.

"Shut up you idiot!" Pam snapped at him. "Ignore my boyfriend Nicola, he's a mental patient. It was very nice to meet you. David, have a good time in Amsterdam and watch over this fool for me will you?"

Dave agreed to do what he could and said his goodbyes.

"Don't forget *Stud*, five o'clock at the bus station, shagging or no shagging," called *Brain-Dead* as Dave and Nicola walked towards the door.

"Sorry about that," said Dave.

The two of them walked up the hill in the direction of the 'halls of residence'. Apparently, according to Nicola, Rivelin Hall was very close to Sheaf Hall, Dave had just never noticed it. Dave hardly spoke a word, not only because he was feeling tired, but because he couldn't get a word in edgeways; Nicola never stopped talking. At one point Dave began wondering if she could breathe through her ears or something, as she didn't even pause to draw breath. But the worst of all was that by the time they approached Rivelin Hall, he couldn't remember a single thing Nicola had been talking about. This was possibly because he didn't care; the snippets he had tuned into were trivial in the extreme and he had tuned out again just as quickly. But he'd promised to walk her home and walk her home he would. As they entered Rivelin Hall, Dave felt strangely uneasy; it was as though he was entering an alien and potentially hostile environment. He knew it was ridiculous, but Sheaf Hall already felt like home and this place unnerved him, as though he was intruding on someone else's territory. Rivelin Hall was much more of a high-rise, without the center quad of Sheaf Hall, and felt bleaker as a result. Where Sheaf Hall had wooden floors and the accompanying smell of polish, Rivelin had concrete floors and a colder, harsher ambience as a result. A security guard in a front office with glass windows glanced up from his television as they pushed open the big front doors, but at once ignored them. Dave had half expected him to ask him who he was and what he was doing there, but then again how could the guard know all the residents one week into the new semester? Even if he had questioned him, presumably there was no rule banning guests. It was co-ed after all, not a convent! Finally, Dave decided that the joints he had smoked were giving him 'The Horrors' and that he should just pull himself together, so he followed Nicola past the front desk to the elevator.

"You're obviously coming up for a coffee then?" smiled Nicola.

"Er..." Dave had been in so deep in his trance that he hadn't thought to stop outside and bid her goodnight.

"Er...OK".

The elevator was very 1960's. A big, black push button, with the word 'Up' rubbed out by decades of use, called it and when it came the metal doors screeched open. Once inside, the doors screeched closed again, scraping off

319

a few more microns of metal. Then, as the elevator moved upwards, it sounded as if it was being hoisted up on chains. The elevator was surprisingly small for such building. According to a sign on the wall, it could hold a maximum of six people but, in reality, only four comfortably and Dave imagined the lines that must build up at the busier times of day. It stopped moving at the fourth floor and Dave moved forward expecting the doors to open, but they didn't budge. He stared at the doors, willing them to move, but nothing happened. He felt 'The Horrors' surge through him again and he broke out in a cold sweat.

"Oh shit!" he whispered. "Don't worry," soothed Nicola, "it always does this."

And sure enough, her words were sill hanging in the air as the doors screeched open and Dave leapt out.

"Women and children first, eh?" laughed Nicola.

Nicola strolled out and headed off down the corridor.

"Come on then," she called without looking back.

Dave followed her down the narrow corridor past rows of identical bedroom doors, through two sets of fire doors that crashed behind them and on towards the sound of people laughing and the smell of burnt toast. Nicola paused at the source of this activity, a tiny kitchen, as Dave caught up.

"Evening all," said Nicola to the occupants of the kitchen.

As Dave arrived by her side he found a group of six or seven people crammed into the small space; some standing, a couple sitting on the work surfaces, one buttering toast and another pouring boiling water onto a group of mugs - the latter not worrying that hot water was spilling everywhere as he moved from mug to mug without lifting the kettle. One young man, who was sitting on the counter, sporting a goatee beard and a particularly stupid woolly hat, grinned at Nicola before scowling when Dave arrived.

"Hi Nic, got company?" he asked.

"As sharp as ever Brian!" laughed Nicola. "This is Dave, everyone."

A chorus of 'Hi's' and 'Hello's' was directed at Dave, who responded in kind. Brian merely scowled.

"So, where did you pick up this stray?" asked Brian, menacingly.

Dave bristled.

"Go fuck yourself Brian!" Nicola responded. "Come on Dave."

Taking Dave's hand, she led him off down the corridor. Behind them there was silence for a few moments, before the murmur of whispered conversations began.

"Who's that motherfucker?" Dave asked, with adrenalin still coursing through his veins and his fists clenched.

"That was Brian. He latched onto me on day one and I've been trying to shake him off ever since. He's alright really, but he treats me like I'm his ex-wife. Anyway, here we are."

Nicola stopped at one of the gray doors and fumbled around in her little, black, bead-covered handbag for a key, which she eventually found and used to unlock the door.
Inside, the lamps were on and, yet again, Dave was amazed at how cozy and lived-in it was. Nicola threw her bag on the desk under the window and her coat over the back of the only chair.

"Are you coming in then?" she asked Dave, who was still standing in the corridor.

Dave entered and stood in the middle of the room.

"Well...take your coat off, make yourself at home," Nicola laughed. "Grab a pew," pointing at the bed.

Dave took off his coat and laid it over Nicola's on the chair, before sitting on the edge of the bed.

"Coffee?" asked Nicola. "Er...yes please."

"White?"

"Yes please."

"Will whitener do, I haven't got any milk."

"Yeah sure."

Nicola then grabbed a very trendy kettle from the corner of her desk (Dave made a mental note to get a one himself - good idea!) and pulled open a door that led into a small shower room/toilet.

"You've got your own bathroom!" Dave exclaimed.

"Yeah, haven't you?"

"No, we have to share a bathroom and toilet with everyone on the floor."

"Ergh...gross," called Nicola, filling up the kettle from behind the door.

She then reappeared and plugged the kettle in, before disappearing again, pulling the door only half shut. Dave heard the toilet lid being lifted up and a rustling as, presumably,
Nicola pulled down her jeans.

"That girl you were at Film Studies with, she was very pretty. Is she your girlfriend?" Nicola called from the bathroom.

"Er...no," Dave called back.

Nicola carried on talking but Dave didn't listen to what she was saying. All he could hear was the 'Ssssshhhhh' sound of Nicola's piss streaming into the toilet bowl.

"Oh my God, that's disgusting!" Dave whispered out loud to himself.

Nicola carried on talking over the rumble of the toilet paper being tugged off the roll and Dave, horrified, convinced himself that he could hear a squeaking sound as she dried her 'undercarriage'. She was still talking as she reappeared, zipping up the flies on her jeans as she went. Dave gave her an 'Aren't you going to wash your hands?' look, but she didn't notice it.

"Biscuit?" she asked, pulling a tin off the shelf and shoving a large oatmeal cookie into her mouth.

"No thanks."

Nicola then continued making the coffees, before turning on a CD player by the bed, switching on a lamp and turning off the main light. She handed Dave his coffee before sitting crossed-legged on the bed next to him. Throughout all of this she talked incessantly and laughed at her own jokes without once waiting for a reply from Dave. Dave, meanwhile, had finally realized that Nicola had designs on him. Now to any neutral observer this would have been blatantly obvious long before it came as a revelation to Dave. But, for reasons he could not explain and only partly explained by the cannabis he'd smoked, it came as quite a shock and he didn't know what he thought about this. There was no doubt that she was attractive and, unsurprisingly, he was beginning to get aroused, but his head was still full of Samantha and Nicola's toilet antics had disgusted him somewhat; although he did acknowledge that after his performance earlier he was 'a pot calling the kettle black'.

While Dave was mulling these thoughts over in his mind, Nicola had finished her coffee, taking glugs between the incessant chatter, and moved closer to him. She kept talking as she began patting his thigh, pulling her hand away at first and then leaving it to massage his leg. By the time she leaned over to kiss him, Dave had convinced himself that sleeping with Nicola wasn't such a bad move after all and offered up a raging erection for her to massage through his pants. As their tongues toyed with each other, Dave took her right breast in his hand and tickled her nipple into erection. Nicola was now breathing heavily and had worked her hand into his shorts to find his erection. Then, letting go, she lay back on the bed, pulling Dave onto her as she went. Dave immediately got to work on opening Nicola's shirt buttons, to reveal a white T-shirt underneath. She sat up to let him pull the shirt free and helped by undoing the buttons on the cuffs that Dave was struggling with, before dropping back down again. Dave shuffled down the bed slightly to start kissing her stomach, massaging her breasts and shoving her T-shirt up at the same time. He had just exposed Nicola's bra and had nestled his face between her breasts when he recoiled with horror. Nicola had body odor! This wasn't just the musty smell of sex or the faint whiff of sweat, this was full-on, mature cheese, old sneakers, throat-clawing, terminal body odor - the Mother of all Body Odors. Dave gasped at the light- brown circles under the armpits of her white T-shirt and winced when the inevitable question dawned, 'If her armpits were this bad, what would the inside of her panties be like?'

"What? What is it?" Nicola asked.

"Oh God, what do I say?" Dave asked himself. "I can hardly tell her she

323

stinks!"

"Er...er..." Dave mumbled pathetically.

"What?" Nicola was getting cross now.

"I...um...I...I just remembered..."

"Remembered what?"

"Er...remembered that I've got to go and catch a bus."

"What? There are no busses running now"

"I've got to catch a coach...to Amsterdam."

"What?" said Nicola sitting up, her T-shirt still hunched up over her bra.

"Yes."

"But your coach isn't until five. I heard your friend telling you," Nicola then smiled. "You've got plenty of time, plenty of time to give me a good seeing to!"

She then lay back on the bed and cupped her breasts in her hands.

"But...I've got to pack," Dave pleaded.

"Pack later, fuck me now," Nicola giggled, closing her eyes as she massaged her breasts.

"No, I can't. I...I've got to go."

"What?" yelled Nicola, sitting up as Dave reversed himself away from her, "You're joking?"

"No, no, I've got to go."

"You bastard!"

"Sorry."

"Are you gay or something?" Nicola snarled.

"No...it's just that I've got to go," Dave mumbled as he stood up.

"Well fuck off then!"

Dave didn't respond, he simply grabbed his coat, pulled open the door and fell out into the corridor without looking back as the door closed behind him. He then hurried off down the corridor, pulling on his jacket as he went, crashing through the fire doors and keeping his head down as he passed the kitchen. When he reached the elevator, he pressed the button but, after waiting momentarily and looking nervously back down the corridor to see if Nicola was chasing after him, caught sight of a door marked 'Stairs' and shot through it. He tumbled down each flight, taking five or six stairs at a time and twisting his ankle on one leap, until he finally crashed through the double doors that led into the lobby. The security guard glanced up from his television to see what the commotion was, but Dave just scampered past him in a blur and shot out into the cold, dark night. As he hurried off down the drive, he did take a quick look back towards the building to see if Nicola was at a window, but it was a rather pointless exercise as he didn't know which was her room anyway!

When he finally made it back to his room in Sheaf Hall and locked the door behind him, he started to calm down. He stood by the door panting, still with his jacket on until he took a hold of himself and began laughing.

"You stupid dick!" he laughed out loud. "What did you expect her to do, chase after you and rape you?"

He stopped smiling, however, while brushing his teeth when he suddenly realized that he would have to face Nicola in Film Studies and it was a somewhat preoccupied Dave who turned out the light and fell into bed.

TWELVE

"Wake up man!"

Dave sat bolt upright in bed.

"Are you in there man?"

"What?" mumbled Dave, disorientated.

"Come on man, get up. The taxi's here."

Dave jumped out of bed, his heart pounding and fumbled for the door in the dark. When he found and opened it he also found Paul standing in front of him, coat on and with a bag at his feet.

"Come on man, hurry up, we're late and the taxi's here," Paul continued, walking into the room.

"What time is it?" asked Dave, rubbing his eyes.

"Quarter to five. Come on man, get your shit together or we'll miss the coach,"

"But I haven't had a shower," mumbled Dave, still half asleep.

"No time for that now, just get some clothes on and grab your bag."

Dave did as he was told. He didn't even have time to brush his teeth, he just jumped into some clothes, picked up his bag (congratulating himself on having packed it the day before) and ran after Paul across the Quad to the waiting cab.

"I nearly left you man," Paul confessed as they sat in the back of the cab racing along wet and empty streets towards the center of town, with Indian music blaring out at full blast. "I was knocking for a full five minutes and I nearly went 'cause I thought you'd stayed at the party with *Brain-Dead*."

"No I...I didn't," muttered Dave.

"Hey man, can I smoke in here?" Paul asked the driver, having just licked the gum down on a freshly made roly.

The driver didn't answer, he simply pointed to the 'No Smoking' sign glued to the dashboard.

"I feel like shit," said Dave. "I always feel like shit if I don't have a shower."

"Too fucking late for that man," laughed Paul. "You're gonna feel like total shit after a coach journey all the way to Amsterdam! You'll just have to get totally fucking stoned on the way, that'll make you feel better."

Dave and Paul kept examining their watches as the taxi sped towards the bus station, but they couldn't ask the driver to go any faster as that would have been impossible. As it was they were gripping onto the handles above the doors as the cab skidded around corners and only momentarily slowed down, but didn't stop, for red traffic lights. It was approaching ten past five when they screeched to a halt outside the bus station where, thankfully, a small group of people including *Brain-Dead* and *Lard-Arse* was gathered.

"'Bout bloody time!" yelled *Brain-Dead* as they pulled their bags from the boot of the taxi and Paul paid the fare. "You dirty bastard *Stud*, shagging all night were you?"

Paul raised his eyebrows with a questioning look at Dave as he lit his cigarette. "Oh yeah man, who was she?" he asked, blowing smoke out of his mouth.

"I wasn't screwing actually," replied Dave as they joined *Brain-Dead* and *Lard-Arse* in the bus shelter.

"Oh no?" laughed *Brain-Dead*. "What were you doing with her then?"

"I just walked her home, that's all," Dave protested.

"I had to wake him up, that's why we're late," grinned Paul.

"Shagging, obviously," added *Lard-Arse*.

"Well, you're in luck, *Shag-Meister*," said *Brain-Dead*, "the coach is late."

And he was right, it was late; forty-five minutes late in fact. But it didn't matter as the time was spent with *Brain-Dead* whipping everyone into a frenzy about the debauched time they were going to have on the journey. According to *Brain-Dead* they were going to be so stoned and have such great fun on the 'Party coach from heaven' that they would seriously consider not getting off when it arrived in Amsterdam. The hype was so intense that when the tatty, dirty, noisy heap of junk that was their vehicle to the *Promised Land* did eventually clatter into view instead of the gilded carriage bedecked with fairly lights that Dave was expecting, he felt rather dejected. Worse was to come. As it pulled up and the door hissed open, a dozen or so miserable creatures piled out onto the sidewalk and instantly lit cigarettes. *Brain-Dead* led the way up the steps followed by Paul, with *Lard-Arse* and Dave bringing up the rear; all carrying their bags which, in *Lard-Arse's* case, was particularly large.

"Here you are my good man, four tickets to heaven!" announced *Brain-Dead* to the grumpy-looking driver, handing over their vouchers.

"You can't smoke on here," the driver grunted at Paul, ignoring *Brain-Dead* altogether. "I said you can't smoke on here, son, it's non-smoking."

It took a few moments for this message to sink in with Paul, but when it did the effect was startling.

"What?" he whispered, with a dejected roly hanging from his bottom lip.

"Don't you understand English, son?" grunted the bus driver.

"No smoking?" said an ashen-f aced Paul.

"That's right, this is a *non* smoking coach," grinned the driver, who obviously enjoyed delivering this particular piece of bad news.

"But...but...I can't go all the way to Amsterdam without a smoke!" mumbled Paul in a state of shock.

"Then you've got a long walk son," laughed the driver with the relish of a torturer who really enjoys his work.

"But *Brain-Dead*...you promised me," Paul pleaded.

"There must be some mistake, my good man. Are you having us on?" *Brain-Dead* asked the driver.

"Do I look like I enjoy a joke?" asked the driver, finally examining their travel vouchers.

A youth sitting next to where Dave was standing shook his head.

"He's not joking, " he confided to Dave, as the driver handed the now-clipped vouchers back to *Brain-Dead*.

"Take a seat if you're coming, fuck off if you're not. Come on you weak, miserable junkies, time to go," the driver shouted out of the door to the huddle of smokers, puffing madly on their cigarettes.

One by one they all took one last drag before throwing their cigarettes away and trooping up the steps onto the bus. As they passed the driver, each threw a look of pure, unadulterated hatred at him, which he seemed to revel in. It was as they pushed past a still standing Dave that he looked down the bus to see that not one of the passengers seemed to be in a better mood. The bus was crammed with miserable-looking youths and even those who were asleep appeared really pissed.

"Sit down you lot," grunted the driver as he closed the door and swung the bus out of the bus station, causing all four friends to tumble into seats and into people's laps.

They eventually settled themselves into the nearest available seats, which were two directly behind the driver and two in the row behind them. Paul, still in his coat and with his bag on his lap, stared silently out of the window as the bus set off.

"I don't think I can go on man," he said to Dave after a few minutes. "I can't go all the way to Amsterdam without smoking."

Dave didn't answer because he didn't know what to say. So Paul leaned forward and put his head in the gap between *Brain-Dead* and *Lard-Arse's* headrests.

"*Brain-Dead*, this is serious, man. I can't go that long without a smoke. You promised me we would be smoking and partying all the way to *The Dam*!" Paul gurgled with tears welling up in his eyes.

"It wasn't like this last time, was it *Lardy*?" *Brain-Dead* asked.

"No," *Lard-Arse* assured Paul, "it was fucking great fun last time."

"It's that fucking cunt o' a driver," said a youth sitting across the aisle from Dave. "He fucking loves it 'ee does. I tell yee', every stop we've made since

329

Glasgae he's taken a pleasure in telling people they cannae smoke."

"Glasgow, you've come all the way from Glasgow, Scotland?" Dave asked in disbelief.

"Aye, but it's the fuckers who got on in Aberdeen that I feel sorry for," replied the youth, motioning back down the bus.

"This bus has come from Aberdeen!"

"Aye and stopped at every fucking town in between."

"When did it set off?"

"Yesterdae mornin',"

"But isn't that dangerous?"

"Ooh no, it's nae dangerous. That cunt of a driver keeps tekkin' it in turn with his mate who's asleep on the back row. The biggest danger is that you'll go fuckin' mad with all the fuckin' stops it makes."

"Why, where has got to stop now?"

"Ya' dunnae know?" laughed the Scottish youth.

Dave shook his head, so the youth took a schedule out of his jacket pocket and started reading.

"Nottingham, Derby, Birmingham, Worcester, Cardiff, Bristol, Swindon, Reading, London and then on to Harwich for the ferry."

Dave couldn't speak, but Paul could.

"When do we get to *The Dam*?" he asked, leaning over Dave.

"Tomorrow morning," came the reply. "We're on the night ferry from Harwich".

Paul stood up and put his hands around the headrest in front of him to grab *Brain-Dead* by the throat.

"You bastard!" Paul yelled.

"Calm down *Hippy*, what is it?" croaked *Brain-Dead*, trying to pry Paul's hands away from his neck.

"What have you got us into, you bastard? This is the journey from hell. No, it's worse than that, it's the journey to hell and back, stopping everywhere in between."

"I thought you'd enjoy the ride," pleaded *Brain-Dead*.

"Enjoy the ride? Enjoy the fucking ride?" Paul was now laughing manically. "Twenty-four hours on a coach without a smoke and you thought I'd enjoy the ride?"

"But there' s plenty of stops where you can have a smoke and the ferry's great fun. The bar stays open all night AND they've got a cinema!"

"And I've brought loads of food and beer," added *Lard-Arse*.

"And it's bloody cheap," *Brain-Dead* continued. "There's no cheaper way of getting to *The Dam*!"

"I'm not fucking surprised. They should be paying us!" screamed Paul.

"So how many nights have we got in Amsterdam?" Dave asked.

"Oh, just the one, but that's all you'll need," smiled *Brain-Dead*, rubbing his neck now that Paul had let go and had slumped back in his seat, sobbing.

"Only one night? I can't believe we're going all that way for just one night!" said Dave astonished. "So when do we leave?"

Brain-Dead rummaged in his bag to find his schedule.

"Er...the timetable says 'Depart Amsterdam 5.00pm Sunday. That's to catch the night sailing."

"And when do we get back to Sheffield?" asked Dave, not wanting to hear the answer.

"Er...Sheffield...er...ten o' clock' the next day," replied *Brain-Dead*.

"Oh, that's not too bad," said Dave, brightening. "Come on *Bud*," he said turning to Paul, "We don't leave *The Dam* until five at night and we're back here for ten the following morning. That's not so bad, is it?"

As Paul considered this, Dave overheard *Lard-Arse* whispering to *Brain-Dead.* "You've got to tell 'em."

"Tell us what?" asked Dave.

"Go on, tell them" *Lard-Arse* continued, poking *Brain-Dead* in the ribs.

Brain-Dead stayed silent.

"It's not ten in the morning," said *Lard-Arse* wincing, "it's ten o'clock Monday night!"

Neither Dave nor Paul could speak, but the Scottish youth could.

"Aye, you've got to do another tour of the fucking country first!" he laughed.

"What?" yelled Dave, "You've booked us onto two twenty-four hour bus journeys in one weekend, are you mad?"

"Och, it's mooore than twenty-four 'oours!" added the Scottish youth helpfully, "and it often gets delayed."

"I can't do it man," Paul repeated to Dave, still staring out of the window as the bus hurtled along a highway towards the Ml Motorway.

"Why didn't we just fly?" asked Dave. "We'd have been there in a couple of hours, we'd have three nights in *The Dam* and we could still have flown back on Monday morning."

"Oh, I don't like flying," said *Lard-Arse*. "I couldn't get on a plane."

"Much more expensive, as well," added *Brain-Dead*.

"Well...well why didn't we go by train to the ferry?" Paul asked angrily.

"Oh, we don't want all that messing around, getting on and off trains and getting across London and all that shit," answered *Brain-Dead*, "not when we can just relax, put our feet up on here and have a laugh."

Dave looked behind him to see if anyone was having a laugh, but no one was.

"Come on boys, cheer up. I've brought shit-loads of beer and grub. Here, cop for one of these each," said *Lard-Arse*, fishing into his gargantuan bag, pulling out four cans of beer and passing two back for Paul and Dave. "What do you want to start with, pork pie or sausage roll?"

Paul wasn't hungry but took a beer. Dave decided to try a 'sausage roll', which turned out to be surprisingly tasty. *Brain-Dead* went for a pork pie, which he stuffed whole into his mouth, complete with a glug of beer. *Lard-Arse*, meanwhile, had a pork pie, immediately followed by a sausage roll and then a scotch egg - just because!

"This is fucking ridiculous!" said Paul, grinning like a madman by now. "What are we doing? It's six in the morning and where are we? We're on some crazy deathtrap, careering along in the dark on an epic journey, drinking beer! I tell you what though.
There's no way I'm doing the return journey in this. How do you fancy hopping onto a train when we get back to Harwich and heading back via London?"

"Agreed!" replied Dave.

"Hey Hippy, I've got an idea for you," said *Brain-Dead* turning round. "Why don't you chew some tobacco? You know, like they do in the Westerns."

Paul pondered for a moment, then his face lit up.

"I've got an even better idea, let's chew on some dope instead!" he grinned, opening his bag and pulling out his stash. "That'll help the journey along."

Paul then pulled out a huge block of dope and secretly warmed it under his lighter, before crumbling little pieces off and handing them around.

"This is the bloody life!" sighed *Brain-Dead* an hour later as they sped down the Ml Motorway with dawn breaking on the horizon. "See *Hippy*, I told you it would be a laugh."

"More beers boys?" giggled *Lard-Arse*, pulling another four-pack from his bag and passing them around.

"Don't mind if I do," grinned a now happily stoned Paul.

Dave was starting to feel extremely stoned himself. He had realized this after spending ten minutes staring at the multi-colored dawn and thinking it was the most beautiful thing he'd ever seen. He did wonder, momentarily, if they could keep up this pace of beer drinking and dope chewing, but decided not to worry about it and tugged back the ring pull on another can.

They were soon turning off the M1 and heading along sleepy streets towards downtown Nottingham.

"This is what takes so bloody long; it's all these bloody stops. Still I am looking forward to a well-deserved smoke," said Paul rolling a cigarette.

By the time the bus pulled to a stop by the side of a horrible-looking, concrete monstrosity of a shopping center in the middle of Nottingham, a line of smokers had already formed, stretching back up the aisle. Paul, spotting the first sign of movement from the back of the bus, had scrambled over Dave to make sure he was at the front of the line, so that he could utilize every moment of precious smoking time. Once the bus finally stopped and the door opened with a loud hiss, it took longer to let the smokers off the bus than it took to allow the new passengers on. Dave giggled to himself as he watched Paul from the window puffing desperately on his cigarette.

"Come on you fuckers," yelled the driver, to get the smokers back on the bus.

None of the smokers though wanted to be the first to finish and climb aboard, so no one moved.

"If you twats don't get on this fucking coach right now, I'm closing the door and driving off without you," the driver threatened.

Muttering curses, the smokers one by one inhaled a final lungful before throwing away their cigarettes and slowly clambering back onto the bus, with Paul taking up the rear.

"That's it, come along children," grinned the driver, as he closed the doors and moved off.

"I fucking hate that bloke," snarled Paul, as he climbed over Dave to get back into his seat.

"Yeah, what a tosser," agreed *Lard-Arse*, busily shoving a 'family-sized' bar of chocolate into his mouth.

"Fucking hell *Tubby*," laughed *Brain-Dead*, "Steady on or your larder will be empty half way through the journey."

"Oh there' s no danger of that," gurgled *Lard-Arse* as he took a swig of beer to lubricate the chocolate. "I've got loads. Anyone want some chocolate?"

And that, pretty much, was the story of their journey for the next few hours; a constant supply of dope to chew, beer to drink and fatty foodstuffs to eat. At first, only Paul got off the bus at the stops but, as time wore on, both Dave and *Brain-Dead* joined him to stretch their legs, get some fresh air and to share a joint. *Lard-Arse*, however, just sat and consumed. At every stop the bus made, the same little piece of theater was played out; new passengers would climb aboard, full of smiles, happy expectations and ready-rolled joints. They would then be given the 'No Smoking' news, the horror of which would sink in for a few moments, before a wave of dejection would wash across their faces. The Sheffield party began to feel like veterans as they watched the scene repeat itself over and over again.

"It's incredible how much the *Fat Boy* can put away, isn't it?" mused *Brain-Dead* to Dave and Paul, as all three stood on the sidewalk at the Bristol stop, staring at *Lard-Arse* on the bus. "That's at least six scotch eggs he's had, and fuck knows how many pork pies and sausage rolls have been thrown into that belly of his. Can you imagine what his stomach must look like? It'd look like a fucking washing machine with beer, grease, chocolate and bits of pig all sloshing around together. And as for his shit...woah! Do you know, I followed *The Tubster* into the shitter one day, fuck me. You know when you have an arse explosion and you spray the bowl with shit? You know, when your arse-cheeks part and wham, you pepper the bowl? Well, not only had *Fat Boy* covered the bowl and the rim, but he'd also managed to pepper the fucking bog seat! How did he do that? Was he squatting over the bog when the explosion happened? Did he fire upwards between his butt-cheeks? And you'll never guess where else he managed to hit; the fucking wall! No kidding. There were bits of shit stuck to the wall on the same level as the bog-seat. He must have fired them through the gap between the seat and the porcelain." *Brain-Dead* laughed and then drew on the joint they were sharing. Paul and Dave then both laughed as *Lard-Arse*, seeing his three friends smiling at him, threw the last piece of scotch egg into his mouth, licked his fingers and gave them the thumbs-up.

It was on the Bristol to Swindon leg that Dave realized just how drunk and stoned he had become. By this point he had swapped places with *Brain-Dead* and was sitting next to *Lard-Arse*, just behind the driver. *Lard-Arse* was chatting away to him between mouthfuls, but Dave wasn't listening; he was too busy trying to steady himself and was taking deep breaths in an attempt to cure his churning stomach.

"You OK David?" asked *Lard-Arse*, noticing that Dave was shuffling around in his seat.

"I don't feel great, it has to be said," replied Dave. "I think I'd better go for a shit."

"Oh well, good luck!" replied *Lard-Arse*. "The shitter's at the back but, if it's anything like
last time, it'll be pretty disgusting."

"Well, I'm going to have to risk it," said Dave, standing up to make his way to the back of the bus.

"You're not going to the bog are you?" asked *Brain-Dead*, as Dave passed.

Brain-Dead's eyes were as large as saucers by now and he had a crazy grin etched onto his face.

"It has to be done," answered Dave, pushing onwards down the aisle.

As he neared the back, he could smell the bathroom from about ten rows away. He wondered how the passengers down this end of the bus could cope with the stench, although most of them were asleep. Reaching the back row, Dave squeezed past the slumbering relief driver and opened the concertina door of the bathroom. There he gasped with horror at the sight that greeted his eyes and the smell that clawed at his throat. The bathroom was smaller than one on an aircraft and it was awash with toilet paper in a sea of urine. It was a chemical toilet, that much was obvious from the blue stains around the bowl, but it was full to the brim. In fact, only to the brim would have been a good result because, as the bus swayed, a wave of liquid, paper and turds sloshed over the side and onto Dave's shoes. Dave squealed and crashed back into the door in an attempt to avoid being soaked. Collecting his thoughts, he decided that, even though he could have done with a shit, this was totally out of the question and resolved instead to rid himself of the excess beer into the tiny sink. This he did as quickly and efficiently as he could, given that the sink was at hand washing height and not pissing level. This meant pissing upwards while keeping a sharp eye of the tidal flow in the toilet bowl.

It was a semi-relieved Dave that staggered back down the bus to his seat. One benefit of the experience was that he had completely sobered up, but he also knew that having consumed so much beer a repeat visit was more or less inevitable.

"That was fucking terrible," said Dave as he plunked himself back in his seat next to *Lard-Arse*.

Lard-Arse, however, didn't answer.

"Are you alright?" asked Dave, noticing that *Lard-Arse* had lost all the color from his face.

"I don't feel very well," he mumbled.

Before Dave could ask him in what way he felt unwell, *Lard-Arse's* cheeks suddenly inflated like two balloons and his eyes started watering. Then, as if in slow motion, his face seemed to explode and a torrent of liquid flew out of his mouth. It was like a jet from a four inch wide hose under intense pressure and was aimed perfectly at the bald patch on the back of the driver's head. The liquid that hit the driver sprayed off in all directions while the rest continued on to the windshield, leaving the driver's body shape in clear silhouette on the glass. The bus, which was hurtling down the freeway at seventy miles per hour at the time, swayed violently across the lanes as the driver felt the full impact of the blow and tried to cope with a windshield now covered in barf. As the passengers screamed and fell into the aisle and their bags crashed down from the luggage racks above their heads, the driver made an almost comical attempt to clean his windshield by turning on the wipers. Eventually the flow slowed and then finally stopped. *Lard-Arse* belched and wiped his mouth. The bus driver, meanwhile, had managed to guide the bus to a stop at the side of the freeway amidst a cacophony of blaring horns and screeching tires of cars that had almost been wiped out by the swerving bus.

Inside the bus was deadly quiet as the shocked passengers silently thanked God for their lucky escape, except for the sound of the relief driver running down the aisle. The driver meanwhile, who was dripping with barf and whose hair looked like it had been brushed upwards from the back of his neck with hair gel, just turned around very slowly.

"Sorry," whimpered *Lard-Arse.*

"What the fuck happened, 'Arry?" asked the relief driver, arriving at the front. "Jesus!" he gasped, staring at the barf-covered windshield with its driver-shaped area of clear glass.

The driver was clearly too stunned to speak. He just kept looking at his dripping clothes, to *Lard-Arse* and back to his clothes.

"I was a bit unwell," pleaded *Lard-Arse,* "but it's OK, I feel much better now thanks."

"You could have killed us all, you fat fuck!" screamed the relief driver.

"I say, my good man, there' s no need for that tone," cried *Brain-Dead,* leaping to *Lard-Arse's* defence. "It's not his fault that he was ill."

"Not his fault?" replied the driver, overcoming his shock and now seething with fury. "He's been filling his fat face non-stop since you fuckers boarded. Look what he's done to my coach."

"Maybe he ate something that didn't agree with him?" suggested *Brain-Dead* helpfully.

"Well it fucking didn't agree with me either!" screamed the driver. "You fuckers are off this coach."

"That's not fair!" blubbed *Lard-Arse.* "We only want to go to *The Dam*."

"We'll sue you!" shouted *Brain-Dead.* "The law clearly states that a person cannot be held responsible for an illness."

"What are you, some sort of fucking lawyer or something?" asked the relief driver.

"Actually, yes I am," replied *Brain-Dead,* "and you will be in breach of contract if you pursue you current course, leading to inestimable damages being awarded to my colleague and possibly a custodial sentence for you."

"That's bollocks!" said the relief driver.

"So you're a lawyer now, are you?" grinned *Brain-Dead*. "Coach driving just a part-time job is it? Well then, let's stop this silliness and continue on our journey, if you don't mind."

"I can't drive anywhere with a windscreen I can't see through and I stink!" moaned the driver.

"Ummm," pondered *Brain-Dead*, "may I suggest then that my fat but now empty friend here cleans you window as best he can, so that we may proceed to the next service station. Once there, you can take a shower, while he procures some cleaning materials and cleans your coach. Also, I would have thought it not inappropriate that he should slip you a few 'sobs' so that you may dry clean your clothing and, as a gesture of goodwill, also purchases for you one of those cute little air freshener things for you to dangle off your mirror, thus alleviating this somewhat pungent aroma?"

"That's not fair!" pleaded *Lard-Arse*.

"What d'ya reckon 'Arry?" asked the relief driver.

Driver Harry considered his options.

"I think that's a great idea," Paul chipped in. "I could do with a cup of tea and a proper smoke!"

"Well 'Arry?" the relief driver asked again. "Well...I dunno. It fucking stinks...but I suppose we've got time. Go on then, set to it."

"But I haven't got any cleaning materials," pleaded *Lard-Arse*.

"You can use some beer and one of your shirts for the time being, just to get all that shit off the windscreen and the seat," *Brain-Dead* suggested helpfully.

"No. I won't do it!"

"Look you dumbfuck, either you spend a few minutes cleaning or you don't get to go to *The Dam*," Brain-Dead whispered into *Lard-Arse's* ear.

Lard-Arse considered his options and it was obvious that the cleaning route didn't appeal. However, the draw of The Dam finally won the day and he reluctantly agreed to do the cleaning. Dave felt very sorry for him as he opened up his bag and pulled out a shirt to use as a cloth and, for a moment, Dave considered helping him. But the task in hand was just too awful and the stench so overwhelming that, despite being covered in guilt, he joined the rest of the passengers in climbing down off the bus and marching up the grassy bank by the side of the freeway. As they passed him, *Lard-Arse* asked each passenger if they had any water he could use, but none did (or none admitted to having any). So *Lard-Arse* was forced to open a can of beer, pour it onto his shirt to dampen it, before he set to cleaning the seat and the windshield. The 'gallery' sitting on the grassy bank was absorbed by the theater before them and the mood certainly lightened as they yelled out handy hints to *Lard-Arse* such as 'You've missed a bit'. Paul and *Brain-Dead*, meanwhile, were getting immense pleasure from the proceedings as they lay in the grass, giggling, drinking beer and sharing a joint. Before long there was a general hubbub of merry chatter from the audience, which almost drowned out the roar of the traffic. Even the driver, who by now had changed his shirt, had lightened up and was laughing at *Lard-Arse*.

It really was a filthy task. At first it appeared that the windshield would never be clean as *Lard-Arse* made circular, technicolor smears in the barf but, with a little persistence and more beer, the glass became clearer and the driver gave *Lard-Arse* leave to 'have a quick flick' over the dashboard and seat.

Finally, *Lard-Arse* announced that he had done as much as he could and so the passengers trooped back onto the bus for a fifteen minute journey to the next service area; holding their noses as they went. Here guilt overcame Dave so, while the driver went for a shower and the passengers (including *Brain-Dead* and Paul) went off to the cafeteria, Dave went in search of cleaning materials. He found a very helpful janitor who sympathized with his plight and equipped Dave with a mop, an assortment of cloths, bleach, a bucket full of hot water and even two pairs of heavy-duty rubber gloves. *Lard-Arse* was so touched by Dave's help that he was almost in tears as they set to work and he kept thanking Dave over and over again until it became embarrassing. Dave for his part, thought it was quite mean of Paul and especially *Brain-Dead* (who was supposed to be *Lard-Arse's* best friend) not to help him in his hour of need and to just charge off to the cafeteria for a cup of tea. However, between them, Dave and *Lard-Arse* had the cleaning done in no time, leaving Dave to join Paul and *Brain-Dead* while *Lard-Arse* went off for a shower.

Paul and *Brain-Dead* did redeem themselves somewhat, by buying an air freshener and shirts for both the driver and *Lard-Arse* from the service area shop. So by the time the freshly-scrubbed and rather pink *Lard-Arse* and driver appeared in the cafeteria to summon everyone back onto the bus, there was almost an air of camaraderie about the place. The driver thanked the boys for the nice shirt they'd bought him, even though it was about three sizes too small for his enormous beer gut and had a kid's cartoon character emblazoned all over it, and the relief driver commended *Lard-Arse* and Dave on their cleaning skills. Even the other passengers were full of praise as they filed past *Lard-Arse* and some, patently lying, claimed they could no longer smell barf. This was proved to be a fallacy when the bus pulled up at Swindon and a new group of travellers climbed aboard.

"Fuck me, what's that terrible fucking smell?" asked the first youth.

"Someone' s been ill and if you don't like it, you can fuck off!" replied the driver.

Paul's day was made when the driver announced through the microphone that, as he would prefer the smell of smoke to that of barf, the smoking ban would be temporarily lifted. A great cheer went up as more than half the bus reached for their smoking materials and at least half of those began openly building joints, something both the driver and the relief driver chose to ignore. Dave accepted the joint that Paul passed forward to him and soon found himself giggling with *Lard-Arse* as the bus crawled through the traffic towards the center of London.

It was approaching nine in the evening when the bus arrived at the ferry terminal in the port of Harwich, by which time it was rocking; there was music blaring out, empty beer cans rolling down the aisle and a fog of blue smoke was swirling around. Dave wondered if the driver had become stoned through passive smoking as he'd spent the past hour singing loudly to songs he clearly didn't know the words to. That same thought obviously passed through the mind of the Customs Officer who climbed aboard to check passports.

"What' s that smell?" he asked the driver. "It's not cannabis is it?"

"Oh no, it's just smoke to try to cover up the smell of the puke," grinned the driver in reply.

"You don't usually allow drinking and smoking on your coach do you?"

"Nah, but it's nearly Christmas isn't it?"

"It's only October. Have you been drinking?" asked the Customs Officer, raising an eyebrow.

"No I haven't, but I intend to start as soon as I get on that ferry and finish my shift."

The Customs Officer didn't seem convinced and pointedly took out his notebook to scribble something down, before starting his passport check. His suspicions must have been heightened even more when someone at the back of the bus suddenly noticed him and shouted "Fuck, it's the pigs, hide the stash!" but, if he did hear it, he chose not to acknowledge it.

"Good evening constable, what a fine evening this is for a voyage!" beamed an immensely stoned *Brain-Dead*, sitting bolt upright in his seat with huge eyes that didn't blink.

"I'm not a constable, I'm a customs officer. Now can I see you passport please?"

"Ah...er...right, fair point. Well that's good news I suppose. At least if you're not a pig, you don't have to wear a tit on your head. Mind you, I suppose you have to shove your hand up people's arses looking for stuff, don't you? Do you have to do that much? What's the best thing you've found up someone's arse?"

"*Brain-Dead* shut up will you?" Dave cringed from the seat in front.

"Just give me your passport, sonny," snapped the officer.

When *Brain-Dead* did pass it to him, the officer once again made a note in his little book before passing it back. He then made his way up the bus checking everyone's passports, stepping on beer cans and kicking bottles out of the way as he went. Suddenly a howl of anguish came from near the back of the bus.

"That's not fair!"

All the passengers turned around to see what was causing the commotion, but it was hard to tell.

"Oh please, please!" wailed the same voice.

"What' s going on?" *Lard-Arse* asked Dave.

"I'm not sure, I can't tell from here. The customs guy is talking to some guy at the back, but I can't tell what about," replied Dave.

"Och the pooor fucker!" the Scottish youth interjected from across the aisle. "His passport's oot of date and the bastard will nae let him gooo."

"Wow, that's heavy!" coughed Paul.

"Aye and he's one o' them that's bin on since Aberdeen!"

"Oh my god, can you imagine that? You've been on this bloody coach since Aberdeen and now you can't get on the bloody ferry," *Lard-Arse* grimaced, inhaling deeply.

The argument at the back end of the bus continued for a full ten minutes before a youth, looking the very image of dejection, moped to the front of the bus with his bag slung over his shoulder.

"OK driver, carry on," said the Customs Officer as he jumped down from the bus after the youth.

The driver started up the bus again, closed the doors with a hiss and pulled away from the customs area, leaving the mournful youth on the sidewalk.

"It's nae wonder he loooks so pissed off," said the Scottish youth as they drove away. "His girlfriend' s going on withoot him!"

"What?" said *Brain-Dead* spinning around in his seat, "Where is she? Is she fit? She'll need some comforting and my comforter is just the thing for the job."

Brain-Dead rose from his seat and marched up the bus.

"Sit down you stupid bastard!" *Lard-Arse* called after him.

"Never! Not when there' s a damsel in distress."

They all watched as *Brain-Dead* reached the back of the bus and began making enquiries as to which 'young filly' had just been abandoned. Finding his victim, he sat down next to her. They couldn't hear what he said but they did hear the 'Goo fuck yerself!" and the blistering slap that echoed around the bus.

"Bitch! Obviously a dyke," muttered *Brain-Dead*, as he came back to his seat.

Moments later the bus rolled onto the enormous ferry and came to a halt on the massive car deck. Its occupants then streamed off like a group of excited kids on a school trip, each taking a bag; as the driver had warned them that they wouldn't be allowed back on the bus during the voyage. Following *Brain-Dead*, Dave ran up flight after flight of narrow steel stairs in a race to claim the prime seats for the voyage. The higher they climbed the more luxurious the surroundings became. They left the noise and diesel smells of the car deck, climbed up past a level that was full of cabins and past another with bathrooms and slot machines until they arrived on the main deck. They were fortunate in that they were aboard before any of the car passengers and made straight for the empty bar. Here *Brain-Dead* picked out a circle of couches by a window and they staked their claim by covering them with their belongings.

"Fantastic eh? What did I tell you, eh? Just check this place out boys. We've got a bar open all night with cheap booze, a cafe, a cinema and we'll be steaming our way to *The Dam* as we party. What more could you possibly want?" laughed *Brain-Dead*.

There was one thing that Dave wanted even more than all this: sleep. It was now eleven o'clock and he was absolutely exhausted. So, while *Brain-Dead* was busy promoting the ship's many facilities, he made himself a nest on one of the couches using his jacket and a sweater from his bag, lay down and was fast asleep before the ship had even set sail.

THIRTEEN

"Wake up man. Come on man, it's time to wake up."

Dave was angry at being shaken, he just wanted to go to sleep. He didn't need convincing that the ship's bar was fantastic, no doubt the movie they were showing in the cinema was a classic and the food in the cafeteria delicious, but all Dave wanted was to sleep. And yet Paul kept shaking him.

"Please leave me alone, I just want to get some sleep. I'm absolutely exhausted," pleaded Dave without opening his eyes. "If I don't get some sleep I'll feel like shit in the morning."

"It is the morning man," whispered Paul into Dave' s ear.

This information took quite some time to register with Dave. At first it felt like this was a scene out of his dream and not a particularly nice one at that. Anger then welled up within him at this cruel joke that Paul was playing on him. He hadn't been asleep more than ten minutes and he certainly wasn't about to fall for a practical joke like this. In fact, he hadn't really been properly asleep at all because it was far too loud in the bar for anyone to sleep and he was extremely disappointed that Paul of all people had been talked into teasing him, no doubt by *Brain-Dead*.

"Oh fuck off and leave me alone!" Dave yelled, sitting upright and opening his eyes.

What he saw was a rather shocked Paul, obviously upset at being abused, and dawn breaking over a distant coastline out of the windows. Elsewhere, the bar was full of bodies; bodies slumped in chairs, lying on couches and stretched out on the floor. Most were asleep but some were coming to. The bar was closed, with its shutters down and bar debris scattered all over, cigarette ends were overflowing from tiny aluminum foil ashtrays, tables were awash with dirty plates and discarded newspapers and bottles and glasses were flying around the floor as the ship rolled from side to side.

"Oh, I'm sorry," said Dave rubbing his eyes, "I was sure I'd not been to sleep."

"You're joking! You were fast asleep within a minute of getting on board," *Lard-Arse* laughed from a chair opposite.

"I suppose you're right but I ache all over and feel like shit. What time is it?"

"Six o'clock. We'll be arriving at the Hook of Holland in just over an hour," said Paul. "We thought you might like some breakfast before we have to get back on the coach."

"Sounds good," replied Dave, coming round. "I could do with a shower first though. I always feel like shit till I have a shower. So, tell me, did you guys have a good time last night?"

"Oh yeah, a fucking riot!" grinned *Lard-Arse*. "Brain-Dead fell asleep about thirty seconds after you, just after compiling his list of all the great things we were going to do on board. So me and Paul had a couple of beers over a game of cards and then crashed ourselves. Oh, and I had to have something to eat 'cause my stomach was empty after puking over the driver. It was really good grub actually. I went into the lorry drivers' restaurant and nobody asked me to prove I was a lorry driver or anything, so I had a huge feast for fuck all. Our two coach drivers came in but they didn't grass me up."

"So where's *Brain-Dead?*" asked Dave.

"Oh, he's gone for a shit", said Paul, lighting a roly. "He says he'll meet us in the cafe 'cause it takes him at least an hour to have a shit. He said something about how you should let the shit just fall out of your arse rather then push it out, if you don't want to get piles."

"Well, if you don't mind, I'll meet you in the cafe in about half an hour after I've had a shower and changed my clothes," said Dave stretching. "I'll take my bag with me, but who's going to look after all the rest of the gear?"

"Oh, I'll stay here. I'm not hungry," said Paul. "Just get me a coffee, if you don't mind."

So off Dave went in search of a shower, which he found on the deck below. Being on a ship, he had to step over a very high door frame to get in (which presumably prevented water sloshing around the deck) and once inside he found a row of men in various states of undress shaving, brushing their teeth and combing their hair, all in a line facing a row of mirrors. As there wasn't a space in front of a mirror, Dave stood behind one of them, squinting to see himself as he shaved with his electric shaver. Once this was complete (or as complete as possible from such a distance), he didn't have to wait too long for a shower stall to become free, as one was vacated by a bald-headed man whose body was so hairy that he appeared to be wearing a gorilla costume. The first dilemma he had was deciding what to do with the bag that he'd brought. After a few moments considering whether he could balance it on the frame of the shower stall, he decided to leave it outside and to take a chance on someone not wanting to steal a few pairs of shorts and a couple of T-shirts. The next dilemma was deciding whether he really fancied stepping into the six inch deep pool of cloudy water swirling with hair and shampoo bottles (why were all public showers like this?), but the cleansing instinct proved too strong and he took the plunge.

The shower was wonderful! There were gallons of piping hot water and the showerhead was the size of a dinner plate, so Dave spent far longer than was absolutely necessary under the deluge. Once he'd finished, dried himself and put on some clean clothes, which he pulled from the bag that hadn't been stolen, he rolled up his wet towel and headed off to the cafe feeling almost human again. No, he felt better than that, he felt totally refreshed, extremely happy and hungry and excited at the day that lay ahead.

He found the cafe without any problem and was greeted by a friendly shriek of '*Stud*' as he walked in. *Brain-Dead* and *Lard-Arse* were busily wading through the ship's equivalent of a *Bumper*, squeezed into immovable plastic seats at a table by the window.

"It's *Rip Van Studly*," grinned *Brain-Dead*, as Dave approached with his 'Full English Breakfast'. "Did you sleep well *Sleeping Beauty*?"

"Don't try bullshitting me that you were partying all night, 'cause I know that's total crap," laughed Dave putting his plate on the table and his bag on the vacant seat next to him.

"Only because you wimped out, you puff! I'd have been up for it if you hadn't keeled over within seconds of being on board."

"That is total horseshit!" giggled *Lard-Arse*, spitting a piece of sausage onto Dave's plate in the process.

"Oh well, whatever," continued *Brain-Dead*. "Look out of that window boys, we're nearly there. Just a short journey on the coach and we'll be in *The Dam*; the *Promised Land* of drugs and whores."

"Can't bloody wait," agreed *Lard-Arse*, spitting a piece of fried egg through his teeth to join the sausage on Dave's plate, "we'll be there in no time."

Lard-Arse was indeed absolutely correct; they were there in no time. After finishing their breakfast they gathered up Paul and their bags and clambered aboard the bus, which still stank of barf. The ferry docked exactly on time, their bus was one of the first vehicles off and they shot past an unmanned customs post; something Dave was quite relieved about, as he had not checked to see if his visa for the UK was good for The Netherlands. Within minutes they were charging along a turnpike, flying past signposts to Amsterdam displaying ever-diminishing distances. It had just gone eight-thirty when the bus pulled to a halt next to the Central Station and disgorged its happy passengers onto the sidewalk.

"Well man, we're here. We made it!" grinned a delighted Paul.

"I know, I can hardly believe it," replied an excited Dave, looking around. "I can't believe I'm in another country already. I tell you what, it'd better be worth it 'cause I'm dreading getting back on that fucking bus; my ass is red raw!"

"Worry not *Studly*, it'll be worth it and when you get on the coach tomorrow night you'll be so fucking stoned you'll think it's a fucking *Rolls Royce*," laughed *Brain-Dead*.

"So now all we have to do is find our hotel. It's near the Leidseplein apparently," said *Lard-Arse*, Studying a map.

"What's the Leidseplein?" Dave asked.

"The Leidseplein is a square where numerous bars are situated and where you shall be partaking of your first truly legal spliff, my sweet Amsterdam virgin," laughed *Brain-Dead*.

"Well, according to this, we can get a tram from here straight to the Leidseplein but it doesn't say which number tram," continued *Lard-Arse*, his face now buried in a guidebook.

"You mean a tram like that one ten yards from your fat face with 'Leidseplein' in big fucking letters on the front?" asked *Brain-Dead*.

"Yeah, that'll do," replied *Lard-Arse*, looking up.

"How's your Dutch?" *Brain-Dead* asked Dave.

"Ignore him, my son," smiled Paul, "the Dutch speak better English than we do.

The driver did speak perfect English and the journey to the Leidseplein was very pleasant on the clean and spectacularly bendy streetcar that raced through the streets. Throughout the journey, *Brain-Dead* gave his friends (and the rest of the bus passengers) a running commentary on the coffee shops and dens of iniquity they were passing, complete with more than a sprinkling of obscenities, which every passenger clearly understood. As Dave sat listening to *Brain-Dead's* rantings, he wondered what the Dutch felt about having such rude tourists in the midst, tourists whose sole objective was to get absolutely out of their brains as soon as they possibly could. He stopped worrying when an old lady opposite him gave him a very friendly and welcoming smile and concluded that if the Dutch didn't want drugs tourism, they would get rid of the drugs. All the same, he made a conscious effort to admire the passing architecture, fully aware that he would soon be making every effort just to be conscious! The driver helpfully informed the boys when they had reached their destination and they thanked him as they got off.

"Haf a nice time in Omsterdom!" smiled the driver.

They wished him well before failing in behind *Lard-Arse* who, as keeper of the map, had become their guide.

"Not far now, just up this street and around the corner," the *Guide* announced cheerfully, as they wandered up a residential street. "There...there it is, just up there."

"Where? I can't see any hotel," said *Brain-Dead*, squinting.

"There, that's it, *The Hotel Edinburgh*," replied *Lard-Arse* pointing to a white painted house which, with the exception of a small sign outside, looked exactly like all the other houses in the street.

"*The Hotel Edinburgh?*" laughed Dave. "We've come all the way to Holland to stay in *The Hotel Edinburgh?* Doesn't sound very Dutch. This is the hotel you've stayed at before, right?"

"Er...no, we got banned from that one," mumbled *Brain-Dead*. "It wasn't our fault really. We were just sitting in the bar one evening, chatting about how fit the landlady was, how we'd like to fuck her and wondering why she was married to the little tosser who was the landlord. The trouble was, he was sitting just around the corner and got really pissed off with us!"

"Yeah, total wanker!" agreed *Lard-Arse*, marching up to the hotel and heaving the remarkably heavy door open.

Inside the small lobby of *The Hotel Edinburgh* the Scottish theme was even more apparent, as every wall was bedecked with tartans, photographs of Edinburgh castle from every conceivable angle and there was even a rather shabby set of bagpipes.

"Fucking hell, it's like a Jock theme park!" laughed *Brain-Dead*. "Do you think they have caber tossing out the back and haggis for breakfast?"

But before anyone could answer, an enormous man with an amazingly long but impressively stiff mustache suddenly reared up from behind the tiny counter.

"Jesus!" said Paul jumping with shock, his roly failing from his mouth in the process.

"Velcome! Can I help you?" boomed the *Giant*.

"Er...yes, we...we've got a reservation," replied *Lard-Arse*, pulling a voucher from his pocket and handing it over.

"I think I've seen that bloke before," *Brain-Dead* whispered to Dave. "He was in a lager font holding a stein."

The *Giant*, ignoring *Brain-Dead*, took the delicate gold-rimmed glasses that were hanging around his neck in his shovel-like hands and placed them on the end of his nose to study the voucher.

"Oh yes, ve vere expecting you, but not until later."

Lard-Arse was about to explain that their bus had just dropped them off, when he was distracted by a strange scratching sound. They all turned to see a cute little west highland terrier dog with white curls and a friendly face scuttling across the wooden floor towards them. He was going at such a speed that all four of his little legs left the ground as he bounded along like a springbok in full flight.

"Ah, here is Douglas to greet you all," announced the hotelier proudly.

With these words still hanging in the air, Douglas sprang forward and attached himself to *Lard-Arse's* lower left leg with a vice-like grip. Then, with an admirable determination and seemingly with every fiber in his tiny body, he began fucking *Lard-Arse's* leg at such a speed that his hindquarters were a motion blur.

"Ahhhhhhhhh!" yelled *Lard-Arse*, in shock rather than in pain.

It was certainly shocking having a two-inch pink penis ramming into his leg, but the only hurt was to *Lard-Arse's* pride as Douglas ejaculated down his pants. By the time the hotelier had lifted up the hatch in the counter and arrived on the other side to drag the dog off *Lard-Arse's* leg, Douglas had a very satisfied grin on his hairy little face. Despite having oodles of endorphins flowing along in his bloodstream, he had evidently become rather attached to *Lard-Arse's* leg and wasn't overjoyed at the prospect of giving up his new love so soon. As his owner pulled on his collar, he howled and dug his claws deeper into *Lard-Arse's* flesh in an attempt to savor just a few more moments of post-coital bonding.

"I am so sorry," the *Giant* apologized as his yanked Douglas along the floor, "he has never, ever done zat before."

Either Douglas had designs on a bit more humping or he felt that he had found his soul mate in *Lard-Arse's* leg, but either way he wasn't keen to exit Stage Left. He was straining on his collar so much that it looked about ten sizes too big for him and was standing fully upright and walking backwards as he was dragged towards a door at the end of the lobby.

As *Lard-Arse* stared down at his newly-decorated pants, the stunned silence was broken by *Brain-Dead* staggering sideways in fits of laughter.

"I thought you might fuck a dog while you were here, but I never thought a dog would fuck you!" he shrieked.

The hotelier, finally managing to close the door without crushing Douglas's constantly reappearing head, returned to the scene of the crime.

"I must apologize to you, young man. I don't know what has got into him. He has never done zat before," the poor embarrassed man repeated, trying to make himself heard over Douglas's howling and scratching at the door.

"Please, use zis," he added, pulling out a handkerchief   for *Lard-Arse* to wipe the dog semen off his pants. Then, regaining his composure, he opened a huge register and handed *Lard-Arse* a pen.

"I vill put you in room number seven," he said, placing a key with an oversized brass tag attached to it onto the counter. "It is a very nice room and it's empty, so you can go zer now."

As *Lard-Arse* accepted the pen and began writing their names and address in the book, the hotelier's face turned ashen at the sound of the door opening again. Before he could shout to prevent it, Douglas was out again and making a beeline for *Lard-Arse*. Even before he had attached himself to Lard-Arse's leg for a second time, *Brain-Dead* had keeled over laughing once more.

"Hey *Fatty*, he thinks you're his bitch!" laughed Brain-Dead at his clearly upset friend.

The door-opening culprit was a fat, orange-faced lady, who had the appearance of an old parrot, She, presumably, thought she was very attractive and had apparently spent a good deal of time applying the thick crust of orange make up to her wrinkled face. Her hair was similarly shocking. It too was orange, but it had been coiffured so many times with noxious chemicals that the bulk of it had given up the ghost, leaving her bald scalp fully visible through the remaining strands. She put her hand over her mouth in horror at the scene she was witnessing. Once again, the hatch flew up and the hotelier bounded over to pull his pet off *Lard-Arse*, while explaining to the fat lady, in Dutch, the trouble she had caused by opening the door. She was in a state of shock, however, and looked like she would never view her dear, sweet doggie in the same light again. This wasn't the cute ball of hair that for years had sat on her lap for hours on end as she watched television, or who licked her face as a doggy thank you for the treats she fed him. Never before had there been even the slightest hint of a hard-on, yet now her surrogate child had revealed himself as a depraved, sex-crazed rapist-hound-from-hell with a shocking pink penis and do or die determination to fornicate.

As Dave watched the poor woman' s horror, it put him in mind of the wife of a serial rapist discovering the shocking truth about her husband.

"Horny little chap, isn't he?" mused Paul, lighting his reclaimed roly. "Great powers of recovery, don't you think? I don't believe I'd be ready to go for it again so soon. In fact, I know dammed well I wouldn't."

"Don't just stand there talking, you bastards; help get it off me," wailed *Lard-Arse*, shaking his leg in an attempt to loosen Douglas's grip.

"You are fucking joking, aren't you? I could watch this all day," laughed *Brain-Dead*. "In fact I'd have come all this way just to watch this. Anyway, the little lad's enjoying himself. Look, he's grinning."

Douglas was indeed grinning from ear to ear as he pounded away on *Lard-Arse's* leg and this time he'd obviously devised a cunning way of securing a better grip because *Mein Host* was having the devil's own job pulling him off.

"I am so very, very sorry," he kept muttering as he pulled at Douglas's collar.

As he pulled harder he dragged *Lard-Arse* around the lobby without pulling Douglas free, so *Lard-Arse* tried to help by pushing down on Douglas's nose. Douglas did not like that one little bit and snarled at *Lard-Arse* with his teeth bared.

"It's a fucking good job he's not an Alsatian, Tubby," howled *Brain-Dead*, "otherwise he'd have made you give him a blowjob by now."

At last, by tugging on his collar and by prying his front left paw from *Lard-Arse's* pants, the hotelier finally succeeded in dragging Douglas away and literally threw him out of the room. His wife then burst into tears and ran into a little room behind the counter, where her wailing mixed with Douglas's howling meant that before long people in pajamas began appearing in the lobby to find out what was going on. As the hotelier attempted to bring calm to the proceedings, *Lard-Arse* shook himself off and resumed his writing in the register, though glancing anxiously at the scratching sounds coming from the door. Once he had finished, the hotelier handed over the key once more and, after apologizing over and over again, pointed them towards their room.

"Do you mind if I ask you something?" Paul asked as they picked up their bags.

"Vat?" replied the hotelier nervously, in case the question concerned the sex life of dogs.

"Why is your hotel called the Hotel Edinburgh?"

"Ah", smiled the relieved hotelier, "because my vife and I vent on our honeymoon zer. Zat is also vhy we have alvays had Scotty dogs like Douglas."

His curiosity sated, Paul caught up with the others as they made their way through a wooden fire door and down a dimly lit corridor. *Lard-Arse's* hands were still shaking too much to get the key into the lock of room number seven, so Dave took over and let them all in. Inside they found themselves in a large room with a very high ceiling and windows that looked out onto a scruffy yard.

"Oh Jesus," said *Brain-Dead*, "there aren't not enough beds."

He was right. There was a full size double bed, a twin size single bed and a rollaway bed, all crammed together.

"Well I'm not sleeping with *Fatty*. I'm claiming this one," yelled *Brain-Dead*, leaping onto the single bed.

Lard-Arse and Paul glanced at each other for a millisecond before racing towards the rollaway bed. As they passed the end of the double bed they both dived through the air. The poor rollaway bed could barely stand upright at the best of times and having the combined weight of *Lard-Arse* and Paul landing in it from a great height didn't constitute the best of times. Its fragile metal legs flew sideways and it folded its two assailants into a mattress sandwich with a terrible crunching sound.

"You've broken it!" exclaimed *Lard-Arse* once he had extracted himself.

"It wasn't me who broke it," Paul protested.

"Children, children, please behave," grinned *Brain-Dead*, fluffing his pillow and lying back.

"I'll go and ask if they've got another bed or even another room," announced Dave.

Dave closed the door on the ensuing argument and made his way back down the dark corridor to find the hotelier comforting the weeping *Parrot* in the back room.

"Excuse me," called Dave. "Er...sorry to bother you, but do you have any more rooms? It's just that there are four of us and there are only three beds,"

"I am very sorry, but the hotel is full. Zat is the only size of room ve have left. I did explain to zer lady on zer telephone, but she said it vould be OK," explained the hotelier, abandoning the Parrot for a moment.

By the time Dave arrived back at the room, the sleeping arrangements had been sorted out. *Brain-Dead* had refused to move so, between them, Paul and *Lard-Arse* had concluded that Paul and Dave would have to share the double bed, as *Lard-Arse* was far too huge.

"But no funny business, OK man?" said Paul to Dave as he struggled to open a window. "Hey, none of these windows will open. That'll be just what we need if there's a fire."

"Well you'd better not smoke in here then, had you *Hippy*," said *Brain-Dead* from his bed.

Paul considered this severe imposition for a moment.

"OK, I'll only smoke in the bathroom."

"We've got a bathroom?" asked Dave.

"Oh yeah, it's just there," said *Lard-Arse* pointing towards a door to the side of *Brain-Dead's* bed. "The daft thing is, it's as big as this fucking room and it's got a bum-basin, so if you shit yourself you can wash your arse!"

"How convenient!" noted Dave.

Half an hour later, all four of them were marching into the Leidseplein giggling with anticipation. Their pace from the hotel had quickened as they drew nearer but now they came to a halt.

"How do we know which ones sell cannabis?" asked Dave as they looked at the various cafes and bars.

"Well, we don't appear to have much choice at the moment, as most of them are fucking closed, you dipshit!" replied *Brain-Dead*. "Let's just check out the first one we find open."

"Steady, my son," cautioned Paul. "Remember that non-*dooby* smoking bars get upset if you sparkle up a number and I for one haven't come all the way to Amsterdam to sit in a non-smoking cafe."

"Well let's ask in here," replied *Brain-Dead*, striding towards the first open bar.

Everyone followed *Brain-Dead* as he descended a short staircase and threw open the door. Inside it was quite dark but there was a wonderful smell of fresh coffee and warm croissants.

"Oh god, that smells nice," said *Lard-Arse*, sniffing the air.

All the tables, chairs, the floor and the bar itself were fashioned in dark wood, yet somehow it managed to seem cozy as well as atmospheric. The only two occupants were a bartender filling the shelves and a very pretty young woman sitting at a table in the corner with a huge cup of coffee and a morning paper.

"Excuse me, but can we smoke in here?" *Brain-Dead* asked the bartender.

"Yesh foor shure!" smiled the bartender in reply.

"Yeah but, you know, really smoke. Smoke dope?"

"Off course, vould you like to see ze menu?"

"Oh yeah, breakfast!" grinned *Lard-Arse*.

"Ze only breakfast ve do is croissants. I meant the schmoking menu," the bartender added, pulling a menu from the bar and handing it to *Brain-Dead*.

"Alright!" grinned *Brain-Dead*, accepting the menu and opening it with glee.

"Fucking amazing!" smiled Dave in disbelief as they all gathered around *Brain-Dead* to read the descriptions of the marijuana on offer.

As they read, it became apparent to Dave that the price for each variety was all the same, but you got different amounts for your money i.e. you got a small amount of the really good grass but loads of the lesser stuff.

"Well Gentlemen, what tickles your fancy?" *Brain-Dead* asked, still grinning.

"Why don't we get a packet of the best shit to start with, just to see what it's like?" Paul suggested.

"A fine suggestion, *Hippy*," agreed *Brain-Dead*. "So, my good man, we will try some of your finest shit, if you will be so kind."

"Schertainly," smiled the bartender, "and vould you like schome drinks vith zat?"

"Oh, yes please. Coffee please and a couple of croissants," said *Lard-Arse* eagerly.

They all agreed that coffee would be a good idea, as well as some freshly squeezed orange juice plus a croissant each and two for *Lard-Arse*. Then, finding a table by a window overlooking the Leidseplein, they settled themselves down and smiled at each other. After a few minutes, the bartender approached carrying a huge, round tray and set it down on the next table. He then placed their drinks and croissants before them and, finally, set down a plate with a small plastic packet containing marijuana, a packet of very long cigarette papers with the name of the bar on it plus a book of matches.

"Enjoy!" the bartender smiled, as did the girl over her newspaper.

"How civilized," smiled Dave.

"Will you do the honors, my good man?" *Brain-Dead* asked Paul.

"It would be an absolute pleasure," smiled Paul in reply.

They all watched in reverential awe as Paul pulled out two large papers, licked one and attached it to the other, before opening the packet of grass and sniffing the contents, like a sommelier enjoying the aroma of a fine wine. As he sprinkled the grass and then some tobacco from his pouch along the length of the paper, the plastic packet was passed around for everyone to have a sniff. *Brain-Dead* and *Lard-Arse* groaned with pleasure as they inhaled the aroma. Dave said it smelled great, although he didn't know how it was supposed to smell; this stuff just smelled strong. At last Paul gave the joint a last lick and a roll between his fingers and held his creation up in the air. They all applauded as he handed *Brain-Dead* the joint for the honor of lighting it.

"What a generous gesture, *Hippy*. I'm almost overcome," said *Brain-Dead*, before slowly putting the joint in his mouth and lighting it.

It crackled and glowed at the end as *Brain-Dead* inhaled and held his breath.

"Well?" asked *Lard-Arse*.

"Woah!" exclaimed Brain-Dead exhaling, before taking another drag and passing it on to *Lard-Arse*.

"Woah!" gulped *Lard-Arse* as he took his first drag.

"That's great shit!" squeaked *Brain-Dead*.

Dave took a drag and had a coughing fit.

"Slowly my son, take it slowly," said Paul, reassuring him.

Dave tried again and actually managed to hold his breath for a few moments before blowing the smoke out and handing the joint on to Paul. If he were honest, Dave wouldn't have said that the taste was particularly pleasant, it was just much stronger and oilier than the joints he'd had in Sheffield. Paul, however, was in raptures.

"Fucking hell, this is seriously good shit!" he giggled as blue smoke drifted out of his nostrils.

"Come on Hippy, don't hog it," pleaded *Brain-Dead*.

"Shall I roll us another?" asked Paul, taking a drag and passing it onto *Brain-Dead*.

Everyone nodded.

The next few hours carried on in a similar vein with a constant supply of freshly-rolled spliffs, delicious freshly-brewed coffee, freshly-squeezed orange juice (from real oranges, not from a carton) and hot, fluffy croissants. *Brain-Dead* then discovered the jukebox and added non-stop Bruce Springsteen and Elvis Presley to the mix. It only took about half an hour for Dave to feel absolutely out of his brains, but not in a frightening or out-of-control way. There were no 'Horrors' this time; this was magical! He felt unbelievably happy and relaxed in the company of his wonderful friends. Every so often, he sat back in his chair and simply drank in the atmosphere, watching them laughing and joking like they hadn't a care in the world. The jokes and witty observations they made were the funniest things he had ever heard and he laughed until it hurt. And the music affected him like no music before. He sang along with tunes he had never heard before, played air guitar like *Jimi Hendrix*, was close to tears during the sad songs and his soul soared with the uplifting ones. He was absolutely convinced the pretty girl in the corner had 'the hots' for him, as every time he looked over she was looking at him and smiling. Outside the sun had come out and the square began to fill with people going about their Saturday morning business. Inside the bar, the atmosphere the four friends generated was infectious. At intervals, people would stick their heads around the door of the bar and, seeing what fun the occupants were having, would come in and settle themselves down. All sorts of people came in, from a rather evil-looking biker type who turned out to be a very friendly Elvis fan, a group of English yuppies on a Bachelor Party weekend, a very aged Dutch couple who sipped hot chocolate for an hour without saying a word to each other, groups of students and, unfortunately, the boyfriend of the pretty girl in the corner. Dave compared this relaxed, friendly, gentle atmosphere to that of some of the bars at home, dark hovels with a violent undercurrent, and he determined to become an advocate of cannabis legalization the moment he returned.

It was approaching lunchtime when Paul suggested they have 'one for the road' before moving on to take in some of the sights.

"Yeah, could do," nodded *Brain-Dead*. "The red light district isn't far away."

So, after ordering another packet of the finest grass, throwing money into a 'kitty' and settling their check with the bartender, who tried to persuade them to stay, they emerged into the fresh air of the Leidseplein. Even though the other bars were now open and getting busy, they set off for the red light district. As they walked along, Dave decided that Amsterdam was the best place on earth and that he wanted to live here as soon as he finished school. The architecture was stunning, the people were so friendly (apart from the occasional aggressive drug dealer who tried to sell them heroin and wouldn't take 'no' for an answer) and the place was just so civilized, stylish and chilled out. Soon they passed the royal palace and were into the red light district, which was certainly an eye-opener. Dave had never seen anything like this in his life! The streets were lined with cathouses, with prostitutes sitting on chairs in windows in various stages of undress, and sex shops openly displaying the most extreme pornography.

"Look at the size of that guy's knob!" laughed *Lard-Arse*, staring at a magazine cover in the window of one shop featuring a guy with a penis at least eighteen inches long.

"So?" replied *Brain-Dead*.

"Well, it's huge."

"Looks pretty normal to me. What do you think *Hipster*?"

Paul puffed on his cigarette as he considered his answer.

"Yeah, 'bout normal size I would say," he replied with a deadpan look on his face.

"What?" asked *Lard-Arse*, becoming worried.

"Are you trying to tell us that you've got a tiny cock?" asked *Brain-Dead*.

"Well...I...?"

"Just how small is it?" asked *Brain-Dead*, pressing the point.

"Er...normal...normal size."

"And what size is normal size to you then?"

"Er...twelve inches..."

Paul winked at Dave behind *Lard-Arse's* back, while *Brain-Dead* went in for the kill.

"Twelve inches? Jesus *Tubby*, no wonder you can never get a bird. Twelve inches, that's not a cock, that's a foot!"

"Well, how long's yours?" asked *Lard-Arse*, not getting the joke and becoming quite distressed.

"Oh, about eighteen or nineteen inches."

"Fuck off! You're kidding, right?"

"No, straight up. Longer, obviously, when I get a hard on!"

Paul and Dave could not hold out any longer and fell about laughing.

"You fuckers!" muttered *Lard-Arse*.

"My god, that broad's being fucked by a horse!" exclaimed Dave, pointing at another magazine behind a selection of vibrators and 'love eggs'.

Sure enough, on the front cover there was indeed a very attractive woman being fucked by a horse with a huge, unsurprisingly, horse-sized knob.

"How do you think they get the horse to do that?" asked Dave, wiping the tears from his eyes.

"Sugar lumps," replied *Brain-Dead*.

"You're joking?" said *Lard-Arse*, setting himself up for another fall.

"Yeah," *Brain-Dead* continued, "that's what they always give horses to get 'em going. That's why teenage girls always take boxes of sugar lumps down to the stables when they're feeling horny. It's not just horses either; they also give 'em to pigs. Did you know that a pig has a cock like a corkscrew? Oh yes, it curls rounds as it's going in. That's why you shouldn't disturb a pig mid-shag, 'cause he can't get out even if he wanted to, not until it dies down. Anyway, didn't you see that tragic accident with the horse in last year's *Grand National*?"

"The Grand what?" asked Dave

"*Grand National, Yank*. Famous horse race," explained *Brain-Dead*.

"No, why what happened?" asked *Lard-Arse*, puzzled.

"Awful it was. A jockey stupidly gave his horse a sugar lump just before the race. Then as they were jumping the second fence, the horse got a huge boner which shot out and embedded itself in the fence, flipping both off them over like a couple of pole vaulters."

Dave and Paul creased up again.

"Oh fuck off, you twats," said *Lard-Arse*, angrily stomping off down the street.

By the time they caught up with him, *Lard-Arse* had found a semi-permanent structure, the size of a large newsstand that sold burgers and other sorts of fast food.

"Got the munchies, my tubby friend?" asked *Brain-Dead*.

"Oh yeah, I'm fucking starving. Bag of chips please *Luv*," said *Lard-Arse* to a woman in a white coat.

"French fries?" she asked.

"Yes that's right, French fries."

They all decided that a bag of fries sounded wonderful and put in identical orders. Minutes later the woman was pouring fantastic-looking golden fries into a paper cone and covering them with salt.

"They look bloody great!" exclaimed *Lard-Arse*, forgetting his previous travails.

The woman then placed the cone under a large dispenser and thumped down on a plunger, covering the fries in a sea of white sludge.

"Woah," howled *Lard-Arse*, "what the fuck is that stuff?"

As the woman handed *Lard-Arse* his cone of fries, he glared at her with a look of pure hatred.

"Well, what is it?" Dave asked.

Lard-Arse dipped his finger in the white goo and put it in his mouth.

"Mmm...mayonnaise!" he replied, his face brightening.

He then dipped a fry in the mayonnaise and took a bite. "Oh fuck, that's delicious,"

"I don't believe it," laughed *Brain-Dead*. "The *Fat One* has found a way to make chips even more fattening!"

With all of them now armed with cones of fries and mayonnaise, they strolled by the side of a canal checking out the bars, cathouses and sex shops they passed along the way. Every few yards someone would offer them drugs or invite them into a brothel or sex show, which added to the entertainment. The most fascinating game though was rating the prostitutes sitting in the windows or standing outside the cathouses they passed. Some were unbelievably gorgeous, some unbelievably hideous. Eventually, however, they reached a very pleasant bar with large open windows facing the canal and a lively crowd inside.

"Anyone fancy a beer?" asked *Lard-Arse*.

"I most certainly do, *Chubster*," replied *Brain-Dead*.

So in they went and, after checking with the mustached bartender that they could smoke hash, they settled down in some extremely comfortable leather chairs by the window and watched their beers being poured, the froth being whipped off using a spatula and then brought over to their table. The first beers hardly touched the sides and so another four were ordered straight away.

"Can we have large beers this time, please?" *Lard-Arse* asked the bartender.

"You are English, yes?" asked the bartender. "The English always ask for big beers."

But he was more than happy to supply them in the shape of four enormous steins, just as a huge ginger tomcat ambled up to their table and began rubbing himself up Paul's leg. Paul responded by tickling the feline brute under his many chins, something the cat obviously enjoyed as it arched its back, closed its eyes and purred with delight.

"Fuck me *Tubby*, that cat looks just like you," laughed *Brain-Dead*. "You're not related are you?"

As they sat drinking beer and smoking joint after joint, with Paul playing with his newly found furry friend, they were fascinated by the steady stream of men visiting the prostitutes on the opposite side of the canal. The process was the same every time. Some guy would stroll along past the brothels pretending to take no more than a casual interest in the prostitutes. He would then turn around and retrace his steps, furtively look around him (as if his wife or a private detective might be following him) before approaching the prostitute he had chosen and following her into the room as quickly as possible. The drapes would then close over the windows and anywhere between ten minutes and half an hour would pass before the man would reappear and shoot out of the room, head down, and charge off into the distance. The girl would then open the drapes and take up her position again, either in the window or standing outside.

What was particularly interesting was the choice of prostitute. In this particular row there were six women. Some were actively plying for trade, by chatting to all the men who passed, but some appeared bored out of their brains, reading books or magazines as they sat in the window. One was an absolute stunner dressed in a bustier with stockings and garters, a couple were reasonably good looking although one of them was incredibly tall, one was a fat, old woman dressed in dominatrix gear and holding a whip, one was very plain with dreadful acne and the last was a possibly the ugliest troll the guys had ever seen. And who was the busiest? The troll! Dave was amazed by this.

"Why is the ugliest one the busiest?" he asked.

"An interesting question, my son," Paul replied thoughtfully puffing on the latest joint. "Perhaps they find her less intimidating."

"I think I might have to shag the one in the sexy gear," announced *Brain-Dead*.

"Oh jeez, you are joking aren't you?" said a stunned Dave. "What about Pam?"

"If Pam was here I'd shag her but, as she's not, I've got to get rid of the 'bone' I've got somehow."

"That's terrible," spluttered Paul.

"Chill out *Hippy*. As long as she doesn't find out and I wear a 'raincoat' on my 'old man', there's no harm done. Anyway, all these tarts are checked every week to make sure you don't go home with a big mushroom growing on your cock. D'ya fancy a go with one of 'em *Fat Boy*; it'll be the only chance of a shag that you'll get."

"I do actually," smiled *Lard-Arse*. "I quite fancy that tall one on the left."

"Oh yeah, why her? She's a bit of an *Amazon*. Are you worried you'd crush the others?" laughed *Brain-Dead*.

"Right then Hippy, pass over the kitty money."

"You've got to be kidding. Me and Dave aren't paying for you two to get your nuts off," protested Paul.

"Miserable fuckers! Come on *Lardy*, let's go treat these birds to a good seeing to."

Dave and Paul watched with morbid fascination as *Brain-Dead* and *Lard-Arse* stood up and left the bar. They disappeared out of sight for a while to find a bridge to cross the canal, before reappearing outside the row of windows.

"I don't believe I'm watching this," said Dave open-mouthed.

"It is rather surreal, my son. We're not tripping this, are we?" laughed Paul.

Brain-Dead, without any hesitation whatsoever, marched up to the girl in the bustier and spoke to her. After a brief conversation, he followed her into the little room, giving *Lard-Arse* and then Paul and Dave a 'thumbs up' as he went. As the prostitute pulled the drapes across, they could distinctly see *Brain-Dead* inside already pulling his pants down.

"He's keen, isn't he?" laughed Paul.

Lard-Arse, meanwhile, watched *Brain-Dead* disappear before approaching the very tall girl standing outside the room next door.

"She's very big, isn't she?" Dave noted.

"She's not big, my son, she's huge. Look at the size of her hands!" laughed Paul.

The negotiations completed, *Lard-Arse* followed the *Amazon* into the room and could be seen fumbling for his wallet as she closed the drapes. Paul and Dave decided that it would be hilarious to time how long *Brain-Dead* and *Lard-Arse* spent 'on the job' and they speculated what depravity each would be up to. The hand on Dave's watch had just passed the three minutes mark when, to their surprise and intense amusement, the door of *Lard-Arse's* room flew open and *Lard-Arse* shot out like a bullet out of a gun, tugging up his pants as he ran off. He looked like he'd seen a ghost! Dave and Paul gave each other quizzical looks but, before they had chance to speculate on what could have possibly happened, *Lard-Arse* crashed into the bar like an angry bull elephant, charged up to the table and, without saying a word, grabbed hold of Paul's three-quarter full liter glass of beer and downed it in one.

"I need a whisky, please get me a whisky," he croaked pitifully.

"What happened?" asked Dave, staring at *Lard-Arse's* shaking hands.

"She...she...had a cock!" he spluttered.

"What?" said Paul, spitting his joint six feet across the floor.

"A whisky, I need a whisky," pleaded *Lard-Arse.*

"We'll get you a whisky, but just repeat what you said," laughed Paul.

"She...she wasn't a she, she was a he," mumbled *Lard-Arse* sitting down.

"What do you mean?" asked Dave.

"I mean that I got in there, paid her a load of cash and got my clothes off like she told me to. Then she got on the bed and told me to come over and play with her tits, which I did. And then...then I stuck my hands down her knickers and...and she had a fucking cock!"

Paul and Dave fell about laughing.

"Don't laugh you bastards, it's not bloody funny!" wailed *Lard-Arse.*

If Paul and Dave had been stone cold sober, they couldn't have stopped laughing even if they'd wanted to but, being totally wasted, this was the funniest thing they'd ever heard and they laughed until tears rolled down their faces and their tummies hurt. *Lard-Arse* wasn't impressed by this at all and stormed off to the bar to get himself a large whisky. They had only just started to calm down when *Lard-Arse* returned, but just seeing his face was enough to set them off again and it grew in intensity to such a pitch that Dave thought he was going to wet himself.

"I'm sorry man, but it's just so funny!" howled Paul.

"Glad you think so," mumbled *Lard-Arse*, swallowing his whisky.

"Didn't she...I mean 'he' tell you he was a guy before you went in?" asked Dave, trying to calm down as he could see he was upsetting *Lard-Arse*.

"What do you think? D'ya think I'd have gone in there if he had?" replied *Lard-Arse*, becoming angry.

Dave had to turn away to hide his smirk from *Lard-Arse* and at that very moment saw *Brain-Dead* reappearing from his room. Seeing Dave, *Brain-Dead* waved and gave a thumbs up. Then, noticing that the room *Lard-Arse* had been in had its drapes closed and presuming that *Lard-Arse* must still be in there, *Brain-Dead* mimed out a little sketch presumably featuring *Lard-Arse* screwing. Dave, in return, motioned that *Lard-Arse* was back in the bar rather than behind the drapes, so *Brain-Dead* set off towards the bridge.

"*Brain-Dead's* on his way," said Dave.

"Oh God no!" wailed *Lard-Arse*. "Don't say a fucking word, do you understand me? Not a fucking word. He'll make my life an absolute misery."

Dave and Paul looked at each other. Both could try not to talk but there was no way on earth that they wouldn't start laughing the second they saw *Brain-Dead* and they didn't have long to wait.

"Ta dah!" yelled *Brain-Dead*, throwing the door of the bar open with a flourish. "Well boys, I fucked her to within an inch of her life. I was so fucking good she wanted to give me my money back, as long as I promised to shag her again tomorrow."

Several of the customers in the bar turned to see the source of the obscene ranting.

"Come and sit down you idiot, you're making a show of us," Dave hissed at him.

"Now, now *Studly*, don't get upset just 'cause you're in the presence of a *Super Stud* and your sacks haven't been emptied," laughed *Brain-Dead*, sitting down. "So *Tubby*, how was yours? I presume she had to go on top."

Dave and Paul bit their lips.

"Er...it was OK," mumbled *Lard-Arse*.

"That's not enough information, my fat friend. We need all the gory details. Did you make her squeal like a stuck pig? Did you fulfill any bizarre kinky fantasies? Tell us all and omit no detail."

"I said it was OK, OK?" snapped *Lard-Arse*.

"Ah ha, do I detect a little bitterness, *Flabmeister*? Is it possible that your performance wasn't quite up to the required standard, eh? What happened, couldn't you find your cock under all your tires, or did your 'old fella' shoot the moment he saw the light of day?"

"Just fuck off, will you? I don't want to talk about it."

Paul couldn't hold his laughter any longer as he had tears seeping out of his eyes, so he exploded. *Lard-Arse* glared at him.

"Methinks you aren't giving old *Brain-Dead* information you've obviously given to these two nerks. So, the question is, are you going to spill the beans *Lard-Boy*, or do I have to extract the truth from you, by fair means or foul? You know it's only a matter of time until I find out what happened, so you might as well get it over with and stop torturing yourself. Think of it like choosing to do that essay at he beginning of the weekend, as opposed to having it hanging over you and rushing it through on a Sunday night after a skin full of beers."

Lard-Arse looked nervously at Dave and Paul and, deciding that he couldn't trust them to keep his secret, decided to get it over with.

"I didn't fuck her 'cause she was a bloke," he mumbled.

"What?" laughed *Brain-Dead*.

"You heard me, you fucker. Don't make this any worse for me than it already is and don't tell anyone else about it."

"Oh mate, I'm so sorry. That must have been a terrible shock," cooed *Brain-Dead* in a sympathetic voice. "Tell me all."

Lard-Arse fell for it and, with *Brain-Dead* listening intently without so much as a flicker across his face, described his experience down to the last detail. When he had finished, *Brain-Dead* took a moment before looking up from his beer. When he did, he had an evil smirk on his face.

"So, you would like us to believe that you didn't know it was a bloke before you went in there and dropped your *trollies*?" he asked.

"Yeah!" replied *Lard-Arse*, indignantly.

"So, there wasn't just a little corner of your mind that fancied a spot of 'Hide the Sausage' with *Ladyboy* over there?" *Brain-Dead* grinned.

"Absolutely not!"

"Not even the slightest inclination to get your botty cheeks parted and to chomp down on the pillow while the *Arse Bandit* lifted your shirt and packed your fudge for you?" *Brain-Dead* continued.

"Just fuck off!"

"Or did you fancy doing the uphill gardening? Was he your bitch? Did you fancy riding the arse off him?"

"I don't have to take this," yelled *Lard-Arse* standing up.

"Calm down, *Blubber-Boy*. I'm just trying to get to the *bottom* of this incident to try to establish whether we're safe in our beds tonight or whether we'll wake up with sore arses in the morning!"

"I'm off."

"Oh come on buddy, he's just trying to jerk your chain," smiled Dave, pulling at *Lard-Arse's* arm to prevent him walking away.

"Yeah, I'm sorry. Sit down. I know you' re not gay," laughed *Brain-Dead*, putting his arms up to surrender.

Lard-Arse hesitated and then sat down again.

"And I want to know what you've got against gay people?" asked Paul. "There could be some people in this bar who are gay and who find what you've just said rather offensive."

"Oooh, are you a bit 'ginger beer' yourself *Hippy*?" laughed *Brain-Dead*.

"As it happens I'm not, but I still don't think you should talk like that."

"OK, I won't say anymore on the subject and I accept *Lardy's* explanation. But what everyone back home will make of it, I cannot say," grinned *Brain-Dead*.

"Oh please don't shoot your mouth off about it at home," begged *Lard-Arse* with the color draining from his cheeks.

"I think they have a right to know and draw their own conclusions. It's in the public interest"

"You wouldn't? Oh you bastard, please don't tell anyone. I'm not gay, I really thought he was a woman," sobbed *Lard-Arse*.

"Come on," Dave interjected, "stop teasing or you'll ruin his weekend."

"And why should I?" grinned *Brain-Dead*, clearly enjoying the pain he was causing.

Paul considered this for a moment, dragging on his spliff.

"Er...how about 'cause if you do tell anyone, we'll all say it was actually you who had the gay experience? That'd be three against one," smiled Paul.

"Yes!" shouted *Lard-Arse*, punching the air. "Got you, you fucker! Oh, thank you Paul, I owe you one."
"Judas," muttered *Brain-Dead*, accepting defeat.

"Just chill out man, we don't want a load of stress and heavy shit when we're on our *Dam* weekend. Here, tug on that and tell us about your bit of nookie," smiled Paul, handing the spliff over to *Brain-Dead*.

Dave was very impressed with Paul's diplomatic intervention. *Brain-Dead* settled back to recount his experience in graphic detail, as he puffed on the spliff and glugged down his beer. *Lard-Arse*, meanwhile, finally calmed down and accepted another joint that Paul had prepared for him.

And this was how the rest of the afternoon was passed; joint after joint was smoked and beer after beer was consumed as they laughed and chatted, watched the world go by, scored every passing woman out of ten and continued to be fascinated by the prostitutes plying their trade on the other side of the canal.

"Another beer?" slurred *Brain-Dead*, a few hours later.

"Oh no thanks man, I've had enough alcohol. I'll just stick to the drugs now," replied Paul.

"You big girl," retorted *Brain-Dead*, nearly falling over as he tried to stand up. "You bloody, southern hippies are all the bloody same, you just can't take your beer."

"I'll just have a glass please," said Dave.

"Another bloody puff! Oops, sorry *Luv*," said *Brain-Dead*, crashing into a woman sitting behind him who was trying to enjoy a quiet coffee.

"I'll have a beer, but I'm still feeling a bit horny. How about we go and find some *wank booths*?" grinned *Lard-Arse*.

"What?" laughed Dave.

"*Wank booths*. In the sex shops you pick a porn film and take it into a little booth and have a wank. It's all very civilized," *Lard-Arse* explained.

"Say what?" laughed Dave.

"Oh yeah, it's true *Studly*," interjected *Brain-Dead*. "They cater for every perversion you could possibly think of and some you'd never have thought of in a million fucking years.
We'll have these beers and then we'll go and check 'em out."

As they were enjoying their last beers, Dave suddenly gasped. He was convinced he was tripping on the drugs because he had just seen a cat's face appear in *Lard-Arse's* hair. It reminded him of a scene in *Alice in Wonderland* where the Cheshire Cat's face keeps appearing, because he could just make out the eyes, nose and mouth amidst the shock of ginger hair on *Lard-Arse's* head. Dave was trying to pull himself together when two paws also appeared. *Lard-Arse* meanwhile was chatting to Paul while slumped back in a soft, leather armchair. Dave rubbed his eyes to rid himself of the apparition, but it was still there.

"You OK, *Yank*?" asked *Brain-Dead*. "You look like you've seen a ghost."

Before Dave could answer, *Lard-Arse* leapt into the air with what looked like a Daniel Boone dead animal hat on his head. But this animal wasn't dead. This animal was a twenty-pound cat, fucking *Lard-Arse's* head. *Lard-Arse* screamed and set off across the bar, crashing into tables with arms flailing as he tried to remove the horny headgear. Quite where he thought he was going, no one could say. But, as there isn't a manual for the removal of fornicating felines from one's head, no one could criticize his choice of action, not even the customers now wearing their drinks or collecting their belongings from the floor. The cat, meanwhile, didn't seem to be able to choose between the obviously pleasurable head-fuck and the less than pleasurable high-speed pirouetting. He grimaced at the latter during the more violent maneuvers, before getting back to the 'vinegar strokes' with a grin even bigger than that of his relative in Cheshire. The customers in the bar began clapping in time to *Lard-Arse's* dance moves, egged on by an enthusiastic compere in *Brain-Dead* shouting encouragement to *Lard-Arse's* head-rapist.

"Go on pussy, fuck his head. There's a boy. Look, he's smiling," yelled *Brain-Dead*.

"I'm not fucking smiling. Help me get this bastard thing off my head, you twat!" screamed *Lard-Arse*, shortly before landing a backward punch straight in the cat's smiling kisser that Bruce Lee would have been proud of.

A large ball of ginger hair flew through the air, before landing like a gymnast on a four paws. Even if he could have stood up on his back paws and bowed he could not have been more cool, nor more appreciated by his adoring audience, who broke into spontaneous applause. *Lard-Arse* was not at all happy at his abuser's newly found popularity or on discovering a damp patch on his head. He resented being this pussy's piece of pussy and decided to kick his ginger ass into the middle of next week. He lined himself up with the precision of a football kicker in the final seconds of a Super Bowl and began his run up. This preparation, however, had alerted his target to *Lard-Arse's* dastardly scheme so, as *Lard-Arse* was on his final approach, he performed his other party trick; namely puffing out his fur so that he became three times his already substantial size and hissing like a venom-spitting snake.

The crowd gasped at their champion's remarkable transformation, which stopped *Lard-Arse* mid-run up, and applauded once again as their hero swaggered off behind the bar, his passion sated and with his head held high.

"It's a pity no woman wants to fuck you like all these animals do," noted

Brain-Dead. "It must be a gift you have. You're like some fuck me *Dr. Doolittle.*"

"Can we just get the fuck out of here please," moaned *Lard-Arse*, wiping cat ejaculate out of his hair with a beer mat.

Forty minutes later, the four of them were in a sex shop that was so huge it was more like a supermarket. All the fetishes and perversions had their own area of the shop and, in the middle, was a massive table covered with porno movies of every description.

"See, what did I tell ya'?" grinned *Brain-Dead.* "They've got everything you could ever want here. So what'll it be? Animals shagging birds, birds pissing on blokes, birds tied up, blokes tied up, rubber, leather, S & M, group shagging, shagging up the arse, shagging in the gob?"

"Haven' t they got any normal stuff?" asked Paul, rifling through the boxes.

"Normal stuff? The Dutch don't do normal stuff, you stupid fucking *Hippy.* No, the Dutch are like the Scandinavians, they like their shagging kinky. I tell ya', if you went out with a Dutch bird and didn't stick it up her arse or ask her mother to blow you off on the first date, she'd think you were fucking weird."

"Oh Jeez, I can't imagine screwing someone up the ass. The very thought of it makes me shudder," said Dave, shuddering.

"Well *Studly*, I'm surprised at you. You've never done it up the arse? You haven't lived man. It's excellent sport at the best of times, but it's especially useful when your bird's up on blocks."

"Up on blocks?"

"You know, got the monthly decorators in. Oh yeah, it's very useful in 'Blowjob week'. When you get that whiff of shit..."

"Oh please stop, you're making me sick," pleaded Dave.

"This one looks OK," said Paul, reading the back cover, 'Hot lesbian action'."

"A fine choice *Hippy*. And you *Tubster*, a bit of *ladyboy* fun for you maybe or some animal action?"

"Fuck off. No, I'll take this one."

"Let me see," said *Brain-Dead*, "'Mary sucks cocks', an excellent selection. So, it's just you now *Stud*. Come on, pick a bloody film."

Dave chose 'Horny Housewives' and followed the others to the cash desk, past mannequins in rubber suits, a startling array of vibrators and ducking under a dozen blow up dolls hanging from the ceiling.

"Buy or view?" asked the man behind the counter.

The boys replied that they wanted to 'view' and paid their money before heading towards one corner of the store. Here they found four tiny rooms in a row, each the size of a toilet cubicle or a confessional and constructed out of plywood. Dave entered his and locked the door behind him. Inside were a chair, a television and a DVD player into which he shoved his movie and pressed the play button. Next to him on the wall was a roll of toilet paper, with a step-on trashcan below it. Listening to Paul and *Lard-Arse* doing exactly the same through the paper-thin walls, Dave laughed at the ridiculousness of the situation. But he still dropped his pants and sat down to watch his film. It didn't take long for him to finish, so he wiped himself down with the toilet paper and threw it into the bin.

"Well?" asked *Brain-Dead* as Dave appeared.

"That was a totally bizarre experience," Dave laughed.

"Come on *Lardy*, we're all waiting for you and I want a drink," *Brain-Dead* yelled.

"Fuck off will you, I'm nearly there," came the reply from the little booth.

Once *Lard-Arse* reappeared they set off on a tour of bars in the red light district. The whole place had a party atmosphere to it, somehow managing to avoid seediness, despite sex being on sale at every turn. Dave decided that this was due to the mix of people strolling around and populating the bars and cafes. All ages and all nationalities were represented in this adult theme park and there were as many couples as there were bachelor parties and dirty old men. Everyone seemed out to enjoy themselves and wherever the boys went they were met by cheery bar staff and equally friendly customers who wanted to know where they were from and if they were enjoying themselves; something that should have been very obvious.

It was approaching three o'clock in the morning when they finally decided to call it a night, as the bars had begun to close and the streets started to empty. Paul hadn't touched any alcohol for hours, preferring coffee and orange juice, but had been chain-smoking joint after joint with clockwork regularity. Dave hadn't drunk as much as *Brain-Dead* or *Lard-Arse* nor smoked as much as Paul, but he was decidedly unsteady on his feet as they staggered along. *Lard-Arse* and *Brain-Dead*, meanwhile, were absolutely stewed. They had consumed a steady flow of beer all evening, as well as smoking enough grass to put a bull elephant to sleep. But the one thing they all had in common, in addition to an inability to walk in a straight line or to stop laughing, was a desperate hunger. *Lard-Arse* was suffering from this in particular and shrieked with delight when they rounded a corner to find an operational burger truck. By the time they had waited in a line of fellow drunks for fifteen minutes, his order had become a distress purchase. He almost cried on being informed that he would have to wait ten minutes for either a burger or some fries to be cooked, but agreed to take two hot dogs while he was waiting. The others went for the hot dog option and were busy piling ketchup and mustard onto them when they were approached by an old gypsy-looking woman dressed in colorful but grubby clothes and with a shawl around her head.

"You wanna fuck my daughter?" she hissed at Paul.

"What?" spluttered Paul, who had just taken a bite from the end of his hot dog.

"You wanna fuck my daughter?" repeated the woman, pushing forward a tubby girl who proved, categorically, that ugliness is hereditary.

"No thanks," replied Paul recoiling.

The old woman then turned to Dave who, that very moment, had bitten into his hot dog to find that not only was it stone cold and full of water, but that it contained a single piece of gristle which ran the entire length of the frankfurter.

"What about you, do you wanna fuck her? She'll do anything you want," the hag insisted.

Dave was busily extracting the gristle with his teeth and could only shake his head.

"What's wrong with you, are you a homo or something?" asked the woman before grabbing hold of Dave's crotch and squeezing. "She'll suck you off!"

Dave howled and spat the gristle out onto the sidewalk, dropping his hot dog in the process.

"Get off me," he yelled, fighting her off.

The old woman, giving up on Paul and Dave, turned to *Brain-Dead*.

"What about you?" she asked.

"I don't fancy her, but I'll fuck you, you sexy beast," grinned *Brain-Dead*, extending his enormous tongue.

The old woman recoiled and dragged her daughter away.

"Pervert," she yelled, as the two of them scuttled off down the street.

It was only once Lard-Arse had his burger and fries and moved on that they realized they hadn't got a clue where their hotel was. They had managed to find the Leidseplein, but couldn't remember which of the many streets off the square they should take. They couldn't even remember the name of the hotel!

"I remember it had a funny name," slurred *Lard-Arse*.

"Oh brilliant! That's a big fucking help, *Sherlock*," said *Brain-Dead*, urinating into a litterbin.

"No, he's right," said Paul. "It was something like...like..."

"Like what?" laughed *Brain-Dead*, shaking the last drops of urine from his penis at a couple of horrified passers-by.

"I can't remember," smiled Paul.

"Wasn't it the *Scotty Dog Hotel* or something?" Dave suggested.

"Why don't we ask those policemen?" suggested *Lard-Arse,* pointing at the two figures approaching them from across the square.

"I'll handle this," said *Brain-Dead*, furiously stuffing his penis back into his shorts.

"Speaky English? Speaky English?" asked *Brain-Dead*, once the immaculately dressed policemen had reached them.

"Of course," replied the younger, blonde-haired one of the two, rolling his eyes at his mustached, plumper colleague.

"Oh, right ho then, just checking. We were wondering if you could point us in the direction of our hotel," *Brain-Dead* continued. "It's just that we can't remember what it's called."

The two policemen laughed.

"Do you have a key?" asked one.

"Oh yeah, I've got the key," replied *Lard-Arse*, fumbling around in his pockets to find it.

"Yes, here it is."

"And does it have the hotel name on it?" grinned the policeman.

"Oh yeah, will you look at that, *Hotel Edinburgh*," grinned *Lard-Arse*.

"You dumb, fucking moron," growled *Brain-Dead*.

"Ze *Hotel Edinburgh* is down zat road zere, on ze right," said the second policeman, pointing the way. "Have a nice time in Omsterdom, but please not to use our litterbins as toilets."

As the crow flies, the journey from the Leidseplein to the *Hotel Edinburgh* is no distance at all unless, that is, the crow is stoned and juiced out of its tiny mind. In which case the crow would have to cover three times the distance, flying from one side of the street to the other and crashing off lampposts and walls as it went; not to mention stopping to piss every few yards and singing badly at the top of its voice. The hotel, however, was eventually found.

377

"Evening all," yelled *Lard-Arse*, holding his finger on the bell.

"I don't think we're going to be very popular," noted Paul as lights came on and the sound of approaching feet could be heard behind the door.

"Fucking hell!" screamed *Lard-Arse* as the door swung open to reveal the lady of the house in a hideous nightgown with her hair in curlers and some sort of pack on her face.

"Yes?" she asked, pulling *Lard-Arse's* finger off the bell.

"Ah, good evening Madam", interjected *Brain-Dead*. "I'm sorry to disturb you, but the time just slipped by in this wonderful city of yours. I trust you had a pleasant evening and that you weren't servicing *Mr. Hotel* when we rang the bell."

It was not evident whether the lady hotelier understood *Brain-Dead* or whether she just decided to ignore him, as her face didn't flicker. Instead she looked at *Lard-Arse* and asked, "Have you lost your key?"

"Oh no, it's right here," smiled *Lard-Arse*, holding up the key ring.

"Vell, zer are two keys. Von for your room and von for zis door and..."

Before she finished what she was trying to say *Lard-Arse* collapsed forward, knocking her backwards off her feet and fell on top of her. If he had been a professional wrestler leaping from the ropes, he couldn't have performed a more perfect 'splash'. The other three stood open-mouthed, worried at first that she might have been crushed to death, but then worried that they might be arrested as she screamed the house down. Movement could be heard all over the hotel but still *Lard-Arse* didn't move. Then, as a door opened, a white blur shot across the floor, making a scratching sound as it went and a moment later Douglas had leapt up astride *Lard-Arse* and was busily ass-fucking him. Douglas's attentions stirred *Lard-Arse* and he began waving his arm behind him in an attempt to remove the horny hound. He made no effort to get up, however, and his writhing simply crushed the poor woman underneath into the floor, causing her to gasp for breath.

"Vat is going on!" yelled *Mr. Hotelier*, making an appearance at last and finding the kinkiest threesome the world has ever seen writhing around on his lobby floor.

"Get that bastard off me!" yelled *Lard-Arse*, still wafting his arms at the grinning dog pumping away on his backside.

Madam yelled something at her husband in Dutch which, presumably, also meant 'Get that bastard off me!" but which referred to *Lard-Arse* rather than the dog. So, with help from Dave (*Brain-Dead* was too busy crying with laughter and Paul was too busy lighting a joint), the hotelier dragged *Lard-Arse* to his feet. Then, as *Lard-Arse* hopped around the lobby with the little dog still attached, the hotelier pulled his sobbing wife to her feet. A small crowd had gathered as the wife ran off down the corridor in floods of tears and a flurry of man-made fibers, leaving them to enjoy the 'Dog-fucking-fat-Englishman' floorshow. And enjoy it they did! Amidst the laughter came applause as the odd couple pirouetted around all four corners of the lobby, pursued by the hotelier intent on putting an end to this early morning entertainment. Douglas, however, was a canny dog and every time his master's hand came within striking distance of his collar, he skillfully guided his dancing partner out of harm' s way. At one point, he had to give *Lard-Arse* a little nip with his teeth to up the tempo, but generally he simply grinned a hairy grin and lapped up the plaudits of his audience. All good things have to come to an end, however, and when Douglas reached the climax of his performance in the most literal of ways, covering his partner for the third time in twenty-four hours, he dropped his guard, allowing his weary master to get a hand on his collar and wrench him off a now-exhausted *Lard-Arse*. The crowd clearly wanted more and hissed their disapproval as their hero was led away, a spent force.

"That fucking dog!" puffed *Lard-Arse*, feeling the damp patch on the back of his pants.

As *Brain-Dead* was still sobbing with silent laughter and clearly not in a consoling mood, Dave put his arm around the clearly upset *Lard-Arse* and led him off through the crowd towards their room. They had nearly reached the door when *Lard-Arse* stopped and barfed violently over a passing Yucca plant.

"That'll be a nice surprise for them in the morning," noted *Brain-Dead*, without a great deal of sensitivity for his friend's already wounded feelings.

Dave, feeling somewhat more compassionate, took the room key off the now very distressed *Lard-Arse* and hurriedly unlocked the door. *Lard-Arse* staggered in, pulling his clothes off as he went and dropping them onto the floor and, in one smooth movement, climbed into his bed and pulled the covers over his head.

"Aren't you even going to brush your teeth?" asked *Brain-Dead*. "Douglas won't want to kiss you in the morning if you've got pukey breath."

"Just fuck off and leave me alone," came the muffled reply.

It was as he was sitting on the toilet that Dave realized just how 'out of it' he really was. He had made the very big mistake of closing his eyes as he strained and that was when it hit him. The room started spinning, he started shaking and, bizarrely, his forearms started sweating.

"Oh God, I hope I don't do an Elvis and die on the shitter!" he moaned out loud, imagining his parents arriving to inspect the place of his demise and being shown a bathroom in a cheap hotel in Amsterdam. For one crazy moment, he could see his mother laying flowers by the side of the toilet, like the floral tributes seen by the side of a road after a fatal accident.

Brain-Dead, however, managed to bring him to his senses in *Brain-Dead*'s inimitable style.

"Will you hurry up in there, *Studly*, I'm touching cloth. You' re not having another wank, are you?"

When Dave eventually pulled himself together and vacated the bathroom, Paul had forgotten his 'no smoking in the bedroom' rule and was sitting up in bed having a 'spliff for the road'. *Lard-Arse*, meanwhile, was dead to the world. No part of him was visible; there was just a mountain of heaving duvet emitting snores and the occasional rasping fart. This, not surprisingly, lead to a farting competition between *Brain-Dead* and Paul, both of whom seemed able to fart at will in various musical tones. To a neutral observer Paul was the hands-down winner of this particular contest, possibly thanks to his musical background, but *Brain-Dead* felt hard done by, as he had put himself at a disadvantage by having a 'dump', thus robbing himself of the required ammunition. The two of them were still mid competition when Dave fell asleep. The last thing he remembered was having the terrible 'swirling pits', thinking how he would never get to sleep and even considering making himself sick.

FOURTEEN

It was during a particularly deep phase of sleep and an exceptionally vivid dream that Dave became aware of a noise disturbing him. He tried to dismiss it at first, hoping that either it would go away or that it was part of his dream, but it didn't and it wasn't. As his brain kicked into gear, he lay in the darkness trying to figure out what the noise was. It sounded like running water but not like water from a faucet. Then it struck him; it was someone urinating!

"Jeez," thought Dave, now awake, "*Brain-Dead's* pissing out of the window."

He knew it wasn't *Lard-Arse* because he could see his huge slumbering bulk, like a hibernating bear. He knew it wasn't Paul, because Paul was asleep in the bed next to him. So it must be *Brain-Dead*, the filthy bastard!

"Why is he pissing out of the window, when we've got a bathroom?" thought Dave.

The pissing had now stopped and in the gloom Dave saw *Brain-Dead's* distinctive form climb back into his bed. Dave sighed to himself and turned onto his side to try to get back to sleep.

"Hold up a minute," he suddenly thought. "The windows wouldn't open, so where has *Brain-Dead* just pissed? Oh my God, he's pissed on the carpet!"

Now wide awake, Dave jumped out of bed and in the darkness started patting the floor with his hand, looking for a damp patch.

"*Brain-Dead*," he hissed. "*Brain-Dead* wake up."

Brain-Dead just groaned.

"*Brain-Dead*!"

"What is it? What' s wrong?" asked Paul, coming to.

"*Brain-Dead's* pissed all over the fucking carpet," replied Dave across the darkened room.

"Urgh, what...what's up?" asked *Lard-Arse*, who had also been disturbed.

"*Brain-Dead's* just pissed on the carpet apparently," said Paul, turning on the lamp by the side of his bed.

Everyone covered their eyes and howled with pain at the light, except *Brain-Dead* who was still asleep. When their eyes had got used to the light, *Lard-Arse* and Paul joined Dave on the floor to try to find where *Brain-Dead* had urinated, patting their way around the carpet.

"There's nothing here man," said Paul, climbing back into bed after a couple of minutes. "Maybe you dreamt it?"

"No...no, I didn't. I distinctly heard him pissing and it can't have been out of the window and it wasn't in the bathroom."

"Oi, *Brain-Dead* wake up. Wake up you twat," said *Lard-Arse* poking *Brain-Dead* in the abdomen through his duvet.

"What? What is it? Turn off the light you fuckers," he groaned.

"No, wake up and tell us where you pissed."

Brain-Dead was getting angry now.

"What is it? What do you want?" he growled, sitting up in bed. "What the fuck are you doing?"

"You've pissed somewhere and we're trying to find out where," said Dave, still patting.

"No I haven't."

"You have, I heard you. Get up and help us look."

Brain-Dead moaned as he threw back his duvet and climbed down onto the floor to help with the search.

"There's nothing here, you wankers," he said after a few token pats.

"Well it's a mystery," said Dave puzzled. "I distinctly heard you piss...wait up a minute, you're wringing wet!"

They all stared at *Brain-Dead*, who was sporting a pair of very old-fashioned stripy pajamas and they were indeed wet. Even *Brain-Dead* looked puzzled.

"How?" he mumbled.

Dave pulled back the duvet on *Brain-Dead's* bed.

"Oh my God, he's pissed in his bed."

"What?" grinned Paul, "He's wet the bed?"

"No, you don't understand," laughed Dave. "He got out of bed, pissed into it and then got back in and fell asleep."

"You dirty fucker!" laughed *Lard-Arse*. "Wait 'till everyone hears about this!"

"I...I haven't pissed, I've just...I've just been sweating," mumbled *Brain-Dead*, staring at the evidence.
"Sweating? Jesus man, that's a shit-load of sweat," smiled Paul, rolling himself a 'being-awaken-in-the-middle-of-the-night' roly.

Brain-Dead pulled back the duvet further to reveal the true extent of the damp patch. He then pulled the sheet off the mattress, which showed an identically shaped patch. Intrigued, he then turned the mattress over to find that the 'sweat' had made it through to the base.

"You sweat piss, do ya'?" giggled *Lard-Arse*.

"Oh fuck!" said *Brain-Dead*, reality finally dawning.

"Don't know how we're going to explain that one away," said Paul, lighting up. "I don't expect we're particular popular since *Lard-Arse* went trampolining on the old lady."

"Dunno how much a bed's gonna cost you, *Buddy*!" laughed *Lard-Arse*.

"What?" said *Brain-Dead* horrified.

"Oh yeah, they're bound to charge you for a new bed. Could cost a fortune as well, looks like a quality piece of furniture," *Lard-Arse* continued.

"Er...we've got to think of something," stuttered *Brain-Dead* uncomfortably. "We've got to think of some excuse."

"What's with the 'we'?" laughed *Lard-Arse*. "You were the one who pissed his bed, not us,"

Brain-Dead was now becoming frantic and began dancing from foot to foot.

"Oh Christ, oh Christ! Come on you bastards, help me," he babbled, ripping the sheets off the mattress and stuffing them in the pants press.

"What the fuck are you doing?" laughed Dave.

"I thought I'd make some soup! What do you think I'm doing you stupid Yank bastard? I'm going to dry the sheets out," snapped *Brain-Dead*.

"And what's going to happen when they take the sheets off?" laughed Paul, blowing a particularly impressive smoke ring.

"I'll...I'll say...er...I'll say I spilled a cup of tea."

"A cup of tea? There's a gallon of piss in that mattress," howled *Lard-Arse*.

"OK, I'll say I dropped the kettle on the bed," suggested *Brain-Dead*.

"'Well *Mr. Hotel-owner*, I was walking across the room with a kettle full of piss when I tripped and spilled it on the bed. So I went and pissed another kettle full and guess what happened? Yes, I dropped that one as well. So I got a third and a fourth and guess what happened...'"

"Oh, just fuck off you fat bastard," snarled *Brain-Dead*. "If you can't make any positive suggestions, why don't you just shut the fuck up?"

"Does Pam know you're a bed-wetter?" smiled Paul.

"*Hippy*, if you breathe a fucking word, you'll be puffing your fucking joints through your asshole. And as for you *Fat Boy*, correct me if I'm wrong, but I do believe this room was booked on your credit card, not mine. So, I suggest you get your fat butt over here and assist me before they slam the cost of a bed on your card!"

Lard-Arse went white.

"You ...you wouldn't."

Brain-Dead merely grinned at him.

"You fucker!"

Paul, meanwhile, began guiding operations from his bed.

"Why don't you turn the radiator all the way up and lean the mattress against it? And you're probably better off drying one sheet at a time in the trouser press."

"Oh thank you *Hippy*," snapped *Brain-Dead*. "And why don't you stop cuddling the *Yank* and get your soft, public school ass out of your pit to come and help us?"

Paul just laughed and blew another smoke ring before passing the joint to Dave.

"Seeing as you two are up, would you mind putting to kettle on and making us all a nice cup of tea?" asked Paul.

"I'll swing for you *Hippy*," replied *Brain-Dead* aggressively.

"Oh and while you're at it, you might as well open the drapes, it'll be dawn soon," giggled Dave.

After the sheets had been put in the pants press and the mattress had been leant against the piping-hot radiator, cups of tea were made and *Brain-Dead* and *Lard-Arse* settled themselves on the end of Dave and Paul's bed to take their share of the joints that Paul kept rolling. Before long they were all laughing about the situation and inventing ridiculous excuses that *Brain-Dead* could give to the hotelier. As they sat drinking tea and giggling Dave, yet again, leaned back and lapped up the humor and friendship he'd found with people he had only met ten days before. It didn't seem possible that they could be so at ease and naturally relaxed in each others' company in such a short space of time, but he felt privileged that they had adopted him and felt that they would always be his friends. Why they had decided to take him under their wings, he didn't quite understand. He was shy and was always nervy in new company and he was the least quirky or comic of any of them. Maybe that was it? Maybe they needed a straight guy or maybe it was just the copious amount of cannabis and alcohol that was making him get all soppy.

"You're a bit quiet *Yank*," noted *Brain-Dead*. "The public schoolboy didn't make you bite the pillow last night, did he?"

"No," laughed Dave, "but I was thinking that it might be best if we make a speedy exit. We could do with being out of here before the cleaner does our room."

"But what about breakfast?" moaned *Lard-Arse*. "I'm hungry and it's included in the price."

"I do despair about you at times, *Fat Boy*," sighed *Brain-Dead*. "You can go to breakfast if you really want to, chewing on some cardboard croissant while that dog rides the arse off you again and then you can explain to the hotel owner dude why you tried to pork his wife at four in the morning and why he's got a set of yellow sheets and a mattress leaning against a radiator with a gallon of piss seeping out of it."

Lard-Arse considered this for a moment.

"Yeah, maybe it is time for a sharp exit," he conceded. "Then we could find a *McDonald's* for breakfast, I saw one on the way back last night, but it was closed."

And so it was agreed that they would indeed make a discreet exit after showering and leaving the room as tidy as possible. It was just before eight o'clock when the four freshly-scrubbed friends picked up their bags, closed the door on a perfectly tidy room and made their way down the corridor towards the lobby.

"Won't they be suspicious when they see that we've made the beds?" asked Dave.

"Nobody makes their beds in hotels."

"Good point *Studly*," noted *Brain-Dead*. "I'll hang the 'Do not disturb' notice on the door. That'll give the bed a bit more time to dry out. We'll just leave the key behind reception on the way out."

"Woah, check out the stink of puke in this corridor," said Paul, holding his nose. "Some dirty bastard has chucked all over that plant. Look, you can see bits on it!"

"And where were you last night when *Lardy* gave the Yucca plant the benefit of a psychedelic yawn, you crazy bloody Hippy?" laughed *Brain-*

Dead.

"I must have missed that one," mused Paul, to himself as much as anyone else.

"The coast looks clear," whispered *Lard-Arse* as he ignored the conversation and poked his head around the lobby door. "The dude is nowhere to be seen and neither is that fucking dog."

"OK, let's go for it!" whispered *Brain-Dead*, pushing *Lard-Arse* forward.

Lard-Arse tiptoed up to the counter to deposit the key as the other three made for the door. He was just lowering the key over the counter, when a teenage girl with bright purple hair and three rings in one of her nostrils shot up like a jack-in-a-box.

"Fuck!" screamed *Lard-Arse*.

"Good Morning," grinned the girl. "Are you leaving so schoon?"

"Oh yes," replied *Brain-Dead*, noting that *Lard-Arse* was too shocked to speak. "Our coach leaves for England very early."

"Oh, that's a shame. Did you enjoy your stay?"

"Er...very nice thank you. We did have a little accident though."

"Oh yesh?"

"Yeah, I'm afraid I spilled a cup of water on the bed."

"Oh, zat's not a problem. You didn't wet ze bed did you?" laughed the girl.

All four boys laughed along with the girl at the very thought of such a thing.

"Oh no, no, no, cheeky!" giggled *Brain-Dead* unconvincingly.

"Oh veil, have a good journey and ve hope to shee you again schoon."

They all bade her 'Goodbye' and were edging quickly towards the exit when there came the now-familiar sound of paws scratching along wooden floorboards. At the sound of this, *Lard-Arse* started panicking and began pushing the others out of the door into the street, but he wasn't quick enough because Douglas suddenly flew around the corner. He had a sadistic grin on his furry face and his tongue was flapping in the breeze, as if he could already taste *Lard-Arse's* delicious rump. With the boys still fighting to get through the doorway, Douglas very gracefully took off and flew through the air with, it has to be said, a certain arrogance. As he began his descent into *Lard-Arse's* posterior, a missile in the shape of *Lard-Arse's* boot streaked up from the ground and towards the furry fiend.

The projectile was too fast and too unexpected for the hound to take evasive action, resulting in him taking a direct hit to his undercarriage. With the exception of *Lard-Arse*, whose delight was palpable, every male in the vicinity winced in sympathy as the now-pitiful animal took the full force of this testicle-parting, erection-destroying blow. As his momentum met that of *Lard-Arse's* size twelve, there was a moment when time stood still, when his paws seemed to wrap themselves around the boot and his tongue and eyes nearly popped out of his head. But he had met a much greater force than his tiny form could ever have coped with and with a violent jolt he went into full reverse. When *Lard-Arse's* leg reached the top of its arc, the dog parted company with the boot and retraced his flight path at a far greater speed than he had arrived. He sailed across the lobby and over the counter, narrowly missing the purple-haired desk clerk's head and on into the back office. Where he landed, none of the boys will ever know because they were already stampeding out of the door into the street and away.

"Did you see that?" laughed *Lard-Arse* when they'd reached the end of the street. "I got the little bastard. That'll teach him to fuck with me!"

"It was indeed a good performance, my fat friend. But, for the sake of accuracy, I must point out that the little fellow didn't fuck with you, he fucked you. Although I have to concede that you well and truly fucked him with that boot to the knackers."

"I don't think we'd better go back to the *Hotel Edinburgh* in a hurry," laughed Paul. "Anyone fancy a coffee and a spliff in that bar we went to yesterday morning?"

"Oh yeah!" grinned *Lard-Arse*. "And some breakfast. I think I deserve it."

It was midday when they eventually rolled out of the bar in the Leidseplein. All four of them were stoned out of their brains and were giggling uncontrollably. The bartender's face had lit up when they had walked in again and his grin didn't subside until they announced that they were off to 'take in a bit of culture'. All morning he had kept them topped up with a constant flow of coffee, orange juice, croissants and cannabis and, in an attempt to entice them and their money back, had offered to look after their bags to save them dragging them around Amsterdam. His offer had been gratefully accepted and they had waved him a cheery goodbye as they set off in search of the Rijksmuseum and the famous *Night Watch* painting by Rembrandt.

"This had better be worth it, *Hippy*," said *Brain-Dead*, as they consulted the map yet again.

Paul ignored him. He had spent at least an hour persuading his companions that they should see Amsterdam's equivalent of the *Mona Lisa* and another half an hour rolling a bundle of joints to keep them going on their journey. Dave, meanwhile, was enjoying the fresh air as they ambled along a canal watching tourist cruises glide by and cricking his neck to take in the tall canalside buildings. As they were crossing a small park, Dave became aware that his shoelace was undone and bent down to tie it. While he was in the crouched position, he suddenly felt himself being shoved downwards as *Brain-Dead* leapfrogged over him. As he looked up, *Brain-Dead* crouched down himself and Paul, joint in mouth, leapfrogged over him. Paul then took up the position and *Lard-Arse* leapfrogged over him.

"You crazy bastards," laughed Dave as *Lard-Arse* crouched down.

"Brace yourself *Tubby*," laughed *Brain-Dead*. "I'm gonna need a long run up to get over your fat chops."

With *Lard-Arse* bent over, *Brain-Dead* made a point of pacing away like a long jumper at the Olympics, before turning and charging towards his friend. Then, with more force than necessary, he shoved down on *Lard-Arse's* back and sailed over him.

"Awwww! You kicked me you clumsy twat," cried *Lard-Arse*, standing up and rubbing his ear.

"Oh my god," he yelled, staring at his hand before at sniffing it. "You stupid bastard, you've stood in dog shit and now it's all over my ear!"

"Oh hell, it's in your hair as well. You're covered in it," winced Paul.

Dave walked over to examine a clearly distressed *Lard-Arse*, who was whimpering as he stared at his dog shit covered fingers. It wasn't a pretty sight.

"It must have been a huge dog to shit that much," noted Paul. "And I think it must have a stomach upset 'cause its shit's really sloppy and it doesn't half stink. Poor dog."

"Poor dog?" howled *Lard-Arse*.

"Yeah, it must have really distressed the poor dog to squeeze that lot out. But look at my shoe, it's covered in the fucking stuff," moaned *Brain-Dead*, wiping his shoe sideways through the grass.

"Poor fucking dog?" repeated *Lard-Arse*.

"I wonder what sort of dog it was?" mused Dave.

"Poor fucking dog?" said *Lard-Arse* again, standing like a statue.

"Come on *Chubster*, shake a leg. You can't just stand there like some sort of fucking idiot covered in dog shit," said *Brain-Dead*.

"I can't believe you lot are worried about the fucking dog when it's me who's covered in shit," *Lard-Arse* protested.

"Not just you, my fat friend. I've got it on my fucking shoe."

"Well I've got it on my hand and in my hair and in my fucking ear and you're the bastard who put it there. So what I want to know is what the fuck you're gonna' do about it."

Lard-Arse was sobbing now.

"I have to point out to you that for one thing I didn't shit the shit, some poor dog did. And if you hadn't moved when I was mid leapfrog, you wouldn't have got it all over you."

"So it's all my fault, is it? It's my fault that you didn't fucking look where you were fucking going and piled through a load of fucking dog shit and stuck it all over my fucking head?" *Lard-Arse* now had big, hot tears streaming down his face. "It's my fucking fault that, thanks to you, I now stink of fucking dog shit and all you're fucking worried about is your fucking shoe? And another thing, if you say 'Poor fucking dog' once fucking more, I'll kick the fucking crap out of you!"

A particularly well-dressed Dutch couple who were taking a Sunday morning stroll in the park with their young son, who in turn was trying to get to grips with his tricycle, stopped and stared in open-mouthed horror at the stream of expletives pouring from this crazed Englishman dripping in malodorous canine feces. The mother lifted the boy from his tricycle and covered his ears as the father picked up the bike. They then made off across the park as quickly as they could, in case the English lunatic became violent.

"Fucking dog shit, fucking dog shit," repeated the grinning boy, as he was carried away.

"Can I suggest the fountain?" asked Paul, quietly.

"The what?" asked *Lard-Arse*.

"The fountain over there. Why don't you wash yourself off in the fountain?"

"It comes with shower gel does it?" snarled Lard-Arse.

"It was just a suggestion," grumbled Paul. "If you've got a better one..."

Lard-Arse stared across at the fountain in the middle of the park, visibly weighing up his options.

"We can hardly go back to the hotel and ask to use the shower," added Dave. "Not now you've crippled their dog."

"There's a certain poetic justice in this, isn't there?" mused Brain-Dead. "You'll have to wash it off somewhere 'cause you can hardly march around all day covered in shite and then jump back on the coach for a twenty-four hour journey home."

Five minutes later, to the bemusement of the Sunday strollers, *Lard-Arse* was sticking his head under the cascading water of the ornamental fountain, washing dog shit out of his ear. It was unanimously agreed that he couldn't take his coat or shirt off first, as they would get covered in shit as well, so Dave helped zip his coat up to the top to stop him getting soaked.

"That better?" asked Paul when he'd finished.

"It's better, but I still stink of shit. Can't we go back to the bar? I've got some shampoo in my bag."

"Oh, there' s no point going all the way back there," said *Brain-Dead*. "We're nearly at the museum now. You can wash your hair in the bogs there."

Lard-Arse was eventually persuaded that this was the better plan and they trooped off to the museum. The security guards on duty at the entrance gave him some puzzled looks, wondering why he was soaking wet on such a sunny day and trying to work out where the awful smell was coming from. But it was a much happier *Lard-Arse* who appeared from the Men's Room ten minutes later, smelling of soap and just a faint trace of shit. He had, however, lost his enthusiasm for all things cultural and could only be persuaded only to give the *Night Watch* a cursory glance on the grounds that it was a famous and that a trip to Amsterdam wouldn't be complete without seeing it, before demanding that they go for something to eat because his 'blood sugar levels were low due to the shock'.

His mood soared when they found a mobile 'fish and chip' van down the road, although his joy was tempered somewhat on discovering that the battered fish he was eating was some sort of herring instead of the cod he had expected and that everything still smelled of dog shit. It was only when they found a bar, ordered him an unfeasibly large beer and stuck a joint in his hand that he finally came around and a smile reappeared on his poor, sad face.

It was a little after four in the afternoon when Dave glanced at his watch and reminded all those assembled that their bus was leaving at five and wouldn't it be a good idea to go and retrieve their bags? So, after smoking a spliff for the road and spending the last of the kitty money on some hash cakes for the journey, they left the cozy bar they had been in all afternoon, collected their bags from a non-too-happy bartender at the bar they had promised to return to and caught a street car back to the station. Despite being completely stoned, it was with great sadness that they climbed on board their bus to be greeted by a crowd of equally miserable faces.

"You're not sitting behind me," growled the driver at *Lard-Arse*. "And it's back to no smoking."

"Those six words have just convinced me, not that I needed any convincing, to get the train when we get to Harwich," Paul said to Dave as they sat down near the back of the bus. "You coming?"

"Yeah, I couldn't face another journey like the last one."

They asked *Brain-Dead* and *Lard-Arse* if they would join them but, as before, the answer was negative on the grounds that they were now 'skint' and didn't want to spend 'a fortune' on a train ticket when they had already paid for the bus. The being 'skint' argument, however, was apparently forgotten when they got on board the ferry and discovered that all the best seats in the bar and elsewhere had been taken.

"We've got to find somewhere private to smoke the rest of our stash. We've still got half an ounce to get through before morning," noted Paul as they surveyed the crowded decks.

"Well, I need a shower and a kip," added *Lard-Arse*, not mentioning needing food for the first time that anyone could remember.

"And we shouldn't smuggle any drugs through Customs, so I suppose we'll have to smoke it or get rid of it," said Dave.

Paul winced at the very mention of 'getting rid' of such excellent stash, but he was made to promise that he wouldn't try to smuggle it through.

"Why don't we get a cabin, then?" suggested *Brain-Dead*.

They all agreed and, on being informed at the front desk, that there were indeed some cabins still available and that they were at a special 'Give Away' price, they paid the appropriate fee and took possession of the key to Cabin number 36. According to the lady behind the front desk, getting a cabin on a night crossing without booking was very rare, but this particular route was different to the others. Instead of being full of vacationers returning from southern Europe with *Volvos* full of children and cheap wine, this ferry was full of 'junkies' returning from 'drug dens' in Amsterdam. Naturally, these dregs of society didn't have two pennies to rub together, having spent everything they owned on their 'habit', were heading home merely 'to pick up their next social security check and were so 'drugged up' that they would simply sleep on the floor if they couldn't find a couch in the bar to lie across. The last thing on their mind would be to enjoy the unashamed luxury of a fourth-berth cabin with a shower and a porthole.

The desk clerk may have been mistaken in believing that the four friends were anything but 'junkies returning from drug dens in Amsterdam', but she was absolutely correct in her assessment of the cabin; it was fantastic. Within minutes it had become a tiny home from home. While *Lard-Arse* took a shower to finally rid himself of the last traces of dog shit and Dave and *Brain-Dead* went off to buy some sandwiches and some cans of beer, Paul limbered up his rolling fingers to build a line of joints to last them the voyage. The first of these was 'sparked' as *Lard-Arse* reappeared complete with a towel around his waist that, on him, looked like a washcloth. *Brain-Dead* and Dave then arrived back and reclined on their bunks with a can of beer each as the ship edged away from the dock and made for the open sea.

"This is the fucking life!" grinned *Brain-Dead*, dropping a 'coal' from the joint onto his pillow and burning a surprisingly large hole into it.

"Yeah, that was a great weekend," agreed Dave, spilling some beer down his front as the ship began to roll.

Lard-Arse farted theatrically in agreement and Paul simply smiled as he held some precious grass smoke in his lungs to get the full effect.

Before long, the 'non smoking' cabin was thick with smoke and Dave kept glancing nervously at the smoke alarm in the ceiling. Nobody else seemed bothered, however. Paul wasn't about to stop smoking, *Lard-Arse* was nodding off and *Brain-Dead's* attitude was 'Fuck 'em!' The calm was rudely interrupted, however, when there was a knock at the door.

"Jesus, hide the stash!" ordered *Lard-Arse*, as he helped Dave waft the smoke with a couple of towels. Quite where they expected the smoke to go in a cabin with sealed windows was anyone's guess.

"Coming!" trilled *Brain-Dead*, trying to win them more time.

But the knocking continued so Dave was forced to open the door, ever so slightly at first.
Outside were two youths.

"You're smoking dope, aren't you?" said the first youth.

"Er...no," stuttered Dave in reply.

"Don't be soft, we can smell it," said the second youth, as a cloud of smoke blew out of the cabin and over his head.

"We've come to tell you that they can smell it in Reception; some people have complained and they're searching for who's smoking it," added the first youth. "It's just that we found you first and, if you give us some, we won't tell them it's you."

Paul was horrified at what he regarded as blackmail, but *Brain-Dead* took a surprisingly pragmatic approach.

"Thanks lads," said *Brain-Dead*. "Here, have a couple of joints."

He picked two joints up off the table and, much to Paul's chagrin, dropped them into the youths' waiting hands, before shutting the door on their beaming faces.

"Quick, 'Operation Remove Smoke'," *Brain-Dead* announced, rummaging in his bag for a can of deodorant spray.

The other three all took up towels and started whirling them above their heads as *Brain-Dead* sprayed into the air until it choked them and they ordered him to stop. It was then decided to head off to the bar for an hour while the smoke and the deodorant dispersed, working on the principle that the ship's crew or security guards wouldn't open an unoccupied cabin without having to open every cabin. On the way to the bar, they passed a search party of four meaty sailors, sniffing the air and knocking on cabin doors.
Brain-Dead even had the balls to ask them what they were doing before giving them the descriptions of the two youths they had just handed the joints to.

"I'm not sure if that was mean or just stupid," said Dave once they were out of earshot.

"Both," replied *Lard-Arse*.

Neither need have worry, however, as the youths were sitting in the bar when they entered and gave them a friendly wave. After a hour and a couple of beers in the bar, they were all fading fast and, deciding that the coast must be clear by now, they returned to their sweet-smelling cabin and were all asleep within minutes.

FIFTEEN

More hammering on the cabin door made everyone but Paul leap up in terror. Dave nearly fell from the top bunk, *Lard-Arse* banged his head on the upper bunk as he sat up asking where he was and *Brain-Dead* began manically wafting his towel over his head again. It took a few moments before they realized that this knocking was to warn them it was time to vacate the cabin, as the ship was entering Harwich harbor.

"Jesus, that gave me the shock of my life," spluttered *Lard-Arse*.

Dave agreed, trying to catch his breath with his heart beating wildly. Paul, meanwhile, peered down from his bunk with a very stoned grin on his face.

"Chill out Dudes!" he grinned.

"How long have you been awake?" asked Dave. "Oh, 'bout an hour or so. Couldn't let all that lovely grass go to waste down the bog."

"Bloody hell *Hippy*, have you smoked it all?" asked *Brain-Dead*.

Paul examined the tiny plastic pouch containing what remained of the stash.

"Er...not all of it. Anyone fancy a spliff for the road, seeing as we're parting company in a few minutes?"

The others agreed that a 'Mexican breakfast' was in order, so Paul built a final joint from the remnants of the stash, which was passed around as they gathered their belongings together and brushed their teeth.

"So you two are definitely not 'letting the train take the strain'?" asked Paul of *Brain-Dead* and *Lard-Arse*.

But they had made their minds up to return to Sheffield by bus, so it was with not a little sadness that Dave and Paul wished them good luck and goodbye. As *Lard-Arse* and *Brain-Dead* set off for the Car Deck to rejoin the bus, Dave and Paul made their way to the Foot Passengers' exit. As they walked over the covered walkway, they could see the bus driving off the ship and thanked their lucky stars that they weren't about to begin the torturous journey back home. Once they were off, they followed a line of people into the Customs Hall and came to a halt. The line stretched ahead of them like that for the most popular ride at a theme park and it moved just as slowly.

"I wonder why it's taking so long?" asked Dave, trying to make out what was going on at the front. But his efforts were in vain and Paul was too stoned to even bother trying.

It took over an hour for them to shuffle along far enough to see to front of the line and the cause of the hold-up. Ahead of them the line split in two and each person was being interviewed by a Customs Officer. This wasn't the usual cursory glance at a passport, this appeared to be an inquisition and it seemed that everyone was having their bags searched.
"They're searching everyone!" noted Dave to the still-grinning Paul.

"Nazis!"

"You' re not carrying any stash are you?" asked Dave nervously. "'Cause anyone they don't like the look of is being taken off through that door over there, probably for an anal search."

"Chill man, I promised not to smuggle any through."

"Good fucking job. They've also got a big fucking dog and it's heading our way down the line. A sniffer dog I guess."

At first, Paul seemed totally disinterested but, as the dog and its Customs Officer handler moved up the line towards them sniffing at everyone' s bags and clothes, he suddenly jumped into the air as if he'd stuck his finger into a power socket.

"Oh fuck, oh fuck!" he hissed, crouching down and ripping his bag open.

Dave went white and immediately began shaking.

"Oh jeez Paul, you promised!" he hissed.

"It's not the stash, we finished that. But I've just remembered those hash cookies we bought. I put them in my bag for the journey."

Paul pulled out a plastic bag containing four huge cookies, each five inches in diameter.

"Quick, we've got to eat them," he said, handing one to Dave as he began chewing frantically.

Dave started taking huge bites out of the cookie and swallowing as quickly as he could. As he did so, he was staring at the dog approaching and aware that a young couple behind them in the line were laughing at them.

"Hurry up man!" whispered Paul desperately as he finished his first cookie and started on his second.

"I'm going as quick as I can," replied Dave, spitting out cookie crumbs in the process, before accepting his second cookie.

The dog and handler were now dangerously close and would most certainly have reached them mid-chew had the dog not become highly agitated by a couple of youths ahead of them in the line. It started barking and running around in circles in front of them as they tried to back away.

"Good girl Jess, good girl!" smiled the Customs Officer, patting the crazed dog in an attempt to calm it down.

Meanwhile, two other massive officers had appeared from nowhere to stand next to the youths.

"Are you carrying any drugs?" asked the officer.

"No man," pleaded the first youth, who now had sweat pouring down his face.

"No *Guv*," agreed the second.

"Well, would you please empty your pockets?" ordered the second officer.

The youths stared at each other for a moment then, as the first one seemed to be reaching for his pocket, the second turned on his heels and shot off down the line of people. Quite where he thought he was going to get to or what good it was going to do him when he got there, Dave couldn't quite see. But, whatever it was, Dave was overcome with both sorrow and relief. Sorrow, because the youth only got about twenty yards before he was caught by the two original officers and four more who had also magically appeared. And relief, because he'd had just swallowed his last piece of the second cookie and had seen Paul drop the plastic bag they had been in onto the floor.
Paul grinned at Dave, squeezing the masticated cookie through his teeth in the process, before swallowing it with a dramatically loud gulp.

The youth, meanwhile, was being 'escorted' back along the line past Dave and Paul, towards the threatening white door that led to unimaginable tortures. It was as he was passing that Dave recognized him as the youth who had demanded the spliffs off them the evening before. This was confirmed when the second youth emptied his pockets to reveal a joint that Paul had so expertly designed and built. Paul, seeing this as well, dropped his head to avoid being recognized; all his previous bravado draining out of him. As the second youth was being led away to join his friend in the torture chamber, Paul secretly pulled a ripped-up beer mat out of his pocket and pointed to a missing piece that now, presumably, could be found being employed as 'roaches' in the end of the two items of evidence currently being studied by the Customs Officers. Paul discreetly dropped the beer mat on the floor as well, as the line shuffled forward to fill the gap left by the two 'smugglers'.

Paul and Dave had just exchanged furtive glances of relief when the dog resumed its duties and reached them. It looked up at Paul before barking madly and dancing on the spot. Paul's eyes bulged and the Customs Officer stared closely at him when suddenly the dog careered off, yanking the officer's arm and dragging him away. Dave and Paul turned to see the dog scamper up to the plastic bag Paul had dropped and begin tearing it apart, howling with delight in the process. It was only after the handler had pulled the dog away and calmed it down, that he looked up to find a black guy with dreadlocks and a woolly hat knitted in the colors of the Jamaican flag standing on the exact spot where the bag was found by the hound.

"Are you carrying any drugs?" he asked the Rastafarian, as a new contingent of massive officers arrived.

"You're only asking me that because I'm black," replied the new suspect, before being escorted away.

After all this excitement, the Customs Officers on questioning duty at the front seemed less interested in the task in hand. It was as if they had caught their quota of smugglers for the day and they asked only cursory questions about Dave and Paul's reasons for visiting Amsterdam. When Paul launched into an extremely verbose and boring monologue describing the art galleries and museums they had visited, the canal cruises they had enjoyed and the architecture they had admired, the officer's eyes glazed over and he interrupted Paul mid flow to tell them they were free to go. They walked out of the Customs Hall and made their way towards the railway station in total silence, not even looking at each other in case there was some camera trained on them to capture any give away display of rejoicing.

It was only after they had purchased their mind-bogglingly expensive train tickets and taken a seat on the platform to await their train that they felt secure enough to let it all out.

"Phew!" exclaimed Dave. "That was too close for comfort."

"We were never really in any danger," replied Paul, but his shaking hands fumbling with his tobacco told another story.

"Thank God those guys didn't recognize us. Poor guys, what do you think happened to them?"

"Someone' s probably got their hand up their arses searching for contraband even as we speak," laughed Paul, finally succeeding in getting the tobacco to lie on the cigarette paper.

"I feel a bit guilty."

"Why? The bastards tried to blackmail us."

"Yeah, but they did warn us about the search on the ship. And I wonder why they hadn't smoked the joints we gave them?"

"Dick brains!"

"And what about that poor black guy getting pulled for our cookie bag?"

"What about him? They'd have nicked him anyway, cookie bag or no fucking cookie bag. If he's clean, he'll be cool. They can't do him for standing near a plastic bag that smells of dope."

"What if they saw you drop the bag? Or what if a security camera recorded us eating the cookies? Or what if the youths give them our description and they trace us through the cabin we booked?"

"Dave, will you please chill out man, you're getting totally paranoid. They can't nick us for eating cookies and they're not going to believe some half-cocked 'we were given these joints by some naughty students on the boat' story. Fuck 'em!"

Dave was mulling over other things to be paranoid about when the loudspeaker above their heads announced that 'due to operational difficulties' the next train to London, 'The Amsterdam Express', had been cancelled.

"Oh excellent, that's just what we need," moaned Dave. "We should have stayed on the bus with *Lard-Arse* and *Brain-Dead*. They'll be half way to London by now."

"Yeah, but then they're off to Cardiff and every other town in Britain, while we sit back and relax as we flick up to Sheffield on our luxury train."

"Guess you're right," agreed Dave.

Unfortunately Dave guessed wrong. If they had thought the bus journey was the journey from hell, then their train journey was the Devil's finest work. Not only was the first train to London cancelled, but the one after that was an hour and a half late. By that the time that train pulled in to the station, there was such a crowd thronging the platform that Dave was panicking he would be pushed under the wheels in the crush. And, despite the fact that they had been waiting for three hours for this train, when it did arrive it stopped with the First Class cars adjacent to them. This meant that when they had fought their way along the platform and on board in the coach section, every seat, every luggage space and every aisle was full, leaving them standing all the way to London outside the bathroom and next to a very distressed and vocal baby. They had so little space that every time the motion of the train jostled them (and it jostled them so often that Dave wondered if it had square wheels) either they would crash into someone or someone else would crash into them. When a constant stream of toilet users was added to the mix, the crush became unbearable to any rational human being. Dave was not a rational human being, however. Dave, by now, was a drugged-crazed ball of paranoia. The huge amount of cannabis contained in the two cookies he'd eaten began 'kicking in' while he was on the platform. By the time he was on the train, every fear he had ever dreamt and a few he had never imagined in his worst nightmares raced around his petrified brain. First he was convinced that the train was going to crash, then that he was going to choke, then that the door would open and he would fall out, then that the man staring at him was really an undercover Customs Officer who had been tracking him since Amsterdam, then that he would be expelled from school for missing Friday and Monday, then that they would get lost in London, then that he couldn't find his wallet, then that he could feel cancer growing in his lungs due to all the tobacco and cannabis he'd smoked....and so it went on.

"Calm down man," soothed Paul, sensing Dave's paranoia.

"I...I can't," spluttered Dave. "I can't breathe in here, I've got to get off."

"Now chill out man. You're just a bit stoned but it'll subside in a few minutes. Anyway, you can't get off a moving train."

"Oh Jesus, I feel terrible. I'm never smoking any of that stuff again."

"What you've got to remember is that you've just eaten enough stash to put a horse to sleep and you're having a bit of a paranoia trip. But it'll be cool, you'll see. It's not like alcohol or any serious shit, it'll just fade away."

"My mouth's not going to get massive again is it? I don't think I could stand it if my mouth got massive again."

"No man, you're mouth's going to be cool. By the time we get to London and get off this fucking train everything will be cool. I don't believe we're on yet another mode of transport where I can't have a bloody smoke. I tell you man, next time we do Amsterdam, I'm coming in *Spermy*."

Paul was correct that Dave's paranoia would subside, but it took an excruciatingly long time to do so and it left him exhausted in the process. By the time the train pulled into Liverpool Street station in London, Dave felt as if he had been wrung out and was quite happy to sit with Paul on a bench in the sunshine while Paul chain-smoked three rollies, before they went off to get the subway. They would have got the subway if the subway had been running, but it wasn't. At the entrance to the underground station beneath Liverpool Street station was a sign announcing that 'due to industrial action' no services would be running that day. Dave moaned that this journey was turning into an ordeal, a belief that was re-enforced when they saw the enormous line at the bus stop and watched three buses sail past them without stopping because they were full. When they eventually did manage to get on a bus and ask the conductor for two tickets for St. Pancras station, the conductor just laughed and informed them they were on the wrong bus and that they were heading in exactly the opposite direction. By now they were becoming rather desperate and, not having a clue where they were, they decided to bite the bullet and grab a taxi to St. Pancras, whatever the cost.

It took several minutes of watching the fare click round at a depressingly high speed, which contrasted perfectly with the lack of progress the taxi was making in the jammed London streets, before they both recognized the bus line outside Liverpool Street station they had been waiting in half an hour before.

Traffic's bleedin' terrible today," moaned the taxi driver from the front of the cab. "All due to the bleedin' tube strike. Bleedin' commie bastards! String 'em all up, that's what I say."

Dave and Paul had nervously counted up what money they had between them and realized that they would have to get out of the taxi some way short of St. Pancras station, when the taxi pulled up at a set of traffic lights and was immediately hit from behind by a bus.

"Fuckin' 'ell!" screamed the taxi driver, jumping out of his seat to go and abuse the bus driver.

"What do we do now?" Dave asked, watching the meter still clicking up a higher and higher fare.

"Well we can't sit here or we'll be broke," replied Paul, climbing out of the taxi.

The taxi driver was examining the damage to the back of his taxi and telling the bus driver what a 'dozy bleeder' he was when Paul told him that they would walk the rest of the way and offered to pay their dues. Amazingly, he declined their money, on condition that they gave him their names and addresses and would act as witnesses if required because 'getting money out of these cunts is like getting blood out of a bleedin' stone'.
Naturally they agreed and scribbled down their details on a couple of taxi receipts, choosing not to point out the inconsistency in his blood and bleeding stones analogy.

"Fanx boys," said the taxi driver, before pointing them on their way.

As it was, they weren't too far away from their destination at all. They could see Kings Cross station and even *Cockney Paul* knew that St. Pancras station was just next door. So, after marching past some rather unsavory characters hanging around the *McDonald's* opposite Kings Cross, they arrived at St. Pancras to be informed that the train they could see pulling out of the station was the Sheffield train.

"We're making a habit of this," grumbled Paul.

After two hours hanging around on the station concourse and in the cafe, they finally boarded their train just before five o'clock. The train looked like it had been in service since the steam age, but they didn't care. The relief at being on the train at last was palpable and when it pulled out of St. Pancras on time they could have cried with delight. Paul could have cried in pain when the conductor announced that smoking was banned but, as he had been stocking up on nicotine relentlessly for the past two hours, he decided that even he could last the two and a half hour journey to Sheffield.

"There was a moment back there when I thought *Brain-Dead* and *Lard-Arse* might actually make it back before us," laughed Dave as they sped through the countryside.

"Oh don't!" laughed Paul. "That would have been unbearable. Can you imagine what they'd have been like, the shit they would have given us?"

Their laughter was still hanging in the air when there was a deafening clang from underneath the train and it screeched to a grinding halt, throwing a woman returning from the buffet car with a cup of tea flying down the train car and into the lap of a pleasantly surprised old man. Less pleasantly surprised was the old man's 'better half', who copped for half a pint of boiling tea in her lap.

"What the fuck?" asked Paul, after nearly smashing his head on the table.

"That didn't sound good," noted Dave.

It didn't look good either, when two characters, presumably the engineer and the conductor, walked past their window dressed in yellow fluorescent jackets staring at the wheels of the train and shaking their heads. Five minutes later, the bad news was
confirmed.

"Ladies and Gentleman, I apologize for the delay but we have a technical problem. The driver and I have just discovered that the track underneath the train has broken. I'm afraid that we cannot move until the maintenance crew arrives to see if we can proceed. As this will take at least an hour, I can only apologize for the delay to your journey and the inconvenience this will cause."

"Oh fucking great," moaned Dave.

"I'm going to stick my head out of the window and have a smoke and if they want to nick me they can bloody well try," said Paul, standing up and pulling his tobacco out of his pocket.

As it turned out, nobody tried to 'nick' Paul and he had plenty of time for several cigarettes; over three hours to be exact. During that time dozens of trains sailed past them and the buffet ran out of hot water, so no one could get a cup of tea or coffee, which simply rubbed salt into their wounds. Eventually several more men in yellow jackets arrived and studied the underneath of the train before the all clear was given for the train to limp forward along the broken rail. Once this hurdle was overcome, the train continued on its journey. It was ten past ten when it finally reached Sheffield. Luckily a number sixty bus was ready to leave the station and they finally reached Sheaf Hall at twenty-five past ten.

"Oh please God, don't let them be back before us," prayed Dave out loud.

But God undoubtedly had other things on his mind as, when he reached his room, there was a message stuck to it:

Stud, where are you?
We've been back for ages -
great coach trip. We'll be in the bar
BD & LA
xxx

"Oh well, I might as well get it over with," Dave said to himself.

So he threw his bag onto the bed, locked his room and headed off for the bar. As he entered, *Brain-Dead* and *Lard-Arse* greeted his arrival with a huge cheer. They were sitting at a table next to the bar with Pam, Joanne and Samantha. Dave's heart skipped a beat when he saw the latter. She looked absolutely gorgeous and she gave him such a beautiful smile when their eyes met that the horrors of his journey melted away.

"Hey, hey *Stud*. What kept ya'?" yelled *Brain-Dead*. "We've been back hours. We had a great journey. They changed our coach and put us on one that was nearly empty. It had reclining seats that were just like beds and a TV and a bar with a gorgeous barmaid who wanted to fuck us."

"Ignore the lying bastard," smiled Pam as he took a seat at their table. "They've been here ten minutes and all that time they've been moaning about how awful the journey was."

"Arrgh Pam, don't spoil my fun," moaned *Brain-Dead*. "At least let me wind *The Hippy* up when he comes in."

"I do wish you'd stop calling Paul a hippy," tutted Joanne.

Brain-Dead then proceeded, in a very loud voice, to tell everyone at their table and those around them of the fantastic time they had had in Amsterdam and how he had smuggled some fantastic 'grass' back in *Lard-Arse's* talcum powder bottle, unbeknownst to its now horrified owner.

"Hello," said Samantha, ignoring *Brain-Dead* and turning Dave.

"Hi. How's your dad?"

"Oh he's fine thanks, the panic's over. It was just something he'd eaten, though it did have us going for ages. How was your weekend?"

"Totally crazy," laughed Dave. "It was an experience I will never forget, nor want to repeat in a hurry."

"I was looking forward to seeing you," whispered Samantha, looking down at the floor.

"Really? I was looking forward to seeing you as well."

"In fact, I was thinking about you all weekend."

"Were you?" asked Dave, blushing with excitement.

"Yes, I was talking to Lucy about you and she said I should have it out with you."

"Have what out?"

"This sounds so childish but...well I really like you and sometimes I think you like me but then you go off with someone else. So she said I should just ask you straight...well you know...oh God this is embarrassing...what's going on and whether you wanted a relationship with me or not."

Samantha was bright red by this point and still not able to look Dave in the eye. But before Dave could answer, *Brain-Dead* had turned his attention to them.

"Come on *Stud*, you can bonk her later. It's your round so get yourself to the bar, mine's a pint."

"No, you go to the bar *Loverboy*. David' s only just walked in, so leave him alone. Mine's a gin and tonic. What are you having Jo?" said Pam, noting that Dave and Samantha were whispering together and trying to allow them some peace. She winked at Dave as *Brain-Dead* stood up and joined the crowd at the bar and then turned to pull *Lard-Arse* and Joanne into a conversation.

Before Dave and Samantha could continue, however, the door flew open with a loud crash and in stomped a middle-aged woman no more than four feet six inches tall.

"Reginald," she bellowed like a tugboat with a point to make and causing everyone in the bar to either jump out of their skins, spill their drinks or spin around to see the cause of the commotion.

The bar fell totally silent, as it was rare to see a non-student in the bar, let alone a dwarf dressed in a particularly unfashionable tweed suit and spectacularly dreadful hat, screaming her head off.

"Where have you been my lad?" bellowed the *Dwarf*.

Both Dave and Sam were absolutely riveted, as were the other occupants of the bar. They were all intrigued to know who this Reginald was; all except *Lard-Arse*.

"Oh shit, it's *Brain-Dead's* mother!" he whispered.

Dave saw the grin drop from Pam's face.

"Reginald?" she muttered.

"Hello Mum!" grinned *Brain-Dead* at the bar.

"He's called Reginald?" moaned Pam

"Don't you 'Hello Mum' me, my lad. I want to know where you've been all weekend. You've had your father worried sick and now his nerves are playing up again. Aren't they Harold?"

At first Dave couldn't see who the *Dwarf* was talking to, but then a tiny head appeared from behind the *Dwarf* sporting a somewhat crumpled tweed trilby.

"Well, not really dear, I..." whispered the *Midget* in the hat.

"Shut up Harold, I'm talking!" hissed the *Dwarf*, causing the *Midget* to once again disappear behind her.

"I've been away Mum," replied *Brain-Dead*.

"I know you've been away 'cause I've been here every five minutes looking for you, to pick up your washing, haven't I Harold?"

"Er...yes dear", whispered the reappearing head.

"Mum, Dad, this is Pam" said *Brain-Dead* pointing to Pam.

Pam stood up and offered her hand.

"Hello Mrs...er...hello, I'm Pam. Pleased to meet you."

"Don't you try to change the subject," snarled the *Dwarf*, totally ignoring Pam's hovering hand. "I want to know where you've been."

The *Midget*, however, did edge forward to shake Pam's hand, giving her a broad smile at the same time before retreating once more.

Dave, meanwhile, was trying to work out how two people just over four feet in height could possibly produce a giant like *Brain-Dead*. He also wondered what age they had been when they had had him. Neither of them looked a day under seventy.

"I've been to Holland," *Brain-Dead* continued.

With that, the *Dwarf* leapt three feet in the air like an acrobat and planted a stinging slap across *Brain-Dead's* face.

Pam, still holding out her hand, gasped.

"Owwwww. What's that for?" wailed *Brain-Dead*.

"That's for cheeking your mother."

"But I didn't cheek you."

Slap.

"Don't lie to me."

"I'm not lying."

Slap.

"It's true Mrs...er...it's true. He has been to Holland, Amsterdam," said Pam sweetly.

"Who's this?" the *Dwarf* asked *Brain-Dead*, motioning towards Pam.

"I've just told you, this is Pam, Mum. She's my girlfriend," grinned *Brain-Dead* proudly.

Dave thought *Brain-Dead* was going to get another slap for that, but the *Dwarf* was too shocked and rocked back on her clumpy, brown, platform shoes.

"What? You didn't tell me you had a 'girlfriend'."

Pam tried again. "Hello, I'm Pam."

"Hello Pam," whispered the *Midget*, smiling again.

"How long has this been going on?" demanded the *Dwarf*, conspicuously ignoring Pam's still outstretched hand.

"Er..." mumbled *Brain-Dead*, staring at his feet.

"My name's Pam, it's nice to meet you Mrs...er..."

"Say 'Hello' to Pam, Mum," pleaded *Brain-Dead*.

"I'm not shaking hands with her and I don't care what she's called. I just want to know what's been going on, my lad."

Dave winced as he saw Pam's smile drop and her face redden at the same time as she withdrew her hand. He thought he noticed a puff of steam coming out of her ears.

"Look *Luv*," growled Pam, the sweetness in her voice now absent. "My name's Pam and I'm the bird who' s fucking your son, alright?"

Brain-Dead's mother reeled as if she'd been punched.

"I've never been spoken to like that in my life!" protested the *Dwarf.*

"Well, you obviously don't get out enough, do you *Luv*?" grinned Pam, sitting down.

"Reginald, are you going to let this...this hussy speak to your mother like that?"

"She's not a hussy, Mum. She's my girlfriend."

"Harold, are you going to stand by and allow this...this wanton woman to speak to me like that?"

"I'm not sure she's a wanton woman dear, she seems very nice to..."

"Reginald, get your bag packed, we're taking you home. I'm not leaving you here another minute, if this is the sort of company you've been keeping."

"No, Mum."

"What did you say?"

"I said 'No' Mum."

"Don't you dare defy me, my lad."

"Go home Mum."

"I am going home and you're coming with me!"

"I'm not, Mum. I'm staying here with Pam."

"What?"

"I said I'm staying, so please just go home. Dad, please take her home."

"I'm not moving until you've..."

"Mum, just fuck off and leave me alone!" screamed *Brain-Dead*.

"Right, that's it. I'm going."

"Good."

"I'm not staying here for you to insult me like that."

"Good. Go."

"All the tea in China couldn't persuade me to stay after being spoken to like that."

"Bye Mum."

"I dread to think what this'll do to your dad's nerves. I just hope you can live with yourself, that's all."

"My nerves are fine dear", whispered the *Midget*.

"Shut up Harold, I wasn't talking to you."

"Mum, the only thing wrong with Dad's nerves is having to live with you for the last fifty years."

"How dare you? You're a terrible disappointment to me Reginald. You were always such a good boy. But you've obviously been corrupted by hussies like her," the *Dwarf* cried, pointing at Pam.

"Right, that's it," yelled *Brain-Dead* stomping to the door and opening it. "Get out!"

"No I won't."

"Nobody speaks to Pamela like that, not even you Mum. It's time you left, so either you leave of your own accord or I'll pick you up and throw you out."

"Excellent! We could be on for some dwarf tossing," *Lard-Arse* whispered in Dave' s ear.

"You wouldn't," she whispered but, seeing the determination in his face and realising that he would, headed through the door.

"Goodbye Mum."

"Bye Reg", smiled the *Midget* to *Brain-Dead*

"Bye Dad", replied *Brain-Dead*.

The ensuing stunned silence in the bar was finally broken by Pam.

"My hero!" she cried, running up to *Brain-Dead* and throwing her arms around his neck. "You slayed the dragon for me."

Brain-Dead grinned.

"Ooooh, it's made me all moist. Come on 'Regie', let's find somewhere else for you to stick your lance!"

"Wyyyyyyyoooooooooooooo howled *Brain-Dead*, holding open the door for Pam to exit the bar, before turning back to the stunned patrons and extending his tongue to an even more unfeasibly long length.

The patrons held their own tongues until the footsteps had faded away before bursting into excited chatter.

"Well, that was a bit different, wasn't it?" smiled Samantha. "You don't see that every day. Anyway, where were we? Oh yes, I was asking you why you are such a big shit who keeps acting like he wants a relationship with me but then goes off shagging someone else!"

"Of course I want a relationship with you", replied Dave, "But I can't, can I?"

"Why not? Have you got someone else? God, that's a dumb question, ever time I turn around you seem to have someone else."

"It's not me who' s got someone else, it's you!"

"Me? What are you talking about?"

"I can hardly go out with you while Greg's around, can I?"

"Greg's my friend. You' re not saying I can't see my friend, are you? 'Cause

Greg's non-negotiable."

"Well that's the problem. I'm not into kinky threesomes, whether Greg is or not."

"What?" asked Samantha obviously baffled. Then she started laughing. "Oh that's funny."

"What?" a very glum Dave asked.

"You think that me and Greg..." she couldn't carry on because she was laughing too much.

"I'm glad you find it so amusing."

"But it is amusing, you silly thing. You don't know, do you?"

"Don't know what?"

"You haven't realized that, although Greg is my best friend and I love him to bits, we can never be more than just friends?"

"And why not?" asked Dave snootily.

"Because Greg's gay!"

It took a few moments for this information to sink in.

"Did you not think it was odd that Greg was raving about his new boyfriend the other night?"

"Er..."

"Oh that's so funny," laughed Samantha. "It's my fault, I thought that it was obvious. He doesn't try to hide that fact that he's gay, why should he?"

Dave was too stunned to speak.

"Shall we start again?" Samantha asked him.

Dave nodded.

"Hello, my name's Samantha, what's yours?"

"Pleased to meet you Samantha, my name' s Dave. I'm a *Yank*. How about coming back to my place for a coffee?"

"I thought you'd never ask. Do you actually have any coffee?"

"Er...no."

"Excellent, lets go!"

www.ingramcontent.com/pod-product-compliance
Lightning Source LLC
Chambersburg PA
CBHW070752280626
47162CB00016B/169